575

THE FIFTH
GOSPEL

DAVID ALEXANDER

THE FIFTH GOSPEL

MACMILLAN

First published 1997 by Macmillan

an imprint of Macmillan Publishers Ltd
25 Eccleston Place, London SW1W 9NF
and Basingstoke

Associated companies throughout the world

ISBN 0 333 67000 0

1 3 5 7 9 8 6 4 2

A CIP catalogue record for this book is available from
the British Library

Typeset by CentraCet, Cambridge
Printed and bound in Great Britain
by Mackays of Chatham plc, Chatham, Kent

Acknowledgements

The author is grateful for the friendship of Barnaby Hall, Nicole Huber and Billy the dancing cat in whose Manhattan apartment this book began. Handsome Antoine Laurent and dashing Chris Wilson dispensed authorative authorial advice. I am indebted to the fabulous Arabella Stein for editorial assistance and to Kay McCanley, Maria Rejt and Peter Straus for their support. *The Fifth Gospel* would not have been published without Claire Walsh and J. G. Ballard, and I thank them.

For Clare, Thea and Freddie.

PART ONE

THE CANNIBAL'S RAINCOAT

Chapter One

THIS IS the truth, putrescent and black, all that I've seen and heard, smelt and felt, told through a clear glass, no lies, no secrets, truth spilling out like rice through a split sack. I have been corrupt, I have corrupted. I am debauched and I have debauched. I have taken, never given, a drunken glutton while others starved, a hoarder among the infested legions of the poor. Lying, I have caused others to deceive and lived off another's goodness in a rotten house.

I am eighty-eight years old, cardinal in the Holy See of Rome, my home is the Vatican, its central courts and inner chambers, I am the Pope's Counsel, privy to every thought and whisper, repository of two millennia of truths and keeper of a devastating knowledge. I know the fate of man. I know of his wars and his peace, his liberty and his prisons, his schools and his prayers, his history and his future. Man's real story is within me and it is written here.

I was born in Edwardian London and abandoned in a city of smog, given to a convent's cold stone doorstep, eight hours old, a snivelling child in lean swaddling clothes, a poor babe left to the nuns. My mother was unknown. I was taken in, fed, given a name and kept by a legion of sterile women, foster mothers to a tribe of little ones, kept in an orphanage of foundling souls. There was no sunshine in this house, but we were better off than the children of the street, shoeless, scabrous foragers without homes. And in the orphanage I was taught to read and write, to attend matins and vespers, sing and pray. Some freak of genetics gave me an unusual intelligence, a memory that failed to forget. I was pretty and my treble voice was fine. A remarkable child, known by the nuns for his beauty and brains, a boy who had wooden mothers in these shrivelled vestigial women, a surrogate for the children that they did not have.

I was marked from early times by my precocious intellect and bearing which were obvious among the average, extraordinary among the ordinary, a beacon that shone out in the smudgy company of the other children of the East End. Special attention was paid to my religious instruction, and I was taught Latin and Greek, educated in Church history, the tracts and gospels, the hymns and psalms. I excelled. The convent's library became mine, and I wandered through its ancient volumes, edicts and calf-bound treatises.

My progress was interrupted by the jarring call of puberty. I was noticed by an Irish novice whose wild red hair strayed from the clamp of her wimple. The novices were kept from us. However, there were times when the two groups met, when trailing lines of children passed in some dim corridor. I searched those lines for humanity, for eyes that didn't look away and found her. We recognized each other, in the distance, in the dining area, at either end of the abbey and at choir practice, and with time uncertain glances became quick smiles of recognition.

One afternoon, we slipped behind a pillar and kissed, and the memory of that kiss is still with me seventy-five years on. Squeezing my hand, she rushed away, and shaking, not knowing quite why I was quivering, I rejoined my friends.

4

It was a summer taken in fumbling, hands feeling through an orphan's uniform, while I lost my way in my first anatomy classes. In my innocence I didn't know how her skin folded, where I should touch and where I should go. I had only myself as a reference point and no part of my body prepared me for hers. My sweetheart taught me, in quick moments made more delicious by the arresting panic of clicking footsteps. She taught me, and in cupboards and cloakrooms, always in the dark, I learnt a little of women.

Her red hair spoke of her Irish origins. Always wild, she'd loved the boys, and after a pregnancy at fifteen, she'd been put away in this place, locked away from any chance to shame her parents again. But sexuality is strong and desire finds its way, so that even in a convent lust can be fulfilled, and filled was her belly which swelled with my seed, until in the winter even the copious play of her habit could not conceal the evidence of her condition and a shocked Mother Superior sent my freckled love back to her family in damp Ireland.

My studies continued and my academic brilliance burgeoned like my first lover's belly. I loved the routine of the orphanage and grew up happily with my friends. I was a beautiful youth, tall, blond curls, bright green eyes, olive skin, and so clever. By the time I was thirteen years old, there had been so many reports of my ability to the Mother Superior that I was called to her office. I stood in front of her desk, stood in coarse wool shorts and a grey shirt, no tie, hands behind my back, head modestly lowered. She was a small woman with soft skin and a coarse moustache. She squinted at me, then her mouth tightened and her eyes rushed away to a garish statue of poor Christ on his cross, staring down hopelessly from the wall at her awful brown carpet. The mouth loosened with the reassurance of Christ and she was able to look at this poor orphan again.

'So, boy, you're clever. Are you clever?' The words were whispered, and I had to strain to hear. In later times I learnt that to speak quietly was a trick, performed to attract attention, but then it sounded so sinister.

'I am blessed with a good memory, that is true, and I am grateful.'

For some reason this modest reply caused irritation, and she hissed, 'Well, little one, let's see how you do. John 12:27.'

'"Now is my soul troubled; and what shall I say?" . . .'

'That's enough, that will do. John 9:6.'

'"When he had thus spoken" . . .'

'Stop. Stop. Matthew 11:28.'

'"Come unto me, all ye that labour" . . .' She seemed to become more irritated with every correct quotation, sitting more upright in her simple wooden chair, avoiding my face more frequently, referring to the crucified Christ for longer and longer periods. I was sure she thought I was cheating, but how, she really didn't know.

'Do you believe in Christ?'

'I do.'

Her mouth twisted up and her final words were spat at me, forced out between steel lips.

'You will follow a career in God. Do you have any questions?' It was not a question that brooded answers.

I nodded my head in acquiescence and scurried through the stone doorway, pleased to be away from the woman, and entirely uncertain as to what she had meant. We were all brought up to follow God, but a career in God was a thing that I couldn't understand.

But understanding soon came, and gone were the warm

corridors of my youth, shriven by the cold dawn of my fourteenth birthday. A whisper at 4 a.m. told me to bundle up my possessions. There was no more than a bundle, a spare vest and some underpants, a home-knit black jumper and wash things, a worn Bible with black American cloth covers, nothing else. I was portable, an easy refugee, small memories, no substance. I said goodbye to my brothers, small and tall, friends of different ages, took in the lines of poor beds and our thin garret, and I followed in the wake of Sister Thomas' solid bottom.

Down stone stairs and out into the late autumn morning. Dew, white dust on the grass verge, marked the edges of the gravel drive that bordered our orphanage. I glanced back to see the building's heavy mahogany doors closing slowly, closed by a white hand stretching out from a black sleeve, fingers curling around the frame and the door shut silently on the early days of my life.

A hansom cab waited for us in the driveway. The horse looked shabby in the gaslight, tatty mane, loose tail flicking. The driver stooped over his whip, wrapped in a blanket. He made no sign that he knew we were there. We helped ourselves into the cab, which heeled as we clambered in. We settled back, and with a 'Hirrup Danny Boy' and the snap of his whip we were off with a juddering motion as the horse Danny took up slack.

'Where are we going, Sister Thomas?'

'Hush, boy. The seminary.'

'What for, Sister, please?'

'You're to become a monk.'

A monk? I'd had no thought till then of any future. In our orphanage there was nothing beyond the present and the past. It was enough to puzzle over my origins, and wonder what would be for dinner. So much of our time we were hungry, always wanting more and never given enough to grow. There were no fat boys in the orphanage. We roared through meals, staring at each other's plates, protecting our potatoes from the quick poaching forks of our neighbours. He who hesitated lost potatoes and he who ate quickest had the chance of another boy's potatoes. How vivid is the memory of the ache of a hunger that couldn't be eased by belt tightening or water drinking or paper chewing. My dreams were always of food, and those childhood visions of great stews and steaming puddings, roast meats and sweet pastries, decorate my nights.

In other dreams, mothers that we had never known came to us softly, with warmth, with gentleness. For all of us poor orphans there was this common vision, this familiar memory, of a mother loving and good, caressing and comforting, embracing, smiling, our own true mothers. We children would often speak of our lost mothers, providing complicated explanations as to why we had been abandoned. In these conversations we would always express the hope that our beloved mothers would reappear, and in my imagination she came to reclaim me, descending, wrapped in furs, from a grand berlin.

These images of women had no basis in the nuns' behaviour. Barked orders never kindness, terms of dismissal never endearment were all that we had from these crabbed souls. We were hungry and unloved, but our lives were not miserable because of a camaraderie that came from a commonality of lot and dreams.

The hansom's wheels rumbled over granite cobblestones. Outside, mists, night, gas lamps and the click of the horse's hooves. Inside, Sister Thomas, massive, entirely quiet, a plump shadow, rocking in the darkness in which we were wrapped. The journey passed but there was no reference

8

point for time, nor clues as to where we were travelling. In my fourteen years I had not left the immediate neighbourhood of the orphanage, an incredible thought in the context of these times of trains, planes and cars, of mobility even for the poorest, and immobility only for the frightened agoraphobic.

Outside, the air became fresher, dawn came, my friend the sun announcing his arrival in the day's hallways, his calling card low green light. The day began, and brightness woke the birds, whose volume was quite unlike that heard in Limehouse, where a few bronchitic sparrows and starlings sounded the morning's alarm. We were in the country, and I was a fidgety boy bouncing from window to window, and despite Sister Thomas's smacks, keen for a view of the green fields, lakes and streams that were prominent in the Song of Solomon, but invisible in the East End of London. Such excitement to see a hedge, a cow, a swan, the great grids of the plough.

As the sun rose higher and higher, I settled down, content to sit back and behave. Sister Thomas stared through my window, eyes fixed across the far fields. Her demeanour had changed, she was sitting upright, breathing more quickly, her face flushed, and from these obvious signs I could tell that we were nearing our destination.

We made our way through a tiny hamlet. No sign declared its presence, nor announced its sleepy smoking chimneys. A cowherd in a rough sheepskin waistcoat, his black dog stalking, ushered a line of poor cows from a barn. The dog rushed at our cab, snapping at the horse, and then scampered away.

We trotted on, and a few hundred yards from the village entered a driveway bordered by crabbed beech trees, their trailing branches clutching at each other. The horse strained, pulling us uphill to a brooding brick building that seemed to have spilled out on to the hilltop, a crystallized avalanche spreading out from the peak. The heavy building was dominated by a huge stone statue climbing up to the heavens from a green copper roof. The statue could only be Our Saviour, thankfully not in pain on a cross, but at rest, wrapped in long robes, coiled hands clasped in a beneficent prayer, shedding grace on the building and the hillsides, the hamlet and the fields.

In the valley below were woods and a cheerful lake, beehives and vegetable plots, a walled garden, and a collection of neat sheds from which came the cackle of chickens. The life of the valley contrasted with the stillness that emanated from the seminary whose windows were shuttered and whose bricks were dark. From the building's heavily carved architraves and eaves, soot-blackened grotesques, gryphons and gargoyles sneered and scowled.

The hansom stopped in a circle of driveway which curved around a mulberry tree whose berries had made purple stains on the gravel. Sister Thomas and I climbed from our cab. The driver, motionless, slouched over his whip, while his horse steamed and made desperate attempts to trim the grass.

We walked to the seminary and rang the bell-pull. At this moment I had the most awful presentiment that I was about to enter a silent order, condemned never to speak or squeak, whisper or shout. Such a simple thought, and almost irrelevant to the major issues of sterility and passivity, which might be thought to be the significant consequences of life in the Church. I was nervous, I can remember now how nervous, heart trying to jump from my chest, hands sweating, my mouth dry. On the doorstep, I tidied my clothes and bent to tie a shoelace. I stood up as the door opened and my fear left me, banished by the enormous smile of an avuncular giant in a brown cassock, who spread out his arms to greet us.

'Sister Thomas,' he boomed. 'It must be seven years. You are looking well, the good Lord be praised.' And Sister Thomas, becoming almost girlish, looked away shyly from the huge friar and blushed.

'And you, Brother Matthew, you look well, the years have been kind to you.'

'Thank you, my dear. So this is the boy?'

He looked down at me with beetle eyes that searched me, stripped me down, weighed me, checking out the item in Sister Thomas's shopping basket.

'This is the boy,' he repeated, 'that Mother Superior has written about. How strange that such a one be blessed . . . Is it true, boy?'

'What, sir?'

'Your memory, is it that good?'

'They say it is, though I'm not sure by what I'm judged.'

'Well said, boy.' Brother Matthew patted my head, bending to stroke my curls.

At this moment I became aware of my environment. I was in a wood-panelled hallway, lit by candles mounted in ornate wall sconces. A central well of light bore down from a glass dome over a circular staircase that descended to polished grey flagstones. Distracted by a buzzing noise, I looked up at the staircase. The whole seminary seemed to be crowded on to the stairs, pushing together, straining for the best view of the new recruit, popping eyes in peaky faces, peeping between the banisters while I stood aghast, Brother Matthew's fingers still playing with my hair. There was a burst of giggling, and a sudden plop by my foot and I looked down, at excrement. Brother Matthew turned to the disturbance, saw the mess and the commotion on the stairs, and shook his huge fist at our audience.

'Disgusting. Wretches. Come and clear it up or . . .' He hesitated, in deference to Sister Thomas. His face hardened, nasty with anger, and he ushered us away into his study. I trailed behind Sister Thomas and Brother Matthew, and as we turned a corner looked back to the staircase and the lewd gesticulations of a hundred slavering, slobbering monks. We walked through dark corridors to the Friar's study.

The room was more luxurious than any other I had seen. Rich altar cloths and gold-framed icons hung on the walls, exquisite Bokhara and Caucasian rugs lay on the floor. Brother Matthew's bibelots, ivory carvings and jewelled boxes, were arranged in harmony on single-stemmed mahogany tables, workboxes and card tables. Bright light shone through tall gothic windows and in straight lines edged by grey dawn, picked out sparkling motes of dust and made scattered rainbows on the far wall.

The room was sensual and quiet, more the parlour of a rich voluptuary than an ascetic priest. We sat, and Brother Matthew and Sister Thomas's talk was an odd flirtation, which ignored my presence. It was a conversation that was undirected and heavy with allusion. Their eyes were stuck on each other, wondering, fleshy, and sparkled with a common sexual past.

Brother Matthew walked to his desk to ring for tea, squeezing past Sister Thomas. He stood directly behind her and said, gesticulating with a heavily ringed hand, that he hoped I would not let Mother Superior down and would fulfil my early promise. His hands rested on the back of Sister Thomas's armchair, one on either side of her head, and as he spoke I noticed Sister Thomas's head tilt back

12

and press against his groin. Brother Matthew's face flushed, and his voice suddenly boomed halfway through a sentence telling me of my responsibility to the orphanage and to the seminary. He paused for a moment, coughed, straightened out the folds of his habit and then went on to explain how everyone hoped that I would apply myself to the gospel and lead an exemplary life of learning. Sister Thomas' head shook slowly, moving from side to side, as if to emphasize these solemn words. But at the age of fourteen, I was already a sexual tyro and knew what she was up to, knew that her emphasis was on Brother Matthew's groin, rather than on my future path to righteousness and redemption.

At that moment a thin youth with an unpleasantly florid shaving rash knocked and came through the study door. He wore a brown cassock that was much too long for him and carried a silver tray, on which were balanced white porcelain cups and a teapot, milk, honey and bread. He placed the tray on Brother Matthew's desk, bobbed his head to Sister Thomas and retreated from the room.

Sister Thomas poured us tea. Plates were passed, bread was cut, and there was honey fragrant with lavender and soapy with beeswax.

'From our own hives,' said Brother Matthew, and clouds of honey-drenched breadcrumbs fell on his clothes. I drank my tea, warming my hands on the cup.

'My boy,' said Brother Matthew, shaking a finger at me, 'we expect that you will fulfil your duty to the Church and Christ. Go now, it is time for you to be taken to your dormitory.'

With these redolent and solemn words I was dismissed from the room, ushered away by the same callow youth with the ill-fitting cassock who had brought our tea. The heavy study door closed and I scurried along behind the tripping monk, trying to keep up with him.

'Why don't you tie up your cassock?' I asked, and in my innocence went on to suggest that a belt might help. The monk turned to me. We both stopped. His face bent down close to mine.

'Fuck off and mind your own bollocks,' he hissed, and turning again, veered off down the corridor. Taking a big breath I stepped after him, as he dipped and stumbled along the passageway.

The corridors were a maze of dark wood panelling and flagstones. We walked in candlelit twilight, the images of our journey fluttering in a hundred breezes, our shadows black rats that rushed from dark corners, scurrying across our paths.

We walked for many minutes turning here, turning there. We passed closed doors which screened coarse voices, loud laughter, the clinking of glasses and the occasional squeak of women surprised. A door opened behind me, swung open with a bang, and the candles blew out. We were in darkness and I was lost, hands out, feeling for a wall. The monk stumbled on, leaving me alone.

My desperate fingers stabbed the panelling, and I edged forward, slowly, slowly, feeling my way around sharp bends until I was back in light. I rushed forward, panicking, looking for my guide, and the corridor suddenly divided, split into two. I stopped; which direction should I take? I took the right fork, running, desperate, turned a sharp bend and smacked into the hissing monk. He was waiting for me, leaning against a wall, smoking a cigarette. He caught me as I bounced off him, and held me painfully by the back of my neck, held me with his thumb and forefinger.

'Where are you going, little one? What's your hurry?'

He held his cigarette between the ends of his index and second fingers, slowly brought it to his mouth and sucked and its bright end burned red. He was silent. After a moment he exhaled, and two columns of smoke poured from his dragon nostrils and made their deliberate spreading way to heaven. I bowed my head. His finger and thumb squeezed tightly, hurting. He sucked at his cigarette, pinched out its lit end and placed it in his pocket.

'Well, little one, you are a pretty boy.' He pushed me away from him and kicked me hard. I fell forward, saving my face from the ground with my arms. My hands were grazed and blood seeped through torn skin.

'Get up.' I was getting up. He kicked me again, this time on my thighs, and I fell once more. He stooped down, wrenching me up, pulling at my shirt, and my buttons spilt on to the flagstones, pearls on stone.

'Get up, get up.' He pushed me roughly, and I stumbled forward, to punches and more kicks, faltering, onward, upstairs, to the first floor, and then to a second floor, a narrow staircase turning at sharp angles in the darkness to a third-floor landing. We continued to a fourth level, where the stairs stopped at a closed doorway. The monk screwed up my collar in his fist and holding on to me so that I couldn't escape, turned the door handle, opened the door and pushed me roughly into the room. I straightened up to a view of eight leery-eyed monks slumped around a dining table on which lay the picked grey carcass of a stringy goose.

'Pretty boy isn't he?' said my guide. He tickled me under the chin with a dirty finger.

'Hold him,' he shouted.

The monks rushed at me, and tore at my clothes. They bent me over the edge of the table and slapped my face into

15

the cold shiny wood. They giggled and strutted, puncturing my poor arse again and again. Such pain as they buggered me and laughed. Two or three of them held me still, encouraging each new violator, admiring his big prick and fine ball bag, while I was torn by pain, riven, shredded, ripped, seared, soiled, consumed, taken, and abused in a scalding procession of agony. They danced around me, cackling while I was fixed on a bed of thorns and initiated into religion and learning.

I shook while the clawing monks took me. I shivered and they squealed. They stood behind me encouraging each other to greater beastliness and my face remained jammed hard into the table.

They had had enough, and red-faced they took their places again at the round table. I was released from my pinioning and scuffling around the room gathered up my orphan's clothes. They slumped in their chairs, smirking, scratching, while I struggled into my trousers, socks and shoes. I wrapped my torn self into my buttonless shirt, and, feeling dampness trickle along my legs, looked down to a line of blood. The monks remained silent and I waited on their silence, an orphan alone.

The silence was split by my guide.

'Well, boy, you're obviously going to enjoy life here.' I bent my head in misery and his friends hooted with amusement. The sardonic one continued to more hooting and honking from his friends, 'We have finished your entrance examination and found, in you, satisfaction.' Even more unpleasant laughter. 'Now that we've taken you by your hindquarters, it's time for you to be taken to your quarters.'

The brown-habited monks stared at me with obvious delight at the prospect of my future years of 'education'.

My guide got up from his chair and tripped to the doorway. I remained by the table, hesitant, wary of the lurking terrors.

'Oh hurry up. Do come on.' He turned sharply and his habit splayed out in a circle that followed him in a swirling arc through the door.

Chapter Two

S O, LIFE in the seminary had begun. My guide ushered me disdainfully before him to a basement clothes store presided over by a fat monk. Brother Bernard, the queen of the basement, sat on a high stool picking his nose and singing in a high falsetto. He winked at me lewdly, and, lasciviously licking a chicken bone, issued me with a habit.

I was delivered to my dormitory. The door closed and I was alone. In this attic room a valley roof sloped low over two narrow rows of beds. The room was without carpets, sink, cupboard or books. A single roof-mounted window gave a barred view of the sky and a wicked wind whispered hard lies.

I sat on the nearest lonely bed, hugged my knees and shook with tears, sobbed and sobbed, shaking with misery. I lay on my back and hid under the sheets staring up at the grey panes of glass. The window was flecked with dollops of bird shit, and muddy light dusted the room. I pulled the blankets up over my head, coarse blankets that grazed my face with their roughness. My sobbing gradually eased and the fear ceased. My early years in the orphanage had given me strength. I was used to misery and could deal with loneliness. The great joy of my encounters with my beautiful redhead had made me sure of my sexuality, and the beastliness of the morning was seen as a physical assault which left me unassailed. It had been an attack, not a violation, and although I was hurt I was not mentally broken.

Things might have been worse. I could have been thrown out of the orphanage, thrown on to the streets like the other graduates of that hard school. Instead I was here, in this seminary, placed for a training. I lay in the bed, nose peeking out over the edge of the blankets and waited. The musky tang of my new robes drifted around the room, softening the air. I stared at the walls and the patterns of cracks in the plasterwork made fairies and faces, lions and tigers stalking the wild woods. There was birdsong on the roof, the chirrups and squeaks letting me know of a sweeter world outside.

From the corridors came the noise of footsteps, the door swung open and a novice in a brown habit walked into the room. He stood by my bed and peered at my face. His arms were lost in the depths of his wide sleeves. His face was thin, his eyes bulged, his ears stuck out, and he had a huge hooked nose. We held each other's gaze searching for clues. Then he looked away, and spoke.

'You're the new boy.' His voice was gentle, I nodded. 'Why don't you get out of bed and dress?'

He walked away, looking the room over, swinging the tassel that hung from his waist. I pushed aside the sheets and started to put on my new clothes. The habit itched and was much too big, but its billowing depths kept in my body heat and warmed me. I tucked up the sleeves and rucked up the waist over my belt. Meanwhile my companion tidied my bed.

'Come,' he said and we walked from the room. He asked where I came from and I told him of the orphanage. I echoed his posture and pace as we walked through the building. My steps were slow and emphatic, my head bowed.

At the end of a corridor my new friend pushed open heavy double doors and we were in a huge dining room, where about two hundred monks and novices were eating at long refectory tables. The men were stooped over their plates, shovelling food into their mouths. Nobody looked up. We took our places on a low bench and bent over pewter plates laden with a steaming beef stew topped with crisp pastry. My neighbours, spotty boys, ignored me and, avoiding my eyes, ate with fierce speed. A monk passed through the aisle between the benches, carrying a huge pitcher. He stopped to tip soapy beer into extended glasses, bending from side to side, inclining the pitcher to the thirsty monks. I held out my glass and he spilt beer over my hand. I drank. It was good beer, thick and mild. The stew was delicious, its pastry rich with lard.

Suddenly we were called to prayer. Cutlery was thrown on to the tables with a great rattle and we all stood to pray, hands clasped, thanking the holy ones for their goodness, blessing the meal and our day. I looked wistfully down at my place. My meal was unfinished, whereas every other plate was gleaming clean, scrubbed down to pure white. I realized then why everyone had been in such a hurry with their meal. I mournfully eyed the remnants of the stew as we filed from the refectory.

As we left the room the constraint of silence lifted and a great chattering swelled through the corridor, and among the slur of noise the occasional rush of words lodged and was discernible. I kept pace with my guide and we left the darkness of the monastery for the bright fields.

I was to work that afternoon with the chickens. The fields were ploughed for autumn, the hedgerows trimmed.

Brambles leaped over the neat beech hedges, bright berries ripening in September's light. We pressed on around the edge of the field, our sandals making deep prints in the soft wet earth. A red butterfly with Turkish carpet wings hauled its way through the heavy air.

'A red admiral,' said the boy. I had no knowledge of the country, could not name the commonest beast. Such a wonderful name, conjuring an image of a bloody pirate, captain of a fierce crew, soaring through a wild sea. We crossed over a stile into pastureland dotted with sheep. From a distance the sheep were tiny maggots, wriggling on flesh green with decay. At the edge of the pasture was a ring of low huts. I'd seen them when I'd arrived at the seminary, and heard the screeching of chickens. We came closer to the wooden sheds, and the wind blew into our faces carrying the smell of chicken shit. An elderly monk came from the huts to greet us, leaning heavily on his stick. His eyes were sharp dots in a vinous face, splattered with broken veins.

'Good afternoon, Brother Aquinas,' said my guide. 'I've brought you our new boy.'

'It is your first day with us?' His voice rumbled low. I nodded and averted my eyes, looking around at the slatted huts, the piles of chicken manure, the stone water-trough, the weeds and the few tatty trees. My guide left us and we turned towards the huts, Brother Aquinas hobbling, his staff a third leg.

'Well, boy, you wish to become a monk.' I nodded. 'Not everyone is acceptable, you know.' I knew. 'It is a hard life.' This had already been demonstrated to me. 'Your reward will be prayer.' What reward was prayer?

Brother Aquinas opened the door of the nearest chicken hut. We lowered our heads and entered to a view of rows of cages on low benches, and the chicken prisoners turned to us, their heavy wattles swaying and shaking. Brother Aquinas handed me a heavy metal bucket and a trowel.

'Clean out the cages.' He closed the door on me. I was left alone and confined by the closed door, the birds' cackles and squawks echoed and swelled, dancing through the shed with the stench of the chickens. I opened the first cage. In it were three white birds, red-eyed, curly-beaked, straw, shed feathers and spilt corn.

I trowelled the rubbish into my bucket and closed the door. I continued along the rows of cages, until my bucket became full. I opened the door of the hut and emptied my bucket on the pile of manure.

Church bells rang the hour. It was 4 p.m., and as the low chimes spilled out from the monastery, birdsong ceased and the whole valley hushed, deadened by the oppressive tones. I returned to my tasks. I opened another cage, to the horror of a dead chicken, flies at its eyes, caked blood at its comb.

I screeched with fright and rushed from the hut and there in profile under the scraggy trees was Brother Aquinas, his robes pulled up over his shoulder, a chicken in his hands, wings pinioned in his grasp. He was purple faced, busy with himself, his erect penis making its way purposefully in and out of the chicken's arse.

I rushed back into the chicken shed and vomited. Palpitating, I caught my breath. Then, gathering myself together, I returned to my job. Time walked by and the great bells chimed five.

I was called out of the chicken hut as the last chime of six sounded. Brother Aquinas pointed at the trough and told me to clean myself and we both returned to the seminary.

Monks filed through the corridors of the building, and

we joined them walking silently to vespers. We took our
places in the abbey, Brother Aquinas pointing me to a row
near the back, where my friend of the morning was sitting
among a group of very young novices. He smiled as I took
my place.

The abbey was hushed, the only sound the smacking of
the monks' sandals on the stone floor. Each monk as he
entered the abbey bowed his head to the great cross that
dominated the nave, crossed himself and then walked on.
The monks were of all ages, from youth to great age; all
humanity was here, every Caucasian variant, hook-nosed,
snub-nosed, curly-haired, straight-haired, the fat, the thin,
the plethoric. I watched them as they took their places,
dropping to their knees for a moment's prayer before
assuming their seats.

The abbey was built in the gothic style, and its stones
were more ancient than the buildings that surrounded it.
High windows of stained glass sprayed coloured light on to
the whitewashed walls, statues of blessed saints stood in
niches on the walls. Rows of carved pews reached forward
to a dominant altar covered with white cloth edged with
heavy silver. On the altar was a gold chalice. By the side of
the altar was a lectern, a soaring gilded eagle. I looked back
as the abbey's doors closed. A stout man pushed along the
nave, his tonsured hair brown and short, brushed forward
from the crown. His nose was strong and his jaw brutish.
He was close shaven, and his lips were thick and voluptuous. His presence was strong and noisy, echoing out around
the abbey, so that one became aware of him before he was
seen. He reminded me of the pictures I'd seen in the
orphanage of Julius Caesar. He walked along the nave and
took up position at the lectern.

My companion whispered to me, 'The Abbot.'

The Abbot rested his elbow on the lectern and stared down at the mass of men. He scanned his audience slowly, deliberately, taking time to peer into the eyes of all of his monks. I felt him take in our row of young things, sweep over us and then move on. His eyes were judgmental, powerful, frightening.

'Let us pray.' We fell to our knees and the Abbot led us in prayer. There were no hassocks, our knees were on stone, and the chanting echo of our voices filled the building with its rise and swell. The prayers continued until the stroke of seven sounded on the church bells. Then, stiff and sore and hungry, we rose to our feet as the Abbot walked along the nave and filed out in his wake.

We went to our room in the roofs, and lay on our beds. More boys came in and lay in their habits on their beds, brown bags of dust, forlorn, on grey-white pallets, two rows of poor humanity. The lights were blown out. The room was dark. The snuffle of adenoidal breathing filled our bedroom. Regular snoring bubbled and burst.

I tucked myself into my bed and despite my hunger fell quickly asleep, and, it seemed almost immediately, was shaken awake by a gentle hand rocking at my chest.

'Prayers,' a voice whispered, and we took ourselves together back down to the abbey. Candles lit the church, and on the high altar splendid candlesticks glistened, heavy gold, capped by cones of blue-yellow flame. On the borders of sleep we were on our knees again, the stone floor so much colder than at vespers. The chanting began, echoing voices, following the Abbot's call.

The Abbot stepped down to the altar. A monk rose from his knees and standing by his side filled a huge goblet with wine. The Abbot mumbled in Latin and sipped from the wine. He was passed a white wafer, and first kissing it, he touched it to his tongue and withdrew it into the cave of his mouth. Two monks then took the goblet and the host, and stepped beside a third monk who waved a huge censer from which spilled the scent of a thousand spices. As he waved the thurible he chanted a Latin plainsong in a low voice, and although the words had absolutely no meaning for me, in the gentle cadence was comfort, reassurance. The monks filed forward to take wafer and wine then turned back to their seats. The Abbot rose up and left the church.

We returned once more to our rooms and very quickly fell asleep. My sleep was without images, broken sharply in the middle of the night by loud sobbing, bursting, rending, panic filled. The crying stopped almost immediately as I woke and I felt the tears on my face and realized that the sound had come from me, that I'd woken myself with my own misery, misery that had taken me without thought, spinning out of my body in dreams. I dried my eyes and blew my nose, and huddled back under the covers. The night came again and I was asleep. And then the dawn was announced by a parade of birds gathered on the roof, strutting among the tiles, shouting at each other in a clamouring rivalry of decibels, a rippling cacophony that shook the eaves. I looked around at the other boys, caught in silent motion, stretching, yawning, rubbing their eyes. Some sat on the edges of their beds, others pulled on their habits, beds were being made.

Four bells sounded, it was time for matins, and in a procession of sleepiness we entered the abbey once more to pray. A choir sang, a cascade of voices shrilling, booming, ranging through the octaves, treble, alto, tenor, baritone, bass, greeting the faithful.

We were gathered, and on our knees the morning devotions were done.

The different periods of the day were marked by the temperature of the stones upon which I knelt. Coldest and hardest in the early morning for matins, warmest for vespers. On our sore knees we prayed in silence for the souls of the damned, and it seemed to me that we were praying for our own lost souls, we were the damned, lost in this world, never to take our places in heaven.

We stumbled to our feet, and I followed my room-mates into a classroom. We took our places at uncomfortable desks, on which were placed a scratchy pen and a Bible. Inset into each desk was a brass inkwell with a sliding lid. We faced a raised platform, home to a clean blackboard, a comfortable chair and a large desk. Our teacher entered and we rose to our feet. He motioned for us to take our places and we sat down. He sought me out.

'You are the new boy?'

I rose to my feet. 'Yes, sir.'

'Your name will be John.' That was it, christened, I was now Brother John. The others were staring at me and I flushed. Our teacher paced the podium, hands clasped behind his back. He turned to us. 'We will take for our lesson today these verses. "Sing and rejoice, daughter of Zion: for, lo, I come, and I will dwell in the midst of thee, saith the Lord." Well, boys, where was that from?'

There was no reply from my classmates but I knew, my memory that sometimes to my sadness fails to forget had located these verses. Our master pointed at me.

'Well, boy?'

'Zechariah, chapter 2, verse 10.'

'Correct, and why, you horrible boys, is it the new boy who tells us this? What is wrong with you? Are you all idiots?' Our teacher paced his little stage, waving his arms at us. 'Remember this, Zechariah told of the coming of our

Lord. He told how our Messiah would ride into Jerusalem, on a humble donkey. And as it was predicted, so he came, amid cheering crowds, to a Temple Mount corrupted by the Sadducees. And what did he do there, boys?'

This, it seems, the boys remembered, and a chorus of them started to shout.

'One at a time,' he boomed, a sergeant major drilling his troops. He pointed at a boy in the front row.

'Cleansed the Temple.'

'That is correct. During the Roman occupation, boys, the Temple Mount had become abased, abused. It was a market place for traders, where redemption could be bought and sins redeemed. The Temple Mount, the holiest place in Judaea, was rotten, sick and spoilt. Redemption and prayers were the property of usurers and the Levites and Cohens had grown fat on this grotesque trade. For a few shekels, a loathsome sinner's place in heaven could be restored. For a few shekels more, adultery, theft and base lies could be forgiven.

'Boys, can you imagine the scene, the holiest place of Israel a souk?

'This was a shocking unholy thing and it rankled God. And the Son of God saw this corruption, this poisoned thorn in the side of God's great house and with a great sway of people cleansed this rottenness.

'Boys, stop a moment, and imagine the great rush of people led by our Saviour, gathering in the city, then sweeping up in a great swell, rushing on to those corrupt traders, knocking away their filth, chasing away the goats and sheep, freeing the pigeons and doves, flushing out the prostitutes, clearing that great and holy area. The market was dismantled, and its wooden struts and its cotton shrouds were passed piece by piece into the city beyond.

'At that moment there came a stream of priests from the Temple, at their head the Great Cohen, leader of them all, direct descendant of Aaron, the first priest. The Sadducees had heard the cheering and baying and from their windows observed the activities below. Imagine that line of corrupt men surprised in voluptuous abandon, imagine them hurriedly wrapping themselves in their holy robes, as if caught in prayer, imagine their fringed shawls, their heavy phylacteries. And it was all a sham. A sham, I tell you.

'No, boys, let me tell you there was no truth in those men. These priests had betrayed their faith, spent their time with prostitutes, eaten pigs' flesh, wiped their arses with pages torn from their holy scriptures, had become fat, while their own poor people starved.'

Our teacher had become most excited with the idea of corruption and deceit and had descended from his podium to our level. He walked past our desks gesticulating, emphasizing each colourful point in his story by prodding one of us with his sharp finger. We were all fascinated, and indeed it was fascinating, this marvellous adventure story.

Our teacher turned and rushed back to his desk. Leaning against it, his bottom wedged on its edge, he faced us.

'Boys, let me take you back to that day, 1,900 years ago. Can you imagine our good Lord, pale, robed in white, flanked by the disciples, the people of Jerusalem behind him, confronting the priests. Imagine the contrast between the pure face of the Holy One and the wine-reddened features of that unholy High Priest.'

At that moment I lost the thread of his presentation, struck by the remarkable similarity between our squint-eyed teacher's florid features, corkscrew veins decorating his face and bulbous nose, and the image conjured by him of the villainous High Priest. Then starting, I returned from my daydream to his imagery.

'Boys, let me take you there. Our Blessed One looks in the eyes of the High Priest. Words were not exchanged, but that Priest knew at that moment that, unless Jesus was stopped, he and his Cohens and Levites would be cut away from their livelihood. No more would their hours be comfortable, no longer would their food and wine be fine. In future, their greatest choices would not be between a beautiful red-headed whore or an even more beautiful brunette, but which stone they should use as their desert pillow. At that moment, boys, the priests knew of the danger their whole society faced from Jesus and they turned, went back to their temple, and proceeded to organize our Saviour's destruction, the result of a monstrous alliance between Jews and Romans.

'Now, boys, I'm going to leave the room and I want you to write an essay, I want you to go back to these times and write about that confrontation, but I want facts, I want to know how Jesus entered Jerusalem, who followed him, give me some background. I want you to tell me how the Jews were organized in Israel. Tell me about the divisions between Pharisees, Essenes and Sadducees, what they believed in, how they acted out their faith. Write about the Romans and their government of the Hebrews. Use your brains, and remember you have a source that you can always rely on, a fount of knowledge that will provide you with all the facts.' He held the Bible high, waved it at us around the axis of his wrist, flourished the holy book, the source of all information. He reverently replaced the Bible on his desk and with a nod to us all, left the room, banging the door.

This sort of task I found easy to perform. At the

orphanage I'd been drilled on ancient history, pressed to learn enormously long passages from the Bible, taught an elementary Latin. The New Testament provided a volume of historical information from those times, so that with a little sense it was easy to possess an understanding of the state of the Hebrew nation at the time of Jesus's coming. I knew from my time with the nuns exactly how Roman and Hebrew society was ordered in those years, and with very little effort was able to write the essay requested by our teacher. Although the original source of knowledge, the New Testament, was available to us, I was unaware at that time of any of the later commentaries, and this original text caused me some confusion.

This confusion came from the enormous number of discrepancies between the four gospels, differing even in their description of the most revered scene in Christ's history.

Mark 16: 2–5 reads as follows. 'And very early in the morning the first day of the week, they came unto the sepulchre at the rising of the sun. And they said among themselves, who shall roll us away the stone from the door of the sepulchre? And when they looked, they saw that the stone was rolled away: for it was very great. And entering into the sepulchre, they saw a young man sitting on the right side clothed in a long white garment; and they were affrighted.'

Yet Luke 24: 1–4 describes the scene differently. 'Now upon the first day of the week, very early in the morning, they came unto the sepulchre, bringing the spices which they had prepared, and certain others with them. And they found the stone rolled away from the sepulchre. And they entered in, and found not the body of the Lord Jesus. And it came to pass, as they were much perplexed thereabout, behold, two men stood by them in shining garments.'

And Matthew 28: 1–4: 'In the end of the Sabbath, as it began to dawn toward the first day of the week, came Mary Magdalene and the other Mary to see the sepulchre. And, behold, there was a great earthquake: for the angel of the Lord descended from heaven, and came and rolled back the stone from the door, and sat upon it. His countenance was like lightning, and his raiment white as snow: and for fear of him the keepers did shake, and became as dead men.'

I slid open the brass lip of the inkwell and dipped my pen. I wrote in my pretty copperplate, wrote without errors, without blot, my spelling perfect. The nuns who had taught me had been brought up in another century and their values and ideals came from a time when the great Queen was on the throne. Victorian England had given them their education, and those standards were mine, courtesy of the nuns. I finished my essay and blotted my paper.

Around me the other boys were scribbling away, squinting, legs sprawled, faces hovering over their pens, frantically chasing for hidden references through the pages of the great book.

One other boy had finished his essay. He sat in quarter profile, back terribly straight, staring through the window at six ducks waddling across the damp lawn. The birds delicately picked their way through the bright rain, heads bobbing to trim choice blades of grass. The boy felt my eyes on him, turned towards me and looked me up and down with great suspicion. At that moment our master charged in, robes flaring out in his wake.

'Time to stop, boys, you've had your time. Essay monitor, collect the work.' A rachitic child scurried from his front row desk and grabbed at finished and unfinished essays, piling high our scribblings, rushing along the aisles. 'Right, boys, to the refectory.'

And it was luncheon time, the rows of low refectory tables, mumbled protracted toothless grace, racing meal, eyes down, and a spooning in of food at a rate that challenged tongues and stomachs. The monks rushed out and I was left alone. Remembering yesterday, I took myself down through the fields to the chicken huts, and the chicken lover.

Brother Aquinas limped towards me, sandals squelching low in mud puddles, ooze rippling over the webs of his feet. The vinous one sucked in his cheeks as he handed me a trowel and bucket, and I passed into chicken hut hell, its noise and bullied birds, its smell and damp darkness. But at least I was alone, and by myself there could be some sort of peace, a peace separated from the morbid festering nag of prayers, a peace secured from bum-loving, perverted monks. By myself I could dream, plan, aim for some other sort of life.

The work had rhythm, a repetitive pentameter of opening cages, trowelling shit, filling buckets and closing cages, marked by the chiming of the monastery bells. Six times each hour my bucket was full, each time an excuse to rush out into the fresh air where I ladled the chicken dung on to the manure heap.

Brother Aquinas had his own wooden hut, in the shelter of three oak trees, by the side of a lily pond. The shed was a little taller than the chicken huts, tall enough to allow a man to stand, and approximately six feet square. Its sides were clapboard, long planks fiercely nailed together. Its roof was covered by a green tarpaulin that flapped and flickered in the autumn breeze. Its door was open and faced the chicken sheds. Brother Aquinas sat on a three-legged stool, hunched over a wood-burning stove, despite the mildness of the weather. Each time I left the sheds with my heavy bucket he'd look up and his face would turn slowly, tracking my passage to the manure heap. In his hands was a heavy book, which I presumed in my verdant naivety held the thoughts of some saint, or a collection of biblical commentaries.

Five o'clock sounded and I'd finished clearing out the sheds. I put down my bucket and trowel, washed my hands in the trough and sprinkled cold water on my face. I pulled up my robe to dry my cheeks and wondered what to do next.

I crossed the yard to Brother Aquinas's hut. The door was open; Brother Aquinas was not there. I stood at the entrance and peered in, half expecting the chicken lover to leer out at me, but no, his home was definitely empty. Its interior was unexpected, extraordinary. The walls were hung with dark red velvet and on the floor was a Persian carpet, subtle mixtures of madders, powder blues, greens and browns, heavily overlaid with thick dry mud. On the stove was a pewter flagon, and from the flagon came the rich smell of spices and warm wine. Brother Aquinas had left his saintly book face down on his stool. I looked back through the doorway at the chicken huts. He was not to be seen. Curious, I took up the leather-bound volume and started to read where Brother Aquinas had left off. . .

'Lord Cuthbert,' announced the butler. Cuthbert strode into Lady Jane's library smacking his cane against his gleaming riding boots. She looked up from the yellow damask chaise longue, embroidery in her fair hands, light falling through her red hair, a halo for her beautiful face. She stood as he entered, and the butler withdrew, closing the rosewood library doors.

Lord Cuthbert bowed, top hat sweeping down around his waist and she walked towards him. Facing him, she clasped her hands together, her breath coming heavily.

Lord Cuthbert smoothed his silken hair, and straightened his waxed moustache. Lady Jane took his gloved hand and led him to the chaise longue. They sat together facing galleries of books, myriad spines of different coloured leather, on shelves that soared to a double height ceiling. Stained glass panels were set in the library roof. The library was a maze of bookcases, and in its corners, spiral staircases climbed to high galleries of delicate wrought iron. Heavy Cuban mahogany library tables and red leather armchairs clustered around an ornate white marble serpentine-fronted fireplace where coals glimmered in a broad black grate. In this library was the greatest collection of pornography in the world, books gathered from the furthest reaches of Victoria's empire by Lady Jane's father, Lord Myddelton, a man of perverse desires.

Lady Jane reached for a silver bell that rested on a marvellous coromandel side table. She rang vigorously and its bright peal brought in James the butler, splendidly bald, and extravagantly frail and elderly.

'M'lady?'

'Tea, James, would you mind.' He bowed and, retreating into the hallway, returned a few moments later followed by a solemn line of three unsmiling footmen dressed in red and gold livery. The first footman carried a folding table that he set up in front of Lord Cuthbert and Lady Jane. The second bore a heavy gilt tray laden with fine porcelain, crumpets, strawberry preserves and thick yellow double cream; the third poured tea from an antique silver teapot. The quartet bowed with great solemnity and in single file trooped from the library. Lady Jane turned to Lord Cuthbert.

'Do help yourself, my lord.'

'I don't mind if I do,' he said, twirling his moustache, and taking her in his arms kissed her lips and neck, then sank his teeth into her shoulder drawing blood, salt and iron in his mouth. Lady Jane turned from his lips and, cutting crumpets, decorated them with preserves and cream with neat strokes of a fine ivory-handled knife. As she concentrated her face puckered charmingly, her mouth making a pouting circle. Their thighs touched, and Lord Cuthbert's lips fell to her shoulder to lick away the tiny drops of red blood that gathered where he'd bitten. His hands racked up her skirt, drifting up along the coolness of her thighs, and pushed deep into her quim. Lady Jane continued to cut crumpets and spread jam as though nothing was happening. She shifted a little on the chaise longue to make herself more comfortable, and spoke of the weather and Lady Salamander's most recent ball.

She placed two crumpets on a fine bone china plate and passed it to Lord Cuthbert. He took it from her, and removing his hand from her dress started to eat. As he ate, Lady Jane's hands went to his breeches and felt him out. His trouser buttons were undone one by one, and his penis, released from its prison, stood up straight and free. Lady Jane bent over his lap and kissed him, then taking a knife laden with thick cream, smeared his penis from its root to its head. Once more she bent down, sucking and licking until his penis was quite, quite clean. Lady

Jane looked down at its flaming length, then reaching behind her head, pulled away her ruby and amethyst hairpins. Her thick auburn hair cascaded to her shoulders and fell rippling to her waist. She bent her head over Lord Cuthbert's groin and swayed backwards and forwards, her hair tickling his penis. Clasping his penis in her hand and hair she rubbed and rubbed, watching closely as his penis appeared and disappeared in her fist. Lord Cuthbert groaned, and his penis jerked, spurting out over her face and hair. She wiped a streak of his semen from her face and licked her finger . . .

'Well, Brother John. Have you quite finished your afternoon's work?' Brother Aquinas's nasal voice, its vowels blurred by his West Country origins and several tankards of hot toddy, broke in on my study of his amorous holy book.

'Brother Aquinas, I'm sorry to have burst in on you, I just wondered what I was to do next?' I put the book down, turning bright red, absolutely flustered. Brother Aquinas smiled, a sickly smile, black toothed, sinister, lopsided.

'Well, little one. You've an enquiring mind, haven't you?' His hand rested on my shoulder. 'And did your enquiries lead you to any conclusion?' His hand traced down my chest to my waist.

'No, Brother Aquinas.' I broke away from his touch as the church bells rang for vespers, and walked up the hill and through the fields to pray.

Although I'd been in the seminary for only a short period, I'd already become used to the rhythm of life, and its order lulled and calmed. We knelt for prayers, and the Abbot's voice rang out from above the eagle's head lectern, rattling the windows, shaking the sconces.

We retired to our rooftop room and lay on our beds. The candles were snuffed. Within a few moments the sounds of darkness filled the dormitory and I fell asleep to dream of packs of wolves chasing me across the snows of wild northern lands.

Dawn came, and we shuffled down to matins and then to lessons. We sat in our schoolroom, waiting for our teacher. Unlike most normal children waiting for their master we were quiet. We had formed no real relationships with one another, there were no conversations about conkers or sweets or girls, no alliances formed, no gangs. There were no bullies, no bullied, no triumphant athletes, no feted football or cricket team: we were solemn, serious, as drab in spirit as our brown robes. The corridor outside our room clattered with the slap of sandalled footsteps that came closer, closer, and bursting into our classroom came our teacher. He stomped on to the podium and hurled our essays down on his desk.

'Essay monitor.' The essay monitor rushed forward and awaited his command. 'Give out the marked texts.' The skinny child, bow-legged, toothless at thirteen, gathered the essays under his arm and scurried around dropping marked papers on to our desks.

The teacher's eyes ranged around his pupils, and it was as if those eyes were making judgements, predicting futures, corroborating decisions taken at an earlier time with regard to our abilities, our lives. The essay monitor went back to his desk. Where was my essay? The other boys looked through their marked work, some smiling, others puzzling over our master's comments, scribbled in bold flashes of turquoise ink. Our teacher took a breath in, assuming with that breath a greater mass, fatter and taller than before. He stepped on to the centre of the podium and coughed deliberately, a tetchy scratchy cough that caught our attention, focused panic. We all leaned forward wondering what was to be said.

'Boys.' He paused, scanning the room, a soaring condor in search of prey. 'Who wrote this?' From his pocket he pulled out a sheaf of paper and waved it at us. I recognized my copperplate script and was absolutely terrified. The essay floated ominously before me. Was I to be beaten, returned to the orphanage?

'This essay is unnamed. Who wrote it?'

Our teacher stepped down from the podium and paced up and down between our desks, staring at each boy as he passed. I raised my hand, ashen, palpitating. He saw me and unbelievably, smiled. 'This, Brother John, is excellent. Your first essay is exemplary. Why did you not write your name on it?'

'I'm sorry, master.' He put my essay down on my desk and beamed down at me. He bent forward and patted me on my back, and as he bent I caught his smell, an odd echo of spices mixed with cloying, startling body odour. Our master leaned over me and he tapped my essay with his forefinger.

'Brother John, I hope you can keep up this standard of work for the rest of your time here.' As he spoke his breath, hot with the carrion smell of vomit, alcohol and foul meat, fell on my face. I gagged and he returned to his desk to talk to us of the good Samaritan, a moral tale for every century, for all time. The lesson had yesterday's pattern in which our master told us a biblical story and then, giving us an essay title based on the story, left the classroom while we wrote. The story of the good Samaritan was a familiar one to me, and as yesterday I had no difficulty writing, remembering, thanks to my photographic memory, whole passages of testament which I quoted. My essay completed well within the time limit, I blotted my writing and looked around at my classmates, sprawling, staring, scratching, abandoned to the solitary pressure of work. Our essays were collected, and we trailed off to lunch, to work, to vespers, to sleep, to matins, to class, to lunch, to work.

And so the days passed. Winter came. The days were short and cold. Our monastery was unheated, we had no winter issue of extra blankets or warm underclothes. We were cold and our existence was spartan, frozen. It was difficult to sleep at night, and we were so chilled in our rooftop home that some of us huddled together in a common bed, warmed by a marriage whose dowry was heat.

Snow fell and covered the fields and buildings, our houses and hedges. The lake was frozen and frost sparkled on our morning windows. Every day I would trudge down to see my friends the chickens, and each day deliver a new burden of frozen corpses to the manure heap. My responsibilities increased, and my duties included the gathering of the eggs, fewer in these winter months than in the warmer spring and summer, and the feeding of the birds.

Brother Aquinas had withdrawn to the solitude of his hut, emerging from his hibernation every two to three days to climb up to the monastery, returning, ploughing through the snow, dragging behind him a sackful of provisions and a wooden barrel of sweet liqueur, distilled from herbs gathered in the woods and hedgerows. Coming back to the chicken huts, his habit covered with a crust of snow, his hair caked white with ice, an icicle on the end of his nose, I would hear him spitting, hawking, coughing, grumbling loudly at the inclemency of winter, screeching vile curses at God's foul weather.

Back in his velvet-lined hut he'd liven up his stove and great puffs of smoke would drift up from the teetering chimney that topped his shelter.

Every afternoon after I'd collected the eggs, I'd knock at his door. Piratical cursing would greet my timid rattles and after a great harrumphing the door would open for me to stack calcific pearls in wooden pallets in the darkest corner of the hut. Each time I entered Brother Aquinas would stumble up from his drink and attempt to paw me, grabbing me as I bent over to pack the eggs, and each time I would rebuff him, becoming more and more aggressive with the unpleasant old dissolute. Every week, Brother Aquinas and I would pile the trays of eggs on to a huge old sled, then, whipping up a poor black donkey, Brother Aquinas would ride off to the village, to sell the eggs and buy essentials for the monastery.

He'd come back leery-eyed, rolling drunk, often asleep, collapsed snoring on his seat, reins fallen at his side, brought home by the reliable beast, who knew his way better than Aquinas.

One particularly drunken January morning, Brother Aquinas was completely incapacitated. The donkey waited patiently in his halter, flicking his tail at imaginary flies, chewing at his bit, pawing at the ground. Aquinas rolled around slapping his belly and giggling, watching me as I worked, guffawing, swigging at his pewter tankard. He slipped on the ground, cursed God and the winter, and, splay-legged, attempted to get up. His red wine had spilt, staining the white snow. He clutched at his tankard, struggling to rise, unable through immense drunkenness to find purchase on the slippery snow.

'Help me up, boy,' he shouted. 'Help me, you disgusting little monster, spawn of a syphilitic whore, help me.' He struggled again and fell back. I gave him my hand and his serpents' nails cut into my flesh as he pulled himself to his feet. He tried to clamber up, missed his step, and fell again, shrieking as he struck his temple on one of the runners. Angered by pain, energized by anger, he grabbed the side of the sled and tried to pull himself up, arse out, legs sliding.

'Help me on, boy,' he shouted. His roars were accompanied by an ocean spray of spittle shooting from his mouth, and I pushed so hard at his arse that he tipped up and over, landing on his nose in the back of the sled crushing dozens of our eggs. He staggered to his feet and crashed down on to the leather-padded driver's seat. Blood dripped from his nose on to his egg-spattered habit. Oblivious of the bleeding, he clutched at the reins, and missed in his drunkenness. He looked down at me, swaying on his tipsy seat, and it was obvious that he'd never make it to the village in his bibulous state. He seemed to realize this too, and, beckoning me on to the seat next to him, shouted at me to drive him into the village. I took the reins and we set off along the snow-covered lane.

Although I'd passed through the village only once, on my way to the monastery, to remember the route was no effort, so strongly had that late September morning been imprinted on my mind. Now icicles decorated the trees, the hedgerows were lost in drifts of snow, and the silent fields curved away to a cotton-wool horizon. Snowflakes were caught up in the rattle of a breeze and billowed in pretty flurries around the ears of our good donkey whose delicate hooves rose and fell, muffled by the snow. No birds sang in this deep white winter where all was quiet and still. Except for the noise of Brother Aquinas's drunken snoring, peace seemed to be in our little world.

Our donkey panted, its steaming breath rushed out, two storm clouds of condensation swirling around its head as it heaved us up to the little hamlet of houses that crested the next hillock. The monastery could not be seen and away from its lowering menace I felt free. Every step our donkey took away from its bulk eased the blackness, cleared the dark oppression from my head. Although the village was close, the journey was slow, and it took almost an hour to travel the mile.

We came to the village. The streets had been cleared of snow and the runners of our sled rattled over frozen cobblestones. The little brick houses were silent-faced, shutters drawn, lifeless, and might have been thought abandoned but for the shivering clouds of mean smoke that rushed from stubby chimneypots.

I pulled at the reins and we clattered to a halt. Brother Aquinas jerked awake, yawned and cursed and, rubbing his fists into his bulging eyes, farted vigorously, then stretched. He sat forward and stared at his surroundings. Bewildered then orientated, he pointed a tremulous finger at the nearest house, shouting, 'That one, horrible child.' I obediently climbed down from the sled and knocked with my fist at the door.

A face appeared at the window, turned and disappeared, and I heard noises in the house, voices that told that the monks were here. The front door was opened by a woman in a check apron. Her grey-streaked hair was tied back in a tight bun and her dress was full, with an old-fashioned bustle. She wiped her hands and waited for me to speak, hostile, guarded.

'Go on, boy, give her the eggs, stupid ugly bitch,' roared Aquinas. The donkey's eyes twitched in distaste, and the poor woman shivered and shuddered. I started to unload the eggs and hand them to the waiting woman. Again Aquinas roared, 'Leave them to the bitch to unload, the devil blast the lazy sluggard.' The woman took the trays of eggs from the sled and staggered into the house.

Aquinas belched, and slumping back in his seat snored loudly. I lifted out the remaining trays of eggs and followed the woman back into her home. The doorway opened into a single small room and into the room plunged a flight of bare stairs. The room contained a rocking chair, a pine table, and a crude Welsh dresser laden with orange and blue patterned plates. Two china Staffordshire houses, rococo fantasies, were on the mantelpiece, one for each of the two barefoot children who played on the floor. By the far wall, under the garden window, the woman was placing the eggs on a wooden draining board that slipped down to a white china sink.

I stood behind her holding the eggs. She turned unsmiling, and with no words took the eggs from me, carefully placing them with the others. I waited, half expecting to be paid, or to receive goods in exchange. None was given; the woman stood silent, arms folded, waiting for me to leave her home. I looked around wondering where her man was, and then realized that there would be no men in the village. It was 1916, and the men had been taken for the war. The children looked up at me from the floor, big-eyed, tense. Their spinning tops and marbles were abandoned. They were waiting for me to leave. I realized then that we were unwelcome in this village, where the monks and the monastery were regarded as evil, ugly.

I flicked the reins and we turned slowly, gathering up speed, retreating from the village, rambling across the blackened cobblestones, making towards our home. The visit to the village had unsettled me, and the countryside no longer felt peaceful, its vista no longer beautiful, just damnably cold.

I rolled Aquinas off the sled, and pushing and shoving at the unpleasant, stinking sotbag, managed to settle him down in the sulphurous shed that he used as his home. I freed the donkey from his halter, stabled him, broke the ice on his water, forked fresh clean straw into his manger, and returned to the monastery and evening prayers.

Chapter Three

WE HAD started to learn classics, and a new master taught us Greek, Latin and Hebrew. Rather unfortunately for a language teacher, this monk had a treacherous stutter. Explosions of consonants shattered the agony of silence that lay in the jerky ruins of his speech. Although the stutter didn't seem to bother him, it bothered us, and in desperate moments, head jerking with the effort of overcoming the hurdles of 'the' and 'this', we'd shout our guesses at the missing words, willing him on to leap the fences of his impediment.

I loved the ancient languages, enjoyed the depths and rhythms of declensions in secret tongues, revelled in the arrogance of blind vowels and verbs. In my hours with the chickens I'd sing hymns out loud in Greek and Hebrew, gesticulating flamboyantly at my congregation of feathered co-religionists, shifting from language to language, exuberant with the joy of my new learning. How wonderfully droll to quote from the Edict of Nantes in ancient Greek, how amusing to sing out Augustus's doctrines in Hebrew. The chickens were impressed. They seemed especially to love Latin, its whistling susurrus bringing a new joy to their laying. They liked Greek less, and its slippery echoes brought out an increased tendency for the creatures to bully each other. They loved Hebrew least, refusing to feed, chasing each other in circles around their cages.

To learn was so easy. At fourteen my intellect was at its zenith, and all that I saw was literally blotted on to the pages of my memory. The columns of a dictionary or an algebraic formula, when recalled, were as vivid as when first seen and this attracted attention in the classroom. At first when I'd shown my abilities, I'd been regarded suspiciously, the boys and masters thinking that I'd cheated, but never quite able to work out in which way I'd managed to cheat. My desk had been searched for hidden books and my pockets checked for secret scraps of paper. Nothing was ever found, for nothing needed to be hidden, it was all in my brain, and if I wanted a fact it was there, never forgotten, as brilliantly etched in my mind as on the printer's original stone.

Once in my first few months in class I'd been called to the front and publicly humiliated, shouted at, exposed as a vile sham, a mean cheat. I'd been asked how I'd known, how I could know so much, and there before the novices had been tested, rigorously grilled, asked for gospel quotations, logarithm numbers, square roots, geography, history. My answers were of course perfect, and as each more complex problem was posed my peers became more vacuous, more idiotically agog as the answers came out invariably correct. The language master and our religious instructor were first bemused at my answers, looking carefully at me and then around the class for clues as to how exactly I was cheating. And then when it was obvious that I wasn't cheating they seemed to become angry, irritated at my knowledge, and their questions were harder, sharper. Finally they became incredulous, their questions became more ridiculously intricate and the spaces between them longer as if they needed more time to comprehend the extent of my extraordinary memory. I remember them, little and tall, side by side in their flapping habits, open-mouthed, pin-eyed, more and more amazed at each perfect answer. I describe this now, not out of vanity but merely to portray those moments and the reasons for my fortune, impossible were it not for my glorious gift.

From this time I seemed to be marked. Special attention was paid to my performance in school and I seemed to be watched at prayers. There were no specific incidents in which I was aware of being spied upon, but always, at all times my innate sensitivity told me that the rulers of our small world were paying me attention.

It was late February and the snow still sat on the land. The rituals and routines of everyday life proceeded in their quiet lulling way and the days slipped by. The winter was long. The monks had difficulty remembering a time when the lake had been so deeply frozen.

I walked from the monastery following the footsteps of yesterday's journey, the flat imprints of sandals echoed by the paw marks of a cat and the occasional imprints of England's tattered sparrows. The chicken sheds were shielded from the monastery by hedgerows, stark oaks and the swell of fields. I wandered in their direction and, child that I still was, played games with yesterday's footsteps, walking backwards matching my steps, then rushing off to make false trails into the fields, trails that suddenly stopped, as I retreated in my own tracks, leaving mysteries for the pirates and vagabonds who were my imagined pursuers.

I clambered up the last hillock before the chicken huts. Cold snow flickered up, clutching at my bare calves, and I slipped, falling lightly into a deep drift. I stood up and brushed off the snow, and moving more carefully on squelching sandals, pulled myself along by the hedgerow's bare elder branches.

I breasted the brow of the hillock to an extraordinary sight. Aquinas's hut was afire. Flames soared, roared, popped. Black smoke billowed. And then Aquinas's searing scream. I ran to the hut, raced to a mass of flames. I stood panting, unable to move near for the heat, and under the crackle of flames came mad drumming, a host of barbarians battering at the hut's door. The flaming door burst open, hinges broken. Aquinas staggered forward, his robes and hair on fire, a great orange flame flickering from the top of his head. He collapsed, falling on his face into the snow. Hissing acrid smoke and foul leaping flames rushed from him. I threw great armfuls of snow over his twitching mass. The snow covered the flames, turned to trickling water then billowing steam. Aquinas was still. The fire was out. He lay splayed in a greasy puddle. Then his body spasmed and shook, his arms and legs twitching. Quiet again, he lay unmoving, limbs twisted, contorted.

I came to him, crouched, and caught the smell of his charred bitter meat. I vomited, choked on sourness, spewed and coughed. Then, controlling myself as best I could, I tried, tried to roll Aquinas over on to his back, a monstrous effort in the slush and slip, tipping that great larded pig. Pushing, panting, I pulled him and his hand tore away. I screamed with fright. Then calming down, and breathless with effort, I managed to flip him around and the splash of melted snow soaked my clothes. The fire had taken his face and stripped it down to black bone and teeth. His habit had been completely consumed, leaving his chest stripped to a bare barbecue of roasted ribs. The skin over his abdomen had gone, leaving great sausages of guts spilling out on to the snow. Blood oozed from the stump of his right arm where his hand had pulled away. Separated, spider-fingered, tendons and muscles exposed, it lay glistening by his side.

There was a crackling and a sudden bang. Terrified, I spun around. The hut had collapsed, into a strangely cosy bonfire, harmless, cheering, it blazed, an innocent winter observer, a gardener's fire, clearing away useless twigs and roots. Bright sparks caught in the uprise of heat, took to the heavens, shooting up in shivering streams.

I felt nothing for Aquinas, no sorrow, no pity. And this body, that lay on winter's mattress, had left no inheritance but bones, no memorial, no memory, no love. He lay there, master of chickens, sot, sybarite, parasite. Who would mourn the beast? I remembered his ways, his loathsome touch, his elaborate pornography, his staggering drunkenness, his bestiality, his sodden, stinking rudeness. There were no qualities that redeemed him, nothing that promised redemption, the only piece of him that would touch heaven the sparks that had flown from his flesh.

Looking down on his body, I wondered what had brought him here, what had happened to him in his other life, what had turned him, if turned he had been, into corruption, into debauch, into filth, into lascivious disgrace. This lack of grace, putrid, dirty, was expressed in his vinous cheeks, and the stench of his rotten breath, a fat man vile and corrupt, respecting only the hot wine bubbling on his stove, and the clear pictures painted by Victorian pornographers of twisting couples, writhing triplets, grasping quadruplets, Siamese conjoints.

Aquinas, what made you? And something from a time when he was innocent, having some echo in my own past, took me to sympathy and I looked through the huts for material to cover his body. I'm not sure why I searched, for

I knew there was nothing to find except wine and chicken shit. I knew that there was wine and chicken shit, yet I still looked, and coming back to his bones, covered him with snow, heaping white over the empty holes of his flesh, until I had built him a decent mound, made him a home, made him a Saxon barrow for a home.

I turned from him, back to the monastery, walking slowly uphill to that dark mass, white in its winter coat but still black and brooding. It was the time of our early evening prayers. The service had started. I pushed open the abbey doors, they creaked ajar, and their scratching echoes, amplified by the abbey's lofty acoustic, clattered around the church, turning it into an alleyway of rolling dustbins and screaming cats breaking the solemn meditation of a thousand monks on silent knees. The monks turned to the noise, to see me, little one, caught in the freeze frame of the doorway. In the razor of their opprobrium, I turned to tears, and sobbing, crying, I burst out with the news, shouting to the hollow nave and peering eyes, 'Brother Aquinas is dead, he's dead, burnt, burnt in his hut. Brother Aquinas is dead, dead.'

Shaking with agitation I fell into a pew, catching my hip painfully against an armrest. The monks rushed to their feet, gasping, buzzing, the same questions echoing between them, in some crazy synchrony. The Abbot leaned down from his eagle lectern searching me out from the murmuring monks. Then, gathering his robes tightly to him, clutching his arms across his chest, he swept from his eyrie out into the nave, and from the church. After a moment's hesitation, the rest of the monks followed, lines of men streaming from their pews into the aisles, crushing against one another in their hurry to leave the church. I followed them, last through the doors, and stood at the monastery's entrance, watching the lines of brown, tracing down, dipping away across the white, to the chicken huts below, their tracks a rake's marks through February snow.

After some moments of quietness, I followed them down leaving the monastery deserted. All of its huddling monks old and young, fat and thin, rapacious and ascetic, had poured out, dripping down over the land to the chicken huts, leaving the monastery, a *Marie Celeste*, empty of all life.

The sun was bright, and its light sharp, February bright, almost warm, promised spring. Hurrying, I caught up with a group of old men, habits flapping, tottering down in their shaky way, sticks waving, prissy paced, fussy, crotchety, grumbling at each other, telling each other, none of them listening, all of them shouting, about how right they'd always been, told you so told you so, and as I passed I left their conversation with its memories of the mysteries of Aquinas. Racing on I passed another flock of elderly crows, slightly more sprightly than the last group, eager-faced, crowding forward, curious to see the charred bones of Aquinas the cooked.

Panting now, I ran downhill, slipping, sliding, making my way forward through the clustering monks and over the final hill to Aquinas's empire and frosty grave. A ring of monks surrounded the mound. I pushed through the tight whispering group, elbowing my way and being sharply elbowed back, squeezing between legs and being cursed. Shoving through the stinking mass of unwashed men, Breughel men, garlic and onions, farting, beer breath, until I was finally through the last of them, into the centre of the circle of men.

The Abbot stood, one hand on his hip, the other circling his chin, staring myopically through gold lorgnettes at the hump of ground where Aquinas lay in death's dark dream.

He paced around the grave, hands raised together in contemplative prayer, eyebrows rammed down tight over puzzled eyes. I stepped forward and he ignored me, circling around Aquinas's grave, head down, lost in some puzzle, fingering the heavy ivory cross on his breast. He stopped, and his head turned, surveying the surrounding pop-eyed, gawking, jostling men, and found them distasteful. He tipped his chin and scowled. His sneer caught me, and stretched unpleasantly as he looked me up and down. The Abbot was fat, very fat, folds of stomach billowing out, filling his capacious robes. Every piece of his body was suffused, his dumpling fingers, his steamed pudding ear-lobes, his bulging serried chins. His face was covered with unpleasant fatty cysts, pearls that studded his cheeks, popped through the bushes of his eyebrows and wobbled oddly on his nostrils. He was old, yet his hair remained brown, no whisper of frost at his temples, and his skin was good around his eyes and lips, where the crows of time imprint. He turned a heavy gold ring set with a huge ruby on his finger and spoke to me. His words were spaced and came in a sing-song voice, high pitched, oddly threatening, as if I was to blame for this apparent disaster. He drew close to me, staring.

'Well, child ... what did you see?' He took off his lorgnettes and flourished them at me.

'Sir, it was like this. I'd finished morning class—'

'Boy, I do not ... wish to know what you had for lunch ... Come to the point.'

'Sir, I came over the hill to find Aquinas's hut on fire. He was screaming, battering at the door to get out.'

The monks were straining to hear, pushing forward to find out details. The Abbot felt himself hemmed in by the excited men and shouted for them to fall back, swinging out his arm at them in annoyance.

'Continue, boy.'

'Sir, he broke free, staggered from the hut and collapsed in flames in the snow. I couldn't help him. It was too late.' The Abbot nodded, and pointing at three young monks said, 'You, dig him up, and carry him to the abbey.' He pointed at another group of gawking men. 'Prepare a grave,' he commanded, and then to the milling multitude he shouted, 'We will bury Aquinas tonight.' Turning away, he cut through the crowd, and the monks fell back, clearing a space for his imperious path. I had absolutely no wish to see Aquinas disinterred, and followed the Abbot away from the bier, keeping a sensible distance as he stalked back to the monastery. As we walked, there came a hush from the monks and then a rising, gushing gasp as the snow was brushed away from the charred corpse.

In the monastery, I hurried through the dark corridors and made my way to my dormitory room. The monastery was oddly noisy, and passing closed doors I was conscious of women's squeaking giggles, bursting choruses of ribald laughter, shouting, plates crashing, noises that I'd heard before but never so clearly as now. Voices liberated by the absence of the monks. Women in the monastery, how strange, who were they, why were they there?

My room had changed little over the last six months; the walls were bare, the beds crammed together, neat rows of tidily folded blankets and sheets. I lay on my bed and was soon asleep, to be woken, it seemed, in a moment, by the great bells ringing out, enticing us to prayer. The chiming ceased, and the tingling clamour of the bells gradually faded. We rose from our beds in the darkness, to the accompaniment of plangent chanting. The aves of the monks reverberated around our rooms, carried up to us, it seemed, from directly below, by the odd acoustics of the wooden-beamed building. The abbey was quite separate from the seminary; it stood free, a stone building guarded by gargoyles and ravens. It was connected to the rest of the monastery by a number of passageways, not all of which were in regular use, and it was these passages that were responsible for the strange acoustics.

We dressed and, in our half-sleep, stumbled down to pray. Aquinas's coffin had been placed by the side of the altar. It was a cheap, rough assembly of plain pine planks, and it rested on a low bier covered with white silk cloth heavily embroidered with gold crosses, fringed and tasselled. A hundred candles sparkled in the chancel. They were the only source of light in the church, and as the flames caught and flickered, the shadows of a thousand mice chased around the edges of the church. We knelt, and the mass for Aquinas proceeded, a Latin dirge of dark notes, repeated, repeated.

The Abbot stood at his pulpit and spoke to the assembled monks of Aquinas's pure life, his dedication to the monastery, his care of his fellow man, his tirelessness, content, peace and goodness. The Abbot told us of his angelic nature, sympathy for animals, concern for the community of man, his endless study of holy books, his curiosity for the ways of nature, his love of solitude, his life of contemplation, and all I could think of was his drunkenness, foulness, bestiality, coarseness, laziness and corruption. Who was this Aquinas that the Abbot remembered?

The Abbot knelt and we all prayed for Aquinas's soul. He needed our prayer. The Abbot called for our silence, and asked us to contemplate the message of Aquinas's life.

To me, the message was quite clear. We kneeled and, heads bowed, thought of Aquinas.

The Abbot creaked to his feet and nodding at the choirmaster indicated that the mass should continue. 'Amen' we sang, and the candles flickered. From the front line of pews eight monks stood up and walked in file to Aquinas's coffin, grouping in two lines of four silently by its side. The singing stopped, they hoisted the coffin on their shoulders and, with a slow and deliberate step, marched solemnly along the nave, towards the church's door. A young seminarist stepped forward from the back of the church and took his place by the door. When the pall-bearers were six paces away the boy opened it wide. A great rush of wind roared into the church, tearing around the building, swirling around our robes. The altar candles blew out. We were in darkness and the monks squeaked with fear. There was a tremendous report, the unmistakable noise of splitting wood, then screams. Chaos. Monks ran around the church squealing. A novice tripped over me. Someone sobbed. Then the Abbot shouted, his voice clearing through the din and calming the storm.

'Everyone quiet. Remain in your seats. Someone at the back bring in light from the passageway.'

And as suddenly as the disturbance had broken, so calmness came. The Abbot's commands were immediately obeyed and the disorder settled. The monks felt their way to the nearest pew and sat down, quietly. While we waited for light, the Abbot spoke again.

'Has anyone gone for light?' A voice answered that light was being fetched. The community waited in their pews. From behind me a mad giggle bubbled and shook, and then an uncontrollable hysteria spread around the church, wild laughter echoing between the monks.

'Quiet!' shouted the Abbot, and the hysteria was amplified by the imperative command, so that laughter and sobbing shook the pews. He shouted again, this time intolerably loudly, and the noise generated fear that sobered the monks and shut them up. Light came into the church. Three monks carrying lighted tapers appeared, the white of their faces made stark by flames. They lit the altar candles, and as the light grew, the disorder caused by the roaring wind was revealed. The neat lines of pews were disturbed, crooked. The silk-covered platform upon which Aquinas had lain was thrown over. The monks were agitated, whispering. The umbra of darkness retracted as more candles were lit, and flicker by flicker, inch by inch, the whole of the church was redrawn by light. And with the light came a great gasp. The monks turned to the fallen bier: Aquinas's coffin had splintered open. Hitting the flagstone it had split, and thrown Aquinas out on to his face. He lay splayed out on the stone floor of the church. He had been dressed in a simple white surplice, and for this I thanked God, glad not to have to see those terrible wounds again.

The Abbot took charge, and striding forward, shouting orders at trembling monks, had Aquinas lifted from the stone floor and replaced in his coffin. They had trouble fitting him back into the coffin because of rigor mortis, but somehow his limbs were wedged in and the lid fitted back over the dead man. The pall-bearers took up their load and we filed from our pews in silent procession behind Aquinas's burnt bones. As I shuffled along the nave, I stubbed my toe on a soft lump, and looking down I saw that I'd kicked Aquinas's hand, left over, forgotten in the high drama. It seemed best to leave it lying and I continued on with my colleagues, to the little graveyard bordered by box privet and yew.

We walked in procession carrying flaming torches, walked out into the black night, while the church bells tolled, slowly, slowly, and their slow resonance fitted perfectly with the metre of our chanting. The graveyard was thick with snow, except for a small rectangle of ground that had been cleared and dug deep. Two monks, one with a pickaxe over his shoulder, one with a spade at his feet, awaited the procession. We came close to the burial plot and formed a respectful circle, the Abbot its epicentre, not the grave. Bright tapers sparkled white, and light shone down deep into the hole in the ground, bridging the grave. The pall-bearers laid the coffin down over the ropes, while the two monks at the graveside took up strain, digging the heels of their sandals into the frozen earth. Slowly the coffin drifted down in its cradle of rope, the monks easing off, turned to sailors by rope passing through their hands. In English now the Abbot laid Aquinas to rest, ashes to ashes, dust to dust, and then the grave-diggers covered the coffin with clay, the coffin a drum for the beating earth.

The muttering, tutting monks drew away from the grave back to their beastly home, leaving the grave-diggers at their work, humping frozen earth, snow and wriggling worms on to Aquinas's body.

In the middle of the night I became aware of bizarre noises, singing, carousing, laughter, bubbling up through a conduit of boards and walls. Our room's strange acoustic meant that these sounds could be only from the abbey. On the borders of sleep, I lay in bed and it seemed as if I was awake, sharp, terribly alert, sparked into life by the squeals and giggles, laughter and chatter. The night appeared very deep, the moon sang out and our room shimmered in the grey light.

As if in a dream I put on my habit and placing my cowl

over my head for warmth, slipped out into the passageways below. Candles flared in sconces lighting my way down towards the abbey. In the passages it was quiet again. If I hadn't been aware of the building's strange flow of noise, it would have been reasonable to assume that the disturbance had been imagined, an hallucination, some fictitious trick of the mad moon. Inquisitive boy that I was, I skipped along, taking a familiar and automatic path to prayers.

The lights were bright in the abbey, the doors were wide, noise and ribaldry spilling out into the anteroom. I drew back, slipping into the shadow, and peered in. The pews had been cleared, and a great sway of naked men and women staggered and bucked. In the centre of the abbey, by the altar, a shivering ring of men and women were joined together in a complex circle of writhing, sucking and fucking. Shrieks burst from the women, and the men groaned and sighed.

In the centre of the circle was a black goat, curly-horned. Under his flanks a blonde woman lay, legs in the air, slobbering and sucking at the animal's penis while a grey-haired monk, holding her legs high on to his shoulders, fucked her.

Above the crowd, on a raised platform, four gypsy violinists played wild swirling music. Their clothes were bright and loose. Their hair was long, tied back with black bows, and silk scarves were drawn around their waists. Their faces were impassive, and they seemed uninvolved with the orgy below, playing as if at some family wedding. Suddenly a dark woman jumped on to the stage and dancing sinuously passed in and out among the group of men, brushing them with her breasts, rubbing her pubic hair against their hips. She danced behind the violinists, then slithering sensuously, her arms snakes around a violinist's neck, she dropped to his waist. She unravelled his scarf, then, pushing between the musicians, she made her way to the front of the stage. Swaying and dipping with the screaming violins, she bent back from her knees, so that her long hair touched the floorboards. Her thighs spread, she flicked the scarf down between her legs, drawing it against her cunt.

She sprang forward and still dancing, turned back towards the musicians who continued playing, regarding her with passivity, ignoring her moves. Challenged, she leapt forward, and pacing in front of them, waved the swirling scarf across each of their faces. The three older musicians ignored her, the pace of their music unchanged. The youngest, caught by her heat, smiled. She came to him and pressed the scarf into his face, smothering him with her scent. The music whirled then shivered as her hand went to his breeches and rubbed his groin. She knelt on the floor, down on her knees before him, arse pointing out at her slithering audience, and took his penis from his pants and sucked him, then stood up, leaving his trousers undone, his dagger cock on display. She danced forward to the front of the stage and bent backwards again, her long body arching, muscles flexing, straining. Hands between her legs she touched herself, shoving her fingers up, rubbing slowly then with more agitation.

Suddenly a cheer came from the audience and an immensely fat man, penis lost in folds of wobbling flesh, jumped on to the stage. It was the Abbot. He waddled towards the dark dancer, and falling on his knees bent over her taut form. He licked and sucked while she rubbed herself. Another cheer as another man rushed onstage, and pitched himself vigorously into the Abbot's backside.

On the other side of this desecrated abbey a spit turned

over a fire and a pig spilt its fat into the flames. A huge
monk in a leather apron sharpened carving knives, then
stripped away flesh from the roasting meat. I recognized
the monk, it was Brother Matthew. By the side of the spit a
young boy sat on a low stool. He turned the griddle's iron
handle and the pig slowly revolved over the flames. The
novice's face turned to me and I recognized my classmate,
the boy who stared through windows instead of writing his
essays.

A line of naked men and women stood before Brother
Matthew, and he greeted them all in turn with resounding
smacks on their shoulders or great slobbering kisses, feeling
them up with his greasy fingers, then laying meat on pewter
plates. He wiped his knives on his leather apron and kicked
out at a louche young monk with too long hair. The monk
fell on his knees before Brother Matthew, who, with a great
harrumph, struck out with the flat of his carving knife at
the monk's arse. His arm rose, swayed at the top of its arc
and then came down with great force, and came again, each
blow catching and shaking the young monk's body. Brother
Matthew, red-faced, puffed, tired of the game and kicking
out, he pushed the monk sprawling to the floor.

The queue of waiting sybarites shouted for food and he
cursed them, screaming that they would be pigs roasting in
the hungry flames of Hell turning on the Devil's spit unless
they shut up, and they did shut up when they saw the great
cuts of meat fall on their plate. The barbecue's flames flared,
and caught the pig's fat. The animal burned, and my
classmate doused the flames with water from a leather
bucket.

The abbey was a busy ocean, waves of men and women
bobbing and breaking on each other's shore. Old men
slithered and shook over imagined virgins, many of whom

were suddenly, shockingly remembered as grey-haired nuns from my orphanage, home of my childhood, land of sweet innocence lost, stern, saintly succubi cavorting with priapic incubi, pierced and heaving, voluptuously writhing with their brothers in Christ.

The wind rattled the abbey's windows and the candle-light shook. The walls swayed and I crouched deep into the shadows, falling back into darkness, then peeked around the doorposts into the Devil's room. The black-haired goat was being dragged around the body of the abbey, pulled on a gold chain by a simpering woman. The links bound them both together, tied in choking loops around their necks. Her breasts hung low, sagging, empty, and an enormous bush of grey pubic hair sprouted high up her belly, to her deep navel. She carried the abbey's great thurible, swinging it as she walked, dispensing holy spice to the baying crowd.

She paraded around the bounds of the abbey, and as she passed, encouraged by the goat's butting challenge, the orgy's tempo became more frantic. They walked towards the altar, and as they came closer, the baying voice of sex quietened. The cavorting, pouncing, bellowing, stinking, writhing decay calmed itself, and the mass of men and women detached themselves stickily from one another, turning together, like sunbathers to the sun, to stare at the woman and the goat. As they walked through the crowd, the people separated to let them through, retreating like the Red Sea from the Children of Israel. Closer they came to the altar, and the great mass of men and women seemed fixed on the chained pair. On the altar, two great golden candelabra threw light on the monastery's gold cross, which burnt with the fire of reflected flames. The goat was passive, quiet, tossing its head back in gentle slow motion as it was patted by the surrounding crowds. The great goat must have been drugged, responding so tamely to the stroking and patting of the cooing, clucking monks and nuns.

The goat was held still, and from out of the hellfire a miniature saddle was produced, ornate, byzantine, golden and studded. The saddle was strapped around the goat, leather tied tightly around its abdomen, and it was mounted by my classmate, who had changed into a simple white shirt. The boy was astride the goat, mounted backwards, face to tail, bum to horns. In solemn procession, the trio wandered the abbey, and every person that they passed touched them, claw fingers pinching the boy's cheeks, calloused palms patting the goat's flanks. They walked in a fixed pattern pacing from wall to wall, then at the centre of the abbey suddenly changed direction by ninety degrees, swinging around. So strange this pattern, suddenly discovered as the form of a cross. Through the crowds they passed, on a broken, crying route, greeted by silent touch, in a wistful, leaden hour, turning, turning, until they came at last to the altar. The boy jumped from the goat, heaved it up on to the altar and threw off its chain. The goat padded around the white altar cloth, challenging its audience with soft eyes, stooping to nuzzle the golden cross, pawing with delicate tentative cloven hooves at the virgin cloth.

Suddenly a magnificent thunderclap broke. The abbey vibrated, reverberating with the fierce noise. The monks and nuns gasped, squealed. The storm flashed and roared. Rain pounded on the roof, hissing on the windows, tapping down from heaven's clouds. Against the rules of science, disordered lightning flashed, bizarrely answering the challenge of thunder, forked electric whiteness piercing the dark colours of the stained glass, reaching right into the heart of darkness, hissing around the goat and the terrified clerics. The wind whined then screamed, blowing louder, calling for retribution, asking for answers of the blackness of night. The abbey rattled in the storm, and the black goat raised its head and sniffed the sulphurous air. The nuns and monks clutched at one another, drawing close, finding shelter in each other's sweaty fear.

The storm found no answer in the abbey's madness and, its energy spent, huffed around England's fields playing games with snow, chasing February's crystal frosts.

As the winds calmed, the panic settled, and the rushing, mewing men and women calmed themselves, concentrating once again on the altar centre stage. From the far corners of the abbey they watched the goat who stood steady and still. I peered more closely, and in a dazed and frightened dream, imagined from my crack-line view a wriggling disturbance, sneaking out from the corner of the altar cloth, an apostrophe of flashy gold and black, slithering out towards the goat. Like the bends of a river meeting the giving sea, this wriggle became larger, thicker, longer, an exclamation mark, then a writhing arm, looping and curving towards the unaware animal who wobbled on four cloven feet, gazing out benignly with seeing, uncomprehending, oval pupils on its friends below. And its friends watched it and the burgeoning scenario on the altar stage.

I moved forward a little to find a better view, peering out into the caverns of the abbey to the strangest scene. The writhing arm had become a thick and ugly snake, reaching out slowly, heaving itself towards the curly-haired goat. The creature dragged its bulk up into the altar cloth. Enormously long, hypnotically writhing, yards and yards of slithering serpent pulling itself forward, encircling the goat. Brother Matthew surveyed the cruel scene, arms folded over his greasy apron, carving knives dangling loosely from his belt. A tight circle of a hundred sweating monks and nuns, intent, anticipating eyes fixed on the stumbling goat and the stalking snake, packed around the altar. There was no obvious end to the coils of the snake, as it pulled itself up from the darkness of the depths of the abbey. A great hypnotic ouroboros, unending, sunk in the centre of the earth, it reached around the goat, forming circle on circle, coiling, laying its piling circumference around its stumbling innocent prey. The snake's head reared up, danced, shimmied, and its fork tongue darted from its gawping monster mouth.

Demented lightning crashed through the abbey, and the blinded crowd stumbled. I pressed back against the wall, and then peeked out again to see the snake wrapping itself around the forelegs of the goat, encircling the creature, climbing higher, darting around its chest, hauling itself up around the placid blinking beast. The snake's head hinged on its body, flapping, creaking, darting, seeking its constricting way up and up, over the goat's back and then to his neck.

The goat licked its lips, stock still, caught in the great writhing coils that settled, then shifted, the snake taking up the animal in its huge muscular bulk. And still the unending length of the snake came up and up, over the edge of the altar, yard after yard, from its hidden place in the darkest sediments of the earth. The goat's body was completely hidden by the serpent's coils, encircled, caught in the choking reptile. The snake pulled itself upwards and twisted around the goat's neck, once, twice, thrice, and the goat's eyes bulged. The goat sagged and wobbled, then toppled over, falling down on to the altar in quiet slow motion, pulled over by the leaning mass of the snake, noiseless, muffled by the great constricting loops.

And the chanting started, the swaying monks and nuns

humming repetitively. They spread out, chanting, then dropped to the flagstone floor, bellies down, faces flattened against the stone, holding hands. They formed circles around the altar, hand in hand, feet touching heads, and the whole of the abbey floor was covered by a wobbling field of pink and white. On the altar stage, the goat had disappeared, covered completely by the monster snake, engulfed in a hillock of scales, flashing, gleaming, metallic, anodized iridescence in the sparking light. And above the lumpen bulge of snake and goat, the gold cross of Our Saviour shone, witness to death, lonely, lovely, glistening. Slowly, slowly, the hillock became a lava flow, shifting in a silky ebb, and with its flow the altar cloth rucked up, moving with the ghastly mire of sacrifice and snake god. The cross fell, clanked to the floor and bounced, and the goat and snake slithered downwards together and were gone.

A great muttering rose from the circles of prostrate worshippers, celebrants of ritual sacrifice, and then a dull thump as death and the dead retreated from the altar to the whispering shadows, leaving nothing, nothing but the altar bare.

Brother Matthew hauled his knives from his belt and clashed them together, and steely echoes ricocheted around the abbey. The clash of knives was a signal and the naked crowd stopped their chanting and got to their feet, dusting themselves down, rubbing dirt from their stinking skin. The noise was a signal to me too, and I rushed away, running through the corridors, sickened with fright and horror, suddenly understanding the essence of the community, whose way was that of rotten flesh. All that had been mysterious, everything that had been a puzzle, was alarmingly and violently explained, the mysterious cacophony behind the closed doors, the sordid welcome, the debauchery and decadence, the drunken perversion, the stench and disquiet. The community had no grace, loved nothing but itself, revelled in evil and vileness. God was dead in his own abbey, and the devil had taken his throne. Blackness and blood, the colours of the dark night, ruled in bubbling decay. Sacrifice and bestiality, sodomy and bile were the corrupt monarchs of this rotten house.

I ran to my room, through the candlelit passages, panting, clutching, racing towards a safer space. But there was no safety, only darkness. There was no security, only ugliness. Barbed arms flailed out and there was poison at my heels. I reached out for peace and breathed sulphur fumes. No safety, only the madness of this dark building, its foundations burning purgatory. I swam through the corridor maze, drowning, bursting, seeking air and finding only burnt oxygen. My path had no signpost, a stinking quagmire surrounded me and the corridor's shadows bayed and roared. Satyrs and ravens rushed out at me screaming, and I staggered aside as vast flocks of sizzling devils clutched at me through searing flames. And then suddenly I was safe in my room, shivering under the sheets, hidden in the eaves, adrift in an ugly place.

Chapter Four

SUDDENLY, THE joy of spring, winter's brooding king checked by March's shining knight, his lance a shovel clearing away the deep snow, parting night's curtain, bringing light and warmth to our valley. The snow shone as it melted, silver edges lighting the drifts, trickling into puddles, oozing into streams, bubbling down the hillside into the lake below. The trees' new buds broke through their shells and stretched out witches' fingers at the morning sky. Apple blossom sparkled and sweet daffodils burst through the new green grass. Birdsong came back to the fields and lanes. The earth was ploughed, heavy carthorses dragging pickaxe steel, pulling the teeth of the field, making neat combed lines in the orange clay.

It was springtime and I was fifteen years old, growing tall on a diet of prayer. The pretence of prayer, the sanctification of suffering, was for me a cloth covering the true beliefs of the monks as their habits clothed their foetid flesh. I knew the charade, understood the act, knew as they did the reality of their moves. Solemn prayer, mass and psalms, the bread, wine and the holy cross, in this place were blasphemous madness, a game that they played in the open spaces, while behind closed doors dwelt drunkenness and ribaldry, violence and bacchanal, ordure and depravity. The monks appeared to me as they truly were, their habits costumes, their prayers lies. I understood their manners and ways, reinterpreted their glances and conversations. Their florid faces and trembling hands marked their indulgence, revealed their gross consumption. Those contemplative moments of prayer held dreams of the night's options and took no cognizance of sanctity and righteousness.

In the abbey I trembled, and shook over the flagstone shield that hid the tunnels and runnels of their sinuous, serpiginous god. Sometimes I imagined a deep rumbling conducted up through the stones to my knees, the hissing of an unfurling snake, touring his caverns below, empire of rattling bones. And when the earth shook, I held my breath and my prayers were sincere, that this dark kingdom would cease.

In this monastery it seemed that there was no innocence, no purity, no sanity, and I looked at my classmates with suspicion, wondering if they all knew of the devilry below. Was I the only being apparently unaware, while around me a web of conspiracy quivered, its silken strands the monastery's corridors? These children concentrating on their Bibles, in the peace of the classroom, how could it be possible that they were aware of the end point of their studies? If they were, then surely they would all be staring through the classroom window lost in images of the night.

So here we were, with our catechisms and revelations, miracles and blessings, learning, memorizing, dealing with histories of the early and late saints, wandering through the gospels, edicts and revelations, our aim to know Christ and all his work, the inheritance of the disciples, the history of the Church. But to what purpose? So that we could live a corrupt life taking the best from the land in the people's tithes, our bellies always contented, our journey bloated? Was this my fate, orphan child, mnemosyne, to be a keeper of chickens and a terrified witness? And was this my colleagues' end? Difficult to imagine these earnest creatures, disciplined by God's goodness, suddenly shifting allegiance, moving from freshness to decay, from light to dark, from the Father, Son and Holy Ghost to a fork-toothed, goat-bearded, trident-waving gatekeeper in hell. But the persuasive charms of a full belly . . .

Caught in the rhythm of the days, time passed, and I thrived in the ritual of an ordered life. Spring grew into summer and wobbly-legged foals and tender lambs browsed in verdant meadows lush with wild flowers and Kent's fine grass. The days were long. June came and the summer solstice. Armies of flies hovered over the chicken shit, a woodpecker knocked at the beech trees, and a kingfisher, sharp blue and emerald, patrolled the edges of the lake. The monastery's golden harvest was brought in, villagers helping the monks cutting the wheat and barley. Their men gone to war, it was the women who worked, earth women, sweating, heaving at the bales, tossing them from field to cart. Their children helped, toiling beside them, adding their small bundles to their mother's loads. They worked to dusk, without pay. After nightfall, they were free to glean the harvested fields. Walking the stubble, bending, stopping, filling jute sacks with fallen ears, this was their wage for the day. In the moonlight they worked, their shadows in the field, grey on black, their lives forever toil.

In the autumn of 1916, the worst battle of the First World War was being waged, murder stalking death. The bloody Somme would, like those of Ypres, take most of their men leaving these women widowed, without promise or joy, their burden to be forever alone.

My masters cultivated the promise of my memory. Extra tasks, extra lessons filled my hours. And I continued to perform well. I was more than able, better than gifted, and when called to recite could recall verse after verse, page on page of learned work and holy gospel. A year had passed and I was perfectly fluent in the classics, able to translate on sight, quote the ancients, Josephus, Pliny, Homer, Maimonides, but we had avoided any sight of the modern.

I had formed no friendships with my peers. Our time was spent in study, at work, sleeping, eating, a purely functional life without call for companions. Our tutelage was strict and worked towards a final examination in which we were to be tested on biblical studies. All other learning was considered to be superfluous. Literature, modern languages, science and mathematics were a garnish that decorated our main course, a great beef stew that was perfect by itself, standing alone, complete. These additional subjects were considered to be dilettantism, unnecessary information, that, it was allowed by the monks, perhaps added a little to our appreciation of the holy book, but which was in no way serious enough to be worth an examination, or merit recognition in the context of the Bible.

We were made aware of the exam's importance in terms of the rest of our poor lives. That importance was clearly defined by a single shrieking statement from our school teacher. He'd come into class one morning, wild, red-eyed, unshaven, rushing as usual, trailing his wake of rippling habit and he'd screamed, 'In one month you'll all be out on the streets.'

The statement had no immediate impact, caused no ripple of anxiety, until he started to explain precisely what he meant. Then we understood the import of the test, knew that if we failed, we really would be out on the streets. Until that time we had thought of the examination as a simple test without repercussion, not knowing that failure meant poverty and insecurity, and with this insight, panic set its course in our jumping hearts. For some reason this awareness bound us together, gave us friendship, where before there'd been no camaraderie. Until that time, quite extraordinarily, we'd had no real conversations, performing tasks, asking questions and making demands that were pertinent solely to the moment's needs, all expedient only to our work. But now with the drama of an imminent examination, panic set us to enquire as to each other's previous existences, establishing by these means the identities of the different environments into which we might be thrown again.

Quite remarkably, with only two exceptions, there was an almost exact similarity in our past situations. My classmates came from orphanages, selected out for their academic ability by the sterile nuns. The two boys who came from family environments did so from missionary traditions, the romance of the wilder continents luring them to the seminary. For the majority, without a family mythology of foreign adventure, failure literally did mean the streets, and this threat kept us awake into the far night, cramming after prayers. Frequent sobbing panic came from under the sheets as a poor boy broke, his nightmare starvation. My own anxieties were contained, estimable, circumscribed. I knew that I was by far the best scholar in the class and it seemed unlikely that I would do badly. I flicked the pages of the Testaments, rehearsing my memory, engraving the verses on the pages of my brain, remembering, recalling, a voice in my head reciting the Bible taking me into sleep, leading me through the chicken cages, telling me in the schoolroom about the life and lessons of the crucified one.

The days passed, and each one as it went added a brick

to the barrier of the examination's wall. Higher and higher it grew, hugely daunting, possibly unleapable. In our class-room we sat studying, and in the days before the exam even the dreamer paid attention to his lessons, staring no more through the window to the free fields. Our work was serious, our aim survival. All our moments echoed with the details of our good Lord's days. I don't think that I have ever known the New Testament better. Even when the Bible became my profession, my knowledge was less, for in those early days I had to learn to achieve stability, displace poverty, while in latter times I had been granted a place and power and had no need to fight to keep from the streets.

The day came, and on the dawn of our struggle, the line of boys knelt together at matins, our prayers from our hearts, our hearts entirely selfish, pleading for just this one favour, just this small inch of grace. We sat in our school-room, essay titles chalked on the blackboard, pens dipping in treacle ink, trailing our spider lines on coarse white paper. Thirty heads ducked low, foreheads creased, lips tightened, hands running through tousled hair, bodies taut, while our master paced between the rows of wooden desks flexing his cane, peering at our papers, checking that we were not cheating. His pacing interrupted my concen-tration, and I looked up at him, then through the window to a woodfire burning in the fields below. A tentative S of smoke drifted upwards and I imagined traces of resinous pine easing into our school.

My muscles hurt, writer's cramp, and so I stopped for a moment, stopped and thought for the first time of the consequences of actually passing the examination. If I passed, my commitment was to a monk's life. Although success primarily meant being kept from the hoar-frost street and lonely starvation, it also meant being bound to the pedantry of books, the rigours of fasting, dedication to the Word. From my observations in this monastery it also meant leading a secret life, where apparent holiness concealed gluttony and vice. Was this what I wanted? I wasn't sure, but I did know that I didn't want to be hungry tomorrow or next week, and that for the preservation of my immediate future I needed to pass this examination. And so, corrupted by the need for a full belly and a dry place to sleep, I put aside my existential doubts, ignored my writer's cramp and answered the examiner's questions. Looking back, I think that this moment, and this decision, marked in indelible purple the first stage of my corruption. This moment's choice, this move for security signposted the crossroads in my life's path.

Retrospectively, there was no decision, circumstances dictated that. I had no options, there was no real choice. This was my fate, and I greeted it with a pragmatic wave, and wrote my paper not wanting to starve. Had a similar situation confronted the other monks? Had they all come in innocence from backgrounds like my own? In the centuries that had been before, in the years that spread back to the Dark Ages, had similar orphanage sources supplied the world with monks? It seemed likely, for who would wish voluntarily to give up what seemed like freedom? It could only be children like me, without place or position, land or home.

Spurred on by decision, I wrote and wrote, unwrapping from my perfect memory the facts of Jesus's life. Pausing only when I looked up at the blackboard's questions, I covered sheet after sheet of paper, my regular geometric copperplate forming beautiful patterns on the faint lines of the page. I wrote well, my answers seemed perfect. Each essay fitted

73

precisely the time allowed, each a balanced answer where introduction led to discussion and discussion to sensible conclusion supported by quotations from the Book.

The afternoon passed. The examination was over, and our master slammed down his cane on his desk to terminate our work. We shuffled our papers into neat piles, hoping somehow that this placatory tidiness might lead our answers to be received with favour. Our master picked up our papers, stopping at each desk to thread string through punched holes at the corners of each sheaf, and checking that each boy had written his name. I see him now, cross-eyed, sweating, controlling his coarse tremor while trying to knot the string, taking delight in our anxiety as we watched him. He stared at me while he sorted my answers, one eye picking out my person, the other red-veined orb sauntering around the edges of the blackboard. He took more time with my foolscap sheets than with the other boys', weighing the bulk of written pages in his hands, then shuffling off, sandals flipping on the stone floor, to another terrified boy's desk to repeat his performance.

This ordeal must have taken fifteen minutes, and during that time we had to sit silent and still, remaining in our places, contemplative of fate's fine options. He reached the spit-turner's desk, and picking up the boy's paper ruffled his hair and didn't bother to tie the pages together. He smiled at the boy, lingering at his desk, his hand resting on his head, and then moved on to complete the row. We were dismissed, and chased off to the refectory for lunch.

We were late, the meal was finishing, there was grease on the monks' faces, chicken bones and breadcrumbs on the floor. We were hungry and the great copper serving bowls were empty. There was nothing for us to eat, and we were sent off to our dormitory by the sour-faced monks.

A whole week passed, a week of silent dread, when our eyes met one another's on the stairs, or at meal times, and echoed a silent sympathy. Our lessons continued, the pattern of the day ostensibly unchanged, our master roared at us for our stupidity and the numbing procession of prayer ate our time. On the seventh day, which was a Friday, I came back from the chicken sheds to vespers to find that my usual row of pews was empty. I looked around, panicking, wondering where my colleagues were. They were not among the surrounding monks, whose stiff backs hunched over their breviaries. Where were they? I was the only boy in a row of twenty empty seats. Suddenly, from the back of the abbey I heard the hollow click of the abbey doors as they closed. I turned to the noise, half smiling in relief, hopeful that my silent peers were being led in. And my smile was returned by the tousle-headed spit-turner, for whom that look of warmth had not been meant. He came simpering forward and squeezed in besides me, his habit brushing my bent face as he passed by. He sat down and his thighs spread, touching mine with their poisonous warmth. My legs jumped, twitched away, and we knelt at prayer.

During the service, amid the calls and chanted responses, there was no explanation given as to why a whole parade of young boys had disappeared. I had no doubt that they had been brutally assembled, put back in year-old clothes, bundled into some jolting horse-drawn cart, and in a clatter of tears dumped under Bow's gaslights, or in the dark fields of Lincoln's Inn, alone, crying, left to make their way.

We returned to our rooftop dormitory, a desolate place, each empty bed a pinprick reminder of teardrop fate. I felt no real relief that I'd been saved, no joy, just lonely, tired and, at the age of fifteen, old. I didn't sleep that night, spent the empty hours racing through a jangled view of the glowing, flaring future. Time had made me a monk and the prospect seemed bitter.

Then at matins, my limbs cramping with lack of sleep, an announcement was unexpectedly made, welcoming me and my one remaining colleague to our order. Just one brief sentence took us into the rest of our lives, and then another telling the two of us to attend the Abbot's rooms after vespers when a blessing of graduation would be made.

Brother Matthew led us to the Abbot's study. We filed behind him, heads bowed, hands clasped across our stomachs. Brother Matthew had been out in the fields and had trodden in something unfortunate, for a strong smell of manure permeated from his sandals. He knocked at the study door.

'Come.' The soothing deep voice contrasted with the squeaking creak of the heavy mahogany door as it eased open. The room was dominated by the Abbot's presence, and his rolling fatness overflowed the arms of the deep chair, spilling out on to the floor and filling the room. We tiptoed in behind Brother Matthew, hushed, scared, slipping in, keeping tight to the walls in deference to his massive presence. The Abbot's eyes were shut. A pink silk skullcap covered his bald head. Brother Matthew coughed. The eyelids flicked open, and a most imperial beadiness stared out at our horrible, disturbing personages.

'Well?' His mouth opened waiting to catch a reply, and his chins wobbled, caught in a wave of echoing movement.

'These are the boys, your grace.' The Abbot's eyes flicked to Matthew and seemed to catch life.

'The boys?' He queried, nodding enthusiastically. Matthew coughed and winked at the Abbot.

'That graduated, your grace.'

'Oh yes, quite so, not those little boys, the ... other boys.'

'Yes, your grace.'

'Very good, Brother Matthew, the boys.' He leaned forward in his chair, and his folds of fat followed him. He took in a great breath of air and started to speak. 'Come nearer, boys, let me see you in the light.' We edged closer. 'No, nearer.' We stood on the carpet directly in front of him. He leaned forward and swept us both into his great arms, spreading his great thighs to bring us closer to his core. I trembled and shook, wary, scared. He fondled my arm, pinching my thin biceps between his sausage fingers, and the heat that came from him was a palpable roar, a wall that rocked over me. And this warmth had a smell, and the smell was of spices. Then he pushed us away and stared at us.

'Show respect, you two, stand at attention for his grace.' Brother Matthew barked the order, and we braced ourselves, straight backed. The Abbot hauled himself up from his chair, slowly, slowly, pushing himself forward, easing himself up. He waddled around us, finger on the dimple of his chin, looking us up and down.

'You have been blessed,' he said. 'Blessed with the opportunity of a holy life, a life with us in this house of God, a life of study, a life of contemplation, a life in which you will preserve the word of our Lord for the future generations. And why have you been blessed, and why have you been chosen? You have been chosen for your abilities but you must at all times remember that these abilities are not your own, they are a gift, granted by the grace of God. The Almighty has entrusted you with intelligence and memory, and at all times you must remember that they are a loan for which you are for ever in debt and your debt is to the Almighty and his Son on Earth, Jesus Christ.'

He paused and caught his breath, then walked away from us, towards a desk laden with huge, leather-bound books. His back to us, fat belly resting on the jutting edge of the desk, he continued, 'And how are you to repay this debt? For this debt is not only to God, but it is also to this monastery and the priests who have chosen you. Let me tell you, let me answer for you. You will repay your debt with unquestioning loyalty, loyalty to your brother monks, and to myself, the leader of this community. You will be silent and observant. You will be trained in our ways, you will continue your studies, you will bless your days with the labour of your industry. I have seen the reports of your masters in school and I know of your talents.'

He paused again, and with the surprising agility of a ballet dancer spun around to face us and pondering over the prospect of our talents leered at my fellow graduate, who blew a kiss at him.

'Brother John, you will work in the library from now on. Your task is to help the librarian in the restoration of holy works. And you, Brother Simon . . .' he walked forward and scratched my colleague's chest with a ticking, teasing finger, 'will work in the kitchens.'

He hesitated, and Brother Matthew, a sergeant major for our order, shouted, 'On your knees, on your knees.' We knelt before the Abbot, who waved his hands over us, a butterfly blessing.

'May the Lord bless you and keep you for ever in grace, may holiness guide your days and goodness light your nights.' The waving hand ceased, replaced by a breathless waiting.

'Amen!' shrieked Brother Matthew, and 'Amen!' we repeated too. After a moment's contemplation, we were dismissed.

Oh, the library, its parade of books, its catalogues, its shelves, its hush, its dust. The library, its rotten leather, its dryness, its inheritance, its hours, its silence. The library, its burden of knowledge, its sourness, its conceit, its learning, its secrets.

The library was at the centre of the monastery, a huge hushed room. The books were racked up to twice the height of a man. Narrow gothic windows let in a smoky light. The roof was supported by coarse rough beams from which dust drifted and cobwebs dangled and sparkled. Rows of tables supported reading lamps, bookrests, blotting pads and the elbows of a host of elderly monks. From the main room, doorways led into discrete cells, quiet places, where the holiest tomes rested in a brooding peace.

The library was the only part of the monastery to have electricity, and a great chandelier, a complex mass of crystal and ormolu, more appropriate to a palace than a monastery, sparkled and pointed spears of light on to the library desks. The library had its kings and slaves. Brother Mark and Brother Phillip, two ancient men, shuffling, slow, were its monarchs, and they ruthlessly ruled a group of ten serfs, almost as old, and certainly just as slow. The serfs seemed identical, all decrepit, all worn and all bald. Their job was to restore and copy the holy books, keeping them in place and in repair.

The library was a central repository for the whole order of monks, and from it were issued volumes for consumption in Northumberland and Cornwall, Lancashire and Wales, where our brothers in Christ had no libraries of their own. Requests were received by Brothers Mark and Phillip, and they kept intricate files of the books that had been loaned. It was my job to act as their clerk, taking their indignant dictation, writing in my best copperplate to those scurrilous, desperate individuals who had failed to return their books. I kept the library's files in order, in a series of black and gold lacquered metal boxes.

The library was regulated like a schoolroom, governed by Brothers Mark and Phillip, who sat at a huge partner's desk at the entrance. They worked at leather-bound ledgers, and wrote at an identical pace with quill pens. They wore tiny gold spectacles that corrected, I'm sure, an identical myopia, and peering out over the rims watched over their minions, schoolmasters surveying their class, making sure that everyone was at work, keeping up with the pace of repair. If they saw any monk daydreaming, I would be summoned from the desk where I stood and, with a nod of their heads, they would indicate the culprit. Solemnly I'd walk to the monk and knock with my knuckle on the table beside him. He'd jump to startled attention, and all the other monks would look up from their work to the dreamer.

The monks were skilled colourists and artists, repairers of medieval illuminations, consummate letterists, reproducing on vellum decaying scripts dating from before the Reformation, patching rare volumes, battling with damp and mould and the inexorable, noble rot of the long long years.

Life in the library, the routine of the shelves, the order of the books, the quiet of scholarship, the reassurance of learning, the peace of intellect, all built a thick crust, a deep rind that provided, with its continuity, its links with the long gone past, a great calm to my days. I was at peace, content with my work, and the rigid structure of library life. The security of the shelves gave me permanence and place, where before there had been none. I wrote letters to distant monasteries, took in the mail, filed, stacked shelves, returned books scattered over disordered tables, tidied, dusted, swept and above all did as I was told by Brothers Phillip and Mark. I loved my life, and the continued call to prayers was an annoyance taking me from my work, my only wish to return. And the books were a family for me, I knew them well, they were my brothers and sisters, familiars, friends.

Gradually my responsibility increased, and I took over more and more of the two brothers' work, recalling books, and selecting works that needed repair.

The artisan monks sensed my appreciation of their work, and I was taught their skills, becoming a skilled copyist and a talented colourist, matching new tints based on natural dyes and oils, restoring ancient fraying volumes. The work was intricate and very slow. It might take weeks to repair a few pages of text, retaining where possible the original, gluing decaying pieces of parchment on to a new sheet sewn into an aged leather spine. Sometimes major passages of text had disappeared into a crumble of dust and we would have to research the origins of the piece, cross-referencing from work to work, then produce the synthesized new text, painting words with our badger-hair brushes on to glistening sheets in their original form.

Many of the reconstructed texts were entirely imagined, sketching out conjectured edicts from obscure continental medieval towns, based on a few fragmented facts and taking on a contrived style. I was encouraged to do this by the monks, for they had been taught to do the same by librarians before them, and it was explained that there was no option, for to do anything else would mean the complete loss of the original works, so that eventually nothing would be left, no volumes would remain and then all that could be relied on was the new. They justified their work by claiming an atavistic skill, primed by the years and years spent in the company of the ancients' work. After so much time among books of learning, their souls and senses had become suffused, overburdened, swollen with a sense of the books' creators. They had been taught that through their years in the heart of the library they would become as one with the learning around them. Textual information would eventually be caught by them, a virus infecting their senses, so that their imaginative reconstruction of an elderly text was not imagined, but rather returned information that had been caught by their hearts and minds. The artifice that they used to reconstruct battered books was therefore not faked, but a legitimate restoration of information turned to dust by the mites and fungi, breathed in by the monks during their long residence and returned literally to the page.

I was caught by this idea, so plausible, that by breathing in the dust of decaying knowledge, we acted as a conduit for its reconstitution on new parchment. And the monks had been doing this through the generations, from century to century, from age to age. So how did the books that we read relate to the originals? There had been nearly two thousand years of copying and reconstruction. How much of the original was represented in what we saw?

In my early time in the library I had asked the monks this question and their reply was comforting, reassuring. Because the works were virtually the same from library to library, from country to country, throughout the Catholic world, the spirit of restoration must be legitimate, the reproductions true. I accepted this argument and developed my intuitive skills, recognizing phrases of text as they came into my mind, and placing them delicately in sooty black Latin, Greek or Hebrew on the palimpsest before me.

My skills grew and were acknowledged, and I moved from the stand-up desk by the side of Phillip and Mark to occupy my own place at the library tables. Often at the end of our day I would be surrounded by an assembly of old men, who, pressing close, would hiss and crackle with admiration for the cleverness of my pages of dialectic seemingly issued from a long dead saint, but which in reality had sprung from some deep resonating cave in my brain.

The library was a maze of recessed shelves, room on room lined with books, branching chambers leading off from the main archive. Within these chambers, there were books whose themes were not religious, or if they were religious, celebrated a different god from the one that stretched over the copper roofs of our seminary. Books on witchcraft and sorcery, on wizardry and the occult, dwelt in the far reaches of the library away from a passing glance. These books were often lent out to our own monks who came with requests for volumes from these fevered shelves. The justification for their borrowing was obvious and often made: 'It is best to know the devil in all his ways because only in knowledge is awareness and safety.' An odd logic, but a populist philosophy in our monastery. The borrowing of these books was not entered on to any leather register, but I was bade to remember the borrower and the volume, these sensitive loans being charged to the excellence of my memory. If I tried to place these borrowings into any other context, discretion held me from voicing this to my brother monks. My experience of the devil worm and his black mass had left its strong memories and I was certain that the borrowings related to these dark practices.

There were other oddities that pertained to library life. Twice a month the library would become busy, busy with monks rushing in to find their own way around the books.

These days would be filled with swishing, hustling, bustling lines of men shuffling off to the side rooms of the library's maze. The monks seemed to drift at random around the library, picking books from the shelves, but this was a pretence. The visits had an aim, and it was the northern end of the library, the rooms most distant from Brothers Phillip and Mark.

The scholarly restorers hated these days, days in which their work was disturbed, their concentration disrupted. Distracted by the beehive buzz, they'd sit and fidget, gazing appealingly at the brothers for the return of order and tranquillity. The brothers acted as though there was no disruption, as if these days were routine and not disordered.

After a few hours' absence the monks would reappear from the northern chambers, hot-faced, rambling, distrait, swaying a little as they walked away, almost drunken in their gait.

Bound to my library desk, concentrating on restoration work, I asked my colleagues where the monks were going, why they seemed to disappear, then reappear, and my colleagues would shrug or shake their heads, refusing to acknowledge any mystery or disappearance. There was nothing going on. I was imagining the comings and goings. It was obvious, it was their study day and the monks were merely preoccupied with learning, searching for the origins of truth, endeavouring to achieve the blessing of knowledge.

Young and inquisitive, I was keen to share their know-ledge, and, some paltry excuse on mumbling lips, I'd get up from my place and wander over to the northern rooms to seek out the mysterious source of their scholarly enquiries. But the chambers would be empty, empty rooms, shelves of books, tables and chairs, but no monks, their disappearance complete and magical. It was all terribly puzzling. Regularly, twice each calendar month the monks appeared, thirsting, apparently, for pure knowledge, but more likely, I sensed, thirsting for degenerate vileness.

I continued with my labours, and the work was extremely interesting; it was fascinating to pick through medieval works, books sometimes seven or eight hundred years old, memories of times so different. Although the books were all of a religious nature, there were other lessons to be learned from the text apart from those of religion; there were histories of different times and ways of being, of different manners and moments. And so much suffering described in Christ's name, so much barbarity and torture, so many lurid and complex deaths, by stabbing, by arrows, by fire, by the rack, by pulling apart by horses, by being eaten by wild beasts, by dipping in boiling oil, drowning, suffocation, garrotting, so imaginative, so violent, so varied, so intricate the oppression of man by man. How the people suffered. And always the Jews were blamed. If it were not for them he would have lived. Because of them he died. They were persecuted through the ages, named in these books as sinners who had allowed the holy one to die. It was obvious to me that they had no real blame and that it was entirely a Roman conspiracy that had led to Jesus's death.

The Great War had come to an end and the settlement of Versailles changed Europe. News of the peace diffused into the monastery, and we learnt of the millions dead, as many martyrs to a Balkan death as to Christ's. The information came to us through the village below. We traded the produce of our farmlands with the villagers, eggs for cloth, milk for leather, corn for nails. Through fragmented village conversations, news passed to the library of trenches filled with millions of men rotting in the rain, mustard gas, generals, machine guns, planes, tanks, grand plans, patriotism, death, the Germans and the Turks, war across continents, into the Middle East, America. The global concept of war took me, caught me.

What extraordinary devilry had overtaken the world? I couldn't understand what had encouraged man to such global imaginative slaughter, death beyond dreams, death beyond nightmares. In the battle of the Somme, one million men had died, their cold blood, poppies, and their soft bodies, worms.

And what was the nature of our God if he allowed such inconceivable massacre? How could thirty million people be consumed if God existed and had power on earth, if God existed and he was good, if the Lord was good and had concern for mankind? If the Holy One loved humanity, surely he would have prevented this war. But if he hadn't? There had been no surcease to sacrifice. And for me the triumph of war was proof either that there was no God and that Christ was an invention, or that the Almighty was powerless. In my heart I couldn't believe that there was no powerful force for creation. Life was too complex, too intricate to have evolved from mad molecules. To look at a butterfly or a flower, the stars, the fields, was to have confirmation of the existence of an organizing benign force, a force of creation, of love. But death, bloody death on such a gargantuan, rolling scale? Magnify the pain of one being's extinction by twenty million. Had he not heard the clamour? This was inconceivable, too unbelievable, and I could only believe that there was some monstrous conspiracy of oppression whereby the forces of goodness were damped, suppressed, denied expression by some imponderable, dark, brooding, mighty malignity.

This huge puzzle rolled and rolled in my brain, took over my days and limited my enthusiasm for restoration work. And the conundrum of the disappearing monks also became an endless preoccupation. I wanted to know where they went, break the mystery of the empty rooms, follow the furtive ones to their goal. I evolved a simple plan. I would wait for an elderly monk and follow him as he shuffled off to the northern chambers, creeping behind him, dodging behind bookshelves as he looked around. And I adopted this plan. Making an excuse to my fellow workers, pretending that I needed a reference book from the shelves, I tiptoed away, creeping creeping, shadowing a tatty, grey-haired friar. The old man pottered through the library, passing from bookcase to bookcase, browsing, picking up leather-bound tomes, reaching up, putting away, stopping, picking his nose, playing with the long hairs that bushed out from his ears, while I kept my distance, following him. He drifted from shelf to shelf, making his doddery way towards the far end of the library. He walked with a heavy, dipping limp, leaning on a silver-headed cane. He stopped again, took out another book, opened it and scratched his arse. I stared at him, my nose peeping over the edges of a musty, velvet-covered life of Saint Joan, and he, oblivious of the spy, followed his text, mouthing silently the words that he read. He turned a page, then shaking his head and replacing the book, he croaked out, 'It's not as I remembered,' and turned the corner into the mysterious cul-de-sac.

I followed, darting forward through the narrow doorway to enter the room just a few seconds after him. I faced stacks of shelves in cubic space. There was nobody in the room. He had disappeared. The ceiling light shone, the books rested quietly in their ordered rows. Where was the monk? There were shelves of books, scurrilous dust in a corner pile, ubiquitous cobwebs and spiders, but neither sign nor trace of Brother Friar. I paced around the room, tapping the vertical columns of the bookcases, listening out for the answering hollow of a hidden space. I searched for secret switches, switches that might cause the bookcases to swing out to reveal hidden chambers. I stared at the flagstones, seeking clues in a mosaic inlay that might reveal the monk's path. There was no entry point that I could find. Frustrated, I returned to the library, despondent, head down, and smacked into fat Brother Bernard, storekeeper.

'Oh dear dear, are you all right?' Brother Bernard lifted his hand to his mouth, and tutting and tooting tried to brush me down, a process that consisted more of pawing me than clearing dust from my clothes. Winded, I withdrew from his dusting and tried to catch my breath.

'I'm quite all right. Thank you,' I said in hushed library tones. Brother Bernard smoothed down his hinged hair, pasting flagrantly ginger locks over his terribly bald head. His tongue wobbled lasciviously in and out between whis-tling lips. I turned away and busied myself tidying the library shelves, making neat rows where the books had been disturbed by the day's monks. As I worked, Brother Bernard kept pace with me, patting his hair, hawking and snorting, a foul mirror keeping me company while I moved along the length of the bookcases. He ogled me, feeling deep into his pockets as he rumbled and belched. Fifteen minutes passed in this way, ridiculous minutes, decorated by the old pansy's panting and belching. Then with a wistful look at my arse, he sidled off towards the northern chamber, scuttling along the edges of the library. I watched as he waddled away, and then, as he turned the corner, he stopped and turned to look towards me, hesitated, then winked. I followed him as he disappeared into the chamber, hoping that none of my colleagues were observing the game.

The chamber was empty again, but this time there was an obvious clue to the monk's disappearance. As if reaching from the pages of some old-fashioned mystery novel, a complete section of books swung to, closing on a passageway. I rushed forward. Too late. The section shut, clicking into place. I cursed, and stood back trying to work out how to open up the passageway. I pulled out all of the books methodically, starting at the topmost shelf, clearing away the volumes to reveal whitewashed wall. I replaced the books. I reached out to the next row down, pulling away the complete row of books. I replaced them and reached out again to clear the next shelf down to expose only wall, no secret switches, no hidden levers. And again, and again, and again. Nothing, no clue. Just bookcase, books and wall. Like a frustrated child I pulled and pushed at the carved pilasters that decorated the vertical supports of the bookshelves, and stamped on the ground, banging at the floor in front of the shelves. Nothing moved. The section of bookcase remained still, immobile, dense, solid.

Had I imagined that the shelves had moved? Was it an illusion? No. Two monks had walked into the room and had not reappeared. The shelves had definitely swung open for them and they must for me. I scratched my head, then felt along the sides of the neighbouring shelves. No clues again. I stood back from the shelves and stared. The innocent books stared back at me and stuck out their tongues. I looked up at the ceiling, absolutely puzzled, and was temporarily blinded by the intense electric light that swung low from an ornamental ceiling rose. The light was an art nouveau piece of twisted shining brass and vaseline glass. The lampshades were draped petals around bright electric stamens whose brass stems curled back to a central stalk ending in an incongruous handle that swung low over the room.

And suddenly, I had found my clue. I reached up and pulled the handle. The silent shelves shimmered and glided open, exposing a whitewashed passageway. I hesitated, and the shelf section swung closed. I pulled again, and the bookshelves opened for me once more.

I walked past the shelves into the corridor beyond. The way was narrow, turning, twisting, descending steeply, deep into the monastery's foundations. I walked slowly, carefully, stopping every few steps to listen for voices, sniffing the air, feeling my way. There was no visible light source, yet the corridor was bright. There was no obvious heat source, yet the corridor was warm, so warm that my habit was sticky with my bubbling, trickling sweat.

I kept close to the walls, creeping around the twisting bends, breath desperately quiet, slowly, slowly, tiptoeing along the sloping flagstones. Steeper and steeper, walls thick, covered with a treacle slurry of quicklime, slope so steep that I was almost falling, faster, tripping forward around a tight curve of wall, spiralling downwards into the deep foundations of the monastery and suddenly into a wide and pleasant room.

Thirteen monks were seated at a long table. Before them were piles of books. I broke into their peace, bursting in with such a rush that the velvet drapes that lined the walls rippled and swayed. They turned their innocent faces to me.

'Brother John,' purred the Abbot smiling from his place at the head of the table. He paused and his smile glistened, held its peace in his jowly face, fixed, waiting for my reply. Then the smile decided against waiting and rushed away.

'And to what, Brother John, do we owe the great pleasure of your visit?' All the big faces stared at me, waiting, oh waiting for my poor reply, leaning closer, wanting to know why I had disturbed their seminar. I hung my head, for there was no sensible reply. I had been a spy in the mist, and the mist had suddenly cleared.

Not having anything to say, I coughed, a deep speculative cough that explored my lungs, then again louder, taking in the whole of my chest. I looked up to the waiting monks and coughed again, a rattling cough that roared round the room, chasing the dust, blowing open the heavy pages of the thick books that lay in solemn piles. The Abbot tapped his fingers on the table, and the monks leaned closer checking on this curious boy who couldn't speak but could cough, who had rushed in and now was standing quite still. Queer child, what was he doing? They were waiting for my explanation, and what could I tell them? That I'd watched their bi-monthly processions through the library and I was curious to see where they'd gone? That I was a nosey little squirt who wanted to know every noisy street of the monastery? It was all true. But how could I admit the truth? The monks stared at me, goggle eyes expectant. But I wasn't prepared for revelations, and so I coughed. I coughed and coughed and coughed, great rippling cascades of noise barging, stuttering, echoing around the room. Coughed for a ridiculous time, barking, spluttering, wheezing, filling the corners, hitting the ceiling. I staggered, clapped my hands to my chest, turned purple, hawked, wheezed, spun and heaved, and then Brother Bernard giggled, heed and hawed and his laughter caught, its stupid, tittering, hysterical contagion firing the solemn monks into paroxysms of spurting laughter, waves of side-splitting, stomach-hurting noise shaking and rocking the room. The thirteen men wobbled on the chairs, held their bellies, collapsed, banged each other on the backs, clapped their hands together, stood up, pointed at me, tears toured their fat faces, and I coughed and coughed and coughed, the foolish boy, never a prying, sneaking, prattling, devilish spy, but all the time a grateful clown, a clumsy, tripping, foolish oaf, watching his dangerous audience, gauging their tension, surveying the undercurrent of poisonous mood that might switch in a moment to a threatening inquisition.

And the survey took in the Abbot at the head of the table, who was sitting quietly, quizzical, unamused, watching, puzzled, trying to establish the nature of this anarchic madness. He wasn't fooled and his perception was dangerous. His eyelids tightened and his jaws clenched; I could feel his anger swelling. He sat forward and his fist hit the table.

'Silence.'

Such menace. The monks immediately quietened and resumed their seats. Brother Bernard remained standing, simpered, giggled once, then took his place. The Abbot pushed back his chair, and the grating noise of its legs scraping the flagstones defined the seriousness of my situation. He leaned forward tilting over the table, knuckles pressing down, boring into the wood. And he faced me accusingly, corpulent, ponderous, massive. His right arm extended and its index finger unravelled like a snail uncoiling from its shell to point at me, and, in the empty space where I waited accusation, I heard high-pitched giggling from behind the long velvet drapes that lined the room. The Abbot twitched, his nose wriggling with distaste. He opened his mouth to accuse me and instead of words came an extraordinary clatter and thump. We turned to its source. By the velvet drapes stood a beautiful girl in black silk petticoats; she stooped to the floor to pick up a fallen croquet mallet, then faced us, hands behind her back, green eyes, red-brown bouncing hair, tipsy nose. The Abbot attempted to ignore her, dismissing her presumptuous presence. He stared at me.

'Well, Brother John, if one was curious, one might wonder why you were here.' His voice was icy. 'And we are curious and we do wonder why you are here.' I shuffled and hung my head. 'Well?' There was nothing to say, no defence; I'd been inquisitive beyond my rank, and this was unforgivable. I awaited punishment, mute, still, and the girl waited with me, edging back against the drapes, making herself small, seeking invisibility in the velvet curtains.

'Sir, I've no excuse, I was curious to see where the learned gentleman went.' I stuttered on, clumsy, stupid, a mumbling fool, relegated to idiocy by discovery. And as I bumbled on a series of lumpen thumping noises, heavy weights falling on the flagstones, came from behind the curtains, interrupting my reply and bringing rolling relief. Rainbow balls of varying sizes rumbled towards the table. Coloured spheres, green, red, orange, yellow, violet, bumped along the flagstones, bumped and rolled, pushing their way to the centre of the room. I started my little speech again and as I did the hanging drapes rippled and waved, and the monks turned to the disturbance, looked away from me and I shut up. Even the Abbot was diverted, settling back from his position of dominance, plumping down heavily in his chair to stare, open-mouthed, as the drapes parted and a group of young women carrying croquet mallets pushed forward to surround their friend, grouping around her, a protective phalanx of pretty bodies, variably dressed in variable undress, silk slips, stringed pearls, high shoes, stockings, garters, the bright flush of powder and paint, bobbed hair, cigarette holders, champagne glasses. A curious contrast with the serious seminarists, their learning, their scholarliness, the dry dust of their religion scattered before them, the grey monks and their rainbow girls.

I edged away from centre scene, taking my chance to mix in with my colleagues, moving forward to the table, standing beside Brother Bernard, part of the group, a monk with monks, rather than a spy under interrogation. The women spread out, moving in towards the monks, a battalion of brightness, centring around the girl in the black slip who led the mass of women, pattering forwards, step on step, spreading out around the room, descending on the monks. The girl in black slipped behind the Abbot's chair and reaching her arms around his neck, bent to kiss his forehead and massaged his shoulders.

'Now, where were we, Abbot dear? What were we up to?'

The other women had assumed similar flirtatious positions, lining up behind the monks, caressing, massaging, coquettes with croquet mallets, and the monks, distracted from the fly spy, were persuaded from their chairs. The table was pushed to one side to reveal a wind-up gramophone, its huge horn all brassy glister. The gramophone was placed on the table. Brother Bernard lifted the great black plate of a record on to the machine's turntable and, the pick-up arm in place, blowsy dance-hall music swung through the room. The girls took their partners and bustled through a quickstep one-two, one-two. They shimmied around a short monk who clutched at his girl, chin between her breasts.

Wine bottles and massive crystal glasses were brought from a cupboard and set up on the table on top of the books. Incense burnt in silver gilt holders and its odd sweetness drifted through the room. The monks waddled one-step two-step, shuffle, crab-grabbing at their girls. The wild music burnt, and the crowd roared and crackled, oblivious of me and I shrank back, hiding in the backcloth drapes.

Couples retreated from the circle of dancing, took to the sides of the room, and stood casually talking. Cigarettes appeared from bead handbags, tubes of coloured paper in amber holders against rose lips, heads tilted back, laughter, gossip. The monks smoked too, enjoying themselves chattering.

Another record and the revellers drew back to clear the floor for a charleston. They clapped hands, roared and the Abbot stepped out, bowed and raised a swirling flourishing arm in invitation to the girl in the black slip. She moved out from the group and curtsied, parodying the Abbot's pretty gallantry. The Abbot raised her hand high, and the two walked the length of the dance floor. The music blared and caught, and with a flamenco stamp, hard heels against the floor, the woman set to, slip raised, feet twisting, toes in and out, hands high, palms out, skipping, twisting. And the Abbot copied her movements, surprising in his grace and speed. The two danced together, and the monks and women drew in around them forming an enrapt clapping circle, cheering, whistling as the pair danced faster and faster, the Abbot keeping pace with the woman's quick steps.

The record scratched to a halt and the panting couple embraced each other, then withdrew from the floor to drink and smoke. Different music, the black bottom.

'I do love the black bottom,' said the girl by my side, and she rushed to dance, waving for her friends to join her. They crowded together, holding close, building excitement, and the record played.

The girl in the black slip sat on the edge of the table, legs slightly splayed, the Abbot between her thighs, his hand resting on her shoulder. His face was flushed. She held a cigarette in her hand, and bringing it to her mouth she kissed its tip and exhaled deep grey clouds of nicotine over the monk. He spoke, his words falling on her, while she puffed into his face and looked over his shoulder at me. I was caught by her green eyes and blushed. She smiled, a little crack of a smile that hardly touched her lips, a tinkling smile meant only for me. She stared at me, sought me out, fished in my eyes, and hooked me in. She smoked, cheeks drawing ashes and dust into her lungs, ignoring the Abbot, reeling me in. And I was caught, caught by green-eyed bait, hooked on the finest, thinnest line, hers, in that moment, for ever. She patted the Abbot on his chest. He backed away from her and, shouting, silenced the music.

'Ladies and gentlemen, let me interrupt to remind you that we were interrupted . . .' I caught my breath, knowing that I had been that interruption, and thinking that my inquisition, temporarily abandoned, was to be continued and my punishment pronounced. The Abbot motioned at me, and I came to him. 'Come closer, boy.' I came closer, a pace away from the promontory of his belly. He looked at me and the audience was quiet. He looked hard. I felt myself weighed, analysed, described. In that look I saw him summarizing my reports, reviewing my life, my provenance and capacity. That hard man held me, felt me out, rattled my bones, knew my potential, judged and decided. The surrounding monks watched the little scene, Abbot and monk, old man at the end of his days, and a blond boy at the beginning of life. And the fat man nodded once, then looked away taking in the surrounding people, monks in their shabby habits, women in their silks and pearls. 'We were interrupted . . .' his voice became quiet so that we all strained to hear him, 'by my new secretary, Brother John.' I heard myself gasp. 'He is known to you all, I assume, and he is with us in all we do.' The monks nodded, heads shaking a vigorous agreement. 'So let us proceed now, return back, as sweet Mary suggests, to our game.'

And thus I was judged, the sentence promotion. Panicky, unsure, blinded, I felt for the table to catch myself, steadying myself, supporting my poor shaking knees. The Abbot's secretary, from an orphanage to chicken shit, from chicken shit to a library, from a banquet of books to a dance with the Abbot. Expecting to be vanquished, banished, demoted and, instead, made up to something of importance, a man to mark. I caught my breath and tried to calm down, my thoughts jumping, swirling, sworling, taking me through my poor past to these confusing times of legitimized debauch among a secret group of God's men.

The monks waddled about clearing the floor, pushing aside the detritus of the dance, and pulled back the long velvet drapes to unroll a delicate white screen, approximately ten feet square, that hung from a hook high on the wall. The screen shivered and shook, caught in every unstable current of air. On the table opposite the screen they placed a huge machine, a machine such as I'd never seen before, an arrangement of metal plates and lens with a cable that stretched down to a wall-mounted power point. The machine was switched on, bright light projected ghosts of dust on the screen, wild shadows chasing each other in a delirium across white plains. The monks watched the screen, clanking goblets, swilling wine, winking, nudging each other, waiting for something to happen.

More cigarettes were lit and gambler's den smoke filled the room. Brother Bernard was fiddling with the machine, "oohing" and "aahing" as he traced a piece of tape from one cog to another, over and under, threading the material delicately between two large spiked wheels. And he was ready, and on to the screen was projected a delicate little man with sideways feet, white face, round hat, tight jacket. He jerked his way with oblivious staccato steps to a poor wriggling woman, tied down on tracks, towards whom an enormous cylindrical machine was inexorably moving. His awkward movements were interrupted by awkward prose arranged in blackboard commentary that told of evil fate, heroines and villains, inheritances and treachery, so much so simply placed in five lines. The text shivered away and we returned to the moving image of the woman on the tracks, head bobbing, feet thrashing and ever closer to this poor creature came the monstrous train.

The audience gasped, crowding closer to the screen, edged forward by the horror of anticipated death. The monks and their women reached out at the screen, flapping as if trying to untie the trapped woman themselves. Then entered sweet oblivion the hero, soundless whistles, umbrella atwirl, his bow tie a miracle, always parallel with the ground, regardless of the list of his walk.

But the train, the train, and the woman's tied and bound, please, our hero, please, notice them. He trips over her and falls into love. We sighed, our sighs mirroring the screen sighs of love's lovers. NEVER MIND LOVE. THE TRAIN. HURRY, HURRY. It's so close. Our hero can'tuntietheknots. Desperation. Oh, please help them! The train is so close. Now, this string goes there and that string goes there and so this knot will loosen so and this knot might if this piece of string goes and let's scratch our head oh I do like a nice black hat, let me see. The train is juddering closer. Its driver leans from the cab, shaking his fist. Meanwhile in the bushes a moustachioed villain, hairy and tieless, is laughing evilly. Flash back to blackboard. Will he untie her in time or will the train run them over? Will Black Will take her inheritance? And with a mad scrabbling and scratching the loop of film breaks free from its cogs and brightness bounces into the room.

The tension eases. It's only a film, and the audience backs away from the screen, relaxes, drinks, stretches, visibly released from the ugly realities of the film. Brother Bernard is at the projector, busily winding the film on, sweetie's burnt his fingers, dear, dear. Regardless, simply regardless of his burnt fingers, he does his duty by the projector and his monastery, and inserts thick black tape through the machinery: he is so brave and selfless. He pats his wing of hair into place, looks around at the crowd and sets to work.

Presto, it's there and off we go again. The knots are loosened. Our heroine is free, and she's gathered from under the first wheels of the rushing train by our hero. Breathless, she's in his arms and her heavy eyelids flutter as she looks into his eyes and then into ours. 'Saved' is the caption, and so she is snatched from the steel jaws of cruel, crushing death. The monster in the bushes slips away with an evil twist of his moustachios and a frightening scowl at us, the prying audience. The hero and heroine disappear into the sunset, walking the rainbow road of certain love. At this point the audience, who presumably had been hoping for spurting gore, became bored with the film and began to paw at each other.

Two women separated out from the group and began setting metal hoops into holes in the floor. Such beautiful women, shimmering in eau de Nil beaded dresses, bending down to the hoops, dresses stretching tight over wonderful curves. They stood up and catching my stare smiled and walked towards me. They shook hands.

'I'm Nora.'

'And I'm Peggy.' Nora's dimpled chin and Peggy's cold hand. I felt so awkward. I crossed my legs and folded my arms.

'We're from London you know, just come up for the day, we come twice a month, you know, it's just such fun.' They giggled, touching their lips with their fingers to hide their laughter. I nodded, dumbstruck by their make-up, made speechless by female sunshine. The Abbot clapped his hands.

'Form teams, everybody, it's time for croquet. Come along now. Do get organized, Brother Matthew. You're a team leader, and Mary, darling Mary, why don't you be the women's team captain? Do form up into sides, everyone. Do you all have your croquet mallets? Come along now, come along. Bernard, do stop fiddling with that ridiculous new-fangled damned machine. Do stop fussing, Bernard. We don't wish to watch any more of those bollocking films.'

But Bernard refused to acknowledge the Abbot's commands, and sat cross-legged on the table, squinting cross-eyed at the projector, threading tape over and round cogs and wheels, while bright light sprayed the screen. We all obediently formed into teams, a line of men in brown facing up to a team of butterflies. Then suddenly Brother Bernard squealed.

'Triumph.' And, amid clattering and spluttering a new reel of film was eaten by the projector and shone on to the screen. The two lines of croquet teams shifted and fidgeted, caught by jerking images on a swaying screen. The images came in and out of focus, blurred, then sharp. The scene was set. Pictures of a city in the rain, omnibuses, horse-drawn carriages, rushing crowds. Then to the façade of a smart hotel, doormen, lobby, reception desk, and then to a twisting corridor, where the camera followed the progress of a chambermaid in a full black dress and starched white pinafore. She wheeled a trolley laden with linen, knocked on bedroom doors, changed sheets, scrubbed and cleaned. Brother Bernard inserted a finger in his right nostril and searched for gold. He came out with a nugget that he myopically inspected, rolled between finger and thumb and ate. The line of monks broke rank and fidgeted. The Abbot stared at the screen, the women swallowed cigarette smoke and raised lipstick-rimmed glasses to their lips. Thoughts of croquet seemed to have vanished for a moment as the men and women watched the mundane performance. The chambermaid closed another bedroom door and wheeled her trolley along another five-yard strip of corridor.

The film's audience were bored, and the Abbot, master of ceremonies, clapped his hands together for the croquet to begin. An unlikely coin was produced from the folds of his habit, and flicked into the air. Mary called heads and the Abbot bent to inspect the spinning coin as it settled on to its flagstone bed.

'Heads.' The Abbot stood up, puffing, his lips blue. Mary smiled and curtsied, mocking luck's judgement. A box of coloured balls was opened and leaning over her mallet, she struck off. The ball rattled over the flagstones, rolling towards the first metal hoop, missing it and then struggling on past the hoop to bounce off a wall. It was the monks' turn and Brother Matthew stood sideways on to the croquet ball, concentrating, his eyebrows twisting down over his eyes, his cheeks sucked in. The monks lined up behind him wishing him on, concentrating with him, and in unconscious parody mimicked his position and tentative practice stroke. Then, with a solid chunk, mallet struck, wood on wood, and the croquet ball rumbled slowly and steadily towards the hoop, gradually losing momentum.

'Go on,' shouted the monks, 'go on,' but the ball had stopped just short of its target and it was the women's turn.

Nora took the mallet from Mary and bent over the ball, swinging the mallet between her legs. Unable to achieve a good swing, she hitched her skirts over her thighs, to show the prettiest knees and a rim of darling garter. The monks tensed, and the boggle-eyed brothers caught their breath in a synchronous sigh. Nora swung and the ball bounced wildly off a far wall.

It was the Abbot's turn next and he waddled forward to pot the ball between the legs of the hoop and then sauntered back to the table to take up his wine glass again. He drank deeply, rivers of wine emptying into his gullet. He wiped his mouth with the back of his hand, then wiped his hand on his habit.

Meanwhile, the film seemed to have taken an unusual turn. The chambermaid had knocked on another door and, turning the handle, wheeled in her trolley. The room was occupied. On the bed was a sleeping black man. The sheets were thrown back and he was naked. The chambermaid, throwing up her hands in mock horror, rushed towards the camera in flash-eyed panic. The black man turned over in bed and lay on his stomach, his round buttocks facing heaven. The chambermaid clutched at her trolley and made towards the door. Just as she reached the door, curiosity overcame modesty and she glanced backwards at the sleeping man. He'd turned over again, and the camera focused in on his absolutely enormous penis, a penis that twitched and fidgeted, oblivious of the sleeping state of its master. The game of croquet faltered, and the players rested on their mallets, staring at the flickering scene. The chambermaid turned again to the camera and simulated coyness, screening her eyes with a shivering hand from the snake in the bed. Then, peering through her fingers, she peek-a-booed at the monster and edged closer to the bed. The black man stirred, stretched his limbs, then lay still in deep deep sleep.

On the floor by the bedside was a black hat, identical in style to the hat worn by the hero of the first film. The chambermaid bent to the carpet, picked up the hat, and with a silly smile plopped the hula-hoop hat over the man's genitals.

He woke, and sat straight up in bed, clutching at the sheets. He saw the chambermaid and grinned. She backed away, and turning to the camera simulated terror. At this critical moment the reel jerked and spun and light flashed on to the screen. Brother Bernard, tutting and sighing, wound on the film, then changing reels threaded in the next scenes. In staccato monochrome, the chambermaid continued her retreat before the black man who advanced towards her, their steps a pas de deux, hers backwards, his forwards, the linen trolley between them, she clothed, he naked, holding the hat over his groin. And of course she bumped into a chair and fell backwards, legs splayed, clothes rumpled. He fell on top of her and kissed her. She pushed him away, hands at his chest, then those hands twisted around his back and pulled him towards her. They kissed again, and his hands went to her breasts and pushed up her thighs. Her skirt rolled back to show the whiteness of her garters and her breasts were unpeeled from her trim spencer. He licked her breasts. The camera went to her face, which registered joy. Her eyes were closed and her breath came and went through her open mouth. The naked man stood up and pointed his penis at her face. She took him in her mouth, sucking him, clutching his buttocks.

At this point there seemed to be a good deal of rustling and sighing in the audience. The monks and their women, encouraged by lust's show, were fiddling with each other, competing with the film with their own display of licentiousness. Brother Bernard was on his knees in front of Brother Matthew, his head a mole in the brown field of Brother Matthew's habit. The Abbot, leader of men, held both Nora and Peggy in his embrace, kissing one, disrupting the other's underwear. I turned from the orgy to watch the film. The chambermaid was now bending over the back of the armchair. Her uniform had been pulled up over her ghostly white bum, and the hero was plumbing her depths with a look of deep and philosophic interest. She smiled at the camera, gazing up from her upside-down position. Meanwhile back in the monastery the flappers' dresses were off. One girl stood between two monks who pressed close to her. She rubbed their penises while one sucked her breasts, her pearls wrapped around his ears, and the other, eyes shut, rested his chin on her shoulders. A hand clutched at me, and I turned to my earthly saviour, Mary. We faced each other. Her soft breath dusted my face. Her hair was brown and shone with a red halo of henna, she had green eyes, a one-dimple smile, stepping-stone teeth and high cheekbones.

'Thank you,' I said, and she shrugged her shoulders. She stared at me, stared hard, then said, 'Well, little Brother, won't you come with me?' and, taking my hand, she led me away to the whitewashed corridor, my heart a box of drums in my skinny chest. Cool hand in perspiring hand, we

walked together, past the first twisting bend, and then she
stopped. She turned to kiss me and put her sweet tongue in
my mouth, tracing out my teeth. She pulled me to her,
backing up against the wall, her arms around my neck. She
pressed against me, and I felt the whole soft length of her
body with all of my body. Height for height, shoulders
against shoulders, breasts against chest, groin to groin, her
leg wrapped around mine. The whole of her given to all of
me, and all of me to her. The moment was strong and its
seconds, clicking motes, stretched out for ever.

Maybe love. I think so now. So vivid, this kiss, its
elements florid, solid. I felt all of her. I smelt every bubble
of scent that trickled from her skin. I heard her tongue as it
lapped around mine. Tasted her silver kiss and, eyes open,
traced the lines of her eyebrows as they dipped and ran.
She reached me, passed over some dam of innocence
confined, and the waters of my loveless childhood roared
and broke. I cried, heaving tears rushed down my cheeks,
hoary sobs cracking and bursting. I cried and breathless
grief tore my bones. I cried because I was alone. I cried for
my mother. I cried because I was lost. I cried because I'd
been buggered. I cried because I'd starved. I cried because
I was a child and now I was an adult. I cried for the other
orphans. I cried because it had been winter. I cried because
I was in this prison. I cried because I loved her. She held
me to her and I cried, head hung low, avoiding her eyes.
The tears soaked my habit, and I cried. I cried for Martha,
my first lost love. I cried for the hardness of the nuns. I
cried for the company of girls. I cried for the library. I cried
for the chickens. I cried because of the films. I cried because
I'd seen my first train. I cried for the wine that had allowed
me to cry. And still she held me. She asked for no
explanation, and gave me comfort, gave comfort to a small

child in an adult's clothes. Then suddenly it was enough.
I'd cried out my tears and was strong again. Mary wiped
my face, dabbing away the salt, and I took the cloth from
her to blow my nose. The material was soft and silky. I
looked at it. She'd given me her knickers to dry my tears. I
grinned and then the grin became a laugh. She looked at
me and laughed too.

'One must be practical, Brother John,' she said. I
nodded agreement, took her in my arms and we laughed
together. She reached under my habit and her leg up
around my waist guided me into her. I moved in and out, in
and out, quickly, slowly, silently. We were so close and we
came together and she laughed, deep gurgling giggles,
trilling runs.

'Why are you laughing?'

'I always do when I come. It tickles, you see.' How
wonderful to laugh when you come. That sex should be joy
and not dark guilt, that sex could be wonderful and
registered by laughter. We separated and she kissed me on
the nose. We tidied ourselves and she reached to hug me.
The Abbot's secretary returned her kiss. I held her by her
elbows, held her hard.

'Will we see each other?' I asked.

'We will see each other,' she replied and disengaging
herself from my grip she kissed me again and with clicking
heels and swaying hips she walked away. At the corner she
turned and framed by white narrow walls whispered,
'. . . probably.' She blew me a kiss and I shivered.

Chapter Five

I T WAS 10.30 on a bright June morning in 1926. I knocked
on the door of the Abbot's bedroom and entered. A four-
poster bed dominated the rococo chamber and ancient
tapestries quivered on sandstone walls. Two blue-silk-
covered armchairs gossiped in a window bay and a smug
kingwood escritoire postured under a shimmering oil painting. The bed was masked by crimson velvet curtains and
rested on carved lions' feet. Its valance was gold-edged
chintz, and gilt guardian eagles patrolled its carved cornice.
I stood at the foot of the bed.

'Good morning, sir.' Something beyond the curtains
thrashed and cursed. I swept back the velvet drapes to the
baleful storm of the Abbot's temper.

'Creature,' he rumbled. 'How dare you?' He plumped
up the yellow quilted counterpane and sat up in bed,
while I tidied his pillows. He farted vigorously and billows
of garlic fumed from under the rippling sheets. He rested
back against the pillows, the pearl buttons of his red
silk pyjamas taking the strain of his shining flesh. I handed
him his skullcap which he delicately placed neatly over
his vertex. He flicked back its long tassel and stared
at me. Then, with an exasperated sigh, he sank back in
his pillows and stared at the dark blue canopy of the
tester on which heaven's constellations were embroid-

ered, galaxies of sparkling silvery thread against the night.

I went from the room to the corridor and returned with a trolley bearing his breakfast and the post. I cranked up the trolley until its top shelf rose above the bed, then releasing a catch I swung the tray out over his counterpane. Through thick horn-rimmed spectacles which rested on the tip of his button nose, he inspected his meal. He contemplated the rounds of toast, and lifted the gilt dome that covered writhing bacon and three delicate fried eggs. Butter and orange marmalade reclined in glass bowls and coffee steamed in a turquoise Sèvres pot. I waited by his bedside while he gobbled his breakfast. Huge forkfuls of everything were crammed into his black toothless mouth and rushed into the maw of his throat.

I handed him the morning's mail. There were routine administrative letters that had come in the regular post and special deliveries that had been relayed by the Vatican messenger service. The Abbot was uninterested in the administrative letters. It was my duty to settle bills and draft letters answering religious questions. These letters from our peripheral churches always enquired as to the details of faith, and it was usually I who remembered the answers from the texts of the learned commentaries. The Abbot's knowledge of our religion and its history was remarkably sketchy, and demonstrated an extraordinary obliviousness to the daily reminders of a lifetime spent with God. He was grudgingly grateful for my abilities, nodding with some relief when I settled disputed points.

Why was such an ignorant man our Abbot? This was a question I could answer only if promotion was judged on the basis of sloth and licentiousness, for which, within our order, he had no peer.

The letters that arrived by special papal messenger were dealt with differently. Each letter came individually, written by abbots, from the different ministries of our order, dispatched from the distant corners of England, carried by monks, and delivered personally to me by virtue of my position as the Abbot's secretary. The letters were borne in black leather satchels, hung within the folds of the messenger's habit, dangling on a leather cord around the monk's neck. The envelopes were sealed in red wax and the seal bore the mark of each Abbot's signet ring. Messengers arrived virtually every day, and after signing receipt of their letters I would escort each monk to the refectory, make sure that he was fed, then lead him to rooms so that he could rest overnight. I was not allowed to read these letters. This the Abbot did. His dealings with the papal messenger service represented his only effort for the community of monks, and, as with all his activities, these efforts were highly idiosyncratic, and entirely stylized.

This morning's post came from the Abbot of our monastery in Newcastle.

'Excellency,' I said, 'do excuse me,' and I cleared away the breakfast trolley, pushing it from the room and into the corridor. Then bowing, as instructed by Brother Matthew when he'd trained me for my position as secretary, I handed the papal post on a silver salver to the Abbot.

The Abbot took the heavy cream envelope from the salver, brought it to his nose and sniffed it, smelt its corners and seal, then following the scratchy writing with his nail-bitten index finger traced out his name and address. He brought the envelope to his lips and touching his tongue to the wax seal licked the outline of Newcastle's crest. The Abbot passed the envelope to me. It was my task to open the envelope, and then return the letter to my master to read. The Abbot eased himself into the pillows, his hands resting palms down by his side. I broke the seal, removed the letter from the envelope, and passed it to the Abbot. He read, and although I was never allowed to see the papal post, I knew its contents, as the Abbot mouthed each word he scanned.

The Abbot read the papal post with great care. His lips silently echoed each slow sentence, then paused as he deliberated its import before engaging the next. Sometimes he would take several minutes to read a paragraph, and throwing his head back against the pillow he'd pinch his fingers against his eyelids, mulling over the meaning of a phrase, trying to predict the consequences of the scene described. The Abbot always read each letter thrice, and these readings might take up to an hour. The Abbot was the head of our order in England and it was his duty to act as a relay stage for information concerning the state of our nation.

Every letter that came was paraphrased and interpreted, and its messages sent on to the Vatican. From the borders of our country, from the west and the east, the north and south, we learnt about crops and conditions, the mood of the people, the confessions of the aristocrats. We heard of industries' profits and inventions. We were told of new roads and railways, local corruption and deceit. There were whispers of small alliances and infidelities, of misused power and persuasions. From the abbeys of England, each abbot told their tales of the land and the order of their people's lives. From each abbot came a careful construction of local information, built from the relayed tales of parish priests, stories of every small community and each large town, a spider's web of confession, its centre our abbey, its predatory arachnid our own Abbot.

These reports gave a unique picture of a real England, an England of pettiness and corruption, of adultery and deception. We learnt of the true government of the country, the sources of power, the manipulation of the law, the pursuit of profit, the betrayal of charity, the decline of truth, the rewards of greed, the laws of favours and preference.

Each abbot reported on local power and important lives, gave clues as to how these powerful men might be manipulated if necessary, and when optimally this manipulation should be pursued. And in every report the poor were unimportant, except in terms of how they might be used to increase the wealth of the rich. Power rested in the hands of the few and was not exchangeable, remaining with its trappings of wealth and land in the same families, through the generations.

Each abbot recounted how control was maintained, how industry and agriculture were employed for the profit of small groups of individuals, and each was laudatory when some local coup increased the hegemony of inherited power. This holy information service led inwards from the furthest and nearest sources, dragging in the smallest and the largest details of life in England. Wherever there was a priest, from the borders of government to the centre of the tiniest hamlet, the truth was gathered, then culled and filed by the local abbot who reported to this bed and this man.

Our Abbot processed information relayed by the Vatican's messengers and in his own letters instructed his subordinate abbots as to how best they might control their territories, maintaining order, reinforcing the local command of the church, increasing tithes, ablating sedition and unease by means of the instructions of prayer.

The Abbot lay among his pillows, eyes shut, picking his ears with the long nails of his little fingers. He scratched himself, then shouted for 'More, much more coffee.' I bowed, and, backing away from his bed, pulled the cord that connected with a kitchen bell. A few moments later there was a knocking at the bedroom door. I opened the door, then walked into the corridor to issue discreet instructions to an unshaven, twitching novice.

'Certainly, sir,' said the boy, and rushed away with his orders. I'd become important, a sir for novices. I returned to the bedroom. The Abbot had arranged a black shade over his eyes and was snoring, the sheets rising and falling, echoing his thunder.

I sat on a walnut armchair in the window bay and looked out over the fair lands, to the rushing sparkle that brushed across the lake, the swaying darkness of the woods and the rippling crops in the fair fields of our labour. A horse-drawn carriage tracked downhill and through the silence of glass I imagined the clip of the animal's hooves and the prick of trailing brambles. Over the hedgerows were the chicken huts and my memories. All in times past, but in my mind all past time ran together, each unit equidistant from the present. The past was a stack of pictures, and I sat on blue moiré silk and shuffled the stack, pulling out images of a life gone by. From a smooth-faced child to these shaven cheeks, rifling through memory's files. Some paintings were more vivid than others: in one scene the colours ran, in another the image screamed. I felt the cold of the orphanage, the hunger of infancy, the smack of the nuns, the stink of Aquinas's breath, my hands on Mary.

My ramblings were interrupted by a scratching on the door, and I took the Abbot's coffee from the obsequious kitchen boy, who crossed himself and bowed. I banged the door and the Abbot jumped from sleep, startled, as he was meant to be, by the noise. It was time for him to wake and work. The Abbot reached into his bedside table and pulled out a medicine bottle. He unscrewed the cap and with shaking hands took a mouthful of tincture of opium, then another, smacked his lips and replaced the medicine bottle in the cabinet. This was his tonic. Taken four times a day, it kept him at peace, freed him from the mundane. I gave him coffee, and placed a bolster behind his shoulder. I took a cigarette box from the kingwood escritoire. The desk was placed opposite the bed under a painting by Alma-Tadema of adolescents in Greek costume, playing in a ruined temple on the edges of a blue sea. Their tunics were appropriate to the scene and its time, but somehow the sea and the ruins conspired to make the children victims of pornography, and this I suspected was precisely the reason why the Abbot had this picture placed opposite his bed, the last image before light left him for sleep. I handed the box to the Abbot. He took out a gold-tipped black cigarette and placed it to his lips. I struck a match and he smoked.

'Wretch,' he rumbled, 'you are failing me again.' I knew what I'd done and corrected matters by paying attention to his coffee cup. He smacked his lips, and dribbled on to his exquisite silk pyjamas. I fetched his satin smoking jacket, and waited by his bedside for his pink toes to inspect the day. They came slyly, like foetuses propelled from a rat's womb.

I ran the Abbot's bath, sprinkled bath salts, adjusted the water's temperature. He came in and stared at his magnified face in the Victorian shaving glass. He sat by the sink, the folds of his enormous bottom drooping around the slim bamboo lines of the bathroom stool. I filled the sink with hot water and lathered his face with a badger brush, working the foam with the slapping bristle. I sharpened the cut-throat razor on the barber's leather. Pulling up the flesh over his cheekbones, tightening the skin, I drew the razor across his face, catching the edge of the blade against his beard. I dipped the razor in hot water and pushed up his chin with my thumb. Again I drew the blade across his skin, this time thinking of the nice bright red line I could make if I really wished, but the strange thing was that my time in his service had led me to respect him, so that this idle thought had no substantial basis, no will for action. I dipped the razor in the sink, washing away the scum of stubble and soap. I flicked away at his upper lip and cleared the beard from his chin. Then I pressed a steaming flannel into his face, clearing the shaving cream from his ears and hairy nostrils. He pushed me away from him, and climbed into the bath with his pyjamas on. A tidal wave of foam and water rushed over the edge of the bath and soaked the precious Persian carpet. He lay back in the hissing bubbles and groaned.

'My head, the wine last night. Brother John, did you drink?'

'Yes, your grace.' I had drunk. We had all drunk, and my hangover, was, I'm sure, as jarringly unpleasant as the Abbot's.

'Take off my pyjamas.' I extended my hand to him and he pulled himself upright. I unbuttoned his top and peeled the wet silk from him. He sat back and then threshing in the water tore at his pyjama trousers, ripping off the buttons. He threw his pants at the bathroom wall. 'That's enough,' he roared, and the maddened river buffalo stomped from the water. He faced me, pink, hairless, tyres of flesh lolloping over tyres of flesh, penis almost invisible among the folds of his abdomen. I opened the white bathrobe for him, and he continued to roar. His face was purple. 'Get me medicine!' I opened the bathroom cabinet and searched the serried ranks of panaceas. Clearing back the front line of laxatives and headache powders, I found his medicine, a

114

glass phial of white crystal crumbs. I snapped off the phial's top and passed it to him.

'Your grace.' He snatched the phial from me and inhaled its contents.

'Ah, you rascal, you vicious womanizer.' He wagged his finger at me. 'You foul whoreson, aah aah!' He dribbled from his mouth, and white threads of saliva spotted the lapels of his bathrobe. 'Come here, you monster.' He grabbed my earlobe and pulled me to him. He stared in my eyes and inspected my face. 'As I thought, you've a hangover too. Help yourself to medicine. It's the only good thing to come from that unpleasant Jew, that little Austrian, Freud. Yes, it is good, the rest is rabble-rousing nonsense, the stuff of dreams indeed!' He sat on the edge of the bath, while I towelled his arms and legs and helped him into his red leather slippers.

Having dried the Abbot, I served myself from his medicine cabinet, breaking open a cocaine phial and breathing deep its contents. My headache worsened, arteries throbbing deep in my head, pulsing, banging, slapping away at my poor painful brain. It was certainly no cure for an excess of alcohol. The Abbot waddled back into the bedroom, clambered up the bedstep and, with his slippers still on, snuggled back under the sheets. He grabbed at the Newcastle letter, while I drew up a chair and opened up my note pad. He read slowly, as usual each written word echoed by his dry lips, a soundless reading easily understood, never heard. He dropped the letter.

'Ready, boy, are you ready?' I was. I took his dictation, my nib scratching at the page.

Master, your holiness,
    I have news from the monastery of Durham. It is in the

north of our country near the town of Newcastle, in the county
of Northumberland, near the Scottish borders. There is unrest
among the working classes and it may disturb the structure of
our land. I had written to you earlier this year telling of social
change. Your holiness, it is widely reported from every diocese.
Life in England has altered as a result of the last war. Our
foreign territories have become fewer and our markets have
shrunk. The Americans now dominate manufacture, and our
own industries are in decline. As you know, your holiness, the
allies, encouraged by the Church, engineered the great war.
They did this to destroy Germany's industry. The threat of
German domination of the market place was eventually
shattered, and we thought that with the peace settlement we
would return to the old ways. But no, America has taken
Germany's place and cheap American goods swamp the market.
No words of ridicule and rumour disseminated by our press, the
government, the Church, no rallying patriotism declaimed by
our leaders prevents this onslaught on our manufacturing
systems. We say their goods are shoddy, but the retail trade
know this is untrue and their produce is displayed and sold.
Your holiness, this has caused considerable problems here in
England. This decline in our own industry has been exacerbated
by an accompanying growth of the labour movement. The
nineteen twenties have been difficult for the establishment,
order has been threatened, and our society is changing. Two
years ago, in 1924, as your holiness no doubt knows, the
working man's movement grew to such an extent that a new
political party swept into power. This 'Labour Party' is made up
of a group of strident working-class men who in alliance with
the Liberal middle-class turncoats have granted certain
advantages to the unions, legislating so that the workers are
protected if they should choose to take advantage of the
benevolence of their employers and strike. Can you believe,

your holiness, that it is now possible for the workers to leave their work and refuse to return until they have been granted increased wages or reduced hours? They are in a position to blackmail respectable mill and factory owners in order to get their way. They are irresponsible children. This should not be allowed. Unfortunately the Great War has led to a comparative scarcity of men between the ages of twenty and forty. The unforeseen magnitude of the slaughter of that war has thus put the people into a position of relative strength where they are able to barter their labour against improved conditions. This outrageous situation, where striking workers are no longer responsible for the damage that they cause to their employers, must be radically changed.

As you know, your holiness, we, your Church in England, are currently doing our best to rectify this situation. Men everywhere are corruptible. This corruptibility is a fortunate condition of life on earth. Your holiness, in England, social change as a result of industrial decline, and the increased power of the labour movement, has recently become a serious problem in the mining industry. In order to compete with cheap imported American coal, the mine owners have tried to reduce costs, by reducing the price of labour, asking the miners to work for more hours, for less money. Although this is obviously quite the right way to do things, the people have not seen sense. Ideally, one would wish to deal with the problem at root by using influence to increase American prices. Unfortunately this is not possible. Your holiness is obviously aware that there have been radical changes in the United States, and because of these changes we, the Church, have lost considerable control. I feel that our power will ultimately increase again as our agents use the prohibition laws to reassert their authority.

Forgive me, your holiness, for I am an old man and ramble. Let me describe for you the situation in Great Britain, for

Durham's story is typical of that in the rest of our land. Local mine owners generously offered to keep their mines open, provided that the workers would co-operate. This offer, as I briefly mentioned, was conditional upon the miners working for slightly longer hours and for a little less money. As our Abbot in Newcastle describes, and I quote from his letter, 'Is it not legitimate that the miners co-operate, protecting their own livelihoods by co-operating with the mine owners?' Of course, your eminence, the mine owners were right and our Church supported them.

The local abbot then consulted with your most humble servant, in my position as your representative in this land, and, through his good offices, the local constabulary were advised to arrest the most active of the miners' leaders. Despite the obvious legitimacy of this action, the workers were not controlled, new leaders came forward and dissent spread. Quite outrageously the workers refused to accept the owners' proposals. After further consultation we decided to show the miners the consequences of their idiocy and on 1 May 1926 the mine owners closed down the mines. The miners were locked out, and their wages withheld. The Church in Newcastle counselled the men to return to work, but, your holiness, unfortunately, and despite the greatest efforts of your priests, the ridiculous lower classes continued with their absurdly irresponsible behaviour.

This madness spread through the land and was taken up by the Trades Union Congress, who are, as your holiness knows, the workers' elected representatives. A. J. Cook, their leader, is one of our men, but such was the pressure of the lower orders on him that he was forced to oppose the mine owners' proposals, with the lamentable statement, 'Not a penny off the pay, not a minute on the day.' Your holiness, the poor man had no choice; either he made a statement in support of the workers or he would have lost his office. It was more important that he maintained power and in this action he had our blessing. Still there was no settlement and the miners then proceeded to ask for active support from their fellow trade unionists. I have been in daily contact with Cook, and the inevitability of the events consequent to this demand was quite, quite shocking. The movement gathered momentum and on 4 May 1926, ten days ago, a General Strike was called. Through the good offices of Cook, the strike although described as 'General' was in fact limited. Only the iron and steel, building, printing, gas and electricity workers went on strike, and we were relatively successful in limiting the potential damage. Alarmist stories were run in the newspapers. These stories frightened the population, as they spread rumours of the collapse of society and its potential descent into starvation and chaos if the strike anarchy proceeded. We drafted an enormous new police force and used the troops to control the strike.

Gradually the people were led to believe that the movement was against them, not against the mine owners, and in this view they were encouraged by the troops and police who prevented the supply of food to shops throughout the country. Eventually, so successful was our campaign that the lower classes themselves volunteered for strike-breaking duties, driving omnibuses and lorries through the lines of strikers in order to maintain essential services, services which we ourselves had disrupted.

Your holiness, our control began to reassert itself, questions were raised in the electoral house concerning the legality of the strike and the possibility of imprisonment or onerous fines was raised. Certainly within the context of the law, in our country, this is conceivable.

At this point the relative weakness of government and the Church of England was amusingly displayed. Our Prime

Minister and the Archbishop of Canterbury both appealed to the strikers to return to work, but these appeals were completely ignored. Abbot Durham writes, 'It is noticeable in our diocese that the grim and despondent strike breakers have ignored appeals.'

We used this moment to increase public sympathy for the monarchy. Knowing that the strike was weakening, George V, who as your holiness knows is a Catholic although he must publicly profess Protestantism, expressed sympathy for the miners and their families. This of course was a hypocritical pretence, a charade that led to a considerable increase in the popularity of the monarchy.

Meanwhile the Trades Union Congress were becoming alarmed at the rumours of the illegality of their strike and the rapid consumption of their funds. Your holiness, we had manipulated the situation so that it was as if their strike was against the people rather than the plutocrats. Your holiness, this moment was a joyous one for us. We had successfully reasserted control and suddenly, on 12 May, the strike was called off. We had triumphed. Abbot Durham reports, 'The miners have returned to work, returned grumbling and sour-faced. The men are in the pits, working and working as the owners wished for less money and longer hours.'

Your holiness, once again, our Church has won.

The Abbot scratched his dewlaps. 'Sign off in the usual way.'

I copied out the text. Yours in utmost deference, I am for ever your humblest servant. While I wrote, the Abbot turned over on to his stomach and covered his head with pillows. From the swans' down depths came his mumblings.

'I will rest now until luncheon, leave me. Wake me then.'

'Certainly, sir.'

I folded his letter into an envelope. Reaching into the bed I uncurled the Abbot's left hand from his penis and impressed his signet ring on to the sealing wax.

It was time for our midday meal and I made my way to the refectory to attend the Abbot. I took my place at high table. The monks filed in, the great vats of food steamed. It was meatless Friday and the ugly smell of steamed cod filled the dark room. The food trolleys clattered between the rows of greedy monks, plates were loaded and glasses filled with dull water. The place beside me was empty. The Abbot was late. The monks looked towards the high table. Where was he? They couldn't start eating until grace. They stared at me, as if the Abbot was my responsibility and my negligent care had directly led to this delay in their luncheon. The Abbot hated the refectory, loathed the mass catering, despised fish and Fridays. He was always late on Fridays. At last, here he was, sweeping in through the refectory doors. The monks watched him take his place beside me. The Abbot looked down on his plate, the mashed potatoes, the overcooked puckered peas, the layered chunks of cod.

'Rrru.' He groaned and, fists pressing hard into the refectory table, he pushed himself to his feet for grace. The monks bowed their heads. 'We thank you, Lord, for the goodness that you have provided . . .' His voice trailed away for a moment and he seemed to lose track of the situation. I tugged at his sleeve and he jerked to attention. 'Lord, we break the bread of our labour and remember with each mouthful your sacrifice. Lord, make us worthy of this goodness you give us and bless us this day with your love. For what we are about to receive may the Lord make us truly thankful.'

'Amen,' said the monks, and before the echoes of their amens had died in the refectory's rafters, they were eating, heads swooping down low over their plates, cheeks bulging, mashed potatoes spilling over their clothes on to the floor. The Abbot surveyed his monks with considerable disdain. He took up his fork and pushed a flake of cod around his plate, hiding the fish in a forest of peas, then with his fingers plied the piled potatoes into a pretty pattern. His nose wrinkled. He thrust the plate away. It slid across the table and crashed on the floor. He stamped his foot. The Abbot was always tetchy at meal times; a gourmand, he detested the refectory cooking, loathed the taste, smell and sight of the kitchen's crop. He fidgeted, tying and untying the tasselled cord at his waist, ignoring the mass of greedy monks belching and gobbling before him. The noise of slurping and lip-smacking filled the refectory, greasy fingers waved shining cutlery. The monks were busy at their meal, stealing from each other's plates, eyes popping, cheeks bulging, sweating with the effort of their only honest labour, consumption. In the rush of their greed, scattered food had fallen to the floor, littering the aisle. Spilt gravy glistened on the tables.

The pudding trolley slid forward, great metal bowls of spotted dick, white fluffy mountains encrusted with black currant pebbles floating on rolling lava fields of hot thick custard. The Abbot drummed his fingers on the table, while his neighbours dribbled custard onto their laps. He was bored. It was enough. He was the Abbot. He lumbered to his feet before the monks had finished their meal, and boomed out grace. Sullen faces turned to him, the tinkle of spoons rang out, and, meal abandoned, an ungrateful response was mumbled by the assembly.

'For what we have received, Lord, we are truly grateful.'

Were they grateful? They were not. The monks wanted to finish their pudding and the Abbot had stopped them. Their grace was graceless.

The monks stood as the Abbot left the refectory. I followed and we made our way to the Abbot's day rooms. This suite of chambers occupied most of the top floor of the north wing of the monastery, rooms for relaxation and dining, rooms for debauch and play, rooms for conference, rooms for contemplation, rooms for the Abbot's day. High over the monastery, these rooms commanded the court-yards and countryside, the fields and farms of Kent, the acres of trees, the grey swathe of river, the distant hills and the sudden glare of chalk. The Abbot wasn't a man for views. Dark damask curtains screened the windows and the rooms were lit by the flickering light of huge silver-gilt candelabra.

The Abbot collapsed into a high-backed carver, the only chair at a table set for one. Its velvet seat sagged under his weight. He grabbed his knife and slapped the table top with the blade. He wanted his luncheon. Bring it in, bring it on. I stood at his right shoulder, out of vision, awaiting his fickle orders. He banged the table again and roared, 'Where's my luncheon, you whore? I'm here, where's my meal, bring me my meat!' In all my time in his service I'd never seen him eat anything but meat. He abhorred veget-ables. The Abbot pushed his chair back and banged the table with his fist. 'Where's my fucking lunch?' The curtains quivered and I dodged a little to the side to be more perfectly hidden by his back. He spun around, his face unpleasantly blotched by the thunderous veins of his roar-ing anger. He punched my chest. 'It's your fault.' He hit me again hard. 'See to it.' I bowed my head, went towards the plain door that led to his kitchen and almost knocked over the serving maid carrying a laden tray.

'Sorry, I beg your pardon.' She caught her balance and smiled coquettishly at me.

'No harm's done, don't worry.' She continued her progress into the dining room, a pretty sight. It was Mary, my saviour from so many years back. As was the Abbot's rule for his serving wenches, she wore a linen pinafore but was otherwise naked. She went to serve the Abbot, white apron's bow tied tight across the small of her back, its sharp line demarcating the whiteness of a bottom whose cheeks rose and fell with her steps. She placed the silver serving tray to the side of the Abbot who leaned forward in anticipation, elbows on the table, knife and fork ready raised in his eager fists.

Mary carved the beef, carved through fat, crisp black and then sharp yellow, cut to the meat itself, burnt dark on the outside, centre bright red with life's blood. The Abbot held out his plate and Mary served him thick tranches of meat, piling a high mound on his plate. Meat, only meat. For the Abbot, fish were vegetables, and vegetables a swindle, stealing space in his stomach that ought to be occupied by real food and meat was real food as many times a day as possible, maintaining his body in its state of rolling corpulence.

Mary stood back, her high breasts peeking out over the top of her apron. She watched the Abbot's plate and, as each slab of meat was seized and bolted, she reached forward to refill it. The mound of meat remained piled high, and the Abbot hummed as he ate. He hummed a chorus from Handel's *Messiah*, so unexpected the music, his voice falsetto, his song sweet.

The Abbot was full. He pushed the laden plate away and waved Mary towards him. She had been many years in the service of the monastery, years of orphaned childhood, adolescence and maturity. Her school was depravity, her university corruption. Since my rescue we'd been occasional lovers, stealing time in the broken moments of our masters' errands. The Abbot sang.

'King of Kings, Hallelujah Hallelujah, Lord of Lords, For Ever Hallelujah,' and as he sang Mary bent down under the table and on her hands and knees, apron dragging the floor, shuffled forward, hair falling over her face. The Abbot sang and Mary crawled forward until her shoulders touched his knees. Slowly, slowly she pulled up his habit, higher, then higher, over his snowdrift feet, his calves, his knees. Over his thighs, hairless, creased with unpleasant dimples of cellulite and broken rivers of scarecrow veins, and then the habit stuck under the fasciculating mass of his buttocks. Mary tugged at the cloth. The Abbot shifted, and Mary pulled the material high up over his waist, retying his sash to keep the cloth positioned around his belly. Unpleasant grey curls tickled around the withered stump of the Abbot's shrunken penis, a wrinkled penis sunk in rolling folds of skin, an eye winking in lardy, coarse flesh, flecked with the tired spots of great age.

Mary squeezed forward, her head wedged between the table top and the Abbot's monstrous thighs. With her shuffling effort her breasts popped out over her apron, perfect button nipples, a friendly mole under her right breast winking at me, her part-time disposable lover. The Abbot spread his thighs, 'BRRRRrrrrr,' and the high smell of yesterday's garlic laced the air. Mary pulled a tiny bottle from her pinafore pocket, poured oil on to her hands, and massaged the Abbot's penis between her palms.

The Abbot sang on. 'For the Lord God omnipotent reigneth. Hallelujah Hallelujah, For ever, for ever.' Mary ducked down over his lap, her lips taking the Abbot's penis. She sucked at him, and her head rose and fell, rose and fell, the skin of her neck stretching, relaxing, the tiny hairy birthmark under her jaw appearing, disappearing. 'King of Kings, and Lord of Lords.'

I stepped forward. It was my turn, and my thumbs and fingers were at his shoulders, pressing down, massaging the deep knots of muscle, easing the bunched nerves, loosening the trembling tension that twisted his bones. Deeper and deeper, round and round, pushing in and away, as the Abbot sang Handel. Handel the English German. 'For ever and ever.' Up and down ducked Mary's head, faster, faster, slowly, slower. She pulled away, to inspect her work. The Abbot's penis remained flaccid, wet, limp, detumescent. She bent over again and her tongue flicked out.

Onward went Handel's marching chorus, 'Hallelujah, Hallelujah,' and surprising us all with its sudden life, the Abbot's penis sprang up, horribly purple. Mary bent lower and sucked again. Louder came the falsetto and the chandelier trembled. Higher came the voice, and the tableware shook. Down, up went Mary. Round and round pressed my fingers in his shoulders. Louder came the singing, Mary's hand circled the Abbot's penis. The Abbot reached out and grabbed the table's edge. Handel's *Messiah* climaxed thunderously and so did he. Mary spluttered and backed out from under the table. I stopped my massage. The Abbot untied his sash. His robes fell over his knees. The kitchen door slammed. Mary had left the room.

It was time for the Abbot's dessert and for coffee. The Abbot fidgeted. He played with his cutlery, lining up knives and forks, then attempted to balance the spoon on its side. He inspected the crockery, turning the plates upside down and examining their maker's mark. He took his wine glass to his lips, drained it, then ran his tongue around its edge, faster and faster until the glass sang, resonant, piercing,

126

rattling the glimmering pair of rose lustres on the mahogany chiffonier. He put the glass down on the table. I filled it to the brim with claret and returned to my position behind his shoulder. The Abbot liked his glass full. He drank again. I refilled his glass. The Abbot drained the wine. Another glass. Another.

The kitchen door swung open and Mary returned, carrying a silver tray. The Abbot deliberately knocked over his glass, wine dripped over the immaculate Bokhara. The glass rolled across the table. The Abbot made no effort to prevent it falling. It crashed to the floor, shattered glass spraying out over the room. Mary's feet were bare. She walked to the table treading glass splinters, and her footprints were suddenly red, blood trickling, mixing with the puddle of red red claret at the rug's edge. She neither winced nor faltered, serving a plate of sweetmeats bordered by black chocolate before the loafing, leaning, heavy-eyed Abbot.

Suddenly the Abbot groaned and clutched his belly. 'Ohhh,' he moaned. He raised his head, and rubbed his stomach. What was wrong? The Abbot shuddered and shivered, sighing, whining, and then suddenly belched. Indigestion. The Abbot had indigestion. Seizing my chance I soothed the beast, cooing, sympathetic.

'There, there, your grace, let's sit down, shall we?' I rubbed his back. 'You just relax for a moment and I'll get you some milk.' The amorphous Abbot slumped over the table, head resting on his forearm. I scurried away to the kitchen. Mary stood by the kitchen window, leaning against a white porcelain sink whose bleached pine draining board was loaded with scoured shining coppers. On the corner of the draining board rested a jam jar filled with crimson roses whose scent captured the kitchen.

'Mary, I need some milk.' She pointed to the larder, and I opened the door. The room was cool, dark, and had the sour smell of a lawn wet with spring rain. Round cheeses, bottled preserves and Doulton jars filled the shelves. Hams and smoked fish hung from butchers' hooks. Sacks of flour and rice reclined on the floor.

'Mary, where's the milk?'

She came into the larder, glass in hand. 'There.' She pointed.

'Where?'

She brushed past me and lifted a muslin-covered milk jug from its shelf and filled the glass. She gave me the glass, our fingers touched, and burnt.

'Thanks.' As I left the kitchen, the larder door slammed hard.

'Here, your grace.' The Abbot drank. He leant back in his chair. He burped. He rubbed his best friend, his belly. 'Better, your grace?' He nodded. He held out his hand and I helped him heave his great bulk from the dining-room chair.

It was time for his afternoon sleep and leaning heavily on my arm the Abbot stumbled back to his bedchamber. He rolled on to his bed fully clothed, and in a few moments was snoring viciously, a thousand wasps issuing at regular intervals from his open mouth.

Chapter Six

TIME CHANGES. Time changes everything. The world, its seasons. It was 1929. I was outside the monastery for the first time in more than twelve years. I had travelled thrice in my little life. Once from the orphanage to the monastery in a horse-drawn hackney carriage with Sister Thomas. A second journey on ice and snow, on a sled with Brother Aquinas to the village in the hollow valley. This time in a black Daimler motor car travelling from the monastery to London. We were to see Baldwin. Our mission was delicate. The Church sensed change in Europe and, more immediately, impending economic crisis.

We were to discuss the economic situation with the Prime Minister in order to establish his government's views. We needed to know, for the Church had considerable investments in the stock market, riding the crest of the burgeoning share prices through its agency the Vatican Bank. We had divested ourselves of gold in the mid-1920s when Britain had returned to the gold standard. We had done so then because in the Church's view currency was about to stabilize, and the enormous profits we had made from European inflation would cease. We had moved from gold to the stock markets. Our investment had been wise and the financial implications to the Vatican enormous. As a result, we were as rich as any single European country, keepers of unfathomable, useful wealth.

The papal messengers had communicated to us the worries of the Church as to the stability of world economies. The basis for instability was that the world's farms were over-productive and farm prices in a competitive market had dramatically fallen. The initial impact of this glut of produce was on the farmers themselves. Unable to make a living, peasants had left the land and flooded into the city. This unemployment had repercussions on industry and the demand for manufactured goods had fallen. There were other more complex reasons for the decline in European economies. Since the Great War, the First World had relied on the Second World. In the late 1920s the United States' capital investment in Europe had declined. This diversion of monies resulted from the extraordinary speculative buoyancy of stock markets. Investment in the markets yielded a far greater return than investment in European manufacturing industries. As a result American capital was diverted to the markets and away from the poorer yields of Europe.

Our advisers in the Vatican Bank were most concerned. They felt that this situation might precipitate recession, and they wished to protect the Church's investment. They saw no real basis to the spiralling prices of world stock markets. Share values seemed to be based on speculation and the whimsical movement of cheap borrowed money. Our bankers felt that there was no substance to the extraordinary prices of shares. They were meaningless because the prices failed to reflect a company's value and prospects. We wished to secure our investments, moving the Church's capital from the stock markets to gold. Before we did so, we needed information. We needed to know when to sell. We needed this information from source.

The Abbot and I were being driven towards London, rattling along the lanes of Kent, past the oast houses and orchards of England's garden. In every country, similar processions of abbots and cardinals were addressing this problem, taking themselves to the houses of secular power. The Abbot, as usual, was in a foul mood, particularly foul today because he hated any disruption to his routine, and this journey represented a major disturbance in the rhythm of his day. The Abbot liked the order of the monastery, its fixed times for prayers and meals, the shelter of its labyrinth, the rigidity of its hierarchy, the entertainment of his bathroom medicine cabinet. And this April morning he had been made to travel to town, carrying out the exceptional orders handed him by last week's papal messenger.

On receipt of these instructions, I had telephoned through to the Downing Street Chaplain and organized a private appointment with Baldwin, ostensibly to discuss the ownership of the Order's lands in England. We wore grey suits, dark ties and high stiff collars. Our hair was Brilliantined. We were ordinary, we looked like businessmen. We were businessmen, and driving with us were two government employees.

The Abbot had not looked through the window for the journey's duration, he had not spoken, and only reluctantly deigned to breathe the air outside the corridors of his power. The two men in the Daimler's front seat were speaking with each other, their mouths forming words which we could not hear because of the glass partition between us. What were they discussing? I opened the speaking tube that connected the two compartments.

'Well, I said to Gladys, I said, that's it, three pounds and sixpence is me wages and that's all I get a week and then she says to me well one pound fifteen shillings is the rent and we've four mouths to feed and what does that leave me? I'm sick of it, she says. Sick of it. Sick of it, I tell her. Well, you know what you can do if you're sick of it. You can stuff it, can't you. Go run back to your mother with the screamers, why don't you?'

'Well rid of her, you would be, Jack, well rid of her.'

'She's always nagging, always wanting things. She's jealous, she is. If Mildred her sister's got a new dress Gladys wants one. Always coveting things. That's the word, covetous she is. Lucky she don't know how much I really earn otherwise I'd not be able to buy a bottle of porter of an evening nor nothing.'

So this was the ordinary man's conversation. It could be avoided. I closed the speaking tube and sat back in the comfortable leather seat. We were travelling so quickly, at least five times as fast as the hackney carriage had travelled. And what was the purpose of this speed, how did we benefit? I didn't like the idea of ease of travel and accessible mobility. If travel became an option for all, it would lead to a change in our society's base. We couldn't afford to let all classes have access to these motor-car beasts. People would no longer be content to spend their lives in Scunthorpe or Nuneaton and our control would lapse.

Our companions continued their puerile conversation. I found them annoying, their silent mouthing a distraction. I bent forward to the speaking tube.

'Excuse me, gentlemen, would you mind awfully being quiet. I'm afraid we can't concentrate on our discussion.' I closed the tube and sat back again. For the first time in our journey the Abbot spluttered to life.

'Quite right,' he said. 'Those irritating little worms.' He dribbled, and saliva streamed from the corner of his mouth down his many chins and dropped on to his lap. He reached into his pockets and pulled out a pint-sized hip flask, unscrewed its silver stopper and drank deeply. He passed the flask to me and I took a tug at the fine brandy.

Our journey became smoother as we left Kent's cobble-stones and travelled through the macadamed outskirts of East London. I closed the window as the air was harsh with the smoke of factories. London's industry was mainly based in the east of the city. There were no laws to regulate factory waste and considerable pollution resulted. London's winds came from the west, driving industry's effluent over the inhabitants of East London. This accounted for their vastly greater incidence of pollution-related sickness. There was more bronchial illness in the East End than anywhere else in the world. The effluent was not regulated because the effects of illness were generally insignificant during a working man's life, but shortened his time after retirement and thereby eased the companies' pension burden: a most satisfactory solution.

The streets narrowed again as we drove through Peck-ham, and our vista was of terraced Victorian houses and gas lamps, omnibuses and trams, policemen and bright red letter boxes. I knew of civilization's inventions through the newspapers and it was a wonder to identify them. The streets were busy with hurrying men and women. The men were dressed as we were, but aah! the women. The war had taken so many men. We could never have calculated how many would be lost when our original plans were made. After the war we needed the women to make up the workforce and we fooled them with the apparent freedom of liberation, manipulated them with superficial suffrage, to take work at a wage less than that of their men. Submissive, they were used to less and the fools were grateful. As part of the chanted freedom, they abandoned the wrappings of

Edwardian England. The bustles and high collars, the long
dresses and the layered petticoats were replaced with soft
clinging silks cut short just below the knee, dresses that
revealed their shape, stockinged calves and dimpled ankles.
These women marched the street, rushing, rushing past the
brightly lit shops, the markets and arcades. Glorious, so
many divine legs and ankles. And over there, over there, a
graceful white neck, unbuttoned, exposed.

The Abbot passed me his hip flask again. We were at
the Elephant & Castle, with its grand Palladian church. I
tipped back the flask and, as we crossed the river at
Westminster, drank again. Parliament and Big Ben faced
us, sooty gothic stone and emphatic clock dominating the
silver water. We had made reasonable time, our driver had
done well. The Daimler heaved up over Westminster
Bridge. The river was quiet, at ease, a mirror in the spring
sun. We rounded Parliament Square and drove along a
crowded Whitehall, where cars and buses clogged the road.

Our car was waved down at the entrance to Downing
Street. A tall policeman stooped to lean through the driver's
window. His elbow on the sill, our driver showed him his
identification and we were ushered into the street of
graceful houses. We stopped outside Number 10 and our
doors were opened for us. I got out, the Abbot remained in
his seat. I walked around to his side of the car and offered
the Abbot my hand. He grabbed at my forearm and heaved
himself around until his legs were suspended from the edge
of his seat, dangling down over the kerb. I took both his
butcher's hands in mine and pulled him upright. His hip
flask protruded from his jacket pocket. He noticed and
straightened his clothes.

A pimply policeman stood at attention at Number 10's
doorway, his spots red stars on his shining face. The Abbot

leant heavily on the crook of my arm, stumbling forward, scuffing his feet.

I rang the doorbell, and the front door was opened virtually simultaneously with the chime by a tall butler in black tail-coat and a high stiff collar. He had bushy eyebrows and Victorian mutton-chop whiskers. He nodded at us from a polite height.

'The Abbot Horsmunden and his secretary to see the Prime Minister?' And with a deferential flick of his wrist we were ushered into a marble hallway, to a comfortable anteroom with its cluster of deep leather seats. This reception room was hung with heavy-framed oils of English country scenes, haywains and happy peasants, villages and lakes and fine portraits of race horses. Along one wall rested a Chinese Chippendale settee and on another a Sheraton love seat. Gleaming brass fire-dogs guarded the serpentine fireplace, and a tantalus and four crystal glasses rested on a Regency table. The Abbot shuffled to an armchair. I stood in front of him, my feet against his toes, stopping his feet from sliding away. I held on to his arms, as he lowered himself into the armchair. The chair squeaked and rolled back as his twenty-three stones dropped into its seat. I wasn't looking forward to pulling him upright.

We waited quietly, kept company by the tick of a carriage clock whose fusee movement scratched away the marching seconds. The quarter hour chimed. There was a tap at the door, and the butler entered followed by a liveried footman, bewigged, gold epaulettes, lace cuffs and a red tail-coat. The footman carried a heavy silver tray and a folding table, which he assembled with one hand. He placed the tray on the table.

'Tea, gentlemen. Mr Baldwin sends his apologies. He will be another fifteen minutes.' I answered for the Abbot, sensing his flowering irritation, and trying to head off any obscene outburst of malevolent discontent, precipitated by his being away from home and further compounded by this delay to his return.

'Thank you.' Tea was poured.

'Sugar, gentlemen?'

'Please.' Of course we wanted sugar, we wanted everything. The butler bowed and scurried away. I tipped an extra five spoonfuls of sugar into the Abbot's tea and handed it to him. He placed the cup on the arm of the chair and reaching into his pocket for his hip flask tipped most of its contents into his tea. The tea bubbled with evaporating alcohol and the Abbot lowered his head over the cup to inhale the intoxicating fumes. He drank, then, slamming the cup into its saucer, went to sleep, head low on his chest until startled awake by the invasion of the clock as it chimed the half hour. And precisely fifteen minutes late, exactly as indicated by the butler, Baldwin entered the room. He came with a companion. The door shut behind him.

'Gentlemen, so sorry to keep you. You haven't met Maynard Keynes, but you may know his work.'

I knew his work and I knew the man. Keynes was an economist, a fringe member of the Bloomsbury group, a bisexual, a descendant of Darwin, a secret convert to our faith. He had achieved notoriety after the Great War because of his views on reparations. They contradicted our own, and he had argued against the extortionate level of Germany's economic responsibility to Europe. I knew the man. His holy confession was regularly reported to us because of his importance to the government. He loved a great diva, she loved his money. He enjoyed the mores of the Bloomsbury people, and they humoured his presence because they thought that a Cambridge don gave their group a little more credibility. Keynes loved their parties, they loved his champagne. Keynes was skinny. He dressed badly in dirty bulging clothes; his hair was thin, pasted back over his skull in neat lines. Baldwin bent to shake hands with the Abbot.

'Don't get up, Horace.' So the Abbot had a first name. It seemed inconceivable that the Abbot should have any of the commoner tokens of humanity. 'Horace, we haven't seen each other since the Oxford congress. How are you, dear fellow?' The Abbot grunted at Baldwin, but Baldwin needed no reply. Baldwin and Keynes sat down facing us. They hadn't bothered to shake hands with me. 'You may talk freely,' said Baldwin. 'Keynes is a friend.' He relaxed, uncrossed his legs and stuffed his thumbs in his waistcoat pocket. Keynes leaned forward, attentive, jittery, nervous. He cupped his chin in his hands, rested his elbows on his knees and stared at the Abbot. The Abbot was a toad in a shallow pond, head forward, cheeks bulging, body still. He spoke his only words of that meeting.

'Brother John will speak.'

And I did. 'As you know, Prime Minister, the Church has a great responsibility to the people.' A lie. Our only responsibility was to ourselves. 'And in the context of that responsibility has a considerable investment in the stock market. This investment is for a time when the world may experience major problems such as famine or flood, at which point its resources will be required to help its flock.' Another lie. 'In such a situation of major catastrophe, it is important that the Holy Church is able to relieve the suffering of humanity, and this is, I'm sure, what our good Lord would wish us to do. The Church's economic advisers are worried. They see an immediate future of considerable uncertainty and have predicted the possibility of the collapse of world markets. Such advice is based on the decline of international trade, the protectionist attitudes of the United States, decreased consumption of manufactured goods, the fall in the value of agricultural produce . . .'

Keynes became tetchy. 'Yes, yes, one does know. What is your point, dear?'

I made my point. 'Does the British Government, and in particular yourselves, share this view? Are the stock markets about to collapse?'

'Yes,' from Keynes.

'No,' from Baldwin. Baldwin had always been a pretty poor reader of futures. He deserved to lose the coming June election. Baldwin and Keynes stared at each other. Keynes continued in full Cambridge donnery, dismissing Baldwin's view with a wave. His little speech was staccato.

'It's obvious,' he said. 'The portents are there. Britain is at greater risk from economic collapse than any other European nation. We depend more on the export of industrial products. These exports have been cut by the new limits to free trade. The barriers are up. The import tariffs have restricted exports. Look at the factory yards. See there, the stocks of unsold goods. We're producing but not selling. The stock markets are irrelevant, parasitic. Share values are arbitrary, based on synthesized fantasy. And all the money that's placed on the market, rather than spent – that's missing money, earned and taken out of the economy. If it were spent on goods rather than paper, men would be in work. Share prices are speculative. Current stock-market valuations are unrelated to the true value of our companies. We're looking at a bubble and in the next few months the bubble will burst. I'm no harbinger of doom, no gypsy in a tent reading the leaves. This is fact. You will see what will happen. And it will happen soon. There is now significant unemployment. This has directly resulted from diminished American investment because of protectionism and the glut of cheap agricultural produce. Greater unemployment leads to less money being spent in the shops. If less money is spent, and fewer goods purchased, our factories will start to run down. If the factories are run down, more people will be out of work. If more people are out of work, then less money will be spent. It's a vicious cycle. We have to spend on a grand scale if we're to prevent disaster and to my mind this is the only approach at this time.'

I looked at Baldwin. 'Will your government do this?'

'We will, if we win the election.'

I had no confidence in the man. He'd initially disagreed with Keynes. Keynes had been so coherent, so logical and his views coincided with those of our own advisers. Baldwin was an ignorant politician, fickle, blown by the circumspect winds of opinion and this morning's wind had a Keynesian direction.

'Thank you, Mr Keynes. Do you have any ideas as to when the stock markets will fall?'

'Predictions as to time would, in contrast to the earlier discussion, issue from the gypsy's tent. It is impossible to make any forecast. But I can tell you that the current situation is fragile. All that's required is for a major speculator to unload his investments and the rest of the market would be panicked into selling. Currently, prices are arbitrarily high.'

This was our answer. This information was to be forwarded to the Vatican. We must choose our time carefully and preserve the Church's interest. 'Thank you, Prime Minister. Thank you, Mr Keynes.'

I nodded at the two. Keynes twitchy, Baldwin calm. I got up from my armchair and heaved the Abbot from his.

The Abbot shook hands with Keynes and Baldwin, who both rose from their chairs to wish him a polite goodbye.

'Well,' said Baldwin to the huffing puffing Abbot. 'I hope it's not another thirty years before we meet again. If it is,' and he chuckled, 'I'm sure it'll be beyond the grave.'

These comments were a charade played entirely for Keynes's benefit. The Abbot and Baldwin met and spoke regularly, they were corruption's cousins at home with each other's familiar vices. The Abbot grumped a farewell without any pretence of friendship or good manners and shuffled from the anteroom. The Prime Minister escorted us to the door. Our moronic chauffeur and his associate opened our doors. I ladled the Abbot into his seat. We retired to Kent.

Some hours later we sat in the Abbot's bedchamber. I wrote a report of our meeting to the Vatican, repeating verbatim Keynes's speech and forwarding my views as to Baldwin's fickleness. The Abbot lay in bed asleep. Over the last few months he'd become withdrawn and apathetic. He'd not participated in the proceedings of the monastery, and, although continuing to preside over meals, had taken no active role. Brother Matthew had read grace and ordered the psalms, while I had become more and more involved in our information network. The Abbot had continued to consume enormous quantities of drugs and alcohol, but his appetite for food had declined. He picked at his meals, and was no longer interested in the piquant 'dessert' so favoured by the monks in the oligarchy of our order.

I was quite able to cope with our communications system and considerably enjoyed documenting the social changes reported by our contacts throughout the kingdom. Our network was extraordinary in its variety of sources. So many different individuals came to confession, and so many old friends were in power. Only to the innocent did power seem to shift and policies change. To the prescient, power remained in a closed space guarded by the military, industry and the Church. The unholy triumvirate. This collusion was not at all surprising. Wherever men sat together, took meals together, went to clubs together, they sought security and the known safety of old friends. Change was abhorred by everyone, everywhere, and at all levels, and the men who were in power were the most capable of resisting any force for change. Change meant uncertainty, insecurity, loss of income, loss of food, loss of shelter. Why should the rich suffer this? They were in charge and could dictate conditions. The lower classes grouped in their pubs or formed unions. The upper classes met in their clubs or in parliament. And these groups struggled to preserve themselves. But the upper-class groups were stronger than the lower classes and were more successful in the maintenance of their own security, more successful in the continued accumulation of their own wealth.

Nowhere was this success more obvious than in the United Kingdom, where over the last one hundred years 7 per cent of the nation had continued to retain 97 per cent of the country's wealth. In the Church's view the social order was stable because the distribution of wealth had not significantly changed over the preceding century.

And I participated in this effort to maintain order, because for us the maintenance of the power of the Church, the continuance of the integrity of established society, meant that our homes and our lives' condition were safe. I did not wish to be a mendicant. I wanted to be a monk, enjoying life, women, food, wine. There was no romance in poverty, no attraction in asceticism. Give me Catholicism, its riches and its regular meals. Guilt was for our flock, and the rewards of their guilt were rightly reaped by righteous priests.

So I reported to the Vatican, describing the threats to the Church and to the social order, distributing messages from our headquarters to the leaders of society, advising, suggesting. The Abbot snored and I wrote, reporting the morning's meeting to Cardinal Buscheim in the Vatican Information Ministry. My summary was succinct: to protect our investment, we needed to sell before any other major investor. Keynes had been clear in his view. The market was ridiculously overvalued. One push and it would fall. Our responsibility was to secure our investment. We needed to sell first and sell at the market's peak.

The silken counterpane covering the Abbot rose and fell, rose and fell. I tugged the bell-pull, and Brother Luke came quickly into the room. Brother Luke was tall, young and intelligent. He was comely and I liked him. He reminded me of my own youth and the echoing innocence of days that had no misleading nostalgic memory, days of a remarkable blindness. I knew now how the world ran, and in my little way I was part of the perfectly oiled machine that ran it. Luke took my letter and left the room. I inhaled the scent of his warm wake and settled into a chair by the Abbot's bed. I sat comfortably, a pillow on my lap, and tried to sleep.

We had company that night, and the abbey was set to entertain a portentous group of distinguished guests, guests of power and reputation, a cabal of the righteous that ruled our English world. The entertainment was to start at 8 p.m., and I was tired from the day's journey and business. I needed to rest, take strength from sleep, but sleep would not come, daylight laughed at me and my mind ran. I tried to relax, but the chair had angry springs, my back ached, and pins and needles punctured my fingers, toes and lips. My heart beat hard and my breathing came quickly, panting breathlessness springing from a roaring panic that all would go badly this evening. I tried to calm myself. It was so stupid to worry. All had been organized, and everything would go well. The monks had practised for weeks, the women were experienced and had been vetted by our colleagues in the police force, the food had been delivered and the wine, the glorious wine, had lain in our cellars for decades. Nothing could go wrong. I calmed myself with these thoughts, and my breathing slowed, and gradually the tingling needles eased away from my lips, fingers and toes.

Time passed, its moments and minutes, and then I lightened up, my sleep became shallower, and I was aware of the sound of the sea, tossing waves sweeping by and breaking on a beach. The water pouring in and rushing away, a furious regular tide piling up sand on white sand on to an imagined shoreline of mangroves and bright beach, arching around into distance's blue horizon. An imagined shoreline, conjured from books without pictures, travellers' tales of missionary journeys to the East Indies, South America, barbarous Africa, the furthest places of our planet. The sea broke on the beach, ebbed away, flooded in and the tide flung down exotic shells and seaweed, gifts for his bride the shore. But the virgin shore rejected her suitor's tributes and the cowries and conches rolled down the fickle shingle slope, trickling back to the ocean's edge. The rejected waters roared at the sand who tucked in her skirts and kissed away the frothing seas in the evaporating heat of Capricorn's tropic sun. And I was on a rocking boat, on monstrous waves, ducking up and down on screaming water. The noise of the tide became louder, the rocking more insistent, my boat caught on the edge of a storm. It seemed that I had a companion because a voice called to me, 'Brother John, Brother John,' but there was no one in the boat. I was alone in a coracle without oars, bobbing up and down on a mad ocean.

'Brother John, Brother John!' Did the ocean have a voice, could its current talk? The blue blue sea called and I opened my eyes to see darling Luke bending over me, his hands at my habit, shaking me awake, calling me from sleep. He smiled as I woke.

'Sir, it is time to prepare the evening,' and as I clambered back into the life of the monastery, the sounds of the ocean were explained by the regular rise and fall of the bedclothes beside us. The Abbot's snores were the waves on the beach, his breath the tide, his body ocean's water. I stuttered awake, and the Abbot snored. Luke left us. I pissed in the bathroom, washed my face and dried myself on the Abbot's bathrobe. I prepared the Abbot's medicines, for it wouldn't do to wake him without them ready. He'd scream and roar, threshing in the bed with a hideous anger that was best avoided. I took the brown glass laudanum bottle and the clear glass cocaine phials from the medicine cabinet and placed them on the marble shelf above the bathroom sink. I sawed at the tops of the glass phials with a toothed metal blade and collected the cocaine dust in a white porcelain pharmacist's mortar.

I shuffled back into the bedroom and gently shook the Abbot awake, just as Luke had woken me. The Abbot snuffled and snorted, starting awake with fright. He grabbed at me to haul himself upright and his heaving weight pulled me down into the bed. We righted ourselves and, without speaking, he reached out for his drugs. He tipped back the laudanum and then, touching a finger to the cocaine, tasted the white powder. The quality was acceptable and bending down over the bowl he breathed deep, inhaling summer's snow. I helped the Abbot dress, guiding his arms and legs into his fine silk underclothes. His flesh hung loose, its rolls thinner. He'd lost weight and it was as if his skin was borrowed from another much bigger man, a pygmy's bones dressed in a cannibal's raincoat. The Abbot held up his arms and I pulled his habit down over his head. The Abbot's habit looked like any other monk's, but it felt different, soft and warm. No coarse flax for him, but the finest Egyptian cotton, dyed and woven to resemble the lesser priests' clothes. He pushed his fists deep into the bed and heaved himself to his feet, his habit falling down over his buttocks, and then, remembering that he'd forgotten to put on his sandals, sat back heavily on his bed.

I knelt on the floor and took his right foot in my hands, his heel on my thigh. The toenails had not been cut for many months; they were curling ram's horns, yellow and enormously long. His toes were twisted and malformed, rambling over each other, joints deranged. His feet smelt badly, a dark sour smell of rotten meat and curdled milk.

I strapped on his sandals and he hardly noticed my efforts. Normally, he would abuse me as I helped him dress, but over the last few weeks he'd become quiet, withdrawn, dreaming in some secret street. I strapped on the Abbot's left sandal, pulling the leather straps tight over his puffy ankle.

The Abbot took my arm and, leaning heavily on me for support, we made our slow, limping way to the reception rooms, where refreshments were laid out for our guests. The walls had been draped with white cotton sheets, painted with huge green apples and equally enormous oranges,

145

peaches and strawberries. A voluptuous buffet was arranged on four long tables which were covered with red lace. Mounds of caviar, grey-green and gleaming, sparkled adrift in a crystal sea of dishes of foie gras, periwinkles, clams, queen scallops, whelks, mussels and oysters piled in tumbling mountains on heavy silver trays. Hairy-legged lobsters, langoustines and crabs snapped at each other with dead jaws, disputing the possession of the seaweed lawns. Jacobean lead glass sparkled, lined up in soldierly rows between regiments of the abbey's best German silver. Glorious turquoise Sèvres porcelain, made for Louis XV's Versailles, ringed the glasses and cutlery. Blocks of ice, impaled on wrought-iron stakes, were at each of the four corners of the four laden tables. The melting ice dripped to the floor, and pools of black water stained the deal boards. Marooned within each block was a buried bottle of Russian vodka. This was our buffet. The real meal was to be taken after the evening's performance, but this snack would cool our burning appetites.

The Abbot and I sat on Carolean chairs of heavy silver. These had been made for Nell Gwyn's bedchamber and had been in the abbey's possession for the last two hundred years. They looked pretty but were numbingly uncomfortable. A low hum came from the Abbot, an unpleasant moan, like a cow mooing for her lost calf, stolen from her udders by the slaughterhouse man. His eyes were shut, and under the false colour of the patina of broken veins that decorated his face, he looked unwell. He swayed in his chair then leaned heavily back and opened his eyes. He looked dazed, confused, unsure of where he was. Suddenly his body twitched, his head jerked and he was awake. The confusion lifted and his grey eyes were malevolently alive again: the toad croaked, in control of his environment once more. He looked around the room and fixed on the vodka. His arms reached out, his hands cupping an imaginary glass. The Abbot's lips pressed together then opened. His tongue reached out, circling slowly around his lips, tasting flaking skin, feeling out the tiny sore that decorated his columella, touching the sharp line of vermilion. At such moments my role was clearly defined, and I took a bottle of vodka from its stand and poured the thick steaming liquid into a glass. Ice formed around the glass. I closed the Abbot's fingers around his drink. Some moments passed until he became aware of its cold presence in his hand, and then he drank, and it was a relief to see him behave normally, come back into our little world and consume as he used to.

It was 8 p.m. and, as if to cue, the double doors that led into the reception rooms opened. Luke pushed them wide, then politely withdrew to let our guests enter. They trooped in, masked, draped in long black cloaks, announced by clicking heels, anonymous, but of course all known.

I stood to greet them, welcoming them to our humble house. They ignored me and circled around the dining tables, their cloaks billowing, masked conspirators. These black raiding ravens swooped low over the tables and helped themselves to food, shouldering each other aside, piling their plates high with the crustacean sacrifice. I was knocked back by the rush and, winded, plumped myself down to watch the feast.

Vodka bottles were dragged from their frozen nests and clutched in jealous grips. Slavering lips sucked at the salty flesh of oysters and fleshy fingers poked into crystal dishes of caviar. Foie gras was licked from upended silver gilt bowls. The cloaked figures swilled drink, and tore into the soft pink bodies of lobsters and crayfish. A muscular man, shaven-headed, bristle-necked, his plate desperately empty, rushed at the table and banged into a vodka stand. It crashed to the floor, and oleaginous vodka oozed from the broken bottle in a spreading puddle that crept past the table's legs, making its way to the unknowing shoes of the cluster of masked guests.

I brought food to the Abbot but his plate sat in his lap, untouched, a pretty picture, a Dutch still life of leaping claws and gaping shells. I poured him more vodka and he drank disinterestedly.

There were twelve guests and they were significant in our society, rulers of the land. There in cloaks and masks stood the mightiest masons, a Lord of the Admiralty, the head of the police force, the Governor of the Bank of England, Baldwin, Beaverbrook, and a relatively new friend of our Church, Mosley, a man, apparently, of rare force and strength: all utterly trustworthy, all completely dependable. A prestigious coterie, gourmands, sensualists, believers, all known to each other and known to ourselves, most important rulers of England's immediate destiny. This network of leaders, spreading across an apparent political gulf, leaping from the law to the dissemination of information, had our country in their grip. All that mattered was theirs. Grouped together around the empty plates and bottles, the detritus of their feast, they looked like actors in their cloaks and masks, fit for the stage, needing only bejewelled scabbards and ferocious curved swords to become buccaneers, pirates or musketeers. And the truth was that they were actors, their stage was England, their theatre the world. It was time for the performance. I cleared my throat and announced, 'The evening's entertainment is to begin. Gentlemen, this way please.'

The audience were to be entertained by a series of

medieval scenes, each dissolving into a pornographic vignette. I led them through the corridors to the abbey, which had been transformed for the evening. The front rows of pews had been removed and comfortable chairs put in their place for our honoured guests. The twelve men took their seats, lined up between myself and the Abbot. The altar had been cleared away and in its place a small stage assembled. On the stage stood a screen painted to resemble the towering walls of a tall castle. A high window opened, and Matthew's bearded face poked through.

The lights dimmed and Mosley cursed. The Abbot snored and the masons gossiped, wondering whether there would be hot chocolate and ice cream. There would be neither. A hawking noise came from Mosley's direction, then gross foul sounds of spitting and snorting.

From my seat in the wings, I could see Luke gather up the skirt of his habit and clamber up the ladder carrying a huge bucket. He reached the summit and leaned out over the castle ramparts, holding tight to the castellated cardboard. The castle swayed, and he clutched at the ladder. Suddenly the audience were enjoying themselves. The masons were simpering, Beaverbrook was smoking, and Mosley had clutched the hand of his bull-necked neighbour, the Rear Admiral, and was dragging it across his lap while with his other he searched for the Rear Admiral's groin. On to the stage walked two blindfolded harlequins, leading a unicorn by gilded reins. On the shoulder of one was a red parrot, and holding the hand of the other was a gambolling ape. The unicorn's head ducked past the curtains and the burden of its body was revealed. On its back rode a naked woman. Her hair hung long and straight, trickling down over her breasts. Between its strands her nipples peeped, tipped with jewelled cones. She rode side-saddle and with each bouncing step her legs parted slightly. Brother Matthew's bass voice rang out.

'Lady Godiva in the streets of Coventry. Let no one look, respect her modesty, please.'

The lights were turned up and we were all peeping Toms. One of the masons held his hands in front of his eyes. His fingers were not clamped tight. Beaverbrook puffed at his cigarette and blew furious smoke. The Rear Admiral gasped as Mosley rubbed his cock. The unicorn, parading across the stage, raised its tail and had a steaming shit.

The unicorn turned, and Godiva's back was to the audience, false bosoms strapped invisibly to her scapulae, a clown's grinning mask over the back of her head, two straw-filled dummy legs hanging over the leather saddle. Mosley liked this and reached deeper into the Rear Admiral's pocket.

Mary appeared at the castle's window and leaned out, a spectator for the scene below. Swaying dangerously, Luke stretched down from his perch and tipped out the contents of the bucket. Paper snow dribbled on to the unicorn below. The Rear Admiral squealed and Mosley removed his hand from the man's groin. He pulled a vodka bottle from his pocket and tipped its remaining contents into his mouth. His cheeks bulged and his unshaven Adam's apple bobbed. Mosley threw the empty bottle over his shoulder and it shattered in the chancel. The masons shifted uneasily.

Luke leaned forward and emptied the rest of the bucket. His ladder swayed. He grasped at the castle ramparts to catch his balance and dropped the bucket. The unicorn reared in fright and threw poor Godiva to the boards. Godiva got to her feet and catching the unicorn by the tail

150

tried to calm the beast. It kicked out and she reeled away. Luke, following his script, climbed down from the ladder and beat at a metal sheet. Thunder rang and the unicorn bolted into the nave. The Abbot snored and Mosley, incensed by the debacle, jumped to his feet. He shook his fist at the performers and cursed. Waving an unpleasantly realistic-looking revolver, he rushed the stage and leaped up on the set, running towards Godiva. Mosley fired at the ceiling and roared, 'Stop this useless charade! Clear this fucking stage!' Temper bubbling, he hurled his revolver at Luke's ladder. It rattled to the floor and three loose shots ripped out.

'Stop!' Mosley screamed, his eyes popping with a monstrous anger. He smashed at Godiva, knocking her to the floor. Beaverbrook got to his feet, burning cigarette clamped tight between his lips, and made for the door. The frightened masons scuttled after him. The Rear Admiral struggled up and his trousers fell to the floor. Hauling them to his waist he ran from the church.

Mosley thrashed at the set. The phoney walls rocked. The castle wavered, then crashed down on top of him. The madman was knocked to the floor, buried beneath the scenery. Unable to get to his feet he kicked out, prisoner in a cardboard castle, struts of wood and broken props muffling his awful cursing. The din woke the Abbot. He rubbed his eyes and stared at the dust clouds and the crumpled paper rubble that heaved and rippled as Mosley struggled to free himself. Clearly puzzled, he shut his eyes and within moments began to snore again.

On stage Luke, Matthew and I cleared the scenery from Mosley and Godiva. I helped Godiva to her feet and, with splinters in her long hair, strips of paper sticking to her sweating back, she climbed down from the stage and slowly made her meandering weaving way along the nave and through the open abbey door.

Mosley stood without assistance and brushed dust from his clothes. He spanked hard at his suit lapels and ripped off his cloak. He threw the tattered cloak to the ground and stared at me, his baleful bloodshot eyes shrivelling me up, drying out my waters. Such hate, and then he punched me hard. I saw his fist come up. He clipped my jaw and rattled my teeth. Blood filled my mouth. He turned to Luke, letting loose another punch, but the boy ducked, and with sense and discretion retreated from the stage. It was Matthew's turn and Mosley spun around to fix him. But Matthew had taken up a boxer's stance and fists cocked stood ready for the madman. Matthew was a formidable eighteen stone and Mosley let his fists drop.

'Sir, didn't you just ask if your driver could take you back to London?' enquired Matthew. Mosley harrumphed and folded his arms over his chest. 'You did, sir, and I think that you'll find him waiting. Your car's by the front door.' Mosley spun around and, with me as his sore-jawed guide and Matthew guarding his rear, he stamped through the monastery, his iron-heeled shoes ringing on the flagstones. Matthew's jolly 'Good night' was cut short by a slamming limousine door, and tyres spinning on churning gravel the the long black car roared away from the monastery.

Chapter Seven

THE ABBOT was sick. Thinner, haggard, weak, exhausted, he huffed his way around the monastery,
dragging himself from chair to bed, losing his way in
the daily services. He was ill and the monks noticed. Too
callous to be concerned, too self-centred to care, they
gossiped and pointed, nodding towards the crumpled man
leaning heavily on my arm who shuffled into the refectory.
The Abbot was sick and sallow-skinned; he coughed his
way through August's days. I took over more and more of
his work, directing monastery business, settling accounts,
conspiring with Cardinal Buscheim at the Vatican, organizing our friends in the land, co-ordinating the machinations
of the Holy Church. Life was busy and the Abbot suffered.
He suffered like the beasts and silently wasted away. In the
dark of his rooms, I counted his days, days of darkness in
the yellow summer sun.

August. The crops were in and tributes paid. August,
and the Abbot's underwear slipped from his skinny hips as
I helped him dress. August, and the Abbot's vomit stained
his damask counterpane. August, and the Abbot's coughing
kept me awake in its humid nights. August, and it was time
to call in a physician. Dr Rash was the monastery's general
practitioner. A particularly unfortunate name for a medical
man, but we were fortunate in our doctor. He was steady

and competent, and the comfort of his touch brought cure. He dressed in grey, eschewing the pompousness of the Harley Street clinicians, their pinstripes and black jackets abandoned for a simple suit. His collar was soft and he drove out to his patients in a rattling open-topped Riley, accompanied by his blond Labrador, who pointed the way from his front seat. Dr Rash carried humbugs in his Gladstone bag, sweets for the children of his country practice, and sweets to keep him company in Kent's winding lanes.

The doctor sat on the Abbot's bed and felt his pulse while I briefly sketched out the story of the Abbot's decline.

The Abbot scowled at us as his tale was told. Then he coughed and clutched at his chest. The doctor released the Abbot's wrist and pulled a conical wooden stethoscope from his case.

'Please take off the Abbot's shirt.'

I hauled the Abbot up from his pillows and pulled off his nightshirt. A streak of brown faeces decorated his shirt-tails. I threw the nightshirt through the bathroom door, and the Abbot slumped back on his lace-covered pillows. Dr Rash placed the instrument on the Abbot's chest and bent down, his ear against the listening piece. He lifted the stethoscope and placed it down again, edging it from place to place across the Abbot's chest. The Abbot was a hairy man, his body covered with grey coiled wires, hair in his ears, hair on his neck, hair over his shoulders, hair over his stomach. He bristled with hair; it had all slipped from his head, falling with age to decorate his body, migrating with the seasons from the coldness of his crown to warmer parts where the follicles could snuggle amid clothes.

Dr Rash edged the stethoscope inch by inch across the Abbot's chest, listening to his heartbeat, listening to the whisper of his hoarse breathing. I pulled the Abbot forward and Dr Rash listened to the back of the Abbot's chest, the instrument jammed tight against his ribs. I helped the Abbot back on to his pillows, and Dr Rash pulled away the piled blankets and sheets to examine Abbot Horsmunden's abdomen. Using the ball of his hand as an axis for his fingers, he pressed deeply into the Abbot's soft flesh, feeling out the vibrant borborygmi of his bowel, touching the edge of his liver, seeking his spleen, palpating his kidneys. Dr Rash shook his head slowly, and then pulled the Abbot's pyjama trousers down over his thighs to examine the Abbot's testicles.

One didn't need to be a clinician to know that there was something terribly wrong. One testicle was hugely enlarged, and the overlying scrotal skin was thickened and coarse, its veins terrifyingly engorged. The good doctor bent down to examine the Abbot's privates, an odd term to apply to what up to a few months ago had been so public. The doctor first examined the normal testicle, rolling the quail's egg between his index finger and thumb. He then examined the diseased ball. The testis was heavy, and fixed. Dr Rash then examined the Abbot's groin. How embarrassing. All the fiddling around had excited the Abbot. The old dog had an erection, and was looking around with interest at the proceedings. To be honest I was pleased, rather than embarrassed. This was the first time for many months that the Abbot had expressed any interest in life. The doctor continued with his examination, and felt the left side of the Abbot's neck with prying fingers. He nodded his head and pursed his lips, ominous signs in a doctor, unless they occur at a time when he is being paid in cash for his service. Then, rather strangely, he examined the Abbot's breasts in the way that a slave merchant might prod a slave girl.

'May we talk freely?' asked the doctor.

'Of course.'

The doctor drew me away from the Abbot, tugging at my sleeve and whispering conspiratorially. This conspiracy was entirely unnecessary as the Abbot was snoring, in deep sleep, away with his favourite fairies.

'The Abbot has cancer.'

I started. Such a blunt approach to death.

'And I'm afraid that he's terminally ill. It may be only a few weeks that he has left.' The doctor looked in my eyes, measuring the effect of his sentences, then finding me strong, continued: 'There is very little hope for cure, but I must assure you there is some hope in that I can promise that he will not suffer. There will be no pain. We have modern medicines that will keep any distress at bay.' I knew these modern medicines. The Abbot had consumed a whole plantation of them in his efforts to avoid the needless pain of being.

The doctor paused and turned away to look at the Abbot.

'He's a great man, you know.' Great in parts, I thought, or more specifically great in his parts. The doctor continued with his monologue, continued with his serious discourse on death and suffering, all the while disconcertingly smiling as he pronounced sentence on Horsmunden's lively corpse.

'There are two approaches to this situation and I would appreciate your views as to which you think the more appropriate. The first is relatively straightforward. We can . . .' and I noted the defensive use of the collective pronoun, 'keep him comfortable, leaving him here in the abbey and nursing him through his last days. Or . . .' He paused once more to note the effect of his words. 'We can treat him actively, hoping that we may obtain a remission of his illness.'

'What do you mean by active treatment?'

The doctor stroked his chin, tugging at an imaginary beard. 'We could operate.' I didn't quite like the sound of this, and the doctor could see it in my face. 'By this I mean a limited operation to remove the primary tumour. This would not mean major surgery.'

'Doctor, I have no idea as to what would be best for the Abbot.'

'It's a very difficult decision. We obviously should not do anything that would cause additional suffering. Let me put a proposition to you. I would like to propose that we take the Abbot up to town to seek the advice of a surgeon.' Before I could interrupt, the doctor continued. 'I would like the Abbot to see Geoffrey Keynes at St Bartholomew's Hospital. He is eminent within the profession and a radical thinker.' To my mind radical thoughts and the Church were in diametric opposition. 'In my view,' said Dr Rash, 'his is the finest opinion. He taught me, and I respect him greatly.' I looked at the sleeping Abbot and I looked at the earnest doctor. Was it worth disturbing Horsmunden? The option was to leave him. Leave him? Let him die? It was too big a decision to make by myself. I would phone Rome and discuss the situation with Cardinal Buscheim.

'Dr Rash, thank you for your visit and considered opinion which, of course, I respect. The decision to treat or not to treat is too great for me to take alone. I must seek advice. May I call you later at the surgery?'

'Certainly.' The doctor bowed and closing his Gladstone bag left the Abbot's room. Luke, who was waiting outside the door, escorted him through the abbey.

I took up the phone and waited for the operator to connect my call. The line was poor; crackling consumed our electronic conversation. The earpiece spluttered, temporarily deafening me. I replaced the receiver and tried again, volunteering another ear for this transcontinental torture. This time my call was placed and the effete voice of Buscheim's secretary greeted me. I did not wish to waste time with the cardinal's catamite.

'Your master, please,' I requested, relegating him to servant, and by my brusqueness promoting to enemy a man who beforehand had merely disliked me. I was left holding on to the receiver. A few minutes elapsed, minutes that were unnecessarily extended by Buscheim's malign secretary. I imagined him sitting in Rome, in some splendid antique room in the Vatican, his hand on the receiver's mouthpiece, yawning, thinking, stretching, looking at the sun shining through the window, and eventually, at a time when he imagined that I might have well been irritated by a delay which I must know was due to him keeping me waiting, he connected me with the Cardinal.

'Brother John.' Buscheim's soft voice greeted me. I described the Abbot's illness, the doctor's diagnosis and the choice he'd presented. My description was succinct, its brevity honed by previous hurried conversations I'd had with Buscheim, conversations often closed by his temper. For once there was no interruption from Buscheim, no interrogatory comments, no interlocutory points. He just listened and, at the end of the tale, there was only one brief comment: 'Go to Keynes.' Cardinal Buscheim rang off, and I was left speaking to an empty receiver, stupidly thanking nobody for their help. I pulled the cord to summon Luke and asked the boy to find out about Keynes.

He returned quickly carrying a file card taken from our

index system. He gave it to me and I read the few lines. Brother of Maynard, scion of an eminent Cambridge family, famous and inventive surgeon, art collector. A pity, he was not of our faith, so there would be no local priest from whom we could extract his confessions. We would go up to town. I rang through to Rash and asked him to organize an appointment with the good Mr Keynes.

Two days later we drove into town. The morning was bright and the fields had been cut. The bristle stumps of the hairbrush land were being burnt, and steady lines of flickering orange flames roamed the farmers' fields, sending their warning smoke to the blue, blue heavens. The Abbot was dressed in an old-fashioned frock coat and high collar and I looked rather sombre in a high Homburg hat. Dr Rash was with us, and we sat in a solemn line of three on the back seat of the Hispano-Suiza.

Our appointment was at St Bartholomew's Hospital, house of mercy and suffering and home to two fine churches of a crapulous lesser faith, St Bartholomew's the Less and St Bartholomew's the Great, founded in fields in the twelfth century. During the past eight hundred years its staff had tended the impoverished sick. It was always a great hospital, a house of learning, and it was there that our friend the doctor had been given his trade. Our little doctor was looking forward to seeing his teaching hospital again, looking forward to sitting at learned feet, and he grinned and chirruped so much that I had a mind to tell him to shut up. But no, I had not yet the meanness of spirit to make the man miserable. Let him burble, let him smile, let him have this day for his rusty memory box.

The Abbot slumped against the leather, each knot of the road a jolting pain. Poor man. Spare me from cancer, spare me from pain. Let me die in sunlight. Suddenly, quickly, thrusting into the backside of a beautiful girl. Let me die with pleasure, in pleasure and with love. Give me a good death at ninety in a harlot's arms. Can I go with joy, can I go with spirit, may I go with grace, may I go with life. Don't let me suffer, skin brittle, pointy bones rotten, long, long, long before the sweating earth takes me down. I want life, I want to live. Let my days be strong, puissant, lusty. Let me shout, let me sing, let me eat, let me breathe the good air and, when my days end, may they end with the sudden night.

We passed St Paul's, its magic columns, its heavy dome, its dust and dirt hiding the stink of priests in skirts. St Paul's, mystery and darkness, springing up too suddenly, too large for the city's winding streets. St Paul's, its hugeness engulfing the little prayers that the deluded sinner offers the empty heavens. There is no sin, we are all innocent, every desire is understandable, all needs attainable, every whim natural, all consumption negligible. And in the grand order of life's eternal song, there is no plan, no great scheme or schemer, chaos, just chaos and the echoing crescendo of hate's silence.

Saint Paul, Saint Wren, Saint Hawksmoor, Saint Palladio. The building broods, the building stinks, monumental folly, without grace or beauty, its columns the blunt teeth of a toothless Protestantism. Past the great post office, doors open on bronze grilles and Victorian marble, and our car stopped in the middle of the road, slewed, skidded. We heaved forward, thrown from our seats, jolted. I was on the floor, the Abbot on top of me, his heaviness clamping my arms, weighing down my legs. The car stalled, and I pushed myself upright. Our driver looked around, pop-eyed, frightened that his charges were injured. We were undamaged. He rushed to the door and heaved at the Abbot, pulling him up and pitching him into his seat. He dusted at his jacket with flapping panicking gestures.

'I'm sorry, gents, are you all right?'

I pushed his helping hands away and glared unpleasantly at him. Dr Rash was in his seat, having kept his balance during the incident.

'I'm sorry, sir, it was 'em, wer'n'it?' The driver stood by the side of the car, pointing, and grinning quite inappropriately. There, crossing the road, was a line of ducks, dusty-feathered, bobbing mother and eight little ones, unaware of the relative mass of cars and birds, disdainful of highway codes. They were a pretty line of waddling things, beaks out, wings in, mother and children in a shambling line. Along the river road and then up, up over the precipice kerbstone, across the ravines of city pavement and through graceful wrought-iron gates into a dark grassy park, where evergreens waved and china plaques decorated a crumbling brick wall.

We drove on towards bloody Smithfield and then turned through a stone archway into a courtyard where drunken London plane trees swayed and shook their rusting fists at whistling blackbirds and irritated starlings. Our chauffeur opened the car door and saluted as we climbed out. Then, in a waddling line, we followed Mother Rash around the courtyard square past a hissing fountain where drowned coins were buried in a silver water, admiring the grace of the Georgian buildings where Portland stone assumed a lightness that defied its mass.

Dr Rash was beaming, enjoying his walk through student memories, along dark corridors, labyrinthine as the monastery, and I felt comfortable in the familiarity of gloomy passageways.

We came into the clinic where the city's sick clustered,

washed up on a beach of invalidity, piled up in theme
groups where plaster casts were predominant, where ampu-
tees lingered, where ulcerous faces oozed, and the breathless
panted. In the far corner crowded waiting giants and
dwarfs. Nurses and clerks presided over this whispering
community of the diseased, healthy queens and princes in
this land of the deformed. The clerks lived behind glass
counters, standing at high wooden desks, dispensing tickets
and forms to the lines of the shambling sick. The nurses
wore long uniforms that masking femininity in starchy
drapes only accentuated the voluptuousness of massive
bosoms and broad bustles. This denial of what made a
woman was stirring, exciting, and the strangeness of their
tall white hats brought memories of nuns. But these nuns
with their pinned-back hair smiled and spoke, directed and
organized, dealt with life.

Dr Rash nodded at a woman in magnificent blue, and
asked directions. Regal and pink-cheeked, with pince-nez
and a prickly moustache, she flourished a pair of scissors at
our little doctor who recoiled then waved to us to follow
him. We sat for a moment with the people on straight-
backed benches. I found this most distasteful, so tiresome
that with our wealth and power we had to take our turn,
and whispered to Dr Rash that I didn't find waiting a
pleasant experience.

'But Brother John, if we wish for the best opinion, we
have to seek it where it's available, and Keynes will not
consult out of his own hospital.'

I was irritated by the people, the shuffling poor, the
stinking hordes, the pathetic patients, scratching, coughing,
oozing, hawking, decaying, barbarous, uncultured, unaes-
thetic, here in these lines, the rotting, stinking, sick.

We sat in the second row, shuddering, holding ourselves

separate, hardly breathing the foul, pestilent, infected air. I wished for smelling salts. I wanted my books, I needed the monastery, I hated this place. The Abbot slumped against my shoulder and snored. Dr Rash looked around nervously, fidgeting, grinning inanely at everyone in uniform. Out of his own environment, away from his own practice, he'd become smaller, crook-backed, huddled into himself, a little man in a big institution.

It was enough. I didn't wish to wait. Frankly it was preferable for the Abbot to die, rather than that I should have to put up with these rows of the diseased. A nurse came out of a clinic room and called a name. There was no movement from the waiting room. She called again, her hand a megaphone, and the man in front of me started up from his chair. He turned to me as he stooped to pick up his briefcase from under his seat, and I was shocked by his appearance. He was badly shaven and wore an eye patch. One corner of his mouth drooped down, and saliva trickled out and dribbled over the morning's yellow egg flecked on his chin. He shuffled towards the nurse, stumbling, hesitant, limping with obvious pain. She didn't help him, just stood hand on her hip, pointing for him to come towards her. The consulting-room door closed.

I harrumphed and fidgeted and glared at Dr Rash. Embarrassed, he got to his feet and went towards the room. He knocked. The door creaked open and the nurse's nose poked around the jamb. Dr Rash mumbled then hung his head and the pointy nose moved up and down. The door closed and Dr Rash returned to his seat. Moments later the door re-opened and the nurse summoned us towards the consulting room. I pushed the Abbot's head from my shoulder, and pulled him to his feet. He crooked his arm through mine and we crossed the linoleum floor towards the nurse. She turned away, leaving us to push in front of the waiting sick into the consulting room. Three high-backed chairs were grouped before a mahogany desk. The room was painted cream and an old-fashioned wooden examination couch, covered with brown American cloth, was half-hidden behind screens. A tall man in a black suit was washing his hands at a porcelain sink. He scrubbed at his nails with a large brush, then turned to face us. He held out his hand to Dr Rash. 'Delighted to see you again, Rash, it must be ... let's see ... ten years.' Dr Rash bowed his head, pleased to be recognized.

'Fifteen actually, sir.'

'Of course, of course. You're in practice now, aren't you?'

'Yes, sir, in Kent.'

'It obviously suits you, you look very well, very well.' His eyes were brightest blue, shimmering morning stars behind tiny oval spectacles. His hair was light brown, cut short, clipped close at the sides, glued down with pommade. He was tall and angular, with awkward elbows that struck out at specimen pots. He looked at the Abbot and myself, summed us up with his surgeon's eyes and shook our hands in turn.

'Gentlemen, gentlemen, do sit down.' I helped the Abbot to sit, aware of Keynes's eyes on us, eyes that summarized and defined, classified and collated, eyes that took in our relationships and condition, health and disease. He leaned forward on the desk. A buff folder was open in front of him and a bowl of white lilies unfolded their perfume over the room.

'Dr Rash has given me some of the details of your trouble, Abbot, but perhaps you'd be kind enough to summarize in your own words your recent difficulties.' I looked at the Abbot. He was shaking, sweating, collapsed in the chair. He quivered in his loose city clothes and licked his dry lips. I knew immediately what the problem was. Keynes was staring at the Abbot in a way that made me think that he too had recognized the cause of the Abbot's distress.

'If you'll excuse me, doctors,' I said, and reaching in my pocket I drew out the Abbot's laudanum bottle and, pushing his chin down, tipped the sticky liquid into his throat. 'The Abbot sometimes has these tropical fevers,' I said. 'They're a remnant of his missionary days in Africa.' Keynes smiled at my lie.

'Brother John,' he interrupted and his eyes half shut in amusement. 'Never lie to one's doctor, leave your stories for your accountants . . .'

My attention was taken by the Abbot vomiting over my sleeve. The nurse spluttered in disgust and made no effort to comfort or help. The yellow and green vomit dripped onto the floor, and the claws of its stench nipped at my throat.

The Abbot sank back in his seat, breath gurgling through his wide mouth. Keynes signalled for the nurse to help and clacking and tutting she rushed from the room and returned with damp towels and a kidney dish filled with steaming clouds of blue-tinted water. She wiped the Abbot's face and placed a damp flannel neatly over his forehead. Turning to me she took up my arm and wiped away the vomit from my sleeve. She wore a sweet perfume, memories of honeysuckle that mixed strangely with her barbed-wire manner and the stay-away-from-me starch of her uniform.

We were silent as she cleaned, and in the silence I looked around Keynes's room, with its prim medical cabinets of steel and glass, its wooden filing cabinets and gleaming basins, its examination couch and instrument trays. On the walls were misty orange watercolours, paintings of fiery dreams. Many were written on, moral lessons scrawled in the paintings' corners, captions in the artist's dabbing hand. Keynes interrupted my perusal of the paintings.

'Do you like them? They're by Blake, William Blake.' I remembered Blake, the tiger poet, lover of lights, seer, visionary. Keynes nodded then turned again to his patient.

'Abbot Horsmunden, can you tell me how you feel?' The Abbot made himself more comfortable in his chair. Keynes leaned out over his desk and spoke more loudly. 'Abbot, are you in pain, can we help you?' The Abbot stretched and yawned. His head slumped forward on his chest and he shut his eyes. 'Nurse, could you help the Abbot on to the couch?' Then Keynes, thinking perhaps that the Abbot would be shocked by a woman's help, held up his hand and said, 'Perhaps it would be better if Dr Rash and the Abbot's secretary assisted him.'

The nurse was immensely relieved not to have to touch the sick man again and edged away from us, standing with her back to the door as Dr Rash and I dragged the dangling-legged Abbot behind the screens, undressed him and arranged him under a blanket on the examination couch. Dr Rash lowered the headrest, and the Abbot's head banged down on the thin mattress.

'Are you comfortable, Abbot?'

The Abbot stared at the ceiling. Keynes bent over the mute Horsmunden, and his professional hands felt out his liver and chased around his belly for his spleen and kidneys. Dr Rash pulled the Abbot's pants down over his skinny grey legs and Keynes palpated his patient's scrotum, shaking his head at the heavy testicle and the mass of matted glands in the Abbot's groin. He helped Dr Rash tidy the Abbot, pulling his pants up over his protuberant pelvis, then felt the left side of the Abbot's neck. He shook his head again and left Dr Rash and me to help the Abbot dress, while he sat at his desk.

He leaned over the pages of the buff folder and wrote with an orange fountain pen, filling the sheets with lines of blue, perfectly rounded script, a woman's hand, neat, ordered. His spectacles reflected the spark of the old-fashioned gas lamps, and the rich smell of lilies crept through the room. He looked up from his notes and spoke to the nurse.

'Nurse, would you help our friend, the Abbot? Could you find him a wheelchair?' The nurse scowled, left the room, and returned a few moments later wheeling a creaking Victorian bath chair, the sort that one imagined an elderly widow to be pushed in around Deauville. The chair had tiny front wheels and dramatically spoked back wheels. Its seat curved out like a treble clef and an awning of black cotton kept out the threatening sun. The Abbot was wheeled away and Dr Rash and I faced Keynes.

He looked at us both, then turning to me, asked, 'What do you expect from me?'

'Nothing,' I said. 'It's too late.' Keynes nodded his confirmation of my view, and then folded his arms across his chest.

'I'm sorry there is nothing I can do. You must prepare him for his Maker.' Prepare him for the Devil, I thought, start now, anoint his skin with ground pepper and lemon juice. Keynes turned to Dr Rash. 'I agree with your diagnosis, and share your views. There is nothing that medical science can offer the Abbot. It is up to you and the

Holy Father to make sure that the Abbot does not suffer. I cannot prolong his life. There is no miracle that surgery can offer, there is no cure. Give him morphine, let him sleep, let him sleep away his days until his time comes. Brother John, don't spare the little bottle, give him laudanum, keep him from pain.'

With these words, our audience with the other Keynes was concluded. He could do nothing, and we could only keep the Abbot comfortable with morphine, drowning his agony in poppy juice.

The journey had exhausted him and he slept on the soft leather of the black limousine. He failed to wake as four monks carried him from the car, and continued in oblivion as we wheeled him to his room. Luke helped me put him to bed. We arranged his pillows and tidied his sheets, making him comfortable. He was in deep sleep, a sleep that came only in part from laudanum. We looked down on the sleeping man, his head slumped back, mouth wide, tongue furred, teeth broken and black, mouth gaping, his throat a dark view of death.

Life in the monastery continued in the increasingly cadaverous presence of the Abbot, and as his heart's pulse slowly weakened the cadence of prayer and the rhythm of ritual strongly pounded their beat. He remained in bed, spoke little and ate nothing. When he groaned, I gave him laudanum, when he was restless I fed him more laudanum. His facial bones stuck out, leaping from his cheeks, and his breath had a curious smell, sour sweet, with traces of Keynes's white lilies. The skin on his arse broke, and a red sore formed that stuck to his sheets. In his latter days it was only this sore that brought him to life, springing a shooting fountain of bloody curses when we peeled him from the sheets.

We kept the curtains drawn in his room. Flickering altar candles beat at the darkness, and incense consumed the foulness of his rotting body. I maintained contact with Rome, and my daily calls informed Buscheim of the Abbot's slow decline. Dr Rash visited most days, mumbling his amazement at the continued presence of the Abbot in our world.

Throughout these last days, I kept on with the abbey's work, relaying our messages of this small Britain into the networks of the Vatican. During this time I became close to Beaverbrook, and his strong voice and dominant personality gave me power to continue, power to send messages, power to lift the Abbot's hand and press the great seal into the soft sealing-wax that bubbled on the confidential messages that issued from my hand. Beaverbrook, the fabulous power, the incredible wealth, the beauty of his name, his newspapers bought by the masses and believed by them. News poured out by the rich further to enslave the enslaved.

September came and the Abbot was still alive. We were all unsure how he had managed to live for so long. He had had no solid food for a month, but the ghost lived on, ever thinner, flesh evaporating with the passing days. Dr Rash had provided us with a rubber tube which, fitting over the Abbot's penis, drained his urine into a glass bottle and spared the sheets. As his flesh shrank, the Abbot became older, his hair became white and his skin mottled and greyed. Peculiarly, parts of his body thrived in this procession to death. Blackheads grew rich and bulged from his nose, hair sprouted from the cracks of his body, thrusting out, bristling. His nails grew thick and strong, wax seeped from his ears and his belly button filled with the strangest concretions.

On a late September morning Luke was giving the

Abbot a bed-bath while I was sitting writing at the escritoire. He had pulled back the sheets and exposed the naked
man. The Abbot lay on his back, ribs prominent, breathing
stertorous, muscles wasted. Luke was gently flannelling
the Abbot's flesh with a soapy towel. He wiped his limbs
and belly, then, reaching to clean his face, he suddenly
stopped.

'Brother John.' His voice was terse. 'Look.'

I put down my pen and came to the Abbot's bedside.
'What am I to look at?' Luke pointed at the Abbot's face. I
still couldn't see what the boy had noticed.

'Look, Brother John.' Luke bent over and, with the little
finger of his right hand, pulled down the Abbot's left eyelid.
Then I saw what Luke had seen. The white of the Abbot's
eye had become lemon yellow.

That afternoon Dr Rash explained the meaning of this
observation, his commentary accompanied, as usual by
vigorous head-shaking.

'He's jaundiced. The cancer has spread to his liver. It
won't be long now.'

'How long, Dr Rash?'

'Maybe a week, perhaps two. It's really not possible to
give a precise time.' Dr Rash might not be able to give a
precise time, but I could. I looked at the Abbot. His eyes
were shut, his chin pointed up to the stars embroidered on
the tester. He no longer had humanity. His was an animal
presence, a presence that breathed and shat, a presence that
felt pain and slept. But this presence had no human
qualities, no sense, no feeling. And like that of an animal
whose useful life was at an end, his life must be ended. It
was time. For eyes he had but he did not see, lips he had
but he did not speak, ears he had but he did not hear, hands
he had but he did not feel.

Dr Rash shut his Gladstone bag and bid me good day.
Luke followed him from the room, and I was left in the
flickering candlelight, amid incense, in the splendour of the
Abbot's bedroom, its velvet and rich woods, its oriental
carpets and silver. The shadow of the four-poster bed
played on the walls, and September's wind ruffled the
curtains.

I propped the Abbot high up on his pillows and opening
his mouth tipped laudanum into him. I wanted the Abbot to
be comfortable, to be at peace, without pain, without fear. I
wiped a trickle of spittle from his lips and gently folded the
counterpane over him. Then I sat at his side and talked to
him, told him of life in the monastery and our friends
outside, described the fields and the farms, warmth, the
autumn's skies. I spoke of the harvest and the lakes,
described the winding lanes and trees, then stopped. These
things were of no importance to the Abbott when he was
well. He had abhorred nature and his life had been spent
within the abbey, his curtains drawn against the world. His
time was the night, and his joy opulent food and ornate
complicated sex. So I spoke again but this time of orgies
and unpleasant deaths, of baroque meals and the courtesan's
arts. I fabricated and invented. I ate for him, tasting the
richness of meat and the sweetness of cakes. I had sex for
him, sex with young women, sex with boys. I reminded him
of music and roaring fires, I told him of power and
perversion, of conspiracies and corruption, the easy descent
of man.

My stories were of the substance of his long life, his
years as our Abbot and he lay on his pillows, inert,
breathing shallowly. Was he listening? Could he hear me?
I think he did hear. He was there alone on an injured coast
crouching on a sharp rock, in a dark, dark cave. The sea

171

was banging in, smashing at the cliff face, whispering: I want you, I'm coming for you, I know you're there. The water roared and the Abbot crept back into his cave, knocking his head against the sloping barnacle roof, grazing his skin, blood oozing from his broken cheeks. The water trickled into the cave, swilling around his ankles and he pressed against the rocks. He could retreat no further, escape no more. The water was at his waist, at his neck, and I took his lace pillow and covered his face, pressed deep into him, pushing gently down.

Chapter Eight

THE ABBOT was dead, long lived the Abbot. Long may I live, for I am the Abbot. Long may I live. I had told Buscheim that Horsmunden had gone and he'd congratulated me on my new position.

'What position?' I'd asked.

'You are the Abbot,' he had replied. Apparently, it was traditional that the Abbot's secretary took over, and it was perfectly logical that this should be so. As secretary, I knew all that there was to know about our monastery. As secretary, I'd been part of every secret, knew the sources of all rumours, knew the land, knew the power. Horsmunden, when he had chosen me so many years back, had known my inheritance, for in his time he had been chosen too. His first choice, my predecessor, had died of a rotten heart, died waiting for his chance. I hadn't realized what was promised to me with my appointment, hadn't understood that with Horsmunden's death I would take over, become the next Horsmunden, become king of this little Kentish isle.

In turn, I had chosen a secretary, taken Luke's sleeve as the earth was shovelled on the Abbot's coffin, and to the sound of the soil echoing on the plain pine lid, had proclaimed to the assembly of monks that Brother Luke was my man. There had been no dissent. As the monks trailed from the graveyard, in order and without pomp, each had knelt on the wet grass and kissed the abbey's seal, taken from my predecessor and now rattling loose on the second finger of my left hand. The lips touched the cabochon ruby, brushed across the death's-head skull engraved in its rusty depths. Luke stood behind me while they kissed their fealty, gave themselves again to another man, entrusting themselves to me, giving me their fate.

With Luke in dutiful attendance, I lay abed in silk sheets, wallowed in the soft waters of my marble bath, presided at services and ruled imperiously at mealtimes. I commanded and the abbey obeyed. Like a king, I had my immediate court and into this holy circle I took Matthew and Bernard the clown, John the Lame and Brothers Simon, Mark and Francis. Dependable men all and each one aware of life's priorities. This inner cabinet ran the monastery and to each one I gave limited power. I delegated work and let these courtiers control the mundane aspects of monastery life. John the Lame dealt with recruitment, Matthew, women and wine, Simon, the farmyards, Francis, public relations, Mark, the discipline of the order, and Bernard, well, Bernard was just there to amuse us all.

And behind everything there was Luke, smoothing the way, investigating the authenticity of information, paraphrasing documents, dispensing money to our creatures, listening to the whispers, organizing, learning. And he did well. He had to. There was no choice. Buscheim had told me.

'Watch him, see how he works, make sure he's one of us, and if he's not, if he should fail, we'll deal with him.' So I was careful and I did watch and in those early months he never failed. He fulfilled his promise with efficiency, order and intelligence. 'We have our enemies,' said Buscheim. 'At all times take care.'

My relationship with Buscheim had changed and our conversations were as equals. Although previously courteous, there had been no warmth in our exchanges, but now, with my greater responsibility, I had become his confidant and our conversations dealt with personal matters, as well as the affairs of state. Buscheim loved to chat about his health, and spent much time discussing his piles and his varicose veins, his painful teeth and his thunderous migraines. An inveterate experimenter with patent medicines, he invariably asked that I forward herbal cures to the Vatican, and always enquired as to which miracle medicines were currently being advertised in our papers and on our billboards. Once, for amusement, I sent him my own patent remedy. Sick of his hypochondria, I had had made up a foul mixture of chicken shit and pond water, sent it to the Vatican with one of my reports and told him that it was a gypsy cure for migraine. It had worked. He told me that it had made him profoundly sick, but the vomiting had miraculously aborted the migraine.

'It is a panacea,' said the excited Buscheim. 'Do see if you can send me more.' More I could certainly send him, and more than enough of the remedy to make every Vatican cleric completely sick.

MacDonald, Ramsay MacDonald, was now Prime Minister, but unfortunately not our Prime Minister. He was not of our class, not of our power. Born in poverty in Scotland, the son of an impoverished maid, he had risen, uncorrupted and incorruptible, through the ranks of the evolving left wing. In far Victorian times, he'd stood with Keir Hardie, first as a member of the Independent Labour Party, and then as a founder member of the Labour Party itself. He had had a long parliamentary life and supported everything that we abhorred. He had become an MP in 1906 and had come to our attention in 1914, when he opposed our entry into the Great War. His first term as Prime Minister began in 1924. In office, he struggled to break the monopoly of power which we held. He raised the school leaving age which irritated the industrialists. He sponsored the building of cheap housing and this distressed the landowners. He allied himself with the Bolsheviks and this alienated the military. In September 1924, as a result of our promptings, the Liberal and Conservative parties joined together to rid the country of this scourge. Baldwin formed a government, and our men were in charge again.

The labour movement unfortunately was a popular one. In 1929 MacDonald was again Prime Minister, at last head of the largest party in the Commons. The Labour election manifesto contained more insufferable promises, promises of slum clearance and of limits to the working week. Ridiculous, quite ridiculous. We could not accept this absurd situation and we did our best to bring him down.

The Vatican was worried. Reports had been received from its agencies throughout the western world of economic instability. I had learnt from Buscheim that this instability was being compounded by the stock-market boom. The banks had diverted their monies away from agriculture and industry and into this easy market, because the gain so devastatingly outweighed the return on commercial loans. How wonderful to buy a share for one pound that became a few weeks later a share worth three pounds. How easy, in this heady atmosphere of multiplication, to manipulate the markets with a few of one's friends, control situations, offload valueless 'valuable' stock and double, treble and quadruple your investment. The stock market was wonderful and nobody remembered the South Sea Bubble.

Our friends sat in their clubs, lunching amid the mahogany and leather, remembering fine times, smoking cigars and drinking claret. They arranged things with each other, talked money and made decent honest profits. Such a sensible way to conduct business and business was good. But the boom had no economic reality. The companies were weak, their sales were poor, and the heavy clouds of under-investment in industry and agriculture, unemployment and declining world trade were gathering over our heads. And who would be the rainmaker, who would throw the iodine crystals into the sky? It must be us. We had so much to lose, all that carefully accumulated security that comes from money and its power. We needed to keep it. We had to retain it.

Buscheim called me from the Vatican.

'The moment has come,' he said, 'and there is very little time. You must gather in your crops. You are the farmer, the press is your scythe. Bring Beaverbrook, Rothermere and Harmsworth together. Ask Beaverbrook to organize the meeting. Tell them that the fields are ripe and will rot unless they are cleared. We must bring in our harvest and do so in an opportune and circumspect fashion. Tell them, my dear Abbot, that we will all sell together, sell when we're ready, at a time co-ordinated globally by the Vatican Bank. All this is in our best interests and ultimately in the world's interest too.' Would it really be in the whole world's interest? I wondered.

'Cardinal, could we not stabilize the markets by judicious movement of our money? Is it not possible that this crisis could be averted and markets made to continue their gains?'

'My dear Abbot, a remarkably sensitive and statesman-like view, but you heard Keynes.'

'Yes, Cardinal.'

'This fall in the stock markets is inevitable and we have a responsibility to our Mother Church and to mankind to restore the strength of the Vatican Bank, which as you know has recently been weakened. My dear Abbot, this economic chaos is unavoidable and we, the Holy Church, must survive it. There is no choice, we must survive and survive with strength.'

Buscheim paused again and I could almost feel him rustling through his pockets for the small change of words, words most suitable to explain my foolishness to me, and the correctness of the Church's solutions. But I understood that there was a balance of priorities, a ranking of needs, and the survival of the Church and its capital reserves was crucial.

'Very well, Cardinal, I will, of course, do as you suggest.'

I was speaking into an empty receiver. The line was dead, Buscheim had known my answer and needed to waste no more time with me.

And so, once more, I entered the City of London. How this world was changing, how extraordinary the miracles of modernity. The city rushed, the city swelled. And the complexity of its interacting pulsating components, its people and its transport systems, its merchandise and its transactions. Everywhere and in everything there was interdependence, and if one component of that interactive network was to fail, what would happen? Would the whole structure collapse, would the species fall?

On a cold Friday morning in early October 1929, this man of the Church sat with three men of the press at a walnut table in a magnificent boardroom. The room was furnished in the most modern style, painted in dove grey and cloudy white, and hung with blurred Impressionist paintings. Its tall windows framed the city and the sky. Beaverbrook was at the head of the table. His hair was thin and his features plethoric. He was black-suited, an unlit cigar in his constantly gesticulating hand, a red carnation pinned to his lapel. At Beaverbrook's left hand sat the sweating Rothermere, fat and florid, and at Beaverbrook's right was Harmsworth, austere and emaciated.

These men were not friends, they were competitors, jostling, strident, outdoing each other with their descriptions of their polo ponies and their Scottish estates, their wives and their brilliant children. Beaverbrook strode around the room. Harmsworth shouted for coffee. Beaverbrook poured himself a whisky, and Harmsworth poured soda water. Rothermere picked at his nostrils.

It was time, and I broke through the banter. 'Gentlemen, we have business to discuss,' and Beaverbrook smiled at me, unendingly amused.

'We have,' he said. 'But we haven't a quorum yet.'

'Oh,' I said. 'Are there others to come? I thought that this . . .' Beaverbrook interrupted.

'My dear Abbot, I've taken the liberty of asking a few friends along. We need to co-ordinate our forces. This is not a minor matter. If we're to be successful, we need to act cohesively to maximize the situation's potential.' He leaned back in his chair, double chins spilling around the arc of his celluloid collar, and poked his thumbs into his waistcoat pockets. Harmsworth nodded and Rothermere stroked his belly.

'Any chance of a snack?' Rothermere asked.

'Of course, dear fellow.' Beaverbrook reached under the edge of the board table and a bell rang in the outer office.

A shadow materialized behind the frosted glass door, moved closer, swirled, pirouetted, and became a woman's profile. The woman knocked and was bid enter.

'Miss Smith,' said Beaverbrook. Such a beautiful Miss Smith, silk stockings and bob of golden hair. Miss Smith waited, hands clasped neatly and Rothermere stared, mouth open, breath held tight. 'Would you mind, dear, some refreshments please.'

'Certainly, sir,' and she swished away, pleated skirt twisting around in a glorious rush that showed her serious knees. The door clicked to, and Rothermere breathed again.

'Very nice, Beaverbrook.'

'Thank you, my boy.' Beaverbrook acknowledged the niceness of his possession. There was another knock at the door.

'Come,' and Miss Smith wheeled in a floating palace of profiteroles, millefeuilles, strawberry tarts and éclairs. She poured coffee into green and gold Copeland cups, and as she placed our cups before us, the softness of the passing drift of perfume took me and made my head ache. Miss Smith was the sun, and we were grey dust.

The cakes were piled in the centre of the table, grand confections of lustrous chocolate, custard, berries and cream. So pretty. Rothermere's fingers curled around two éclairs. Elbows on the table, éclairs in his dimpled fists, he snapped at the cakes, ferocious mouthfuls of cream and chocolate slopping around his lips, soft pastry breaking away and fleeing to the silk slopes of his bulging waistcoat.

'That's better,' said Rothermere, his cheeks full, words slapping around his muffled tongue. 'That's much better.' Beaverbrook and Harmsworth sneered at the greedy boy. Harmsworth delicately lifted his coffee cup to his lips.

Beaverbrook pushed himself up from the boardroom

table. He walked to a cabinet and opened its door. He took out a record and placed it face down, pressed a button, rotated a knob, then shut the cabinet door on fairy violins and crackling piano. He sat down.

'Mozart,' he announced.

Rothermere ate cakes. Harmsworth winced and sipped black coffee. Beaverbrook wished to tell us something, but he wanted to be asked. He fidgeted, bursting, and the beautiful music trickled and sang. What did he want to tell us, and why were his friends ignoring the music? I'd not seen or heard anything like it before.

'It's beautiful,' I said and this was Beaverbrook's chance.

'Yes, it is. It's the only one in the world. It's an electric gramophone.' He smiled and nodded emphatically at Harmsworth who ignored him, staring through the windows at Fleet Street below. And I understood Rothermere and Harmsworth's coolness. If Beaverbrook had this machine and they had not, they were certainly not going to acknowledge that the machine was of interest. Why, of course it wasn't. It was mundane, and the quality of its music inferior to existing wind-up gramophones. Electric. So what? Beaverbrook looked at the caps of his Oxfords, clearly disappointed that the machine had made no impression. The telephone rang. Beaverbrook lifted the receiver.

'Yes, do show them in.' He rose to his feet and walked to the door to greet Gibbons, representing the Masons, Hughes-Smith, the Stock Exchange, and Morgan, the Prudential. So confident these men, so much in charge, and so little in doubt. Plump city men in coded clothes. Harmsworth stood to shake hands. Rothermere licked profiterole chocolate from his fingers, and glared at these people who were interrupting his meal.

'You haven't met the Abbot,' said Beaverbrook, and they shook hands, firm handshakes except for Gibbons. Gibbons whose third and fourth fingers were claws at my palm, the Masons' handshake. We sat down and pleasantly discussed the weather, its wind and rain, sunshine and showers, all of us except for Rothermere who was busy with another millefeuille. A yellow rain of confectioner's custard splattered the dove grey carpet, pastry flakes tucked themselves into the folds of his lapels, raspberry jam streaked his collar and dotted his navy blue tie. Rothermere tucked in, and we moved from autumn to Deauville. Beaverbrook pressed the buzzer under the table's edge and Miss Smith came in.

'Miss Smith, would you mind doing the honours?'

'Certainly. What will you have, gentlemen?'

Miss Smith brought the drinks to the table on a heavy silver tray, and, nudging Morgan's shoulder with her breast, passed him his soda. He flushed and edged away. Gibbons and Hughes-Smith ogled her. Perfect Miss Smith left the room, left the room to wonder what she did for Beaverbrook.

'She could mix my drinks any day,' said the mason. Beaverbrook frowned, and Hughes-Smith didn't dare have any opinion. It was Deauville again and how nice it was to be in a resort used to dealing with the English. How nice to be abroad and be able to have decent tea.

'Of course, the problem with Deauville is the weather. It's so unreliable, don't you know? We last went there twelve years ago and it rained for two weeks. One might as well have been in Brighton, frankly,' said Hughes-Smith. He was a little man with a monocle and a waxed moustache. Emphatic in his manner and speech, his words struck at the listener, precisely enunciated, stated, not spoken, too loud, they precluded any other conversation. 'Of course, after that we simply could not waste another summer and we bought a rather nice villa at Juan-les-Pins. It is a much longer journey, but worth it.' The group nodded politely. Rothermere ate another cake.

'I say, Hughes-Smith,' asked Morgan. 'Your son still at Eton?'

'He is.'

'And how does he find it?'

'There's no need for that, the chauffeur takes him to school.'

The plutocrats chuckled and Hughes-Smith looked very pleased with his witticism.

What on earth were they talking about? Here we were, gathered to discuss the most important matters and there they were, chitter-chattering like a flock of cleaning ladies. Rothermere snapped at the end of a huge cigar and spat the end on to his plate.

'I say, Harmsworth, do you have a match?' Harmsworth padded at his pockets.

'Sorry, old boy.'

'Anyone have a match?' No matches. Beaverbrook grinned. Rothermere scowled and stuffed the cigar into his jacket pocket.

It was Hughes-Smith again. 'I say, what do you press chappies think of that Mussolini fellow? Is he a beast?'

Harmsworth replied. 'I think that Mussolini has done a good job for Italy. There is effective central government, marshes drained, malaria controlled, roads built, railways made to run on time, industry encouraged, the civil service organized, and above all the Italians have had a bit of muscle put in them. They have civic pride and a feeling of nationhood. Fascism and Mussolini have organized Italy . . .'

'But I say, Harmsworth, what about the murders, and those frightful blackshirt thugs?'

'My dear Hughes-Smith, I don't think you quite understand. To achieve effective nationhood, the people have to be able to identify with a cause, and there's nothing so rallying as certainty and strength. Now, you asked about the murders and certainly a few people have died. You're a businessman, Hughes-Smith, and as a businessman you'll understand that one must consider the balance sheet and then make a judgement as to the viability of the concern. Extend that analogy, Hughes-Smith, from business to countries, and you'll see that on the whole, Italy has gained, she's in positive balance. One has to transcend the small view, and if a few have died for the good of a nation, so be it. Remember the end is far more important than the means.' Harmsworth turned to me. 'And tell us, Abbot, what is the Church's view?' The Church had a definite view of Mussolini, a view propounded to me by Buscheim, at length.

'Well, gentlemen, to be frank, we opposed Mussolini initially. We viewed him as an unsettling force for change, a force carried by the people, and we are always wary of populist movements. The Church had never been happy with Garibaldi's kingdom of Italy. We found Garibaldi's empire uncomfortable and Victor Emmanuel a useless puppet. Gentlemen, the Church in Italy was in the unique situation of finding the establishment disagreeable and so Fascism opened up possibilities for improvement. Earlier this year our position in Italy became formalized by treaties between the Vatican and the State. In exchange for our loss of temporal power within the kingdom, the Lateran Treaty recognized our rule within the neutral city of the Vatican where we were free from Italy's laws. The Vatican became a country with its own ambassadors and governance. The

184

terms of the treaty led to the overt recognition of covert fact. Catholicism was recognized as the official religion of Italy, and in the new secular state, belief ruled. The Lateran Treaty included a financial settlement, to compensate for our loss of power: 1,750 million lire was paid to the Vatican and this, as you know, gentlemen, has been invested by the Vatican Bank ... The Vatican Bank, gentlemen, is our wise son.'

'Ah yes,' said Beaverbrook. 'Investments, we do need to consider investment. What do you think, Hughes-Smith?' The monocle gleamed.

'October the twenty-fourth.'

Beaverbrook looked around the room. 'Is that convenient for everyone?' It was, and with that the collapse of western stock markets was organized. Simple. Four sentences, and the fate of the world was fixed, a fate that included a decade of depression and a world war. But to more important matters. Rothermere to Gibbons:

'Tell me, old boy, you know about wine, what do you think of this year's Burgundy?'

'Well, it's promising. The year's gone terribly well, rain at the right time, and that glorious summer. Buy. Lay some down. It will be quite drinkable in five years, and if you try and buy then, you may find that the stocks have gone.'

Rothermere leaned forward, belly folding around the edge of the table. 'I don't think, Gibbons, that availability of stock is a significant problem. Everything is always available.'

'Quite, quite.' Beaverbrook glossed over the potential for disagreement within the room. 'Anyone like another stiffener?'

'No thanks, Beaverbrook, it's time I was away, you know. Work to do, very pleasant, very pleasant.' And with a nod to the plutocrats, Hughes-Smith was off. And suddenly they were all off, people to see, places to go, things to do, business to settle.

The room cleared and I was left with Beaverbrook's button eyes. He showed me to the door, arm around my shoulder.

'Well, Abbot, everything seems satisfactory, and if the Church acts expediently, its coffers will be restored. Good day.'

I was dismissed, but in a gentlemanly fashion, so that I was left feeling good, part of the conspiracy and one of the conspirators. It was interesting that play of power, so casual the discussion, just old pals chatting. So that was how it was done. Comfortable conversation in the company of a coterie of friends, friends whom one had known all of one's life, and friends of whom one could be absolutely sure. And the chat had been about family and wine, horses, holidays, the weather and business. Why, it was no more important than any of life's other components, so why make it a big thing? Allocate the same time to work as the rest of life's parts, maybe a little less because it wasn't quite as pleasant, then sort it out with a few refreshments and a couple of drinks. How agreeable. How circumscribed. How defined. How easy . . . but how had Beaverbrook known about the state of the Vatican's coffers? That casual remark at the door. Where had Beaverbrook obtained his information? How had he known that our coffers needed replenishing? This was worrying. Our financial status was meant to be a most secure secret. It wouldn't do for the world to know how much or how little we had. The ledgers at the Vatican Bank were for a few men to know in part and for far fewer men to know in whole. How had Beaverbrook gained access to that information, and why was he letting me, a humble Abbot, know that he knew? The comment must have been considered, it was pointed, and so must have a point. It was a necessary piece of information that required investigation. Was there a leak in our security system, a mordant spy in the house of God? This needed to be reviewed with wise Buscheim.

Back in the monastery, I ordered the masseuse to come to me. She was Japanese, a sweet thing who spent her time, in her little room in the abbey, drawing fine sketches of rice paddies, temples and Mount Fuji in mist. I'd bought her for a thousand pounds from an opium dealer. Brother Luke had organized the purchase on one of his frequent sorties into town to restock our community's pharmacy. The dealer had been described by Luke as a living Fu Manchu, surrounded by bodyguards, reclining in the dangerous light of an opium den, attended by a harem. All a little unbelievable, except that it wasn't Brother Luke who came swishing into my room but my own Madame Butterfly, wrapped in stiff silks. She bowed in the doorway. So formal.

'Do come in, dear,' and she came in and set down her case of emolliments and perfumes. Luke followed her into the room and set up a miniature Primus stove, all spindly legs and twisted metal. I lay on the bed and watched. Luke filled an enamel bowl with water and set it on the stove. Fujita stood still, straight backed, hands clasped, waiting.

'That will be all, Luke.'

'Thank you, excellency.' He left us and I told Fujita bits of my day, how the town looked, the fields, the weather, nothing important but it was good to speak. She nodded, attentive, an easy listener, and I felt unburdened. The water in the basin came up to boil, hubble bubbling on the spider Primus. Fujita bent to her case and brought out a blue glass bottle, and thick white towels. She paraded the bottle.

'Fo yo lun, exellen.' She clicked her heels and bowed, then sprinkled the contents of the bottle for my lungs into the boiling water, which hushed and spurted, steam poking up at the room.

'Come, exellen,' and this Abbot came to Fujita and sat on a low stool by the stove.

'Ben head plea.' I bent over the steaming basin. She loosely folded a towel over my head and turned the Primus off. She tucked the towel under the bowl, so that I was caught in clouds of thymol, dark and damp, wonderfully cleansing, chasing through my sinuses, clearing my throat, searing my larynx, soaring along the generations of my bronchi and deep into my alveoli. How my lungs sang. Deep breaths in, and sweet Fujita squeezed her thumbs into my shoulder-blades and eased away the day.

'Be dee, exellen,' and I did, deep deep, inhaling as she pressed, exhaling as she relaxed, and with her thumbs the tension went, and in the depths of her towel, I felt calmer, easier.

Fujita ran the bath, blending in yellow oils, rainbow slicks on the water, and I looked at myself in the medicine cabinet mirror. With age, my hair had slipped from the skull to my ears and nostrils, shoulder-blades and back. With age, lines had carved my face, criss-crossing under my eyes, leaning into my lips, and twisting my chin. With age, my eyes had dulled, and my nose had become fleshy. I looked at this near image and I didn't dislike what I was. What was the choice, what were the real options? From a foundling to a monk, from a monk to an Abbot, I had done well. My bed was softer than cobblestones, and my house was warmer than snow. I liked it, loved my little Japanese girl, felt comfortable with a full stomach, loved the rooms of my power, disliked the hollow streets.

In the bath Fujita soaped my limbs and paid reverential attention to my member, cooing and clucking, speaking to it with respect, enquiring as to its day. My shoulders heavy against the hard slab of the bath, I saw her little face, its sweetness, its light, and thought of her hairless vulva. Fujita rubbed at my chest with a hard hot sponge, pressing against my breasts, massaging deep and strong. I closed my eyes, and felt soft in the water, soft and slow. She pulled me gently forward and soaped my back.

'Come, exellen,' and she slopped warm water over my body, washing away the snowdrifts of soap, the mire of bubbles. She took my hand and led me from the bath, wrapped me in towels and padded me dry.

Oh Fujita, I remember you. Oh Fujita, I loved your days and now as I write in age and in sin, I melt when I remember your ways. Fujita, Fujita, do you remember me? She dressed me in a black kimono and took me back into the bedroom.

I sat at the kingwood escritoire, looking at her reflection in the gilt overmirror. She clipped a broad metal plate over the Primus stove. She took a white pan from her bag and placed it on the hot plate. She uncorked a bottle and poured sauce into the pan. She turned up the gas light, and the sauce simmered. From her magician's bag she pulled her magician's tricks, pampered meats sliced fine and thin, and she soused them for moments in the boiling sauce. Then, twisting the meat around ivory chopsticks, she tiptoed to my side and fed me, delicately placing the salty meat between my lips.

I had recently grown to dislike vegetables, fruit, bread,

fish. It was meat I wanted, and only meat that I ate. I was surprised at how much I could consume, and wondered at the source of my hunger. Meat of any sort, pig, beef, veal, venison and game, but not chicken. Never chicken, with its memories of perverse, priapic Aquinas.

I relaxed at the escritoire and Fujita fed me, from stove to mouth, chopsticks held out like flagpoles, meat the flapping flag. She fed me, and I lolled, arms slumped, loose at their shoulder joints, legs splayed, completely limp, eating good dark beef. I ate, savouring the orient, and Fujita bent down and fed between my legs. I stroked her hair, and licked the ivory chopsticks, catching the drops of gravy on my tongue, while Fujita caught the drops of me on her lips.

'Fujita, the telephone, my dear,' and my sweetheart tiptoed and brought the machine to the desk.

'Exellen.'

'Abbot John. How was the meeting?'

'All went to plan, agreement was reached, details will arrive by the next messenger from England.' We were still unable to trust the security of the telephone system, all important messages were still relayed by the papal messenger service, a tiresomely slow system but one that was immaculately safe, completely discreet.

'Abbot John, have you dictated your letter?' Cardinal Buscheim seemed to be articulating his words very slowly.

'No, excellency.'

'Good, I wouldn't dictate. Why don't you write it yourself? You do remember how to write, don't you, Abbot dear?'

'Of course, excellency, and you of course remember how to read?'

'Abbot John, there is a reason for my sarcasm and another for my caution.' I guessed that there probably was

190

a reason and regretted my caustic repartee. Buscheim, always a man with a reason.

'Abbot John, exactly how secure do you think the abbey is? Are we safe? Are there spies? Does information leak? Do your people gossip? Tell me, Abbot. Think, man.'

And I thought. What was there to worry about? What on earth was there to worry about?

'Excellency, what do you mean?'

'Abbot John, I would like you to read today's mail. Open all the letters yourself and act appropriately.'

The line was cut, and the clamp of insecurity and panic caught me. I pushed Fujita away and rushed to the morning's post. I roared, scuffing through the pile of mail, throwing letters to the floor until I came to the only letter that mattered, the Vatican missive. I tore open the cream envelope and read Buscheim's filigree script. One sentence.

'You have a spy called Luke,' and my heart died. Luke, a spy. Luke, light of my eyes, made in my image, to be me. Luke a spy. My hands shook. It was beyond reason. Unacceptable. Unbelievable. Incredible. Luke was faithful. Luke was ever there. Luke was pliant. Luke was good. So clever, so clever. If I could not trust Luke then I could not trust myself. Besides, what had leaked, what information had moved from the secure boundaries of our abbey, flown from the borders of our Church? Nothing, there was nothing. We were safe, we were secure. Buscheim was a liar. It could not, just could not be.

I paced the room and Fujita cowered in a corner. Buscheim was a liar, Buscheim was a fool. Luke, never. Never, never. Buscheim. I kicked the wall. Buscheim. I kicked the bed. Fujita scurried from the room. I kicked over the Primus. Buscheim. Kill Buscheim. I smashed at the escritoire with my fist, and crushed my little finger with the weight of my anger. I hopped around the bedroom, tears in my eyes, tears of pain and tears of anger. I slumped in an armchair and wringing my arm, furious with pain, stopped for a moment, stopped and thought. Was it possible? Was there really evidence? Did I have any idea that he could have spied on us, given away vital information to our secular enemies? No. My finger throbbed, pulsed.

But wait. There was something odd, something today that I hadn't understood. I went over the moments of the day, the drive into the town, the meeting, what was it? There had been something odd. It came to me. It was Beaverbrook's final statement. My perfect memory cursed me with that last sentence, so banal, put in such an avuncular fashion.

'Well, Abbot,' he had said, 'everything seems satisfactory, and if the Church acts expediently, its coffers will be restored.'

He had known about the state of the Church's finances. This was classified information. I caught my breath. Buscheim was right. It was Luke. Only Luke and I knew ... and Beaverbrook, and the Vatican. How could he do this? But such betrayal. All my faith and all my heart. He had been my son and he was unworthy. I had picked him. Chosen him from among the others, for his gifts and talents, and he had given me away, given us all away to Beaverbrook. It made no sense, why should he have done it? And yet it made perfect sense. Perhaps he'd been looking for a safe life away from us, and spying would make life's rewards secure.

I felt shocked, and then so bitter. The Vatican had known and I had not. Beaverbrook had known and I had not. Then the emotions of denial and revelation were replaced by a stronger fatal emotion: strong madness to take him and punish him, destroy him and redeem ourselves.

I paced the room kicking the furniture and nursing my poor hand. Luke must go, Luke must die, rid us of this plague, this foul besmirched beast, this Judas monster, this snake. He must die. There was a scrabbling noise at the door, then a knock.

'Come in, you swine,' I shouted, and a rather shocked, lumpen-faced Brother Adam limped into the room, swinging his leg brace.

'What is it?' I hissed and shook a meaty fist at him. He coughed and shuffled.

'Well?' I roared at the blackheads on his red nose and the springs that coiled from his nostrils and ears. 'What is it, disgusting creature?'

'Your grace, I have the first of the season's honey for you.' I was not disarmed. I knew what he was up to. He wanted something, unctuous pervert, sodomite. What did he want?

'A present for you, excellency.'

I was aware of a bizarre humming, a persistent buzzing echoing from deep in the room. Brother Adam patted the pockets of his habit and then reached deep and pulled out a Kilner jar.

'For you, lord.' I took the heavy jar from him. Brown honey, slopping, sticky, thick within the grey glass jar. Brother Adam fell to his knees and clasped at my gown, pulling annoyingly at the soft silk, clawing at my robes.

'What is it, pestilent arsehole?'

'Excellency, nothing, nothing at all. I'm just grateful to you for your beneficence,' Brother Adam sobbed.

'Get up, fool.' I kicked out at him and jerked away from the impertinence of his grasp. Destabilized by my sudden movement he fell on his face.

Adam pulled himself up, and still snivelling took another Kilner jar from his habit.

'Excellency.' He lowered his head, smirked and thrust forward the jar for inspection. It hummed and vibrated. I jerked it from him and peered into its depths. It was full of sodding bees.

'Disgusting, Adam. Why are you showing me these insects?' Adam looked very pleased with himself. 'Stop smirking, pisspants. What is it, fool?'

'These bees, highness.'

'I am aware that they are bees.'

'I've bred them . . .'

'So?'

'They're very special, lord.'

'I don't care, shitsmear.'

'Do let me show your excellency.' Adam suddenly released the clasps clamping the Kilner jar's lid and pushed his fingers into its depths. He pulled out his hand and, clamping the lid tight, showed me his fingers. Wriggling along their length were ten hissing bees. He moved his hand towards me so that I could inspect the insects and I jerked away.

'What are you doing, cretin?'

'Now, don't you worry, Abbot John, you're quite safe.'

'What do you mean safe, with those ferocious-looking creatures. I don't want to be stung.' I rushed to the other side of the room and the lugubrious Adam wiggled his black-gloved hand at me.

'You're quite safe, sire.'

'What the fuck are you talking about? What do you mean safe, shitslime, and what's so special about these fucking bees?'

'Sire, I've bred very unpleasant bees, very irritable bees,

that will sting without provocation. I'm very proud of that.
It's quite an achievement for a mere Kentish beekeeper.'

'Well, so what, shitprick?'

'Well, sire, you're right of course. It's of no consequence
at all.'

Brother Adam's head hung low. I moved towards him
to inspect his bees. They were certainly unpleasant-looking
creatures. Wings whirring, they were trying to pull themselves away from Brother Adam's sticky fingers. Most
curious that despite the rainbow blur of wings they
remained attached to the monk. Brother Adam brought the
insects close to his face and, rotating his hand slowly,
inspected the mass of bees.

'Adam, why are they stuck to you?'

Adam looked up at me, his pop eyes made huge by the
bottle lenses of his tortoise-shell glasses. 'Excellency, they
sting me and they are caught by me.'

'What is this idiotic paradox?'

Adam chuckled. 'No, excellency, there is an easy explanation. The bee's sting is barbed like a fishing hook. For
these insects my skin is thick and strong so that if they sting
me, they're hooked by their own barb.' He pushed his
glasses back up the long slide of his nose, and peered down
at the bumble bees. Then, catching a bee between the finger
and thumb of his left hand, he jerked it away from his right
hand and showed it to me.

'There, my Lord, can you see?'

I recoiled, then stepped nearer to the loathsome Adam
and the bee. Its arse was torn away, and soft sludge oozed
from its shattered abdomen. He brought the torn bee closer
to his eyes, rubbing its ripped carapace between the first
finger and thumb of his right hand. Black, oily body fluid
dribbled on to his skin. He plucked at a wing, pulled it from

the insect's thoracic cage, then pressing translucence to the tip of his tongue, closed his mouth and swallowed. Adam pulled a second bee from his hand, pulled off its wings and ate them.

Adam opened his mouth and scraped a live bee from his index finger on to his lower incisors. He closed his mouth and the insect cracked between his yellow molars. I stared at this creature, thick-lensed, pasty, blown, finding extra-ordinary the sensual delight with which he ate. Eyes closed, lips apart as if for a lover's kiss, he took his creatures into himself, peeling the bumble bees from his broken-nailed fingers. He finished his hors d'oeuvre and I would provide him with his entrée.

'Brother Adam.' He looked up at me. 'Adam. You say that these bees of yours have been bred?'

'Yes, sire.'

'Don't interrupt, stinkswill,' I shouted. Adam's smile became broader, finding satisfaction in my anger. 'They've been bred for their viciousness, you say?'

'I can most humbly confirm their breeding, my liege.'

'Would you like to test them?'

'They have been tested already, excellency.'

'How so?'

'On mice and rats.'

'Adam, test them on something a little larger.'

'Of course, highness. I would like that.'

'Something much larger, Adam.'

'A cat?'

'No, Adam, I like cats.'

'Certainly the bees would not be allowed to kill delicious pussy creatures.'

'Tell me, Adam, what's been your most significant experiment?'

'Excellency, the bees have successfully dispatched a useless senile goat.'

'A nanny goat, Adam?'

'Yes, lordness, not a billy.'

'That's a relief, Adam, otherwise there might have been great trouble for you. Adam, we have a spy in our establishment.' Adam stood straight, thinking that he was accused. 'Relax, you snivelling masturbator.' Adam collapsed again into his normal crawling unctuous kyphotic state. 'This monk is treachery, Adam, and I need your help. No, not just I, but the Church needs your help because this monster threatens our existence. He has betrayed us for useless gold. This Judas has given our secrets to our enemies and made us most vulnerable.' Adam stiffened. He liked the idea of being threatened and vulnerable.

'Excellency, how may I help? What traitor have we here?' Adam hissed, equanimity disturbed by the traitor in his house. He thumped his fist against his heart and the bees rattled in their jar, buzzing, disturbed, catching his mood.

'Adam, this foul traitor is a most evil and calculating monster. He has betrayed everything that we have given him. This Church that has nurtured him, this monastery that has sheltered him, we monks who have taught and cultivated him. This beast has thrown our secrets at our enemies, given our secrets to the armies of the outside world against whom we strive to maintain order. Adam, I will not bother you with the details of our betrayal, but let me tell you this one thing. News of our betrayal has reached the Vatican, and our orders are to dispatch the beast, dispatch him quietly, dispose of him so that we are troubled no more. He is a fly to be swatted away, a subhuman of no feeling to be destroyed, and Adam, dear Adam, it is for you to rid us of the beast. You will do this.'

'Excellency, I will, it will be a signal honour.' Adam was at attention, the jar of bees pulled from his pocket, he was ready and the bees were rattling.

'You will send him to the hives, excellency,' and Adam left me. It was simple, so simple.

I rang for Luke and he was before me, shining brightness, love, clarity, running water, the wind, spring, dark dirt, dishonour, disorder, disgust, death.

'Luke, my dear.'

'Yes, your grace,' and the spy awaited his orders, ready, so ready, blond, cream-skinned, tall, straight, bent, disloyal, ugly, treacherous, limp and squalid. Luke, my heart, my love and my hate. I pulled him to me, grabbed the sleeve of his habit, reached for him.

'Luke, my dear.' He smiled for me. 'Luke, I hear that Brother Adam has a delicious harvest of honey. Fetch me some, would you. Go down to him and bring me honey. Go now.' I released his arm, freed him. He bowed and left me.

Matthew, Adam and I stood in a dark and noisy clearing in the woods, a solemn troika among the wooden slats of a hundred white-painted beehives. Luke was laid out on a bed of pine cones. His body was discoloured, purple, hardly visible beneath an army of writhing bees. Adam tipped a can of fuel over the body and stepping back struck a match against his sandal and threw it at the pile. Luke burnt, flamed by Adam, and the seething bees, trapped in his skin and clothes, soared upwards, caught in a bright rush of orange-blue kerosene. The bees burnt, then his habit and for the smallest moment, Luke's swollen body was exposed, cleared of bees, free of his clothes. His skin was bloated and mottled apart from a flash of white at his waist, where his tight underclothes had saved his flesh from the bees'

198

desperate needles. And then he was gone, gone in secondary flames of burning fat and muscle.

Adam tipped more fuel on to Luke's flesh and the flood of kerosene swallowed the flames, which caught again and roared higher. We three stepped back from the rush of heat and coughing on the char of his flesh covered our mouths and noses with swatches of our habits. We watched the fusillade of sparks snaking up to the treetops on a current of black smoke. The column of smoke wavered in the wind and, suddenly changing direction, blacked out the autumn's sun. And from above, a strange snow fell on us, caught our hair, touched our faces, layered our clothes, Luke's ashes drifting down, in death, brushing our earthly presences.

PART TWO

HOPE'S HORIZON

Chapter Nine

WE HAD co-ordinated our friends throughout the world, and although the massive sales of shares had precipitated universal economic crisis, we had all managed to realize our investments without significant loss. Our money had been successfully transferred from the markets and used to purchase gold. There was no doubt that we had precipitated the crash but we felt no guilt. The crisis was inevitable and our action had been expedient. It was ordered and we were safe. Such crises were cyclical, and, so long as the basic structure of the world was preserved, would be lived through and followed by economic regeneration. We and our friends were the basis of the world, we were the foundation and frame of civilization, its form, its substance, and with our resources preserved, the whole world was ultimately safe.

It had been no great effort to co-ordinate the sales, a few conversations with friends in the private rooms of discreet clubs had settled the day and decided the order of our actions. It had been easy and all had gone well. A few may have suffered for the greater good, but the minimal impact of this suffering on the ultimate community of man was known, calculated. The equation would work well and our ledgers remain in positive balance.

They had called me, called me to Rome, to the castles

and domes of the Vatican City. I was wanted for higher office and Buscheim had sent an escort of the Pope's men to take me to Italy. My work was good, he had said, and had emphasized that I was now considered trustworthy. Had I ever been untrustworthy?

I had stepped from our monastery in the spring of 1930, and driving along the gravel road that led away from our abbey, I had not looked back. It was not necessary. I knew who I was and where I was going. The past did not matter, it was secured; we in the Church had done our best for almost two thousand years to synthesize security.

Brother Matthew had taken over the running of the abbey, had become its new Abbot, master of its days. It suited him, he did well and with this gift of power his deep chest expanded and his voice resonated more loudly, the crown of authority making of the man a king. His was the abbey, and his were the monks, his were the woods, the pastures and the streams. He was welcome to them, let him rule, and I would to Rome, an English cardinal at the Pope's court.

We were driving to Southampton to take the steamer to Naples, and in the back seat of the Daimler I sat between the bulky shoulders of a Swiss Guard and a Vatican messenger, cramped, slightly uncomfortable, caught between the closeness of muscles and bone.

The huge Swiss Guard had initially terrified me, moving too suddenly, speaking too loudly, an unpleasant presence, the lumpiness of his shoulder holster pushing out the padding of his grey suit. Always alert, awake for the chance of assassination and murder, every lampshade hid a booby trap, all food was poisoned. Last night at supper, he had knocked the glass from my mouth. My lips were cut and my blood had dripped on to my beef. 'Poison,' he had muttered. I thought this unlikely in the sanctuary of our abbey, but then he reminded me of Luke, and Matthew was welcome to his inheritance.

The Pope's messenger, pigeon-chested, long-limbed, a pianist's hands, high-voiced, giggly. I would not have trusted this man's discretion and picked him for the service, but he must have been screened.

To Rome, to Rome, Heaven's city, God's home. To Rome, to Rome, the great light, keeper of time. Rome, breathless your name. To Rome, eternity bound.

But before the romance of Rome, on to Southampton, its harbours of twisted metal and burnt fires, its ships and buildings, ramshackle wood, peeling paint, hooting horns, steam blowing from the great funnels of the ocean liners, crowds, sailors, passengers, the burden of separation, the drift of voyage, a striding captain, the customs men, the great coils of rope, the unending jetties, with their clothes of barnacles and green trail of weed, luggage left in tumbling mountains, the crush of cars and buses, spring rain, apparent disorder, seeming order, and what must be the sea. Green and grey liquid mud, ripple caked, froth, swirling, sloshing, teasing the hulls of the great ships, slopping over the quayside. The sea, my first view, I loved its look, its vastness, its smell, its clouds of gulls, its waves and spray. The sea, glorious infinity of proportion, how wide, how deep, how long, how far. And having dismissed Southampton for its rush and bustle, I loved it now for its friend the ocean. On land, my heart was the ocean's.

Our car stopped beside a treacherous gangplank tipped up against the side of a steamer. The shoulders of my travelling companions disengaged themselves from me and relief came with the loss of their pressure. The car doors opened and an enfilade of March wind rushed in, cutting our breath, bringing us the sharpness of spring.

We paraded the steel decks of the *Oceania*, led to my cabin by a blue-uniformed steward. We were a solemn procession in military step. Steward and Cardinal, Swiss Guard and papal messenger, then three porters, each carrying a single small briefcase, for we travelled light, possession-free. The click of our heels on the decks, and then the solemn thud of heavy steps on a steep wooden staircase. I put out my hand to steady myself on the rail, then withdrew it with distaste, for my hand had touched sticky salt. We were shown to our cabins, three adjoining rooms, and the Swiss Guard tipped the servants, dismissing them with pennies.

We entered our rooms together and with a synchrony of motion turned door handles, opened doors, then looked around into the corridor to take stock. The Swiss Guard signalled to me to wait in the corridor. In a burlesque of paranoia, he sniffed around the door frame, then pushed into my cabin slamming open the door. I watched him strip the bed, twitch the curtains, search the cupboards, inspect the doors, follow the trail of light cables, and look underneath chairs. He signalled for me to enter, then searched the bathroom, running the taps, delving inside the cistern and emptying out the bathroom cabinet.

I contemplated the chaotic detritus of open drawers and distressed linen as the door clicked to, then called room service for food, drink and a chambermaid.

The ship's horn sounded, three angry hoots that told the world we were ready to sail and the sea that we were on our way. The engines heaved and the cabin shook as we pulled away from our berth. From the porthole there was a

view of gurgling water and a diminishing dock. I drank
from the whisky bottle, Southampton's chimneys receded
and the voice of the engines settled to a song. I looked
around my cabin, pleased by the softness of the decor. Not
for the Church a spartan odyssey. If sail we must, it was in
comfort, with safety, and at speed. I drank again, whisky
billowing around the heavy warmth of the meat in my
stomach. Meat and whisky settled down well together,
made friends in my innards, took kindly to the acid of my
gastric juices, warming, filling, easing, comforting.

We had been sailing for about thirty minutes when
suddenly I became aware that our passage was no longer
smooth and the boat was no longer a cruising limousine,
but rather a bobbing kite, ducking up, then swooping down
on the sea. I looked through the porthole. We had cleared
guardian land and had reached the open Channel. The sea
was high, and our huge liner rose and fell on drunken
waves. I no longer felt camaraderie with the salt water, and
my communion with the elemental ocean was as far from
me as the safety of Southampton's land. The rocking motion
of the ship was unpleasant, I felt sick, confined, unsteady,
disturbed. I lay on the bed and drank a little more whisky,
tried to find comfort in different positions, tilting my head
to escape the unpleasantness of the waters. I drank more
whisky, hoping that the familiar blur of alcohol would
muffle the screaming sea. We went up and we crashed
down. Drops of water splattered against the glass of the
cabin portholes, distorting my image of the world outside,
confining me more precisely to the misery of my cabin.

The room no longer appeared so pleasant, no longer
discreetly luxurious, no longer suitable, furnished now with
the rush of seasickness, the jarring disjointedness of my
poor stomach and the whirring confusion of my thudding

head. The wind zipped in through a crack in the window's seal, and ripped around the cabin. The ship leaned, and the carafes and glasses on top of the chest of drawers rushed across its surface. Bored with leaning one way, the ship tipped to starboard, and keeping gravity company the glassware sped across the chest.

If this room was disgusting, how was the corridor? Worse, and the inclement English Channel pushed this Cardinal nascent from one leering, looming wall to another, so that it was better to be back in my cabin, back on my bed.

The ghastliness of continued sickness, the awfulness of sour vomit. The pain of abdominal muscles worn with the stitch of repeated vomiting. The unbearableness of a head out of synchrony with the bobbing ship. Up and down, ceaseless misery, senseless misery broken by the occasional quiet of sleep. Comparative quiet, because even in sleep I was not free of the water and its unbearable motion.

The Channel was peaceful compared with the Bay of Biscay. Some twenty-four hours from Southampton, at a time when there seemed nothing left to vomit, and no more space in my head for giddiness, nature revved up, and like a car speeding forward to overtake a tractor the jerking ocean geared up to send me careening from washbasin to lavatory bowl, from bowl to bath.

The Bay of Biscay. The word bay conjured up images of shelter and calm. Foully misnamed Biscay, no bay, just open rolling ocean, roaring waters smashing on the side of our southbound liner and the boat pushed into the waves, bow lifting high against the roaring wind.

The terrible noise of that journey, banging, barging, smacking, water against the vessel's decks and stern, the splat of the waves as the ocean staggered and slopped against the ship's bows, the monstrous motion of a ship

jerked unwillingly to left, right, up, half down, then sideways, irrational thumping clumsy motion, through the
waves, never with them and always into the hissing snapping malignant wind.

The waters became calmer as we cleared the gateway of
the Mediterranean, through the portals guarded by Goliath
Gibraltar and Africa's burning shore. A calmer journey
from thence on. Calmer, in that the waters were quieter and
the wind spent, but exhausting, so exhausting, the seasickness never easing. I lay abed with vomit and piss, abed with
poor companions, ugly reeling souls, howling, mewing, sour
friends, wizened and cruel.

Throughout these six days of misery, I was alone
without solace from my neighbours, no enquiry as to my
state, my journey. The only breaks in the monotony of the
tumbling ship were the arrogant sneers of a lizard with sea
legs, the loathsomely healthy steward who'd knock and ask
if 'Sir' wanted anything. Sir did. Sir wanted something very
badly, O pink-faced boy, Sir wanted to be off this ship on
wonderfully dry land, safe, land lubberingly safe. No food,
no drink, just the good ground of some harbour's stone
shore. Away from this ship, this clumsy dance of gravity
and storm, water and the waves. And the steward in his
navy and braid coughed into the shadows of his sleeve and
said, 'Of course, sir. It is a rough trip, but tomorrow's
forecast is for sunshine, waves two to four feet, sweet wind
straight up our arse, if you will excuse the naval expression,
your honour.'

I threw my slipper at him. A deserved slipper, the gross
indecency, confronting a sick man with pink-faced health.

'But do try a little of our soup, sir.'

To hell with his sick man's consommé and its ghostly
peelings of exhausted vegetables. I writhed in the bed and

kicked out at the sheets, fighting, wriggling, despising the harassing horror of the awful voyage. But never once a thought of Kent, moments spent in regret or memory. Never a look backward to childhood, to youth, adolescence or manhood, to the orphanage, to the seminary. No regret, all time spent in the present without the past, the dimensions of my hours marked in their present minutes, who cares for what's gone, we only know the moment.

And this moment was misery. I screamed, I roared, I moaned, and my storm was a rival to the sea, competition for its anger, its fierceness, its hate for this cockle boat. I hated the ocean as the ocean hated its burden, hated its malignant currents, its slapstick waves, its spray and foam. I hated this bed, this cabin, this ship, I wanted to be away, away from this sickness, this sea. I kicked out at the sheets, then rolled on to my belly and smashed at the pillows with breaking fists. Take me out, take me away, set me on land, take me now to Rome. And the steward bobbed and said, 'There, sir, they do say whisky is a tonic for the seasick and have you tried lying on your side, sir?'

'Be off.' And he scurried away.

Suddenly I stopped vomiting. It was most peculiar. I looked up from my blankets, sniffed the sour air, and cautiously prodded the cabin floor with my cream cheese toes. The nausea had ceased. Ceased because we had berthed, berthed in Naples, home to cholera and our friends the Mafia, home to typhoid, corruption and now home to me, a safe port. I stood up, and I was safe, and I pissed without having to sit like a woman, drank without vomiting, breathed without pain. Such pleasures, the enemy sea beaten. Never again would I travel this way. Never again until the end of my days.

I looked in the bathroom mirror at my puffy bristling

face, and, touching shaving brush to hot water, dabbed at my beard. There was a knock on the cabin door and the Swiss Guard entered. I would have sworn at him for his callousness in leaving me alone, alone for so long, but his hopeless pallor and unsteady stumbling were a check for my tongue. He had been seasick too, and the great muscled man, so proud on land, had been made a weak baby by the sea.

'Excellency, I am sorry.' He bowed deep and low, and kept low until forgiven. Forgiven, he was forgiven, and so was the papal messenger, all of us sick things on this boat of sighs.

We left the liner, a solemn procession of anonymous men, left the darkened port in a discreet limousine, and unbothered by customs were whisked through immigration. Our papal passports exempted us from the normal constraints of travel, and we were ushered through invisible barriers, saluted by customs men, smiled at by sallow clerks. Naples' golden lights twinkled amid the blackness, hostile rivals for the stars. Naples stank, and we shut the car windows against the febrile sewers. Lines of needle rain lanced the mirror puddles that dotted the harbour side.

We sped from Naples and rushed to Rome, racing along Mussolini's new roads through the moonlit countryside, driving through fertile valleys bordered by dark hills humped against a darker sky. Alone on the whispering road we cleaved the night, travelling to a new place, coming home to Rome. The land became more hilly, graced by villages and farms, and the gentle warmth of rural Italy rose to greet us from the wet earth.

It was 1 a.m. when we reached the outskirts of Rome, and we passed quickly through the suburbs, the cobbles of the streets reflecting the car's busy headlights. The car climbed up a hillside, and as we drifted around a slow bend the messenger and the guard strained forward, staring through the raindrops. The car slowed and the solid battlements of the everlasting city loomed. Such a mass of buildings, so much stone, mountains of rock dissembled to form another lowering mountain, massive and mordant, mortared together in an eternal bond of cement and stone, the high towers, the secret doors, the spying windows, the foundations and fortress of our empire. The Vatican, God's city, our power, there, here, at home in Rome.

We halted at a barrier and a uniformed Swiss Guard saluted, then inspected our papers. He waved at his comrades in the gatehouse and the barrier was raised to admit us. The atmosphere in the car lightened, my companions relieved by the security that met them as we entered God's gates.

I was escorted to my rooms through a maze of corridors, a maze that echoed my old home in its complexity. Burning torches lit our way. Exhausted by the journey, I fell on to my bed and fully clothed, the taste of salt on my fingers, I passed immediately into sleep.

Chapter Ten

IN THE gardens of Rome, we sat, two cardinals, scarlet on scarlet, within the security of high walls. I was with Buscheim. He leaned close when he spoke, conspiratorial, confiding, his eyes never fixed, darting, seeking out the spies in the bushes and trees. In a scented place we sat on ancient stone benches, marble patinated with green moss, carvings blurred by time. We sat among the summer roses, their thick blossom heavy with perfume. Bougainvillaea crept over the walls, and oleander in alternate pink and white lined the walkways. In flowerbeds, agapanthus and gerbera. In porphyry pots, exquisite geraniums rivalled the red of our robes. Dwarf cupids confined to earthly lead cavorted among marble angels and shot arrows at spelter Saint Sebastians, captive targets for bows forever drawn taut. The sun was high, and we were cool under the fixed parasols of two slaves. Behind us two Swiss Guards watched over us, submachine-guns held low and ready. Electric fans made a swift breeze, and the whirl of turning blades kept our conversation discreet. Buscheim patted down his Caesar curls and tugged on my gown, pulling me closer. His breath was on my cheek, and the softness of cloves whistled and blew.

'My dear, we do worry about Germany.' We did worry about Germany. We had welcomed Hitler to power and encouraged his rise. We had supported his party financially, finding in him an antidote to Communism, a support for the forces of conservatism. The great German industrialists had seen security in his party, and in the control of labour's radical forces a return to established values, and a suppression of the widespread decadence that sapped and destroyed.

Communism was marching into Europe. Fired by the evangelism of the Third International, it had crept over the heartlands finding a home in the houses of people made poor by the depression. Where unemployment was high, where poverty was widespread, Communism had found company and taken root. Paid for by the Antichrist Stalin, European Communism had become strong. Country by country, we were doing our best to balance the equation, and the conspiracy of capitalism and the Church was countering Communism by supporting Fascist populist movements.

In the early 1930s, in Germany, by deft assassination and judicious movement of monies we had fuelled the National Socialist Party. Our Jesuits had fought alongside the Blackshirts, inspiring their dogma, training their battalions, ordering their confused propaganda, making a force out of a bullying, disordered rabble. And what a rabble, bullies and failures, paranoiacs and butchers, a band of madmen led by hallucinating sadists. But our army was there with them, disguised, unidentifiable, prompting, leading, taking them from the streets, assembling them into a force of power, giving them parades and flags. The Jesuits conjured a philosophy for the Nazis, made steel from the dross, inspired and led, directed their excess, gave them a focus, wrote their speeches, provided them with imagined enemies, gave them ambition, realized their power. The

Jesuits encouraged the National Socialists, branded them with an ideology, gave them pride in the achievements of their nation, directed them towards tradition and loyalty.

The Jesuit generals expanded the Nazi movement and took it into the lives of the people of Germany. From the confused and stumbling Sturmabteilung, the seedling Brownshirts of the early Nazi movement, grew the Schutzstaffel (the SS), the Hitler Youth, the Students' League, the Teachers' League, the Nazi Women's League, the Physicians' League. For every social grouping there was a movement, and the purpose of each movement was to produce conformist behaviour controlling the workers in the factories and on the land, all for Germany, all work for the greater good of Germany, and all ultimately leading to the demise of Communism and the glory of the establishment of Church and industry.

We did well, and rearmament and the great building programmes made Germany strong again. Our agents pushed and prodded, organized and inspired, they led, indistinguishable from native Germans because they were native Germans, taken in by our orphanages and fed into our seminaries, trained, and then retrained, selected and groomed, until they were capable of taking power and doing the Church's bidding, our army, in the uniforms of another country. They were on their side, but they were ours.

The Germans needed an enemy, someone or some group to strive against, someone or some group to blame because they couldn't be to blame for the loss of a war and for the economic miseries of the 1920s and early 1930s. German machismo was such that these terrors were not their fault. An alien force had sapped their strength, weakened their youth, destroyed their trade, sold their factories. The Germans were blameless. That pure blondness, that cleanliness

215

and loyalty, that strength, that purity. No, it was a dangerous outsider, a thief in their midst, a Judas, who was
responsible for the situation.

The Germans were encouraged in their paranoia,
and it was for the best. They were not to know that the
establishment had started the First War, our purpose the
annihilation of German trade competition in the new markets of the Third World. They were not to know that the
oligarchy had caused the inflation of 1923, our purpose to
limit reparations. They were not to know that we had caused
the Depression of the 1930s, our purpose to maximize speculative profit. We could not be to blame, and the German
character could not psychologically accept responsibility.

If we could not be blamed and the Germans were not at
fault, who was responsible? It must be a coterie of conspirators, alien traitors and spies, impure foreigners plotting for
their own good, their own gain, for themselves and not for
the land of love. Who was it? Who were these people?
Where did they come from, what valley of hate, what region
of despair? What were their motives and how deep their
greed?

It was easy to find an enemy, and simple to cast guilt.
Who was the eternal enemy? For who were the strangers,
the aliens, the foreigners, identifiable, separate, who had
taken the pure heart of Germany, spoilt and ruined, defiled
and corrupted, drunk the holy rivers and eaten the land?

It was the Jews, their unleavened bread enriched by the
blood of gentile babies. It was the Jews, their ritual killing,
their hooked noses, their greasy skin, their corrupt
language, their different god, their dietary laws, their
skullcaps, their synagogues, their black-eyed women, their
black-hearted men, always together, a united force against
the simple, honest, unsuspecting Germans. They had sold

the Fatherland, they had enslaved, they had lent, they had bought out bankrupt factories, they had repossessed the mortgaged lands, employing the former factory owners, landlords and farmers, as tenants and menials, forever enslaved, their rotting coffers swelling with gold, gold falsely earned from the labour of Germans. These foreigners fattened themselves, lazing, gibbering, while good Germans sweated in German workplaces.

The International Conspiracy of the Elders of Zion became the focus for the discontent, bankrupt jealous Germans, blameless now, failure projected for ever on the Jews. The Jews, why not the Jews? Christ's killers. The centuries' enemies, the millennias' plague. The Jews, their ghettos and their shtetls, their rabbis and their cheders, their mikvas and their phylacteries, curse them, curse their prayer shawls and their mezuzahs, their sacrificial lambs and their Red Sea.

The Holy Ones. The Chosen Ones. Germany would show them, Germany would have revenge. Sweet revenge for the usurer's commission, sweet revenge for the selling of our land. The strangers in our heartland, let them pay for once, let the Juden pay back what the Juden have taken. *Juden raus, Juden raus.* Jews and Communists, taken from us our inheritance, our right, our life, our light. Stand aside, Shylock, stand out of our sun, your beards are blocking out our good German light. We own the sunlight, get out, foul blight.

This conspiracy theory appealed most mightily to the muddled masses of embittered Germans. It was predictable, for all Europeans hated the Jews, were jealous of this race, suspicious of their separateness. Through all known time, the Jews, quite rightly, had been persecuted, persecuted for their original crime, and the Germans loved this current confirmation of their age-old hatred. This distillate of distrust did well, focusing the populace away from the realities of Germany's division and fall. Jewish shops were shattered, Jewish babies thrown from high windows, Jews kicked out of their jobs, Jew professionals forbidden to practise. And for every Jew that fell, a German took their place, felt the comfort of their leather and silks, their diamonds and furs. A most satisfying justice.

For a time we were in control of Hitler, and the conspiracy of the Church, industry, army and politicians to carry Germany away from the bitter threat of Communism succeeded. Every German took satisfaction in his inherent Aryan superiority. The porter was better than the professor, the dustman was superior to the storekeeper, and the fishwife was nobler than the philosopher. And how good it felt, to be tall and strong and brave and pure, even if you were small and feeble, emasculated and corrupt. In the streets of Germany the Aryans were kings. Pride took the country and consumed its enemies, vanquished Communism and made the mighty mightier.

The battle against the Jews proceeded slowly and quietly so as not to alarm the priggish international community. The Jews were excluded from the law and civil service, from citizenship and intermarriage, from medicine and the universities, and the work camps were opened.

How grateful were the industrialists. These work camps, such simplicity, such cleverness, fruit of the machinations of the Jesuit generals. A marvellous creation, supplying German industry with an enormous labour force, unpaid and skilled, and once again German goods were cheap to manufacture, and German industry set to rule the world.

How grateful were the bankers, for the unfathomable millions left in bulging deposit accounts, unclaimed, confiscated, taken, swelling the profits of these true Aryans. How grateful were the generals, with their regiments of believers, eager to defend Germany's precious borders and provide security for their brethren in the sub-human Slavonic lands. The Church encouraged Hitler, encouraged stability in middle Europe, and Hitler formed a massive bulwark against the acid tide of Russian Communism.

Buscheim and I contemplated all this in the gardens of the Vatican, and amidst the heavy scent of summer flowers we watched the play of the silver fountains on the ponds, water splattering the dark green pads of the water lilies. Sunlight twisted through the fine spray and for a moment, a rainbow shone out. A flicker of breeze rolled over the high stone walls of the hidden courtyard, and we two men sat and reflected on Germany the good, and the worrying.

Hitler needed to be controlled, his madness sedated and directed. He was doing well, but his unpredictability could take the world into chaos again. I clasped the golden pectoral at my chest, touched with tender fingertips the sharp edges of diamonds, the roughness of pearls, the smoothness of ivory, the slip of silver gilt. Buscheim smoothed crimson cloth over his knees and sniffed the air, his nostrils flickering, eyes seeking among the plants for spies. I gestured to the slave. He altered the direction of the electric fan, and a better breeze cooled us, filled our sleeves, gave us ease.

It was time for our afternoon audience with the Pope, and, preceded by our bodyguard, we moved from chamber to ornate chamber, through ormolu and silk rooms hung with fabulous medieval tempera and furnished with voluptuous furniture, rococo, byzantine, the palace of the popes, where the hoarded centuries languished. The procession of chambers fed into each other, doorway led to room led to doorway. There were no discretionary corridors, skirting the outside of audience rooms and dining rooms. If you wished to go somewhere, it had to be through everywhere. As we walked, each successive chamber became more magnificent, more opulent, the paintings brighter, more elaborate, the furniture richer, more ornate, the hangings and plasterwork more detailed. Each room was larger, its scale more panoramic, and then a colonnade of onyx pillars took us through a curving walkway into a vast room, an anteroom, lined on its four walls by a hundred Swiss Guards, shoulder to shoulder, machine-gun wallpaper. They stared out at us as we crossed the darkest blue lapis-lazuli floor to a boule desk where the Pope's third secretary sat scowling. He leant over an old-fashioned quill, seeming to work at a roll of crackling parchment.

We stood before him and our guards clicked to attention, their staffs thumping down on the stone. The machine-guns of the Swiss Guards had followed us through the ante-chamber and were now held still, trained on us. Two hundred Swiss eyes watched, and the man in the purple robes and skullcap sitting at the boule desk flourished his white quill and ignored us. I looked down at the parchment, an ancient Book of Hours, and in its margins the Pope's third secretary was drawing motor cars and airplanes in black ink that dribbled over thirteenth-century script, Christ's agony modernized. This was Cardinal Neuburger, unpleasant Keeper of Power, Gateman to the Pope, Controller of Audiences. Buscheim hated him. We all hated him, but we smiled at the German and waited while he doodled.

After five years at the Vatican, the Swiss Guards no longer made me nervous. They were controlled and steady, always on our side, alert for spies and traitors. Their guns protected us, kept our interest, guarded and watched over us, always ready for assassins. The million bullets, in the stocks of these hundred machine-guns were good bullets, bullets on the side of the Vatican.

Neuburger. So insolent. But there was nothing that we could do, we had to wait our turn, wait until he was ready, his power was great, and our need for regular audience paramount. Of course there was always poison, but the next third secretary might be worse. Better the known. We knew his ways, his weaknesses, the most delicate of his temptations, and so we pandered to whimsy and waited without comment until he was ready to deal with us. We looked down at his embroidered skullcap, the neat blond hair, the rimless glasses, the good strong nose, the billowing purple, and we waited, waited while he drew Messerschmitts and open-topped Mercedes limousines, scratching over the heavy black Latin script, shading in wingtips and wheel hubs over the yellows, golds and blues of the heavenly manuscript.

I felt Buscheim's anger, felt it rise and prick, and was immensely amused. Neuburger was achieving his aim, the emphasis of his importance. Buscheim should try and control himself. Always so quick with his flashing anger, he'd have apoplexy one day. It would be at a moment like this, and his writhing fall would be the ultimate tribute to Neuburger's power, the power of the third secretary to keep us waiting. Then suddenly Neuburger looked up from his script at the Captain of the Guard, and, without a word to us, without a glance at our faces, he pointed his little finger at us, then at grand doors framed in pilasters of malachite.

The Captain of the Guard pulled both doors open and Buscheim and I walked through the malachite frame and fell to our hands and knees, eyes fixed on the ground.

The doors closed behind us. Two inches from my nose a shiny black ant walked across the silk carpet, then marched across the hills and valleys of my knuckles, its tiny feet tickling my skin.

'RRRRRrrrrrrrr,' the tremendous roar of a lion seared the room and was answered by the 'Roooooooooo' of a trumpeting bull elephant. The hot smell of dung and urine trickled through the room. We remained on our hands and knees, and the soft scuff of footsteps came closer and closer. My view of the carpet was interrupted by a white ballet pump that squashed the ant. The ballet pump led to a white silk stocking that compressed the faint blue bulge of varicose veins trailing over the arch and ankle of its owner's foot. Slowly, slowly the pump lifted itself from the carpet, moved closer to my chin, made contact and pulled my head up, stretching my neck, tightening the ripple line of muscle that fell from chin to clavicles. The tension eased and the white pump danced in front of my lips, wriggling, teasing, waiting, then stopped. I pushed forward from my haunches, my hips and shoulder joints an axis for my heavy body. My lips touched the ballet pump. I sucked at the coarse silk, and I was bade rise by the high-pitched whistling voice of Pius XI. Buscheim too kissed the holy foot and staggering to our feet we genuflected seven times, then stood stock still, our hands clasped in prayer, averting our humble eyes from the lewd strabismus of our Lord Pope. Pius slowly pirouetted in front of us and, with a unique plomping plié, flounced around, arms twisting and turning, a belly dancer for his crimson cardinals. We clapped politely and Pius curtsied.

'My dears, do you like my new robes?' He pursed his lips and turned half-profile, left hand on hip, right arm a fencer's thrust. Pius was wearing high-collared white satin, pinched at the waist, flaring wide at mid-calf. He turned to show us neat pleats topped by two golden buttons, and while he turned I looked around. Two dozen Swiss Guards, their backs to us, faced out, guarding the edges of the room. Fourteen bare-chested Nubians dressed in turquoise chiffon harem pants and carrying peacock feathers were arranged around three sides of an enormous bath filled with bubbling mud.

'You look beautiful, your majesty,' said Buscheim gravely and the Pope smirked; he knew he looked good. Buscheim and I paid fervently loyal attention to the Pope. Audiences were formally structured, and the Vatican's conversational code dictated that we spoke only when questioned, and always, always, gave the Pope our entire and respectful attention. Despite these strict restraints, I couldn't help but be diverted from the Pope's new outfit by repeated roars from the far corner of the room. There in a golden cage paced a lion, prowling around the ripped carcass of a small deer. The lion shook its mane and curling back its upper lip roared and slashed at the deer's neck. Pius liked this.

'He's so savage, don't you think, my dears, so strong. Doesn't his roar make those tiny hairs on your back prickle? He's glorious and so majestic.'

The Pope danced away and zipped his painted nails across the bars of the cage. The lion, bloody meat caught in his teeth, growled and shook his head at the Lord of all Catholics. The Pope stepped back. The lion sank down to the floor of the cage, elegant forepaws over the deer's dead body, pulling at the beast's ribcage, tearing away delicate strips of flesh, flickering tongue licking at the pools of blood that gathered in the abdominal and thoracic cavities. The Swiss Guards remained at attention, implacable, unhearing, all hearing, unseeing, all seeing, on guard, watching the walls. The Nubian slaves glistened, the colour of their skin exactly matching the bubbling mud of the Pope's bath.

'Buscheim, do come here.' And lapdog Buscheim scurried across the rich carpets to the Pope's side. The Pope took his hand. 'Let me show you the cages, Buscheim my dear,' and the Pope patrolled the floor, Buscheim trailing behind. He stopped in front of the elephant's cage. 'This, Buscheim, is an African elephant, larger than the Indian. A bull, beautiful isn't he?' The whiskery eyes of the rubber-skinned elephant flickered at the Pope and his cardinal and his trunk slithered out through the bars of the cage, snuffling, checking, interested in the men who kept their careful distance from him.

'His name is Solomon, Buscheim, a gift from that poison dwarf Haile. Can he flatter me with gifts? Will he enlist my help? Of course not. He will not have our aid. Ethiopia is rightfully Italy's, and in October, Ras Tafari will fall. I have told the Duce to take him. Come, Buscheim, let me show you another creature.' I watched the Pope lead Buscheim, hand dragging reluctant hand, to another cage. The door of this cage was open, and its creature, a pile of gold ingots, was piled into a neat pyramid. The elephant's trunk snaked through the cage's bars wriggling towards Pius and the lion chewed meat.

'Gold, Buscheim. You like gold, don't you?' Buscheim was silent, impassive. 'Go on, Buscheim, take a look.' Pius let Buscheim's hand go and the cardinal stood alone and trembled. 'No, Buscheim, take a proper look. No, not from the outside. Step in, pick it up, feel it. Taste it. Go on, why don't you touch it?' Buscheim walked into the cage, lifting his robe to step over the bars. He turned to me, his eyes, his eyes took me, accused, but I was guiltless, blame free, innocent, innocent, Buscheim, can you hear me? It was not I who betrayed you.

'Pick up an ingot, Buscheim.' The Pope's voice screeched and sawed, a rusty hacksaw in the cages of night. Buscheim did as he was bid, stooping to pick up a gold bar, and the Pope skipped forward and slammed the cage door closed. He turned the key then walked towards me.

'Spies, my dear, spies everywhere. Be careful.'

Buscheim screamed.

'Shut up!' the Pope screeched. 'Quiet.' And there was quiet, quiet broken by the snuffling of the lion and the slip of the elephant's feet. Buscheim squatted in the corner of his cage, rubbing his eyes, dabbing at his cheeks with the sleeve of his robe, and bent so the pyramid of gold dwarfed him, overwhelmed him and with its bulky mass made him a child, a child in red skirts, in a wicked corner.

'Pororepoo,' the elephant trumpeted, and folded green shoots into his mouth. The Swiss Guards stood watching the walls. The Nubians flicked their peacock feathers over the bubbling mud of Pius's bath, and with each slice of feathers through the air their chiffon pants rippled and shivered. The Pope scrutinized me, took in my pores and hairs, wrinkles and folds, looked me up, looked me down, judging, confirming, checking. He stepped back two paces, and crooked his forefinger over the hill of his chin. He made up his mind.

'My dear. It's bathtime.' He gambolled over the carpets, skipped and danced, a cumbersome parody of a floating ballerina, then twisting around he slipped his left and right shoulders up and out of his white robe, stepping out of the creased pile with a delicate flick of his green-blue feet. The naked Pope turned from me and dipped his left leg into the bathwater, testing the temperature of the bubbling mire.

'Just right, my dear, just right.' Deeper, deeper into the bathtub, until his chest then shoulders were submerged, and his chin breasted the surface. The peacock feathers swooped low over the mud bath and the elephant's trumpet was echoed by the lion's competitive roar. Buscheim snivelled, and the Pope was just fine. He waved at me.

'John, my dear, won't you join me.'

I took off my clothes, neat pile of crimson, company for the scattered white. Down the marble steps and the sticky mud crept up my calves, wriggled around my genitals, over my belly and chest and formed a neat line at my nipples, a line that clung and oozed, rolling over my skin. The mud felt slippery, oily, restricting movement with its heaviness. My legs floated up, and I bobbed to the surface, on my back, floating high in mud. Black ooze covered me, caught in my hair, filled my ears with bubbles, made a monster of my penis and cannibals of my toes. The Pope stared at me, enjoying my body and its slimy new clothes. He kept his distance, kept to the opposite corner of the bath, arms resting on its edges, holding himself high above the molten mud. Sweat bubbled on my forehead, coalesced, and ran into my eyes. I rubbed my face, leaving a trace of mud on my skin. I licked my lips, and they tasted sweet, they tasted of chocolate. Chocolate? I licked again. It was chocolate. The Pope, revealed every few moments between the lustrous arcs of sweeping peacock feathers, was smiling. Amused at my bewilderment, he pushed aside the iridescent feathers and waded towards me, hands trailing behind him in the 'mud'.

'There, dear Cardinal, you're confused. Can't establish which sense you should believe. Your eyes say mud and your tongue says chocolate. Here.' He poked his finger at me, black, dripping. 'Open wide, there's a good boy.' I opened my mouth and the black finger wriggled its worm way in, pushed in and out, tickled the roof of my mouth, then scraped down, layering blackness over my shivering teeth. I shut my mouth. It was chocolate, we were lying in a bath of bubbling chocolate. The Pope giggled.

'It's fun, my dear, fun. Took some work to get it right. The science boys, you know. They helped. They were useful. Just the right mix of butter and sugar and cocoa powder, Cardinal dear. Now, if this boiling brew was ordinary chocolate we would be boiled alive. Pope stew and cardinal consommé. Think of it. Dreadful. Those science boys. It took a while but they came up trumps. Got the mixture just right: low enough melting point so that it's warm enough to relax in, and not so hot that more than chocolate would melt in it. Delicious confusion, delicious, don't you agree?'

I did my best to look confused but not too delicious, floating on my back, surrounded by a vista of drifting layers of feathers, the stocky columns of Nubian legs, the distant unseeing, all-knowing backs of the Swiss Guards, and the three golden cages. The Pope continued.

'This is my Titian room, my dear, so suitable for a bathroom, Titians, so much to rest one's eyes on, feasts and saints, ornate architecture, glorious colours, crowds, idiots, animals and so on. So much to see and so much to do with what one sees.'

I hadn't appreciated all of the room's contents. The paintings reached forward from out of the darkness of the walls, and in their silence judged the two men floating on their backs in the chocolate bath. The Pope's attention span seemed short, he wandered from subject to subject, then drifted back, Knight's move conversation on an empty chess board, where he was the only Queen. He looked over at

Buscheim who was sucking at a gold bar and staring at the pacing lion. The Pope's gabble ceased, he shook his head and sighed.

'Silly Buscheim, so silly to be disloyal.' He turned to me. 'But you're not disloyal are you, Horsmunden, Horsmunden dear?'

'Your holiness, I am yours, body and soul.'

'Yes, we know, little one, body and soul, you're ours. Body and soul. You're loyal, we know you're loyal, you've given us everything. Always obedient, ever trusted.'

The Pope looked at Buscheim, who had started sobbing again.

'Tut tut tut.' He turned to me, his body floating around, so that I had a view through his feet of his disembodied head, trunk and limbs, lost in black bubbling chocolate. 'Can you hear him? I'm losing patience with the traitor.' And the Pope drifted around, floating away under the swirling peacock feathers. He pushed his feet into the side of the bath and floated back towards me.

'But you're loyal, aren't you, Cardinal? You've been tested and found to be our friend. A friend of the Church, a friend of this Pope.' Pius slapped his hand down hard on the chocolate's surface, splattering a sweet spray over Nubian legs, emphasizing my dependability with a chocolate retort.

'Yes, your holiness.'

Pius floated closer and continued his theme. 'We know you're safe, little Cardinal dear, we know you're safe.' He paddled away again, and I hung on to the soft edge of the marble bath and waited for the conclusion of his rambling, and it came, how it came. Pius floated back, dribbling chocolate falling in fat globules from the stiffened rat tails on the nape of his neck. 'The guards are loyal too.' The

Pope leered at the guards' pantaloons. 'Of course they have to be. We've got our money in Switzerland, their bankers guard our money and their soldiers guard us. Nice arrangement. Quite fair. They know what would happen if the guards were untrue. We'd take our money back. Put it in New York or London. They'd be very sorry if we did that. That nice country would fall, no more watches, no more ski slopes, no cheese. Nothing. Bankrupt. So we're safe with these men. They're dependable, utterly dependable. So comforting, so nice. They do as they're told, all day long, every day. So Swiss, don't you think, Cardinal?' I nodded. 'And you're dependable too. Do what you're told, don't you?'

'Yes, your holiness.'

'See if you can guess, Cardinal dear, how we know that you're not a traitor? By the way, dear, you do have nice toes.'

'Thank you, your holiness.' The Pope sucked chocolate from my toes, hanging on to my calves to stop himself drifting away in the chocolate quagmire. Pius waited for my answer.

'Because I'm loyal?'

'No, dear, quite wrong, quite a silly guess actually. Would you like me to tell you? No I won't. Guess again. Go on, try me, try me.'

'Because everything I am comes from the Church and without the Church I am nothing and have nothing.'

'Yes, that's true, but as is so often the case, part truth. Now, I'm going to tell you, Cardinal.'

Pius squeezed my calves tight and pulled himself upright, a monster emerging from the rippling morass, great streams of chocolate falling from his shoulders. He looked at me, took me with his eyes, so pale, so blue, seized me and waited, judging me by the impact of his words.

'Luke, you remember Luke?' Luke. It had been five years and extraordinarily I hadn't once recalled his name. I nodded at Pius. 'You had him killed, didn't you?' His voice hung low, and softly drew me in.

'On Buscheim's instructions, your holiness. Luke was a traitor.' My words were interrupted by a whine from Buscheim. The Pope shook his head, annoyed at the disturbance. He clamped tight on my knees, pulling himself towards me.

'Cardinal, you killed him. He was an innocent. He was yours and you killed him. That's how we knew that you, Cardinal, were ours.'

And I understood. Oh, my heart, my heart. I had killed him. Luke, my own image, slaughtered. They had tested me and I had passed and lost. The Pope's weight was on my thighs pressing me down. Pius was staring at me but I showed no emotion. I was in control again. How could this be? Had I no feeling? I had killed my creation and yet I felt nothing. And the Pope knew. He recognized the emptiness, and his weight left me, he released me, let me go. He had seen that I was his and could never be free. Wherever I would go, whatever I would be, I would be his, the Church's creature. Buscheim waited.

'Johannes.' Pius trilled at the wall of Swiss Guards. A massive soldier spun round and crunched to attention. His machine-gun hung low at his hip. He was ready.

'Johannes, my captain. See to Buscheim, would you.' Johannes saluted and marched to Buscheim's cage, marched past the parade of soldiers, who stood to attention facing the walls. The Pope continued. 'Of course the guards are all Swiss-German. They're more reliable, less emotional than the Swiss-French. Quite dour in fact. No humour, no imagination. They do their job, serve their time, think of their pay and their little Swiss-Deutsch wives back home in the cantons. That's good. That's just what we want. Service. And we have no trouble with the servants nowadays.'

Meanwhile the Captain of the Guard had marched to Buscheim's cage. The Pope stopped talking, stopped to watch. Buscheim had collapsed on the floor of his cage, crumpled crimson next to an upright mountain of gold. Buscheim was curled up in a foetal ball. His spectacles hung from one ear, he was sucking his thumb and the ingot in his hand was pressed into his face. The captain pushed against the cage, his machine-gun scrabbling against the bars. He pushed, and Buscheim's prison scuffed across exquisite carpets, past the curious elephant, who saluted the cardinal with his rearing trunk, and rolled towards the lion's den. The lion looked up at the approaching cage, trundling across the room. The guard's back and legs formed a straining arch and his gun hung loose, falling down from his belt like an enormous evil penis.

Buscheim started mumbling, and his incoherent rambling broke out over the noise of the rattling wheels. The Pope relaxed against the side of the bath, watching the spectacle. His face was expressionless, his eyes unblinking. The rumbling cage wheeled closer to the lion, who looked up from over the deer's carcass at the approaching pyramid, sniffing out the man who lay behind the gold. What was Buscheim saying? It was Latin. I couldn't make out his meaning, his voice rose and fell, drowned by the noise of his rattling prison, the clank of the machine-gun against the bars of his cage and the sympathetic trumpeting of the African elephant.

Captain Johannes pushed the cage across the floor, closer and closer to the curious lion. The cages crashed together. His majesty rose, and stood stiff and suspicious,

231

one front paw resting on the blood-streaked carcass. Buscheim's mumbling continued, and then became coherent, a tumbling litany of names, lists and lists. French names, German names, Italian names, names that coursed from country to country, through Europe to Russia, from the low countries to the Balkans, the North Sea to the Mediterranean, an unending list, then a name that wasn't a name, two words: mea culpa. This list was his guilt, a blood roll, a view of his life's deaths.

The Swiss Guard lined up the cages, edging them closer, pushing, pulling. The two prisons clicked into place, door against door, bar against bar and Johannes locked them together, pressing giant clamps around the adjacent corners of the cages. The lion's tail veered upwards, and his nose pointed forward towards Buscheim. Johannes crouched down and pulled at two long bars set in the floor of the cages. He pulled them towards him, and the two cage doors cranked back, making a single room for the prisoners. Buscheim's list continued, his voice plangent, low, calm, a catharsis, the Church's executioner, telling us, telling someone else.

The bubbling chocolate popped. We stared at the cages, and the Nubians waved their peacock feathers over the quagmire. Sweat dribbled down my cheeks. The Captain of the Guard turned to salute Pius, then marched back across the room to assume his post. The lion's tail flicked at imaginary flies, whipping his back and buttocks. His head low, shoulders forward, he stalked through the entrance of his cage, then stopped to peek around the edge of the golden pyramid at the crimson rag doll.

Buscheim was on the floor of the cage, clutching his ingot, seemingly oblivious of the curious lion. And now the names were English, and there were many, and one was Luke. The lion backed away, then crept around to sniff at

Buscheim from the other side of the pyramid. He crouched then sprang. He leapt at Buscheim in a furious flurry of fur, then cuffed him, cuffed his head with a heavy forepaw, and I heard the click of Buscheim's breaking spine. The lion sank his jaws into Buscheim's neck, tearing out his larynx, and the Pope raised his hands to his own throat. Buscheim's carotids squirted, bright red, pulsing, pumping. The lion shook his head and Buscheim's body bumped the bars, thrashing against the golden pyramid. The lion worried his prey. He pushed the body against the cage, tearing at his robes, ripped back cloth, then ripped out a chunk of Buscheim's abdomen, and his coiled gut spilled out, white greasy loops tipping out over the golden ingots. And then the animal had had enough, and rippled back into his own cage, elegant, padding, prowling, stepping back to a more refined meal, preferring deer to cardinal. Pius broke the silence.

'Well, that's rid of him.' It certainly was. Buscheim was a dead pile on his prison's bloody floor. Pius swam a languorous, flipping backstroke to the far side of the bath, waves of rippling chocolate streaming away from his body. He pulled himself half out of the bath and shook a silver bell, its shivering tinkling a strange accompaniment to death and the animals. Many yards away, over a vista of marble and carpets, past the lushness of silks and paintings, the double doors opened to a silver fairy in a white tutu and rhinestone tiara. How she sparkled as she danced towards us, sprinkling shimering sunlight with the wave of her wand. She carried a bulging black case, and foil wings were clipped to her back. She came towards us and curtsied. The line of Nubians broke rank to let her through to the bath side.

'Your holiness.' Her voice was high and shining. She curtsied again.

'Tinker Bell, my dear, you've come. How nice to see you.'

'Thank you, your holiness. You'd like your usual, would you, your holiness?'

'Yes, Tinker Bell dear.' And the Pope placed his hands on the edge of the bath, dripping black on the snow-white Carrara marble, pools of chocolate solidifying in tarry drops and rivulets. Tinker Bell took up the Pope's hands and, pulling towels from her bag, cleaned them of smeary chocolate. She took a nail file from a leather case and rubbed delicately at each of the Pope's claws, the action of the nail file the soaring bow of the musician's fiddle. She replaced the nail file and proceeded to buff the Pope's nails with a soft chamois pad.

'A light varnish, your holiness?'

'I think so.'

'Clear or coloured?'

'What do you think suits me best?'

'Oh, I do think a nice pink does you.'

'Pink it is then.'

'Goodie.' And she painted Pius's nails, taking care to trace out the moons of his cuticles.

'That's you done, your holiness. Would you like a hand out of the pool?'

'Thank you, Tinker Bell.'

Leaning down she heaved Pius from the water, drew him out, his hand gripping her white evening gloves, besmirching, befouling, making grubby the pure. He stood on the bathside, this chocolate ogre, and great pools of chocolate mud gathered around his feet, formed from the bilious black lava that streamed from his body. Tinker Bell peered down at me.

'And would your excellency like to be done too?' Fluttering her thick eyelashes, she giggled and took my hand. I chose clear varnish.

234

Chapter Eleven

I HAD Buscheim's job. Mine were the telephones and mine the wires, mine were the informers and mine the messengers. Our information came from the whole world running in electric rivers, along spider's web streams into the Vatican. From the periphery to the epicentre, core of knowledge, hub of hubris, came the storm that was Europe, the screams and the terror of echoing desperate days. By 1938, our systems and our power were dangerously threatened by change. The conspiracy of Masons and military, Church and industry was just holding on, moulding the breath of Europe. Wild was the wind and unsteady the earth, ferocious the fires and poisoned the water. Europe; the steam of our times. We held on making deals, affirming stability, quieting the wind, cementing the stones, quenching the fires, filtering the waters, patching, putting back together, regrouping, ordering, making firm, strengthening the strong, sacrificing the weak.

My office held an extraordinary concentration of technology. It was a command station, with the most modern filing systems, switchboards, monitors, maps, telephones and secretaries, secretaries in cassocks and habits, organizing, busy, rushing. My office was built into the strong walls of the Vatican, an information centre, marshalling and manipulating the world, with our friends the generals, our friends the landowners, our friends the dictators, our friends the grand Masons.

We were everywhere and in everything, linking, organizing, involving, dealing, giving, and always taking. And we did this for our own preservation. Making the system safer made us safer, maintained our status, kept us in our castles and fortresses. And into the room's filing systems, switchboards, monitors, maps and telephones poured the world's sighs and whispers, the stories passed from politician to Mason, from Mason to monk, from the monasteries and seminaries, to the Vatican, to me. I was the voice and ears of a universal briefing system, the master of information, gatherer of knowledge, disseminator of instruction, deceit and guile. Through our agents in every land our power spread, marking men, destroying, corrupting, through the high and low points of the known world.

What it is to know how it is. The running of the world, the way of things, the secret heart of man, the numbness of reality. The truth. How things worked. And making them work, making them happen, a true internationalism, unimagined by the Communists, a continuity of spirit and soul working for world order, working for the order of the world, subtly changing everything. How well we were doing. How well we had done, so important our command, our work, our role.

An apparent new order had established itself in the thirties, not only in Europe but in Asia. We had benefited considerably from the Keynesian-inspired inflationary policies of Takahashi, the Japanese finance minister, who had spent his country out of depression. Against our best advice, Takahashi then decided that this inflationary process might cause economic disaster. This was an unhelpful attitude. Decreased government spending might control the bursting bubbling Japanese economy, but it certainly would not be good for the agricultural monopolies and the manufacturing oligarchies, for bankers and business. It was an incorrect attitude, inappropriate for modern times, and our friends in the army disposed of this man who was afraid of national debt.

In Spain things had gone particularly well for us. Our colleague Franco, after successfully aborting the irritating workers' strikes of the early 1930s, led the conservative crusade against the elected Popular Front Alliance of Socialism and Communism. He stood firm for law, for order, for the Church and tradition and stood proudly against the wild men, the free-thinkers in Lenin's chains. We helped him, and prompted Mussolini and Hitler to assist Franco militarily.

We had tricky times in France, with that spiteful Jew Blum. The Socialists won the 1936 elections, and then agreed with union leaders, under pressure from striking workers, to the ridiculousness of a forty-hour working week and three weeks' annual paid holiday. How impractical, and this Zionist-Marxist coalition nearly ruined France, almost bankrupted this most civilized nation. Blum was disgraced. The year 1938 was a good one for our power, and our men, Daladier and Reynaud, swept away the Jew's changes.

In South America we had no problems. The power of the Church in the countries of Latin America was absolute and immense. The people were fools, kept to innocent uneducated oblivion, paying their tithes, numbed by disease, poverty and coca leaves. Great swatches of land were owned by a few individuals who were related by family and shared power. The secret police obliterated Communism's murmurs. How well the plutocracy was doing.

India was difficult, but we didn't care. India had nothing

but starvation and poverty, and there was little profit in that land. We let the British policemen keep order and that was enough.

With the Arabs, it had been simple. They needed technology to exploit their oil, and the oil companies had provided this. The Arabs couldn't count beyond ten, and so how were they to know how much oil had been pumped from their lands? The oil had to be transported from Arabia and that required ships. Our friend Onassis had the ships and the monopoly of transport. It was a fine situation, profits made at source, in transportation and then at point of sale. Three chances to make money, and prices set at every stage of the enterprise by one group of colleagues.

In the United States, the profits of Prohibition had made us very strong. Our family in America had done well and the money had come home to the Vatican Bank. These holy men were our loyal men and our investment in America was magnificently rewarded. The Jesuit field commanders, Capone, Costello, Marone, Vicenzo, raised billions of dollars from 1929 to 1933, an enormous tribute to the Church, a unique tithe. These monies were wisely invested, and although the great mass of profit came back to Italy, enough was retained in America to allow the diversification of our troops into business, the law and the unions, when Prohibition was lifted. We had foreseen the repeal of the law of Prohibition, and we had had plenty of time to reinvest.

Our planning of the New Deal nearly went awry in its early stages. Huey Long, the Louisiana state governor, came to know of our plot, came to understand how the resources of the people were being appropriated by the few. This foolish man proposed a massive redistribution of wealth, away from the deep pockets of the mighty. This man wished to take away the just fortunes of the rich, and give their deserved capital to the poor. His ironic comments on the New Deal, 'Shuffling the same old pack,' and 'Dealer gets all', were misplaced, but unfortunately populist. His 'Share Our Wealth' campaign was well supported, and the ridiculous offer to banish all poverty was enormously appealing. The masses loved the idea, they all wished to be Rockefellers, but how could they be? The campaign gathered incredible momentum and Huey Long, supported by the tramps and bums, the tenement dwellers and subsistence farmers, became a champion for the masses. He obviously had to be stopped, he was too threatening for the establishment, a terrible danger, a subverter of order, a knife at our throat. Buscheim stopped him. Had him assassinated by one of Capone's men. It was nicely done and allowed Roosevelt to be easily re-elected in 1936. So, taking stock in 1938, we were very pleased with progress in the New World.

But Germany. This was a difficult matter. We were in control but only just, and we were to discuss the situation tonight. Goebbels had done well but there was so much to contend with.

I sat with Cardinal Agnelli in the Vatican Control Room. A stenographer bowed and delivered a note. He waited for my reply. The letter was from Chamberlain. Chamberlain had taken over from Baldwin following his resignation in 1937. Chamberlain was an excellent administrator and England was in good order. Agnelli sat back in his chair and twirled his glasses while I read the letter.

My Dear Cardinal,

I hope that this letter finds you in good health. Spring has come early to London and the Downing Street garden is showing signs of life. We are a little worried about that Hitler

239

fellow, I'm sure that he is essentially a good-hearted, reliable chap, but he does seem to be kicking up a bit of a stink over in Germany. Frankly, he's causing some concern in military circles. You probably remember Fisher, he's the head of our civil service, very sound, Oxford man. Well, Fisher has become very anxious about Germany's military strength. He's made some quite alarmist statements about the United Kingdom being at the mercy of a foreign power. Can you believe it, Cardinal, England, at the mercy of Germany!

Well, as we discussed, in response to his concern I increased budgetary allocations to our defence forces, organizing the construction of these new-fangled radar stations, and increased production of fighter planes. By the way, you should see them, they are very dainty, hard to believe that they are used to kill people. But back to the point. Certain people in our country feel that these precautions are insufficient. Churchill has publicly stated that Germany is attempting European military domination, and that we are to be included within this plan for dominion. Well, honestly. There is enough to worry about without Churchill making a fuss as well. As you know he is not one of us and can't be trusted to be discreet. Well, Cardinal, my concern is that if we re-arm, Germany will only increase its rearmament programme. The whole thing is a vicious cycle. If we manufacture more aeroplanes and ships, then Germany will manufacture even more aeroplanes and ships. I do feel that it must be possible to find some gentlemanly way out of this insane mess of a situation. We are all grown up, and capable of mature discussion. Surely the way forward is through negotiated reconciliation? I would appreciate your views on the matter.

With kindest regards, yours sincerely, Chamberlain

'Agnelli.' My fellow cardinal put on his glasses. 'Agnelli, Chamberlain is worried.'

'And so am I, Horsmunden, worried that we shall be late for supper.'

Agnelli slapped his thigh, pleased with this Italian attempt at English humour, amused by his twist to a conversation in Latin. I snapped my fingers and the sedan chair was brought to us. Agnelli and I got in, Agnelli drew the curtains and we were hoisted on to the strong shoulders of four guardsmen. We were taken through the corridors of the Vatican, our carriage bobbing from side to side despite the attempts of the guards to hold us steady.

I had never got used to these wretched chairs, their up-and-down motion brought memories of that frightful sea voyage from Southampton to Naples, and its echoes on land were of seasickness. To distract myself from nausea, I concentrated on Agnelli's conversation, which was remarkably flippant for a Jesuit. It seemed that he had dressed in secular clothes and visited La Scala.

'*La Bohème*, there's nothing better. And that Vignallini, so beautiful, she must have the best breasts in Italy and I think she knows it. I tell you, Horsmunden, she knows it, has her costumes tailored to show herself. I saw her left nipple when she took her last curtain call. The applause was completely deafening and I'm sure it was for her breasts as much as for Verdi. It was a glorious evening. I returned home, how do you say in English, completely titillated.'

Agnelli laughed, he did like his own jokes. He was very tall and fitted uncomfortably in the sedan chair, head craned forward, legs bent. His complexion was soft and flushed, his cheeks blown, slipping around the rock of his chin, his hair immaculately coiffed, parted on the right, a rose tint to the immaculate grey, quite the suburban housewife. I did like Agnelli.

Arm in arm, magnificent in our robes, made tall by our pointed hats, we walked into our dining rooms, and the guards at the door saluted our arrival with the bellow of their golden trumpets. We were a little late and our colleagues were already at table. The Pope waved a languid hand for us to assume our seats, and bowing our heads to him we glided to our places. We were thirteen at the table, our traditional number, a gathering of the great men of Catholicism, a spreading phalanx around our Pope. Pius stood up, and the noise of our gossip quietened.

'Well, everyone. Haven't you noticed?' We all stared, and no one had. 'Not even you, von Rumbold?' Von Rumbold shook his ancient head. 'Zut, well I'll show you properly, my dears.' Pius clambered on to the table, and walked its length stamping on cutlery, cracking plates, knocking over candles, squashing fruit, spilling salt. He passed us all in turn, the hem of his robes glancing our faces, the detritus of his passage tipping into our laps.

'Nor even you, Zbrinski?' Pius pointed at the gormless Pole. 'You're all senile, poor dears. My new dress, don't you love my new dress?'

Pius gave us a twirl and the white silk spun up and flapped around his podgy knees. Agnelli started to clap and taking our cue from the sensible Italian, we all joined in the applause.

'Very nice, excellency.'

'Nice. Is that all you can say, Agnelli? It's beautiful, it's Schiaparelli.'

'I thought so,' said Agnelli. 'That diva, Vignallini, you remember her, holiness, she's at La Scala this season, she wore a similar outfit to take her curtain call. Of course she didn't look as elegant as you. She's blown, coarsened, not as refined as your holiness.'

The Pope looked suspiciously at Agnelli; was he mocking him? If he was ... Pius ground his golden sandal into
broken crockery, then kicked daintily at a massive silver
candelabrum, which crashed over on to the table. Small
fires kicked up from the tablecloth and the Pope flounced
back across the ruins to his place at the head of the table.
No one dared damp down the flames, spurting and flickering among the broken china and squashed fruit. Water from
a fallen bowl of orchids tumbled on to my robes, dampened
my knees and trickled down my calves. The Pope glowered
and fretted, looking away from us all, his sulking, sickle-
moon profile pouting, furious.

It was Agnelli's fault. The cardinals shifted uncomfortably in their seats and the blaze of the candles became
confluent, alarming. It was up to Agnelli to do something.
The problem was his. Agnelli's attitude was that of a
schoolboy who knew that he had been naughty but was
damned if he would admit guilt. He looked up at us, smiling
benign innocence, as if absolutely nothing had happened.
He twiddled his thumbs and looked around the room,
winking at his colleagues. I caught his attention, and raising
my eyebrows I turned my face towards the Pope and
nodded at Agnelli as if to say, well, you know what to do.
The Pope sniffed loudly, blew his nose between his finger
and thumb, then wiped his fingers on the tablecloth. Tears
glistened on Pius's cheeks. He sniffed again and the bonfire
blossomed on the far end of the table. Agnelli coughed, and
spoke.

'Your holiness, where did Schiaparelli obtain the silk for
your robes? It's really most unusual.' The Pope dabbed at
his salty cheeks and turned full face. 'Most unusual. Is it
Chinese?'

'Yes.'

'I thought so, it has that absolutely characteristic sheen, you know, that exquisite shimmer that very good silk has. Wonderful stuff, quite marvellous.'

'Nice of you to say so, Agnelli.'

The Pope had perked up, and we could relax again. Von Rumbold shouted, 'Service,' and the dining-room doors pushed open to an army of pygmies in loincloths, carrying folded napkins over their arms. They marched into the room and stamped out the fire. They cleared the table, grabbing the tablecloth at its ends, removing the mess en bloc. They filed from the room, bearing the bundled tablecloth between them. The linen sagged in the middle, loaded with the table's detritus, and tiny black hands formed fists at its white edges, jungle men with their trussed prey.

The table was reset, the tazza dainty in its centre, a Renaissance masterpiece of silver fountains and cherubs. Our places were laid and the conversation restarted. The Pope was in good humour again, amusing himself by surreptitiously rolling bread pellets, which he flicked at ancient von Rumbold. Thirteen of us were at table, myself, Agnelli, von Rumbold, corpulent du Plessis, Van Eyck the Dutch Eagle, Van der Moer the Belgian, zu Hohenzollern the Austrian, Corruna la Playa the talented Spaniard, Costanza, shadow-eyed creeping ghoul, representing Brazil, Zbrinski the Pole, Enrico Costa from Sicily, Antonio Caetano the Portuguese, the Pope's cardinals.

The doors opened to three blonde women in Roman togas. They were chained to each other, linked by their ankles they limped into the room dragging each other clumsily along. The first bore a gilt jug and she filled our golden flagons. The women shuffled from the room and the doors closed. Agnelli raised his cup.

'To the Pope, blessed Pius, may he live for ever.'

'Amen,' we echoed, raised our glasses to Pius and chanted, 'The Pope. May he live for ever.'

The Pope's humour further improved and he graced us all with his flickering smile. We drank and the iron of blood filled my mouth. We were drinking Dr Issells's elixir, a concentrate of foetal lamb's serum, sterilized and processed, guaranteed to prolong life and maintain body vigour. My gullet burnt as the elixir tipped down my throat; there was alcohol in the medicine which made it most pleasant, and it had some aphrodisiac quality. The elixir had a narrow range of distribution and apparently was most difficult to manufacture in any quantity. I didn't like Issells, a suspicious ferret of a man, but he had science on his side, and definite results.

We settled back in our chairs, awaiting our meal. It was not right that we should wait, and most unusual that there was any delay to our dinner. We became querulous if kept waiting for food, and on one famous occasion six years ago the Pope had stormed into the Vatican kitchens and shot two sous-chefs, one in the right foot and the other in his buttocks. Service subsequently improved. Von Rumbold smashed his flagon on the table top and belched. Zu Hohenzollern dabbed at the corners of his mouth with a table napkin and the cardinals waited. The dinner had better be worth the delay, otherwise there would be a ruckus. I could feel the cardinals' irritation. The Pope inspected his fingernails and yawned. There was silence, and then fortunately the pygmies entered, carrying our first course. Each pygmy carried a single plate. They grouped before us, then bowed. They were terribly ugly, but for some reason Pius found them amusing. They'd been bought from our Belgian friends who had found them interfering with their business in the copper mines of Central Africa.

245

Apparently the pygmies had tried to frighten away the miners, scared them with totems and magic, hoping to ban them from their ancestral lands. Their magic had no effect and so the pygmies had become more active in their campaign, creeping into the miners' hostels during the night, firing their silent poison darts and killing many hundred of the Belgians' employees. To rid Africa of this ridiculousness, the Belgians had executed an elaborate and costly jungle campaign, marching through the pygmies' equatorial kingdom in a complicated encircling movement that had trapped them in their leafy redoubts. Many of the pygmy women and children had been machine-gunned and a few were taken as curios into captivity, exported to Europe where they could do no harm and could entertain. I was annoyed rather than entertained by their ugliness and oddity, foul size and captivity.

I inspected the hors d'oeuvre. It would do. Roast suckling pig. I jabbed at it and bloody juice dripped on to the bed of calves' brains on which it rested. I sliced through the calves' cerebella, beautifully soft, slightly raw, grey on pink, just as we liked them. The chef had done well.

The pygmies stood behind us, fifteen tiny corporals, attentive, trained, one behind each of the cardinals, and three behind Pius. Wine was poured into crystal glasses. It was good, an 1899 Château Margaux, perfectly cellared, perfectly chambré, perfectly balanced, a beautiful wine. The pygmies watched our glasses, topping them up as we drank, replenishing our glasses with perfection, a distillate of cinnamon and blackberries. As a rule we drank French red wines, and Italian white. Wines from the New World were banned.

Von Rumbold was not using his cutlery. He held the pig in both hands and was munching through flesh, turning the animal as one might an apple. Agnelli had finished his first course. The Pope's food was untouched. The other cardinals ate steadily, fine trenchermen that they were, heads low over their plates, hands cradling their food.

The first course was cleared, and the pygmies returned bearing between them a spit on which hung a huge roast cow, head and legs, body and tail. Behind the pygmies marched a centurion in tunic and armour, the straps of his sandals climbing his shins, short sword in his hand.

'Hail, Caesar,' boomed the centurion and he saluted Pius. 'May you all live for ever, your majesties.' He saluted us all.

The centurion carved beef with his sword, hacked bloody ribs from the beast's back and layered the meat delicately on to our plates held out by the silent pygmies. We ate till we were full, and then we ate again. There was no talk, no conversation. We enjoyed our food, and we loved the wine, a fine Haut-Brion 1872 whose bouquet was of fraises des bois and honeysuckle, nutmeg and almonds. The wine had been well chosen by zu Hohenzollern's aide-de-camp, who was of good family and understood wine's genealogies and regions.

I needed to empty my bladder. It wasn't urgent but it was uncomfortable. I hitched up my robes, pissed into a carafe and then repositioned it on the table. Nobody noticed, for it was unexceptional behaviour.

The pygmies cleared the table. It was time for our planning meeting. They placed full carafes before us and, leaving the room, crossed the paths of six Hawaiian maidens in grass skirts, who were crowned with garlands of tropical flowers and playing tropical blue guitars. They undulated into the room then shuffled away, their retreat surprisingly pleasing, their skirts mown away at the back leaving their loins free to sway in the golden breath of the timid Vatican breeze.

We filled our glasses with brandy, and contemplated business. It was time for me to give an intelligence briefing. This was a tricky business. Presentations had to be short, otherwise drunken, elderly attentions lapsed, and the more senile cardinals slept. Pius was particularly difficult to entertain; his mind tended to wander and we had great problems trying to obtain any sort of decision from him. We were dissatisfied with his leadership, and a cabal of powerful cardinals had started meeting to review his decisions. The time seemed to be coming when we might need to be rid of him. I stood up.

'Excellencies, our power is holding, and through a series of circumspect moves we remain in control in most of Europe. The exception, of course, is Germany. As I have outlined before, Hitler is rearming, we have incontrovertible evidence for this, and his aim is clear to all. He preaches Lebensraum, and Lebensraum he will have aplenty. The allies are weak, unarmed and unready. They preach the idiocy of appeasement.'

Pius yawned, and I hurried through my presentation, confining myself to a skeletal outline of the situation that only Agnelli and I understood in depth. I was not worried about von Rumbold and zu Hohenzollern, their prime loyalty was to the Church, not to Germany and not to Austria. They were in this room as representatives of their countries' churches, useful for their contacts with local power brokers, who had no dominion over them. The Catholic Church was above country and continent, its domain the world, the whole wide world.

My attention was distracted for a moment by van der Moer, the aged sot, whose tremulous hand swung out in a crab's-claw arc and clutched the carafe I'd pissed in. I continued.

'Excellencies, the situation in Europe is likely to lead to war, Hitler will not be content with the Sudetenland, the Nazis will not have enough with Austria. They will be encouraged by the success of acquisition and Anschluss. They will take more. It is unlikely that they will be allowed more, without resistance.' I looked around the table. Pius was snoring, snoring overtly, his head slumped on to the table, cheeks billowing and popping. Eight cardinals were day-dreaming, scratching, picking at themselves, drinking, paying absolutely no attention to my speech. Only von Rumbold, Agnelli and du Plessis were attentive, cast forward, watching, waiting.

'Gentlemen, even if jealous Europe allows Hitler's Germany to continue their expansion, even if the Nazis are allowed to roam free from Brest to Dubrovnik, even if there is no war, we have to come to an understanding with him.'

'What do you mean, Horsmunden?' asked von Rumbold.

'We must negotiate.'

I looked around at the corpses of cardinals, half dead, half drunk, a quarter senile, three-quarters useless, stupid, greedy, hopeless, hopeless, hopeless.

And then Agnelli. 'We must negotiate with him. You're right. We must come to terms, treat with Germany.'

And then von Rumbold. 'We must do this, we must secure him, otherwise he'll notice the Vatican and our gold and take us as he has the Jews.'

And then du Plessis. 'We must talk with him. We need to secure agreements. Secure them so that he cannot, I repeat,' du Plessis chopped at the table and the glassware jumped, 'cannot renege on agreements.'

I sat down. The matter was agreed, sealed by Agnelli,

who leaned into our group, leaned forward into the conspirators and whispered, 'And we, Horsmunden dear, must go
to Berlin and talk with him.' Von Rumbold and du Plessis
nodded. The matter was sealed, our plans were fixed, we
would go to Berlin and settle things with Herr Hitler, fix
Hitler, Agnelli and I.

I finished my brandy, and there was a little small talk
between us, talk of this or that secretary, the quality of the
dinner, the recent opium consignment, the relative dullness
of the nuns, the return on our investments in Switzerland,
the smallness of the pygmies until it was time to retire to
our own rooms, to enjoy the evening in our usual ways.

The Swiss Guards marched in with thirteen sedan chairs
and pectorals, crosses and rosaries jiggling we made our
way through the passages of the Vatican City to our
apartments.

I loved the Renaissance, its colours and scenes, its
furniture, its paintings, its gold and silver, its tapestries, its
discoveries of perspective, its invention, its life, and I had
removed from the distant and close parts of our city citadel
all that I needed to make my chambers everything that I
wished. Beautiful Madonnas graced my walls, Michelan-
gelos, Leonardos, Titians. In golden light, fountains
whistled. Brigades of empty armour, troops in a frozen
frieze, were caught in battle's tumble in my corridors and
halls. Within my apartments I had ordered the building of
a vast birdcage, an architectural assembly of belfries and
ogee domes, an entanglement of gold wire that trapped one
hundred songbirds.

In the depths of these riches, amid peace and beauty, I
sat in my opium den, a dark room hung with silken
watercolours of oriental erotica, priapic, libidinous, salacious. The rosewood opium bench on which I reclined was

a recent acquisition, given by our friends in the Kuomin-
tang. It had been sent with a shipment of green opium,
which I had enjoyed, and was smoking again. I lay back on
the red wood, my head propped on an indented wooden
cube. I liked this room because it was small, a shelter. It
seemed so safe in the quiet light with my women. They had
no names. They came and served me, looked after my needs,
gave me peace. There were three this evening, primitives
from the Ethiopian highlands, more tokens from black
Africa, baubles from Benito, compliments of the season.

The season was summer, and Mussolini was in favour. I
liked the looks of these women, with their high cheekbones,
the smooth curves of their foreheads, the grace of their
walk, their flat bellies. This evening's women had good-
sized breasts. I had recently had to complain to my adjutant
about his dereliction of duty concerning his responsibilities
toward this important aspect of my catholic life. I had
slapped him around a little and the situation had improved.
I liked the degree of menace granted me by rank, this
earthy, redolent power. He knew I could have him flicked
away, my word was life, my words were death. The Swiss
Guards waited, pikestaffs ready, and I had beaten him with
the lion-tamer's whip, banged him up with its ebony handle,
banged him until he bled a little, broke the white skin over
his bony shoulders. He'd fled away from my whip and the
Swiss Guard had prodded him into the centre stage, edged
him back. I understood about the women. He loved boys
and looked for androgynous qualities in the parades of
females that were shown him. He looked for the flat-chested
and the narrow-arsed, the skinny and the lean, but I wanted
flesh, round and formed, comfortable and soft. So, in
annoyance, I beat him, irritated by his stupid choice, and
he scurried away on to the pricking points of pikes, and

came back to my blows. I liked this sort of exercise, and Paul was keener for the beating than punctured death; I saw it in his pleading eyes, as in pain he tried to smile.

From the prosaic to the prosodic. My pipe was being fixed by one of the night's women. She bent over the hubble-bubble, softening the opium between her fingers, crushing it, compressing it, breaking off green-brown crumbs into the shining bowl. I liked the line of her arse and reached to prod her with my cane, running the stick along the falling line of her bent back, then over the curve of her bustle. I pushed at her arse with the cane and she obliged me, pulling aside her buttock with one hand to show me the spread of pink. I pushed at her, attempting to spear her with the ferrule, but missed. I was drunk and my aim was untrue. I lay back and she continued her business. Hot towels were brought in to my opium cave and laid on my face. The steam clamped my skin, orientated me, found me firm, in the waves of alcohol, that took me from here to there and found me swaying on a bandit's bench.

The opium was sparked and the hubble-bubble was brought to me. I inhaled, pulling in the softness and the harshness, cool smoke that clawed my throat in its rush to my lungs. One woman held the pipe, another lent over me, her hands massaging my breasts, and the third Ethiopian lay back on silk pillows and gently played a flute. Her fingers were angels and her music aching fairies in the deep wells of a dripping darkness whose ceiling was the racing clouds. I loved the night and its sweet dreams. My lips were dry, and a sandstorm blew in the desert. Somewhere a sea was lapping on a beach of bliss, where camels leered with turning lips and babies chewed on half-moon melons. Somewhere a child cried and I was that child, I was his tears, I was his pillow. My mother reached for me, pulled me to her sweet breast and I suckled, sucked the sweet milk of a lost inheritance. Bells rang and their chiming filled the summer's meadows, where buttercups and alpine flowers turned for ever to the golden sun. The summer was gone and there was only this room, this room of women and my hubble-bubble.

'Smoke, my child,' but she would have none, shook her head and wiggled her finger in politest denial. Her teeth, such convincing teeth and her smile a lion's grin.

'Come, rub my chest again.' The flat of her hand brushed my nipples and the hairs on my neck prickled up and screamed. I touched her cheek and rubbed my fingertips over the ribs of her lower lip. Her tongue danced with my finger, the lightest waltz, most sensitive rhythm. Her movements slowed and she was clockwork, distorted by opium breath, a cloud behind shadows. From a distant corner the music ached. The whorls and knots of the polished rosewood bench were angels chasing devils and the devils were in me, and the angels had poisoned darts. The music shivered and somewhere in some far life found competition in the hundred songbirds that fretted for freedom, within the wire spirals of their palace prison.

Life seemed so slow, a thousand seconds to each moment, the smiling women, the space between breaths. So gentle these creatures, these pretty pieces and the comforting hands spread lower and lower, across my belly and into my pants, rubbed me, made me strong where I was weak, made a tower of scattered bricks. She bent and kissed me. I stroked her hair, the barbed-wire curls so surprisingly soft, and squeezed the nape of her neck, nipped it tight, held her firm.

Here was my mother squeezing her breast into my face, and this moment was the best, her nipple in my mouth. The two women pulled me to my feet. I tottered forward, a cramped bent figure, unable to straighten out, stuck, bent low, head into my chest. One of the women took my place on the bench, and I was turned gently around to face her, my penis ridiculously firm, pointing out. I straightened a little, felt the press of a body behind me, the warmth of breasts on my back, the soft push of scratching hair at my buttocks and I tottered forward, stubbing my toes. The hubble-bubble tipped and cracked, and cool water trickled, blessing my feet with its streams and rivers. The seated slave pushed her breasts together, and the women behind me guided my penis between them. I was rocked backwards and forwards, pushed and pulled by the warm body behind me. I was pulled away, the rocking stopped, and the seated woman bent to my penis and kissed me, her spit a snail's trail of silver. Then again between her breasts and the motion was easier, more exquisitely sensual, in and out, in the sweetest giving crush. And then I came, a great glob of semen, spurting over her chest. And the relief, the sweet relief. The peace, the calm of quietness, of quiet, for a moment, for a shallow, sobbing moment.

Chapter Twelve

WE WERE in Berlin, Agnelli and I, a Berlin of monuments and clashing heels, a Berlin of shouting and
furious cars, a Berlin of uniforms and badges, a Berlin
daubed with posters. There were two species of mankind in
Berlin, distinguishable by the way they walked through the
streets, head down, avoiding beatings, or head up, looking
for people to beat. So many striding military men, stalking
the city, newly proud, nobly furious.

It was right to rage, and the targets for their rage were
obvious, pointed out, delineated in billboards which
described Jewish physiognomy, not only the obviously
recognizable hooked nose, but subtleties, the narrow forehead, the squinty eyes, the pointy ears, the greasy hair,
haunted hunted rats, spot them, beat them, lynch them,
take their business away, for they are the ones who
bankrupted Germany.

Wake up, Germany, to the crimes of Zion. It is patriotic
to persecute them, as they have persecuted us, weed out
this filth, cleanse this corruption. Too long have they been
tolerated. They are leeches, taking, always taking.

And you are right, Germany O Germany. Blessed is
your youth, your blondness and your strength, and deadly
is the rottenness that in innocence we took to our hearts.
Let us purify the land, liberate our nation, cut away the

curse that saps our Fatherland. Look, there's one. Get him. And the beautiful, the powerful, the upright, the righteous, the courageous man in the black shirt, rushed at the little boy in the velvet coat, with the yellow star on his right arm. The boy ran, the Blackshirt ran faster, knocking him into the gutter, company for his Jewish friends.

And the crowd walked by, but nobody stopped the brave corporal kicking the child's head. He lay unconscious in the kerb, but it was none of their business. And the outstandingly brave non-commissioned officer did his duty. Served them right. Parasites, let them help each other. Another Jew down and one less problem for Germany.

A military band paraded the streets. Our car stopped while the soldiers crossed in front of us, the high-stepping goose-steps, the braveness of brass, the boldness of drums, such perfect Germans, marching with pride, proud of their uniforms, swollen by Hitler to be the warriors that they secretly knew they were. Who could stop them, for this was the Third Reich, a kingdom for ever, on earth until the stars fall. See their civic buildings, how tall, how perfect, how true. Immaculate that arch, that column, that pilaster, classicism reborn, engineered, redefined in the nobility of town halls, barracks and ministries. Be proud, you civil servant, be firm, you bank employee, be brave, you soldier, be emboldened, all of you, by the power of the authorities that had the strength and foresight to plan these architectural monuments. All of the work that you do in these buildings is for the glory of the Fatherland, every pen stroke is historic, and every file a potential piece of history. So go with grace to your homes and to your work, for everything you touch, noble-hearted German, is ennobled.

The light over the Chancellery was beautiful, highlighting in the sharp detail of brilliant shadow the majestic architraves, the massive sculptures, the heavy columns. The windows of the building caught the setting sun, and in their blazing red reflection gave warning to Europe. Tanks ringed the building and their vigilant turrets followed our slowing car.

Our car stopped. A line of guards smashed their boots into the ground, and their arms swooped out to salute Hitler. An officer approached our limousine, inspected our number plate, and with his clipboard checklist, cross-referenced our passports and the car's details. He signalled the gatehouse that we were to proceed. The barrier was raised. The officer opened the car door and settled down next to our chauffeur. He was everything a German officer should be, muscled, blond, manly, and decorated with a hero's slash of crooked cross on his military sleeve. The car pushed forward under an arch, into the depths of the looming building, which bore over us, heavy, dark and low. The grandeur of scale and the echoes of classic beauty had quite the opposite effect to their distant impression. Instead of grandness, there was meanness, instead of lightness, darkness, it overwhelmed, depressed, made dark, was sinister, imposing on the visitor despondency and gloom.

We parked in an inner courtyard next to an open Mercedes-Benz. On the car's bonnet a swastika flag danced with its shadows. The lieutenant opened our door, saluted, clicked his heels, and led us through the corridors of German power. Guardsmen fell in behind us, forming a troop that both guided and followed. We walked along a vast colonnade where massive stone columns held high a distant ceiling. We passed a hundred checkpoints, and a thousand stamping soldiers crashed by. On the walls hung dark oils where legions of armoured knights rode on brave canvases, and their sharp lances pricked out and kept us on the right path. The German soldiers kept a straight line through the corridors, a marching line that took us to a chamber of bare flagstones and walls, without comfort or warmth.

A small man with gold spectacles sat at a plain steel desk. He saluted our guide with a limp 'Heil,' a heil only just heard, a bored whisper, hardly said. His hair was very short and his cheeks freshly shaven. A leather folder lay in front of him. It was bright red and embossed with a black swastika. Everywhere the sign, and on everything this cross. The lieutenant announced these Vatican visitors. He handed over our papal passports, and their details were minutely checked with the information within the red leather file. The clerk's glasses tilted low, reflecting the shining glow of the soldiers' jackboots.

'The papers are in order,' and the passports were shuffled in a dealer's hands and returned to our guard. 'You may enter.'

He saluted again, this time with a little more enthusiasm, then pressed a button on a plaque recessed into the desk, and the doors to Hitler were opened. Seated, they faced us. Uniformed, helmeted fire and night. In the centre, Hitler, at his side the captains of the host of death. The famous moustache, the drifting dip of hair, the white white face. He stood to greet us, curtly nodded and signalled that we sit before him. We sat, sat in a hard place. Rome in Berlin. I scanned the Germans, their backdrop, a hundred swastika flags. Goebbels, Himmler, corpulent Goering, drug addict, degenerate, the elegant Ribbentrop and mad Hess, eyebrows twitching. The Nazis sprawled and played with their guns. Hitler leaned forward, and clasped his hands.

'Well?' Our Jesuit gave no sign of recognition. How

could he? He had been chosen and we had been trained. Hitler's eyes avoided us. He waited, and this was the Vatican's proposition.

'Herr Hitler, greetings from his Holiness the Pope, his blessing is for you and the people of the new Germany.'

Hitler waited, and I was afraid, afraid for a moment of what my negotiations would undoubtedly lead to, responsible, for a millisecond, for mankind, but then doubt was lost and I spoke on.

'Herr Hitler, the Vatican wishes to negotiate with you, negotiate a secular treaty, unwritten, untold. We are of course aware of the situation in Europe and wish you well. His holiness asked me to forward to you his congratulations on the restructuring of Germany. We condone your action in the Sudetenland, and feel that it makes for a better order in Europe. Rationality is the essence of this order and we all desire a rational world.' Hitler's face was expressionless, the dull eyes stones. I continued and the Nazis watched me.

'Führer, may I continue? My mission is a delicate one, and it is to air with you the view that the Vatican may be in a position to make Germany a unique offer, in exchange of course for certain guarantees.'

My pretty speech was broken by Goering. 'So, the petty priests think they have something for us! Ridiculous.'

Goering smashed his fist on the table and a fly jumped into the air. Goebbels raised a trembling hand for Goering to quieten down, and I continued with my message. Agnelli was very still, terribly silent by my side.

'To continue, excellencies, and may I at this stage speak directly. I have come to bargain with you. Our Vatican Council has concluded that Germany's aim is legitimate hegemony over all Europe, the establishment of a greater

259

Reich, the rightful dominion of the Aryan race over lesser Mediterranean peoples of lower stock. The aim of Germany is to cleanse Europe, purge our European world of impurity and weakness, and this idea we have sympathy with.'

The Nazis leaned towards me, took note. Hitler paid no attention at all. He bit his nails and looked away.

'In the Vatican's view, Aryan rule is of course to be welcomed, there is much that a centralized, efficiently run Europe could do that would be infinitely preferable to the degenerate disorder of a hundred tiny states. The opportunities for progress and ultimately for the greater good of mankind are many. To see mankind striving together, working together, in harmony and with common aims, would be welcomed and the advances that a stable culture could offer civilization are extensive. We in the Catholic Church would like to see this, would welcome this change.' I paused, trying to gauge the impression that my words were making. Goering had stopped fuming, Goebbels was taking notes, Hess seemed to be talking to himself, and Himmler stared at me. Hitler's eyes swept from the ceiling and seized me.

'So,' he said, just one word and Agnelli caught its echo and quivered.

'Good point, your excellency, so where does this leave the Church and what does the Vatican wish to negotiate? May I respond to this question.' Hitler nodded permission, solemnly nodded permission. I could continue, he had agreed that I could continue.

'The Vatican wishes to maintain its territorial integrity during the coming struggle for European liberation, and at its legitimate end wishes to continue its independent and peaceful existence in the domains defined by the Lateran Treaty. We wish for no more, no more except for the continuance of Switzerland's neutral status, a status held for so many centuries, a status that has obvious financial importance not only for the Church but for the ultimate safety of the greater Europe. Our bankers must be secure.' I stopped and Goebbels in his whistling tidy voice clipped in.

'A fine speech. Our compliments on your intelligence service but when one negotiates one comes to bargain, and bargaining requires that you have something to bargain with. And what does the Church have that Germany could possibly want? What do you have, Cardinal?' He settled back.

'Excellency, excellencies, the Church has always considered that a certain race bears the responsibility for our beloved Lord's death. From his blessed birth to his pitiful death, they despised him and they abandoned him. And his holy martyrdom, his unending, bleeding suffering, was and is for ever their responsibility. They are guilty. Theirs is the culpability, and theirs is the blame. Theirs is the betrayal, theirs is the loss of Christ. And whose is the responsibility, whose is the guilt? The Jews, excellencies, the Jews. For corrupt is their blood and original their stinking sin. Cut them off, cut them out, destroy them and you will be blessed. You proud men of mighty Germany have made this your aim, and we the Vatican support you.'

'Well,' said Goebbels, 'we obviously have a measure of agreement on essential issues. But how, dear Cardinal, may you help us? Forgive me, but I cannot see what there is to negotiate.'

The Nazi standards rippled, the backdrop of swastikas shivered, caught in an unknown, rustling breeze. Hitler turned to stare at the ghosts behind him and Agnelli caught my sleeve to steady himself, stop himself falling from his shaking, quivering chair. I paused, waited for the little storm to settle, caught the attention of the Nazis with the dramatic device of silence. Silence, for a long moment. I stood up, and Hess jumped with fright and reached for his rattling gun. I leaned on the table, facing the negotiators, an orphan boy among tall men. My fists rested on the table edge, and I swayed towards the uniforms and the cardboard faces.

'Excellencies.' My words were whispered, and they strained to hear me. 'All Europeans agree that the Jews are a sub-human nuisance who carry the weight of history's sentence. Every European, however enlightened, carries the essence of Jew hatred in his soul. Germany is not unique in its sentiments. Jew hatred is in the hearts of the French and the British, the Belgians and the Spanish. It is by chance that Nazism has its root here, the movement could have grown in any European country. Excellencies, at this juncture may I take the opportunity to remind you that man is a complex organism, and for each element of his nature there is an opposite. For this particular aspect of mankind, the potential irrational antithesis is Jew love, a love that springs from the essential goodness of mankind. Do you take my point, gentlemen?' Not a single Nazi nodded his head. They failed to understand my argument.

'At present you have confirmed in the hearts of Germans that the Jews were the cause of Germany's disgrace in the last war and of the economic difficulties that followed. We, the Church, have encouraged the world to believe that the Jews' acquiescence led to the martyrdom of our Saviour, a belief that has marched through the centuries. Now, it might be possible that this sentiment, although correct, could be forgiven, forgotten. Your righteous processing of the Jews in the work camps might just lead, given the right prompting, to a backlash. That populist backlash, demanding the cessation of persecution, might be engineered in the hearts of man by the voice of the Church. Yes, gentlemen, if the Pope spoke up, if the priests denied communion to the wardens and the guards, the soldiers and the police, your power on earth would be ephemeral.'

I stopped and sat down. Waited. Hitler continued his blank-faced staring into the middle distance. Goebbels spoke.

'So, Cardinal, let me summarize, and forgive me this time the sin of reductionism. Is this the essence of your proposal? You, the Church, will not interfere with our activities in Europe, and in particular with our plans for the Jews. And we, the National Socialist party of the glorious Third Reich, will recognize the sovereign integrity of the Vatican and Switzerland, its bank.' Hitler's eyes came back into the room, greeted Agnelli and me. We both nodded.

'Agreed,' said Hitler.

'Heil Hitler!' shouted the Nazis, and the history of Europe was defined.

It was late at night as we left the Reichstag buildings, drove away from the negotiating table on our way to the border. The limousine kicked off from the seat of German power, from darkness into the night. The barriers rose for us, and we spun out into Berlin Platz, away from the imperious statues, the fountains, the pillars and pilasters, the triumphal architraves of Hitler's power. We drove out past the tanks and the guards, the mass of men and armaments. Agnelli sat silent on the rear seat of the limousine and I hummed a phrase from *Tosca*, hummed the same phrase again and again until Agnelli's tolerance was exceeded and he asked that I be quiet.

Agnelli was trembling, his hands shaking as he reached to tip the brim of his Homburg down over his eyes. He looked so dapper in his high starched collar, the pearl pin at his necktie, the formal stripe of his dark suit. He turned away and looked through the window glass.

'What do you think, Horsmunden?' he whispered.

'What do you mean, Agnelli?'

'The terms of our negotiation . . . ?'

'Let's forget the terms for a moment, and let me go over for you the implications of the settlement that we have just made. It has historic import. The settlement means that order, and the natural hierarchy of power, is maintained in Europe, for us, and for the foreseeable future. The Vatican's territorial integrity and its financial base are secure so that whatever may happen in the far future, when this current European crisis has been resolved, we will be able to rebuild again. We will, furthermore, through the maintenance of Switzerland's neutrality, survive with our finances intact and with our monies continuing to gather interest through the coming troubled years we will have lost nothing. Agnelli, our duty is to the Church's future. We must think not only of this little epoch, but the whole spread of history before us. Don't you understand? We have negotiated the security of the generations of cardinals who can now follow us and will follow us.' Agnelli nodded.

The car rattled around a corner and glanced the kerb. How annoying. I rapped the glass partition between us and our chauffeur and catching his eye in the mirror shook a warning finger at the slave. He had better be careful.

'And its cost, the price of the settlement, Horsmunden?'

Agnelli seemed to become smaller, crumpled in his topcoat, contracting with each staccato surge of light that pulsed into our limousine from the passing street lamps.

'My dear Cardinal, you ask me to consider the price of peace. The Church has agreed to condone the Nazis' actions. This is an inconsequential price to pay for our future security. Remember, Agnelli, the Jews bear the guilt of Christ's death, and in their persecution and death will lie their atonement and redemption. Look at it this way, Agnelli, they are atoning for atavistic sin. It is just.'

At that moment our discourse was interrupted by shouts. The car skidded to a halt. So careless, I'd have the driver shot. But what was that over there? It was a huge bonfire, burning, bristling, blazing, filling the street. The shouting became defined, distilled into one clear chant.

'*Juden raus, Juden raus, Juden raus.*' And before me storming Blackshirts ran through the streets. Shots echoed, raged, and the roaring mob rushed and screamed. The fire soared, sparks flew high. The night was bright, and the street lamps ghosts.

'Reverse, get us out of here,' I screamed at the driver and our car backed away, away from the massive street fire and into a crowd of running men and women. Fists banged on the boot and crashed against the windows.

'Forward, driver, forward,' and the car pushed forward again, inched through the crowd, and everywhere the screaming, chanting chorus.

'*Juden raus, Juden raus.*'

Faces pressed against our windows, distorted, angry faces searching inside our limousine. I heard the crash of smashing glass. Shop windows shattered and the people poured in to pillage, stepping over the fallen in their fury to be at the goods. Looters raced from department stores loaded with shoes and coats, food and radios. The police stood by, truncheons at their belts, smiling benignly at the rushing crowd and joining in the ferocious chanting.

Everywhere there were Blackshirts, jackbooted, striding, directing the pillage, encouraging the sack.

'Over there, Agnelli, look.' Mounted police were using megaphones to direct the crowd, through the tight-wound windows I could hear their messages.

'This way, patriots, this way, over there to Goldberg's store.' And the policeman waved his truncheon in the direction of an alleyway where a shop was half hidden, but not the tracing in dripping yellow paint of a star of David over the shop's window.

And the crowd rushed in the direction that they had been pointed, a thousand people pouring across Berlin's stony streets to assault Goldberg's store. Rubble soared over the crowd, a rocky rain falling on the shop. Its windows shattered just as the quickest of the mob were at its steps and then in through the windows, trampling the display of mannequins, grabbing, stealing, taking everything.

Our car rocked and swayed, pushed around by the sheer crush of crowd, the mass of bodies butting against its panels in rhythmic waves. Suddenly two mounted police saw our stranded limousine. The police kicked their heels into their horses' flanks and came together towards us, the horses' legs delicately reaching out through the parting people. Our chauffeur lowered his window, letting in the roar of the howling, screaming, baying crowd. The policemen leaned down towards us and our passports were shown.

'You better get out of here, sirs, this is not for you.'

The officer pointed out a route through the racing riot, and the chauffeur, winding his window high and tight, started the stalled car and edged, yard by yard, through the swelling mob. The crowd was so great that we could not see where we were. Bodies pressed tight, smudging against the glass, noses squashing against the windows, hands rolling across the glass, as we moved slowly forward. Our chauffeur followed the mounted police, and inch by inch by inch we moved along Berlin Platz, until suddenly we were free.

We accelerated a little, past a straggling line of men, women and children trailing behind a platoon of mighty warriors. The people's heads were low, and some of the women had babies at their breasts. A rifle butt fell on the tender skull of a straggler and an old man slumped to the ground. A gang of onlookers were immediately at him, kicking at his face and groin. We drove on past a burning synagogue, tall fires reaching pleading arms to the hard heavens. In the streets another fire surrounded by more Blackshirts, smiling, laughing, drinking, enjoying the blaze of books, the mishnah, the Gemara, the learned commentaries, the holy scrolls.

A tall man struggled from the synagogue door. His long straggly side curls had unfurled, the corners of his hair falling wild. He carried parchments wound on two wooden poles and cuddled the scrolls as if they were his own precious children. A soldier in battledress and helmet tore the scrolls from him, threw them at the high fire, then grabbed him by his side curls and swung him round and round. The man stumbled around the laughing soldier then slipped and fell, bleeding curls torn out in the soldier's hands. He screamed in the gutter, white shirt muddied, blood pouring from his scalp, and the soldier drew his pistol and fired into his face. The tall man was quiet. The soldier put his gun in his holster and warmed his hands at the fire.

We turned the corner, past two mongrels fucking in a shop doorway underneath David's painted star. His front legs cradled her neck, and back arched, he pushed in and out, in and out. We drove on and the dogs were gone.

Chapter Thirteen

INTO POLAND, the fighter planes, the armoured brigades, the Blitzkrieg rumbling forward into the land's soft belly. The surprise of the Russian–German non-aggression pact to the allies, but not to ourselves, for the German Military Academy had been training Russian troops since 1938. Poland was neatly parcelled, and then the Russians were into Finland. The situation was agreeable to the Vatican, trade was booming, massive profits came from war, iron and steel, coal and oil, building, munitions, all on an international basis, from Scandinavia into Germany, from the Balkans into Germany, from Germany into Russia. Everywhere business was having a wonderful time.

'My dears, don't you love my new coiffure?' Pius was late for supper, we were waiting for him, twelve at our long table, waiting, and he'd twisted into the chamber, in a birthday-cake dress, pink-flounced low-cut taffeta and ribbons. He spun on his high heels and patted his curls, curtsied and waited for applause. Du Plessis clapped, the rest of us were silent. The Pope was displeased.

'So, you don't like my tint then, you traitors. I hate you all.' And he was out of the room, leaving us to our own grumbling council.

The Pope had become more petulant, idiosyncratic, moody, unable to make decisions, confused, confabulating, perverse. His life had become more Augustan, he was the last Caesar, an embodiment of Rome's empire, and it was as Roman Emperor that he spent his days. He lived in his zoo, with his pygmies and circus dwarfs, surrounded by pale sycophants and the licking love of whispering catamites. His counsellors were astrologers, hairdressers and manicurists, and he worried about his wrinkles and sagging skin. His days were a folly. Not his, the authority of command, the portentousness of decisions. He loved to dance, and on a silver stage in a brilliant theatre he danced alone to the applause of his creatures.

The Pope was Byzantine madness, ornate, crazed, useless as a figurehead, impossible as a leader. His Christmas speech rang out over St Peter's Square, read by an acolyte standing behind him on a high balcony, and Pius, disorientated and confused, unable even to mime, had spun around, his brain on fire with amphetamine and diamorphine, looking for the imagined cockroaches of his delirium. Below, a million pilgrims shivered in the whistling rain and a slave dipped his umbrella over the Pope's brow, so that his confusion was hidden.

The Christmas message was for a world of peace, but the world was at war and its warriors deaf. I pushed forward to Pius's side, held his upper arm tight and pulled him up and around so that he faced the crowd. I raised his arm to the masses and waved a Christmas benediction. The hum of their amens filled the hollow square and the cheering frightened the scattering pigeons.

The Pope was a liability, his confusion a disordered nuisance, his habits uncontrolled and his delusions a menace. He was kept from foreign emissaries and an actor took his place. And in secret corners, in the quiet places of conspiracy, we gathered and planned. We were unanimous in our decision, uncertain only as to its timing. The Pope had to die. He was too enormous a risk, too great a threat to the security of our state. This dancing, simpering madman was no longer in control, his whimsy and addictions could not be countenanced. He was unpredictable, and lived in the wildness of beastly dreams, mumbling and incoherent, disorientated in his days.

Von Rumbold, Agnelli and I walked around an ancient courtyard in the centre of the Vatican, three statesmen, deliberate in their pace, grand in their demeanour. Von Rumbold leant heavily on a stick, limping a little because his gout was bad. Agnelli and I walked slowly by his side. We whispered together.

'It cannot continue in this way,' muttered von Rumbold.

'In that we are all agreed,' said Agnelli.

We were all agreed. In private meetings in silent sacred corridors, the cardinals had sounded out one another's views. In every instance there had been a uniformity of decision, a uniformity remarkable in the context of the disparate natures of the decision-makers. We all agreed. The Pope was too great a risk. The integrity of the Vatican in these difficult times was paramount and couldn't be left in the hands of a degenerate lunatic. Pius must be disposed of. This was our decision. He had to go. The wind hissed around the cloistered courtyard, disturbing winter's leaves, and turned them into busy twirling capuchins. The cold wind burnt our ears, burnt them as red as the robes of our religion.

Von Rumbold belched. 'I saw it before in the last Pope,' he said. 'In him the madness was controllable, defined, but in this man...' His words trailed away, the sentence incomplete. He shook his head and rubbed the stubble on his purple-blotched chin.

'We have agreed, my dears,' said Agnelli, 'that he must go, but there is no such thing as retirement for God's Popes. They die in office and are buried with ceremony and splendour.'

'Yes,' said von Rumbold. 'They die in office,' he waited, waited until our attention was absolute, 'and die he must.' We nodded. 'The situation cannot continue unchanged. As is written of these circumstances, the death of Pius must not be the task of a single man. His death must be shared.' Von Rumbold continued, 'We must rely on tradition and be fortified by ritual. His death must issue from all of us, from twelve blades, each falling thirteen times. It is written that this is the custom.'

We mumbled our agreement, for after all von Rumbold's particularly Teutonic choice of speciality was Church tradition, and in his knowledge lay our instruction.

'So,' I said, 'our path is defined, and only its circumstance remains undecided.'

'Not at all, Horsmunden. Church tradition prescribes circumstances.'

We continued around the cloistered square. Misty rain settled in the mossy lawn and splattered the dark surface of the ornamental ponds. A disconsolate raven skipped and tugged at an elastic worm and two seagulls settled on the silent fountain. Von Rumbold linked his arm in mine and hobbled on, and the Vatican's shimmering bells claimed the hour and broke the silence of our contemplation.

'So,' asked Agnelli, 'what is it that we must do, von Rumbold?'

'In tradition, so saith the books, if we the cardinals are agreed, and we are – ' I tired a little of the tedium of repetition, for the repeated description of our unanimity and the diktats of tradition was irksome – 'then our action

271

must be immediate. Now, my Cardinals, are we certain that each one of us is determined that the Pope must die?'

'Yes,' I said. 'Agnelli and I have discussed the situation with everyone. We have no doubt, there is no dissension, he must go.'

'Then it must be tonight. Tonight at our usual meeting. Let it be known.'

'One moment, von Rumbold.'

This was Agnelli speaking. He walked in front of us, faced von Rumbold, hand out to the German's chest, stopping his procession through the cloister. We hesitated, waiting for Agnelli.

'The succession, who is to succeed Pius?'

'Good question, Agnelli. Who is next? It is written in the history of the Church that in such times as the Pope should meet a violent death, the eldest of the cardinals should take the holy crown.' It didn't take too long to establish who was the eldest . . . von Rumbold.

'Can you prove this?' Agnelli strangely to the point again, the butterfly Jesuit wanting information, requiring confirmation of von Rumbold's succession.

'Of course I can. In these times there is no election: madness and violent death define succession and preclude a vote. There is no papal election, no parliament of cardinals defining a new leader.'

Von Rumbold looked straight forward at Agnelli, his eyes strip-searching the Jesuit for dissent. Agnelli's hand slowly fell to his side, and the three of us continued our amble for a few more minutes then bid each other good afternoon and proceeded to our chambers.

I opened my door, and hollow flute music rippled through the hallway, inspiration for the goldfinches, competition for the macaws. I walked through my rooms, and the music spun louder. In the dining room, my three Ethiopians waited, lolling naked by the huge open fireplaces that lined the length of a wall. I closed the door, they smiled at me and the flute whistled a greeting. I had eventually given them names, generic names, memories of a distant youth, Phyllis, Nora and Mary, strangely English for these wild women, but warming for me. Phyllis was the flautist, and she stood by the fire, roasting her arse, flute at her lips, wide eyes following me through the room. Nora was sitting on the table and Mary sat on a chair in front of her. Nora's nipples were painted bright coral and her legs were spread wide. She leant on her left elbow, her right thigh pulled back by her right arm. Mary was bending into her groin, intent, concentrating, the back of her head hiding the focus of her attention. I came closer to see what they were doing, and, disturbed from her game, Mary looked up to greet me. She had lipstick in her hand and Nora's labia were bright red. They grinned at me, then Nora slipped from the table and changed places with Mary. Nora dabbed paint on Mary's dark button nipples, then pushed her friend's legs apart, and brushed crimson on a swath of vulva, making a bright mouth under the black curls.

I came closer to watch her work, and touched Nora's breast, which hardened in my hand. I pulled Nora to her feet. Nora pretended obliviousness and bending towards Mary continued with her lipstick. I pushed my hand into Nora's vulva. She bent her head lower and her arse rose high, pretty sight. I pulled up my robes and rode into her, rode her like a Berlin dog.

Nora's hand came to me, squeezed around the base of my penis, made for me a second introitus. Mary wet her index finger with saliva then rubbed her clitoris as Nora's face fell forward into Mary's groin, licking, sucking, while

273

the flute music came closer, came louder. Phyllis was with us, and her soft pubic hair brushed my thighs. The music billowed, my thrusting became more vigorous, and suddenly we all came together and the flute trilled triumph.

I lay back, comfortable in my apartment, safe in the castles of the Vatican. The Ethiopians chirruped in their tribal tongue and, at peace, I relaxed, watching the women giggling and playing.

The room was ancient, dating back to the time of the original Roman Empire. Its floor was mosaic, a bacchanal inlaid within the floor's geometric border. A priapic satyr caught in stone chased three plump nymphs through a verdant arbour to the shimmering borders of a cerulean lake. The hairy, cloven-footed satyr was beautifully pre-served, all his details were bright and fresh. The virginal nymphs had become worn and frayed. Their virginity had challenged the rust of time and lost. The pinkness of their nipples had faded to dull beige, and the roseate tints of their soft flesh had become chalky grey. On the walls of the room a fresco had been painted. It had peeled significantly during half a millennium, but a pretty scene still remained, a feast of wine and meats, Bacchus and the lesser Gods having sport with maidens fair. The peeling of the fresco was particularly pleasant, the missing areas allowing one to imagine clouds, gods, mortals and music, Aeolian harps and silver tympani.

Phyllis left the room then returned carrying her flute and a pharmacist's pestle and mortar. Her back straight, she walked prissily, holding the mortar level, shielding its contents from any breath of air. She crouched on her heels and laid her flute on a shivering nymph's belly. She held the mortar rigid and carefully ground its crystal contents with the white china pestle. The crystals crunched, and became a dull heap of white powder. Phyllis peered at the bowl's contents and satisfied with the powder's consistency detached the mouthpiece from her silver flute and handed it to me.

I pulled myself upright, and contemplated the fine dust of amphetamine sulphate in its ceramic container. Blocking one nostril and holding the mouthpiece's nozzle to the other, I bent over the mortar and inhaled and the powder disappeared. I settled back and gradually I was aware of my heartbeat pounding, beating, a thousand tom-toms within my chest. My thoughts rushed, became incisive, funny, logical and I felt prepared for the evening ahead, more than intelligent, strong, able to deal with any turn, any trick, any plan, any plot.

I loved the crystal compounds, amphetamine and cocaine. They made me soar, they made me more, such welcome products of the German pharmaceutical industry and our own south American plantations. So good to feel so alert, so in touch, so in tune.

Nora helped me into my robes and Mary balanced my crooked mitre over my brow. My pectoral was draped around my neck, and I was ready for the evening.

The sedan chair waited by the door. Flanked by a phalanx of Swiss Guards, we cut through the Vatican walkways, evening made early by winter, night made bright by electric light.

We gathered in the council chamber, gathered in solemn mood for a momentous time. We were all present. The room was bare of decoration. Plain stone, polished by the ages, shone brazen and the bare pillars and floor, ceiling and walls spoke grandly of the portentousness of this time. This was the heart of the Vatican, the soul of our power. Twelve cardinals. The select dozen that ran Catholicism, representatives of the powerful Catholic nations, defenders and keepers of the Roman faith. Our council table had been pushed back against the far wall and we stood in a circle around a smoking crucible, where charcoal flames met and conspired.

Von Rumbold stepped forward from the circle of men and, chanting in ancient Aramaic, swung a thurible out over the flames. A shiver of spices caught in the flames, and heady fumes reeled around our room. The chanting stopped and a cock crowed thrice. I hadn't noticed the black-feathered bird, prisoner in a hanging cage, splendid wattles, triumphant comb, marching, bristling, surveying the scene.

Von Rumbold hung over the flames, filled his lungs with cloying smoke and coughed. He chanted again, then stopped to beckon us forward to the burning brazier. He swung the ornate gothic censer low over the fire and, in turn, we bent low to the flames and inhaled acrid, confusing smoke. The cock crowed for each of us, marked every break in von Rumbold's litany with the fierce cackle of his challenge.

Du Plessis dipped to the smoke, inhaled, then stepping back, reeled. And for me too, confused by von Rumbold's herbs and spices, sped on by amphetamine, the room was a phantasm that swayed and shimmered, rocked in the hallu-cinatory confusion of this drugged moment. Twelve men in solemn order broke from the circle and inhaled ceremonial fumes. We were made increasingly dizzy by the fumes, confused by a numbness that crept from combustion into our lungs, to our blood, into our brains. Again von Rumbold called us, again and again, and seven times eleven cardinals dipped and swayed, our throats parched, our bodies dis-ordered, the room a shivering valley in the enduring Vatican's distant, fortress hills.

Von Rumbold kept himself from the fumes. In control,

commanding, he waved the thurible and kept order among his men. The room was misty with smoke, and in the night's hallucination became the prison dungeons of a powerful king, lord of an unending dominion which stretched in fire and plague from sunset to moonrise. This lord ruled in a bitter place, king of a monstrous realm, subterranean and monotone, he ruled cities of crowded tears and raised crops of jaundice, piss and bile. In this country the king's agents were misshapen and besmirched, rancid and rotten, seared by purulent carbuncles and stinking sores, wall-eyed, foul. In this country the king's people were innocents enslaved. In this country the king's children were sorrow and pain.

The room flickered, its greasy mist cleared, and I saw the king's shimmering servants. They wore fine robes of virulent red, coloured for the people's blood. Von Rumbold swung the censer around his head, faster, faster, swirling, catching in its mirrored silver the burning charcoal of the fire it had fed, becoming the fire itself, sending messages to the room in tumbling silver clouds of burning herbs.

The cock crowed again, crowed for a distant dawn, crowed for the hen he wanted, crowed to a rival cock, in a far and open field. The thurible swung faster, its shape blurred. It flew faster, until it was scarcely visible in the dusty light. It took off and freed from von Rumbold's rheumatic hand became a phantom fluttering, a piping, hooting pipistrelle that soared and flapped, bolting upward into the high rafters, gone, gone.

Von Rumbold faced the surrounding circle of cardinals. He fixed each of us with his gravel eyes, then broke from the circle, strode forward and paced across the room to the cock's cage. He twisted the door open, reached for the clucking bird, and grabbed it by its yellow feet. He pushed into us, knocking Agnelli and du Plessis aside with the clumsiness of his charge, then swung the bird around his own head. The cock flapped, his wings shedding feathers in a frantic effort to right himself, free himself from the crazed man.

Von Rumbold twirled and spun, turned faster and faster, then stopped. He rushed towards us, the bird's neck held tight, its bright coxcomb and yellow beak, wattles and wobbly eyes poking out from his fist. Von Rumbold, stopping at each of us in turn, spoke the same litany.

'In our death there is life, and in all of our lives death, with this bird's blood we will live for ever, live on in the glory of our Church. The Church is our mother, the Church is our father, and to the Church we give our lives. Take this life as a token of another, incorporate this creature's blood in ours and he will live on.'

The brazier flared again, and a trailing smoke lifted up to the ceiling. Von Rumbold pulled a jewelled kris from his belt and scythed the cock's head from its neck. The head bounced once, then lay still. Bright blood pounded from the cock's neck.

Von Rumbold dropped the creature to the floor. Headless, its body was alive. It ran, ran around our feet, searching for its head, a useless blind search. As it ran, the blood pumped high spurting on to the hems of our robes. The bird stumbled and the pouring blood became a riven trickle, until there was no life, only death and the body lay still on the floor.

Von Rumbold bent to the ground and dipped his fingers in the stubby bloodied neck of the twitching cock. He came to us, his hands dripping, and one by one he faced us, pulled open our jaws and jabbed his bloody fingers into our open mouths, wiped blood on to our gagging tongues. He turned back to the bird and shook the dead body until blood trickled again. He grabbed my jaw, his fingers pinching, hurting and twisting my mouth open, his whole hand jammed into me, smearing me with iron blood. I bit his fingers and he laughed.

Von Rumbold danced for us, became a Turkish woman from the deepest chambers of the sultan's harem, a belly dancer, twisting, jerking, swaying, wriggling, and with this dance there was magic music, mad pipes that cawed and hooted, conjured by the cardinal, imagined, surreal.

Von Rumbold danced around the burning brazier, flapping his skirts at the burning coals. The flames hissed, fuelled by the bellows of von Rumbold's robes, and the heat of the furnace blasted our faces.

His back was to me, around his waist a broad leather band, and strapped to the leather band a metal harpoon, a devil's tail bumping over his buttocks. Von Rumbold beat his chest, pummelled his breast with his fists, an ancient panegyric for his jungle gods. He roared and leapt the flames, tail lifting high, spiking the air. We cardinals followed him, chanting, pounding through the flames.

We danced for the fire, fanning the flames with our robes, leaping the swaggering flames. We twelve men swayed through the smoke-filled room, falling through the hissing fire. Our clothes fell to the floor. And our chanting became one music with a single beat. Together we danced to a jungle rhythm, swaying, singing, baritone, bass, recalling a distant memory of a primitive, Neanderthal time of caves and glaciers, flints and beasts. Wrapped in animal skins, filthy, hidden, we danced, and we were in another dry land, hot sand without shelter, in eternal flames, where cruelty was queen, and bitterness her sceptre. We cardinals were a caterpillar line, hands on each other's shoulders, and von Rumbold led our stamping procession, chanting fiercely as he pulled us around the high flames of the brazier.

My hands, slippery with sweat, lost their grip on zu Hohenzollern's hairy shoulders. I gripped them again and twisting my fingers into the mat of curls followed his swaying way around the room. And we were rolling shadows between the stone pillars, in von Rumbold's shabby wake, his harpoon tail banging over the clattering floor.

And suddenly a voice impinged upon our chanting, broke the rhythm of our dance, a voice tinkering and unpleasant that had no definition, that came again from out of the haze, a swarm of hissing wasps, a rainstorm on autumn's leaves.

And whose was this voice that invaded, what was this hardness that dared stop us, this brittle buzzing that broke our peace? I hated this annoyance, this thief, this arsonist, how dare he, how could he, how presumptuous, how pustulant and my fellow cardinals murmured, grew restive, their chant interrupted, their contemplation destroyed.

And who was this who called us, this thin voice from an alien world, this burglar at our feast? My hate grew, bubbled, roared, became an echoing fury feeding on anger. We needed to kill this criminal who had consumed the fire, who had dulled the brightness, who had stolen our glory. Our hate was a storm, brewing, brooding, bursting, and in our sweating, palpating nakedness we turned, blown to it by a furious wind that came from the dungeons of darkness, the prisons beneath the flagstones at our feet. We turned, and there at the door was the burglar, the thief, the vandal, dressed in Tutankhamen's jewels, his gold, his necklaces, his crown, his sceptre. And our hate was directed, focused, focused on this epicene idiot who ruled us with his petulant astrology, who dictated by whimsy and foolishness, tarnished, sapping: Pius. This was the maggot, rotten, stupid. This was the beast, prissy and pestilent. This was the monster, foul and stinking. This was the salop, purulent, ugly.

As of one, we moved towards him, and he was caught rigid, sculpted, captured by terror. The phalanx of naked cardinals advanced, and in our hands were golden daggers. Von Rumbold led, his harpoon tail raised high. Together we pulled our blades from their sheaths, and with this movement became marching soldiers, our captain at our head, leading us onward, forward to our enemy. Closer we came. Pius had turned from us, had pressed himself against the wall, bloody hands scraping at the stone. Onward. Nearer. The room howled, the room whirled, and we were a righteous wind that rushed and stabbed the beast, stabbed, stabbed, sharp blades through softness, catching bone. Again, plunging into the falling body. Again, so many blades, and von Rumbold with the coup de grâce. Neptune Rumbold, his harpoon a trident lunging into the body as it teetered and fell, soaring into the lumpen falling mass, pricking into Pius's neck, hacking into his throat, dispatching this rottenness, as if he were another chicken. Red blood seeped through the white silk, stained, dripped on to the floor. Pius was dead. Arms splayed, head crooked, bleeding. And the pool of blood grew larger, became a red lake, became a red river, and the man was borne away on this river into distant stinking marshes, to murky boglands, to fester and rot. Von Rumbold drew himself up from the emptiness where Pius had lain, drew himself upright, his flabby nakedness hard. He had scooped Tutankhamen's crown and necklace from Pius's death, taken from the dead what was now his. He settled the golden crown on his brow and fastened the flashing necklace. Bloody harpoon in his right hand, he was king. He shook the harpoon at the high heavens, and blood dripped like the answering rain on his head.

Chapter Fourteen

BUSINESS WAS good, the war had proceeded well. Europe was still and Germany had taken over and held dominion over France and Holland, Belgium, Norway, Sweden and Poland. The Czech lands and Austria had been incorporated into a greater Germany. There was peace between Stalin and Hitler, the product of the division of old Europe. Russia had taken the Baltic States, and part of Romania. Hungary and Bulgaria had made their peace with Hitler. Everywhere the industrialists prospered and in the factories of Germany, I. G. Farben, Siemens and Krupps, made more of their fortunes, their machines driven by sub-humans from the work camps of the Reich. Germany was valiant in her efforts to be self-sufficient, but in one essential she was not. She was dependent on imported oil and our friend Onassis, a prince with Arab jewels, fuelled the engines of the enemies, the ships and the armoured cars, the troop carriers and the planes, the tanks and the trains of both the British and the Germans. In the Far East too, order and manufacture had won through. Germany had formed an alliance with the Japanese, settling the frame of the world.

Our new Pope was doing well; auspicious in his presentation, powerful in his Teutonic demeanour, he understood this new order, dealt well with its masters, for they trusted his German manners. Pius XII had been brought up with learning; a master of Church ritual, student of history and scholar of orthodoxy, he was organized and capable. His way was stable, and without capriciousness. He delegated, commanded, dictated and listened.

Secure in Europe, Hitler ached to destroy the Communists. The non-aggression pact co-signed by Molotov and Ribbentrop was merely paper, and the Communists and Communist philosophy were the enemies of National Socialism. For the Germans, the Communists were always a threat, a serious threat because of their massive numbers, their obedince, their strength. The world had room for only one great power. One people must have hegemony and one people rule. It must be Germany and it must be the Germans. The Russian alliance was temporary, a convenience during the operation to cleanse Europe of its filth and dust, the gypsies and Jews, the homosexuals and the handicapped.

The Communists were the Nazis' enemy and the Nazis' enemy was also the Church's enemy. Large and treacherous was the threat of the Communist conspiracy to our dominions and lands. The movement was populist and popular. Its philosophy was a wonder for the working man, a panacea, a cure-all.

'All property is theft,' and so all that was rightfully ours, the legacy of millennia, could be claimed back by the people. What wonderful appeal that phrase had, how infinitely attractive. Of course. But what good would a Leonardo cartoon be in the front room of a labourer's cottage in Southern Italy? Would the peasant truly appreciate this beautiful thing, could he love it as we did? Did he have our eyes? Did he have our sensitivity? Of course not, how could he, how could a being so crude have the education and intelligence to appreciate the subtle sensuality of art? And how would the anarchist redistribute our culture, our achievements? To everyone, to all? Would he peel off the frescoes and rip up the mosaics?

'A stone here for you, brother comrade, and a stone for you.'

'A sack of coloured plaster for you, sister, and another sackful for you.'

'Have a scraping of gold from this altarpiece, a square of embroidery from this tapestry.'

What nonsense, what ridiculous cant. Leave the wealth where it was best loved, leave the beauty where it was most appreciated, leave it in the banks and in the palaces, in the mansions and cathedrals. Keep away those grubby hands and those unseeing greedy eyes.

From many fronts, Germany's military might tore into Russia, from Finland to Hungary, Operation Barbarossa sprang up, ripping into the evil belly of a wizened Mother Russia, her paps dry and rattling, an exhausted mother, worn from suckling her poisoned child. The Germans advanced a thousand miles, straight miles that roared towards the Russian heart.

To Moscow, brave men, to Moscow. And terrible was the German two-edged sword. It slashed and it destroyed and bitter were the Russians' days, dispersed were her armies and dead were her men. By December Russia was starving, and the Germans were in Moscow's suburbs.

Hard winter set in and the Russian counter-attack was launched. On 6 December, General Zhukov attacked, driving the brave Germans from the Russian capital. At this stage the balance of power and order was threatened. Russia and her historic friend, her winter, were together destroying Germany's army. It was possible that Communism might be preserved and the Church and Germany's rightful mission fail. Urgent action was required, for if a powerful and prepared United States were to enter the war on the side of the British and the Russians, all would be lost in our struggle against International Communism. Our response had to be immediate, and through our emissaries and through Hitler the Japanese were prevailed upon to intercede, to act. In one blow effective American intervention in the European war was set back by one year. With their swift attack at Pearl Harbor, the Americans were prevented from acting to save Russia, from helping Zhukov in his attempts to push back the Germans. American aid was impossible, they needed to build up their own strength after this destruction in Hawaii.

But the American recovery came quickly and everywhere, on all fronts, Germany fell back, retreating to the European heartlands. In our chambers and council rooms we regretted this extension of the war, a world at war, a world of chaos, a world out of control. Although the escalation of fighting was of course very good for business, the threat to the stability of global politics was great. There was no doubt in the minds of the strategists and planners at the Vatican that this Second World War would lead to even greater change than the last Great War. The enormous movements of men through the world would eventually lead to a greater expectation of the working class. The troops that had explored continents would have greater aspirations, larger desires, a product of their broader view of the world. This inappropriate greed would in turn lead to a jealous force for change that would, when the conflict had been resolved, lead to greater world instability. We would have to deal with this, plan for this contingency, establish new controls, goals for mankind offering superficial satisfaction, fulfilling seeming needs and desires.

It was, surprisingly, du Plessis who suggested how to deal with the problem. His philosophy came from a striking insight into the essence of humanity, the driven greed of mankind. He had observed the response of the semi-educated Europeans to the GIs, their desire for motor cars, Frigidaires, flashy clothes, radios, and had suggested that man's energies might be redirected. It might be that if an accumulation of these useless possessions could be made to be viewed as being enviable, then not only would manufacturing industry benefit, but the population would also be deflected from any concern with political issues. The man with a car and fridge would want to keep his car and fridge, keep it away from the man who had neither car nor fridge. And the man who had neither fridge nor car would strive to obtain these desired objects. This process would solidify the established system, this drive for consumer durables operating to stabilize political systems, directing the people towards capitalism.

Agnelli had argued that this might not be the case, and that grubby humanity might strive through revolution to obtain what they wished. But Pius, our great logician, swayed our council, describing mankind as essentially placid and non-violent. Von Rumbold's belief was in a passive populace that would strive through legitimate means to obtain defined comforts. So, in our plans for the world after the war, the new consumerism was to be promoted, guaranteeing the continued expansion of the world's manufacturing base, and limiting civil unrest.

We had had bad news from the secular Fascist Government of Italy. The Italians had always been half-hearted in their support for the Germans, and had not desired war, which meant an unpalatable destruction of their peaceful lives. These children loved the sunshine, loved their laughing wine: there was too much beauty in their warm lands distracting them from empire and conquest. The Allied landings in Sicily were for the Italians a most serious event, a reality that was cold and unpleasant, that breached the pantomime amusement of strutting uniforms. They wanted nothing of a bitter war, of death and blood and steel, and the vision of an onslaught on the homelands of Italy, on the fair plains, on the ancient cities was horrible and extreme. The Italians wished for no more to do with the war. Sicily. The Allies were in Sicily, it was time for peace, and a return to the pleasant fields.

Agnelli had information from the Italian cabinet. In late July 1943, the Italians' distaste for war had become harder, angrier. The workers were striking, an expression of the antipathy of the whole nation for the war and its escalation in their land. The mood of the people was for peace, for a settlement prior to the Allies' inevitable invasion from Sicily to the mainland. Agnelli had heard from General Badoglio that Mussolini was wavering in his loyalty to Hitler. He had sensed the mood of the people and had declared himself for peace. This would not do. We could not have Europe's underbelly exposed to the tearing teeth of the Allies. Italy could not be unprotected. Italy could not be an Allied camp. In council our discussion was brief. Italy needed to become neutral, her sovereignty intact, the Allies out of Sicily, Hitler safe from attack from the south. Mussolini had become unreliable and he had to be got rid of. It was simple. The army was the only effective authority in Italy and we had General Badoglio take over. A most satisfactory truce was signed, and there was peace between Italy and the Western powers.

Meanwhile, Mussolini, that treacherous traitor, plotted and fretted, regrouping, attempting to return to power.

Surprisingly the Italian people missed him, missed the jolly parades and the boasting dictator. He gave them joy, he made them feel significant, he was a bright light for Italy, shining sizzling neon that made Italy's men feel manly, and Italy's women feel that Italy had men. Italy missed the man, the ripple-necked dictator, Il Duce, primping, empty symbol of a toytown land. They yearned for him, needed the illusory promise of an infallible strength.

Von Ribbentrop rang through to my control desk to express German governmental concern. I was enjoying a fine cigar, the dung of the Cuban tobacco on my fingers, the grey breath of its smoke at my lips. My right arm encircled a cup of cappuccino. I loved the redness of my robes, loved to see the cloth before me, and the unnecessary protection of my arm was not for the coffee, it was to make my view more perfect, the rim of red, a sea break for a vista of business, a view of the rushing order of the Vatican command post.

'My dear Horsmunden. Good morning. You are well?'

'Thank you, von Ribbentrop, and you are too, I trust?'

I pictured him in his office, book-lined, tidy. I waited for von Ribbentrop to settle into the meat of our discussion. The line was clear, so entirely audible that I could hear him cross his legs, hear him bend to align his trouser creases, hear him think. Von Ribbentrop, so understated, such a perfect gentleman. I felt warm when I spoke with him, his conversation brought me love for the day.

'Cardinal, our government needs to know the Vatican's opinion of Mussolini. May I speak frankly with you?'

'My dear baron, I would be distressed if our conversations were not frank.'

I tipped a little brandy into my coffee, saw with pleasure the alcohol puncture pretty black holes in the white froth.

Von Ribbentrop continued. 'We tire of Mussolini.' This, of course, I knew. Goebbels had told Agnelli, and Agnelli had presented the information to the Vatican cabinet. We had tired of Mussolini too.

'And how does the German Government wish to proceed?' This of course I knew too.

'We wish to remove Mussolini and replace him.' How unusually bluntly put. The Germans would substitute an identical double for Il Duce, a malleable replacement, trained and true. This was absolutely sensible. It fulfilled the needs of both the German and Italian peoples. The Germans would have their southern flank reliably protected and the Italians would have their hero. Already, within the lower echelons of the Italian military the Germans had established control, the SS taking over the soft Italian brigades, reinforcing Italy with uninvited German troops and now, at the highest levels, they would also have security.

'My dear von Ribbentrop, I speak on behalf of the Vatican. The situation has been difficult for too long. We need to act now, to protect the order of Europe. Your government has the Vatican's blessing to do as it sees fit.'

'Thank you, Cardinal. You oblige us greatly. Good day.'

And the Nazis duly acted. A minor putsch was staged by 'dissident' Italians who arrested Mussolini. A few days later, German paratroopers 'rescued' Il Duce, then shot him and replaced him with a stooge. Italy was secured and the Vatican made safe once more.

Chapter Fifteen

IT HAD been a valuable war, but Europe was changed beyond the dreams of any strategic plan. Our priests were active in the immediate post-war period, dispensing prayers to the starving, warming the frozen with incense and clothing the naked with a thousand blessings. The challenges that the Vatican faced were similar to those at the end of the Great War. The challenge's essence was change and our struggle the management of change and the maintenance of our control of world order. Our council's concern was with the limitations of the mad dance of Communism, the disruptive poisonous anarchy oozing from Eastern Europe that threatened to drown our world. A bulwark against Communism in Europe was erected, and the Marshall Plan rebuilt industry and formed the foundations of the wealth that provided the ultimate defence. People who have wealth will not share their comfort, material possession is the securest defence against the ravening hunger of Communism.

So Germany became strong again and our eastern boundaries were made safe. The bright allure of material goods, of comfort, of full stomachs, of unnecessary consumer ephemera, was enormously attractive to the people, and everywhere, through the influence of the media, this allure was made ever brighter. Advertising created icons of desire and the people were given visions of the standard, the average, the mode, whose motes they must strive to attain. The happy housewife, the successful husband, loaded and encumbered by unnecessary goods and accompanying debt, were established as the norm. To be without was an abomination, to be without was failure. Fashion and film were the means by which consumerism was conveyed and, by the magic of transfer, each purchase gave promise of access to this glamorous world. We loved it. And in post-war Europe, the investments of the Marshall Plan were returned a thousandfold, returned in terms of political stability, and returned as financial gain.

The people were not only stabilized by these indirect processes but also directly by physical addictions, the enslavements of alcohol, of cigarettes, addictions that produced enormous gain. Glorious were the legitimate revenues from beer, wine and spirits. No longer did we need Prohibition to support our Church. Nicotine our brightest son, huge are your industries, and immaterial your harvest of death. Immaterial because death saved money, coming when the worker had retired, and therefore having only good revenue implications, limiting pension payments and society's responsibility for care.

In America, McCarthy and Nixon captured the moment and purged the nation in a series of showcase hearings against a few nonentities. The Senator's hearings made electric the paranoia, magnified the population's anti-Communist feelings, made solid and comfortable the materialist order of the second world.

In Asia too our plans were subtle. A broken Japan was rebuilt with Western laws, built as a capitalist edifice, a bulwark against the innumerable Chinese, the sweeping tide that threatened Vietnam, Korea, Cambodia and Laos.

The investment mirrored the Marshall Plan, building stability with each factory, manufacturing legitimacy with each bridge, railway, road and dam. A military confederacy was established. A union of South-East Asian states, backed by American capital and organized by Secretary Dulles. Our best efforts were extended, and military bases, harbours, airfields and depots were constructed to hold back anarchy.

Our world was relatively stable again. We had recovered significant control, and civilization was restructured through the confederacy of our power, through our friends, through our organization, money and will. We needed to extend our power in the United States and to fund European counter-Communist political movements, and this required an enormous financial commitment. America was ever-changing and there was no place for complacency with regard to our current status. The United States in the early 1950s produced over one-third of the industrial world's output, and was of overwhelming importance in our view of the planet.

Pius had convened a planning meeting to review strategies for the decade. He ruled our world with grace and gravity, in control, balanced, sensible and occasionally inspired. Von Rumbold had done unimaginably well. In a time of change, he had been constant, strong, organized, ordered. He had become even more obese with the years of his rule, so that he could no longer carry his own weight, and like some Polynesian potentate he was carried from table to chair. There was no space between meals for von Rumbold, and his cooks provided an unending parade of comestibles for the ravenous one. Von Rumbold, falling on his food, clamping, sweeping, seizing, cramming, from plate to mouth, from new plate to the same mouth.

In the council room of the Vatican we sat, thirteen and

two, planning the financial reinforcement of the European political vanguard against Communism, the flow of cash into the coffers of the French and Italian democratic parties. Thirteen: the Pope and his cardinals. Two: the Capo dei Capi and Europe's *éminence grise*. In a circle of fifteen, men of consequence, men of might, in a room of ancient treasure from the palaces of Rome and Athens, we organized our world.

The Capo was a small man, smiling, benign, grey-haired and anonymous. A man of delicate nature and sensitivity, fastidious, urbane, a Sicilian of Greek ancestry, a man with whom we could deal, and a man who could deal for us. This man had entered the cabinet room on his knees, and crawled, a supplicant, to Pius's throne, where he'd kissed the hem of his robe, his head lowered in appropriate respect. Pius had leaned forward to pull him to his feet, embraced him, blessed the Church's favourite son, and begged him to be seated. Onassis, the roots of his wealth in Prohibition, the foundation of his fortune in drug smuggling, the mansions of his money built from oil shipment during the war, Onassis controlled organized crime in America, Capo dei Capi, head of all the Mafia. He ruled, magisterial, unchallenged, commanded the unions, controlled all illegality. Onassis was as powerful as the leader of any country, his budget billions, his armies the free world's enforcement agencies. And Onassis needed forgiveness, craved cleansing, and for him, only for him, Pius played the charade of dispensation, quieting the black beast of Sicilian superstition.

The *éminence grise* was Retinger, a man of urbanity and sophistry, friend to Emperors and Presidents, a respected philosopher, councillor to governments, manipulator, intellectual, planner and believer, his mission to unify Europe through committees, through legitimate canvassing, through political lobbying, through the wise hands that held the tillers of power. Retinger appeared avuncular, a friendly parish priest to whom all could be told and by whom all could be forgiven. He was a priest and planus his life, he had known everything and everyone. Born in Poland of noble stock, educated at the Sorbonne in the years before the Great War, a devoted and learned Jesuit, master spy, double agent, Retinger had excelled. Through him alone, the First Congress of Europe had been set up at the Hague in 1948, and from this meeting had grown the Council of Europe and eventually the European movement. The Americans realized the significance of this movement in the struggle against Communism, and funded these groups via the Central Intelligence Agency. Through these organizations, Retinger was able to form a unique grouping of the powerful, the élite, the establishment, that took its name from the Bilderberg Hotel, an isolated hotel in rural Holland, where the first meeting was held.

So we sat, we fifteen, and exchanged gentle words, while the rain fell hard on the Vatican's roofs and windows, its noise a million summer flies hitting the tiles and glass.

Before business a pretty diversion. Indian dancers in ceremonial costume came into our circle, and celebrated an irrelevant god. We clapped the wriggling charade, and the waves of the Pope's blessing were on the smiling people as they left the room.

I was at the Pope's left hand, my position defined by my status within the Vatican's hierarchy, second in line to the throne. Agnelli was at his right. We faced Retinger and Onassis who sat side by side, a grey locus in a ring of red and white. Dr Retinger spoke, his voice spittle thickened, husky. He was eloquent, his speech precise and the significance of his statements was emphasized by his right hand which held an imaginary conductor's baton. We listened to his summary of the state of Europe, a précis gleaned from a thousand conversations with the world's real rulers. His summary was for Onassis, who nodded ponderous approval at each mention of the menace of Communism. The Capo's arms rested on his thighs, the tips of his fingers touching each other and forming the apex of a liver-spotted pyramid.

Dr Retinger concluded, 'Gentlemen, today we have to plan for the Church's future. It is vital that we, the Church, are part of populist politics. We need the hearts and minds of the people. These are ours if we invest wisely in the Catholic democratic movements, which by the simple manipulation of the name have a powerful hold on the community. Gentlemen, I ask that you consider the apportioning of funds to these movements. Let us keep Europe strong, let us keep its people. Let us maintain freedom, let us maintain the hegemony of the true Catholic Church.'

Retinger's passion had pulled him from his chair, had taken him over, overwhelmed him. He looked around at us, confused, a blind man, uncertain of his place, disorientated for a clumsy moment by the rushing enthusiasm of his own rhetoric. He felt for his chair and sat down. Agnelli coughed, cleared his throat, and answered for the Vatican Cabinet.

'Monsignor Retinger. On behalf of his holiness and the entire council of ministers, I thank you for your work for Catholicism, for civilization. Monsignor, you have been tireless in your efforts, unremitting in your exertions, exemplary in your contribution. For over thirty years you have toiled, and it is with pleasure that we take this opportunity to bestow upon you the title of Knight Templar, of the order of St Nicholas, honouring your service and dedication to the Catholic Church.'

Dr Retinger flushed, absolutely surprised. Cardinal Agnelli reached into his robes and pulled out a velvet box, opened it, and passed a blue and white enamelled Maltese cross, hung on a showy chain, to Pius.

'Monsignor, would you be good enough to approach his holiness.'

Retinger shuffled forward and knelt before the Pope. Pius extended his hand to Retinger who kissed the heavy ring of office. The cross was draped around his neck, and Retinger, trembling with delight at the honour, the flash of rolled gold at his throat, bowed to us all, his hand held over his heart.

I watched Onassis's face, saw the quick flash of jealousy that had captured him and knew that our plan was working well; we had manipulated the Capo. He wished for recognition, needed reward, and would be prompted into the contributions that we required. Dr Retinger returned to his seat. It was my turn to speak.

'As Information Minister, I have watched the growth of democracy with concern. The power of the common man has increased, and, as we have seen in the last decade, it has been used to promote change in the order of Europe. We have seen the disruption of war, a disruption that would not have come to pass without popular support for the National Socialists. We do not wish for a repetition of this disorder. The Church needs to disestablish Communism, to restore old orders and morality. The new Catholic democratic parties of France and Spain offer the Church a unique opportunity for us to re-establish sense, to reorder Europe, to bring peace, promote industry, restore the establishment, and maintain stability over the coming years.'

At this point Onassis ostentatiously crossed himself and looked around the room to make sure that his gesture had been noted. It hadn't, so he crossed himself again. I continued.

'These political parties need support, and by support I mean financial assistance, to establish credible populist movements that oppose the march of Communism. We have an unparalleled chance to win the hearts and minds of the people, manipulate them, and defeat Communist oppression.' Onassis nodded his emphatic agreement.

'Gentlemen, the Church cannot be seen to be directly supporting these democratic political parties. The Church's coffers cannot be opened to them, because this would bring against us accusations of imperialism, of interference in the politics of secular states.' The audience agreed. 'This funding must be covert.'

I turned to face Onassis, and the Capo, seizing his chance, made his bid.

'Holiness, eminences.' He stood up, bowed deeply to Pius, and with a sweep of his hand extended the bow to include us all in his respect. 'I can see the necessity of supporting the Christian democratic movements, and it gives me only pleasure to pledge aid from my organization.' He bowed again.

That was it. It was done, covert monies from the Mafia families would find their way into the coffers of the Christian Democratic Party in Italy and the Mouvement Républicain Populaire in France. I resumed my seat. It was Agnelli's turn again, and he stood to present Onassis with his honour.

'Capo dei Capi, Aristotle Onassis,' he began, and Onassis, recognizing that he too was about to have a holy order conferred upon him, smiled hugely, then, almost tearful, blew his nose. Agnelli continued. 'On behalf of his holiness and the entire council of ministers, I thank you for your work for Catholicism, for civilization. You have been devoted in your efforts for the Church, the greatest benefactor in our history, a labourer for the Vatican, a valiant knight at the head of a loving army. For over thirty years you have toiled, both in the United States and in the Middle East. You have worked in difficult times and by your efforts brought yourself honour and dignity. Your selflessness . . .'

Agnelli faltered a little at this point, and, knowing him as I did, I recognized that he was having difficulty containing his laughter, laughter at the extraordinary concept of Aristotle Onassis being selfless, honourable and dignified. He was none of these things. He was a hoodlum. Agnelli was in control again.

'Your selflessness has sown the seeds of a great crop, that we, the Church, have reaped over the many years of your loyal service. Capo dei Capi, it is with great pleasure that we take this historic opportunity of bestowing upon you the title of Commander of the Ancient Order of the Holy Cross of St John, honouring your service and your dedication to the Catholic Church.'

Onassis's cheeks puffed out with the sweet pleasure of pride. He was certain that a Commander was much more important than a Knight, that his award had greater significance than Retinger's. And Retinger was just as sure that a Knight Templar was of much greater status than a mere commander. But we all knew that both titles were of no significance and that enamelled brass was worth less than silver. Onassis came forward, shuffled towards the Pope, then flung himself on to the floor, his hands slapping the flagstones. Agnelli bent to raise the prostrate man and Pius slipped around the Capo's neck the vainglorious flashy chain that carried a cheap and glittering cross, while outside there was thunderous applause for our performance from the rain breaking on the cobblestones.

Chapter Sixteen

AGNELLI AND I lay together in the cool waters of a crystal bath. Through the panoramic windows the indigo dusk was livened by the evening's first stars. Yellow lilies crowded the bath chamber and their scent filled the room. Thick white candles burned in silver sconces and their flickering light made ghosts of the hanging tapestries. A Koi carp flashed across my legs and the shivering brush of its fins tickled my skin. I pushed away into the deeper water and relaxed, floating on my back, tied up at the pool's edge by my trailing hand. A bigger fish nibbled at my genitalia, kissed me gently, a young Chinese girl from the mountains of Mongolia, hairless and sweet, trained, artful. Her twin was with dear Agnelli, whose wrinkled crowsfeet drew together, puckering with the pleasure of the sweet moment. Our bathtime had its earlier model, took its paradigm in antiquity from Tiberius's swimming pool on Capri. There in the island sunshine, he had swum with his fish, nibbling children, delight of his rapacious old age. Our twins were mature, aged, I guessed, seventeen or eighteen years. We had bought them in Hong Kong, a most satisfactory purchase, bought from their own mother for $10,000, and the lustre of my twin's shining hair sparkled in the Venetian mirrors that surrounded the bath.

'Enough, my child,' I said and the smiling one floated

away to splash after the orange fish that spasmed from poolside to poolside. Our peace was broken by the shuddering reverberations of a plane's descent to Rome airport. How tiresome, how infuriating; I would ring tomorrow and arrange for the flight paths to be rerouted across the city, leaving the Vatican at peace.

I had been disturbed by the wretched plane, but my discomfort was not felt by Agnelli, who floated on his back, his feet rippling flippers, the occasional happy whale-spout blowing from his mouth. Agnelli was enjoying himself, comfortable, at peace with his pleasure. A rare thing, this contentment. Who had I known who was happy, who enjoyed their time, loved their place, accepted their position? Nobody; except for this placid Italian. Yet in him this comfort had not driven out ambition, had not made him slothful. He ruled the Jesuits, he was able, he was creative, he had attained and achieved, reaching the second highest position in our Church. He was the Pope's heir, Pius's successor.

Champagne was brought to the poolside by a Haitian slave in a loincloth. Agnelli and I drank each other's good health. I tried to tip a little wine into my Chinese girl, but she would not drink, shook her head and wriggled away, frightening the carp with her giggling escape.

At the far side of the pool stood four steel poles. From their tops hung thick leather stirrups, and this modern assembly of brown leather and polished metal contrasted with the ancient mosaics and friezes of the Roman bath.

Through the golden architrave of the entrance to the bath chamber walked the evening's actors, in a show organized for our gracious pleasure. They were Thai, two women and a man, and they bowed deeply and respectfully to their audience, two cardinals and their fish, aquatic and air breathing. Our little women clung to us, holding to us for support in the bath's water. My little one's head rested on my shoulder, her arm draped over the hoary grey of my belly, and her breasts, cool with water and hot with her body's heat, touched my chest.

Before us, the actors drew themselves up from their deep bows. The man was young and strongly built, his chest unusually muscular, his belly flat, his legs bandy, his hair long, his face smiling, clean-shaven, healthy. His feet were bare and he wore blue, chalk-striped trousers. The taller woman was a pastiche dominatrix in a tight leather corset, its bows and buttons wagging, dangerous patent-leather stilettos and elbow-length satin cocktail gloves, and her drunken riding whip danced a hissing waltz with an invisible partner. She had pruned her eyebrows to thin needles, and her mouth was coral cruel. The smaller woman was dumpy, plump and placid, an automaton, her dazed, jerky bows gracelessly out of synch with her fellow actors. She wore a loose-fitting crêpe evening gown cut low over her breasts and billowing out over her soft hips to fall in neat pleated creases to mid-calf.

The actor turned from the group and with a swift movement switched on a tape machine. The machine head clicked into place, and thick metallic tape threaded between the slipping spools. I sipped champagne and listened to the music, the new bossanova rhythm, shuffling, scuffling, scuffing, Latin, strong.

The dominatrix lunged at the yellow man. She cracked her whip. He scurried from its darting snake tongue, backing away from the march of her attack, until he could retreat no more, his shoulders jammed into the dusty orange plaster of the wall. The whip was ripping steel in the burnt air, snapping hooks thrashing at his head and shoulders. He ducked, his arms up high to protect his face, dodging almost with random luck the vicious whip. She smacked the handle of her whip flat into his chest, screamed, 'Don't move, bastard,' and the spiders and flies bounced in fright from the room's dark crevices. She clamped a massive iron collar around his neck, fixed it with a stiff padlock from which a steel chain dangled, and pressed its keys into her fierce brassière.

Across the poolside wandered the automaton, a lost child sucking her thumb, oblivious, enwrapped in a smoky dream. The dominatrix's whip cracked across the man's chest and a broad red welt declared itself in a roseate line that crossed between his nipples. She placed her black-gloved hands on his chest, and they traced down across his ribs and belly, black tarantula, stalking across the slippery skin of their prey. Her hands were at his waist, then ripped at his trousers. Two of his fly buttons sprang across the room and tinkled on the mosaic floor. She fell to her knees before her slave, and was his slave, sucking at his penis. She pulled back to inspect the rearing bird that shone with the polish of her spittle. She stood up, stamped her foot, and grabbed his penis in the clamp of her glove, then smashed him again with her whip, this time with a jarring nastiness that had the reality of broken skin. A thin line of blood prickled from his shoulder. Blood bubbled, then tripped down his chest. She shouted, 'You will come with me,' and dragged him by his penis towards the idiot girl. Golden fish wriggled through the silver bathwater, and our Mongol girls drew shiveringly to their floating cardinals.

'Agnelli, my dear, what are your views on Suez?'

The dominatrix and her slave barred the path of the idiot girl, who looked up with skewed puzzlement and stumbled away, thumb deep in her mouth, cheeks sucking,

sucking. The dominatrix screamed and yanked at her slave's chain. He fell and she kicked him with her sharp shoes. He groaned. Agnelli looked towards me and sipped a little more fine champagne. The Haitian slave tipped more wine in his glass, and as she bent to serve him, her buttocks peeked through the wizened strands of her grassy skirt.

'It's difficult. Nasser is an annoying manipulator. Pity, he's not Catholic, really. We could have use for him. That business with the Dam, inviting American then Russian offers. Quite remarkable. Had them all running around. And now nationalizing the Canal. Outrageous from the viewpoint of the French and the British. Bad for business.'

His conversation was interrupted by the crack of the whip, and his girl pressed to him with fright, pushing Agnelli low into the bathwater, spilling his drink. A slick of champagne bubbles floated away, lodged in the weir of his pubic hair, then disappeared. Agnelli comforted the Mongol with strange softness, patting her damp hair, as one might a nervous poodle.

'Do you think there will be a response, Agnelli?'

'Certainly. There's so much at stake. But it's not money, Horsmunden, it's national pride, jingoism. The Church is well out of it. Things will end badly for the British and French. Nasser rides a tide of Arab nationalism. He's harnessed the people in the same way that Hitler did. He's sensed the moment and it's his. There's no point in our interfering in Egypt, they've nothing to offer. The land is poor, the people wild. The worst that could happen would be a limit to shipping through the Canal. And the blockade would be ultimately too damaging to Nasser for him to sustain. Egypt depends entirely on the Canal for foreign exchange, and eventually it would have to be reopened. The French and British are being stupid. They need to realize that their imperialism is limited, these are modern times, and now we have a new form of colonialism that is pannational, subtle and avoids the petty delineation of territory. It is a financial hegemony, covert and most —'

The whip cracked again and its fizz interrupted Agnelli's soliloquy. The dominatrix and her slave had trapped the dumpy automaton, caught her in a corner. The dominatrix's whip flew, and her prey was snatched from dreams to a land of fear and fire. The two seized the woman and dragged her to the metal poles. Her heels dug into the ground and her body was stiff, resisting. Her eyes jerked between her two masters, wild whites flashing, popping. They strapped her wrists into the leather cuffs, bound her tight then stooped to her feet, hauling her from the ground to bind her pale ankles. She swung like a captured deer between the four steel poles, head back, dark hair loose and tumbling.

The dominatrix scowled and her whip whistled. She ripped off her victim's dress to expose her shivering breasts, and sucked her nipples, pulling and teasing. She heaved her prey's dress high and forced gloved fingers into her vagina, while we drank a little more champagne. The Mongol women were calmer, less tense in our arms.

The dominatrix grabbed at the yellow man, rubbed his penis energetically with her slippery satin glove, then pulled him by his chain, link by link into her embrace. She clung to him, pushed hard into his body, then wriggled and slithered, snaked up and down against his flesh, her stiff corset making tramlines in his skin. Her arms enwrapped him, pulling him closer, closer, then she trapped his penis between her thighs, rode him without him entering her, buttocks juggling backwards and forwards, vaguely in time to the bossanova's beat. Then, keeping hold of his penis with her hand, she fell on top of the limp ragdoll, scratching at her breasts, then reached underneath herself, unhooking her corset. The leather snapped open and her vulva flashed at us. She rubbed herself into the bound woman, grinding her pelvis into the woman's wide crotch, and yanked at her man, cramming his penis into her own vagina. The actor took her from behind, pressing in and out, twitching his penis into her, and the dominatrix writhed over the bound woman, squeezing her breasts, and banging at her pubis with her clitoris. The three meshed together, heaving and grinding, the man standing, pushing into the dominatrix, who curled, shrieking and clawing, over her automaton slave. She swung back at the actor and slapped his buttocks.

'Harder,' she shouted. 'Harder.' And his efforts were spurred on, the bossanova beat, this time, kept by the whack of his scrotum against her buttocks.

I guided my woman's hand to my own groin and she traced delicate lines over my skin. Agnelli's girl's head moved up and down in the water, rising and falling over his penis, and an inquisitive shoal of goldfish sneaked towards us. The Haitian slave stood silently and the music played out, the tape spools thrashing free. I held up my glass and it was filled. On the edge of an orgasm, I clutched my woman's hand, so that she was still, and I could continue to enjoy the play. The dominatrix came with a shriek. Her neck arched back, and her twisting hands pulled the actor's buttocks hard into her. She collapsed forward, and was still for a moment on the automaton's belly.

Agnelli and I politely clapped and my woman bent over me to take my blessing. The automaton was untied and she jumped to her feet. The three actors sprang around the poolside, leaping dancers, at the end of a successful matinée. They bowed, and bounced from the room waving, leaving us the resonating echoes of their smiles.

Chapter Seventeen

THEY CAME towards us from a shining middle distance, a deputation of Africans from a starving country. They wore long white robes and embroidered pill-box hats. They came forward slowly, in a stately rhythmic march. In this mirage there was no sound, then, as they came closer, the light slap of their sandals on the floor was suddenly audible and brought an image of the flickering swish of sand blown across a tumbling dune by a rushing burning wind. They marched forward, these little people, and grew, becoming taller, developing features as they approached our thrones. They came to us along an avenue of marble statues carved in a far Renaissance time, and the stone saints frowned as they watched the Africans' progress through the courts of our power. Autumn's whispering sun bid them welcome through stained-glass windows, and the occasional flash of red or blue lit the pure robes of these equatorial people. They came to us preceded by a tall captain of our Swiss Guard, and their footsteps kept pace with his. From the walls a thousand Holy Virgins inspected the desert men, stared at the strangeness, the flowing robes, the dark faces and the virgins sighed, then turned away. Although it was only midday, there were shadows, and the receiving rooms were lit by the blue and yellow flames of a thousand thick tapers burning on ornate floor-mounted

308

silver-gilt candelabra. The shivering wake of the black men's billowing robes caught the flames which flared high as they passed by, then stuttered and fell.

The delegation stood before us. The captain saluted, stamped his boots into the ground, and marched into the ranks of guards that surrounded our thrones. We were three, Pius XII, Cardinal Agnelli and myself. The Pope bestowed his blessing on the Africans and, as he began his benediction, they fell to their knees before him, eyes averted, hands clasped in prayer. Pius bid them rise, and they stood before the golden thrones, hesitant and tremulous supplicants. Pius began the audience.

'We welcome you to St Peter's Basilica, to the Vatican, to Rome. The Church is honoured by your presence and wishes your people peace . . .'

He continued with these and similar pleasantries and I inspected this delegation of churchmen from the Sudan. Their country was starving and their people tired victims of civil war and drought. Their children were dying of diarrhoea, schistosomiasis and malaria, AIDS and kwashiorkor. Plague and pestilence, disease and bullets were competing equally successfully for the thin legions of desperate souls. The fertile north had become desert, the dry south was fused sand and the sun and the heat's progeny were dust and death. Tanks paraded over the rocky land and fighter planes strafed the columns of refugees, who straggled along invisible trails in innocence, to nowhere.

The African delegates seemed to relax a little with the Pope's felicitations, they were smiling, enjoying their time in history. Why had they come here, these hopeless people? Go back to your mud palaces and your wattle cathedrals, go back to your straw homes and your African sun, go back to your tribes, go back to your slaves, go to your withered

lakes and dry dust, your burnt mountains and sterile plains!
Go from the Vatican, with your infinite needs and irrelevant
plans. Africa was impossible, it threatened, it consumed, it
raged, it starved. Africa was too great a problem, its people
primitive, unable, uneducable, simple. Let them stay in
Africa, let them starve, let them suffer, let them starve and
suffer until they evolve through these natural processes to
civilization, to culture. We had their mines, there was
nothing else that the continent could offer. Pius continued.

'And how is your country, Archbishop?'

The fattest and oldest black man started, then answered.
'Your holiness, our country is at war, strife and starvation
empty the pockets of our people. Our land is tired and our
fields are barren. There has been no rain for seven years and
the storehouses are empty. The people are dispossessed
and the armies run wild. Despair and misery are our ministers and starvation our emperor. Holiness, we come to you
from an exhausted community of souls. We come to you to
plead for aid from the Holy Father. We come to you as
brother Catholics. We come as beggars. Holy Father, feed
the starving, help the poor. Holiness, save our country. In
our poor land our only possession is our belief, and we
believe in God's goodness and the purity of his earthly
emissaries. We beg you, grant our country your assistance.
Let the Church feed its people, let the shepherd Church
succour its flock.' Pius prickled up in anger, and his many
chins settled defiantly into his chest.

The Archbishop carried on, 'Holiness, in our starving
country, a child dies every three seconds, and his death is
from poverty, from poor sanitation, from diseases that died
in Europe in the last century. We have no pure water, no
drains, no inoculation programme, no harvest. In our

country, bacteria and flies are the only creatures that prosper. Yet our country is rich, rich in foreign aid. Our money comes from the Americans, the World Bank, the Russians, the Chinese. It buys guns and tanks, bombs and planes. And these eat each other. More money comes, and the war is sustained. Our country becomes more indebted, and the interest on our loans cripples us, takes the little profit from our mines, leaves us poorer than ever, unable to find credit to import food and medicines. Our debts are bad, bad in their origins, wicked in their result. Holiness, our country starves, our children die. Holiness, we come to you on behalf of our brethren, the needy, the hungry and the dying. Holiness, grant our country the Holy Church's aid, help us to help our people.'

The Archbishop fell to his knees. I stared down at the grey astrakhan that fluffed out under the dome of his black tribal hat, and it annoyed me. The Archbishop clasped his hands together and his mumbled prayer was punctuated by the baritone 'amens' of his fellow churchmen. Pius responded to his pleading without bothering to ask the Archbishop to rise to his feet.

'Archbishop, fellow churchmen, we are saddened by the situation in Africa and you bring us stony news. We were, of course, aware of the bitter war, but not of the decimation of your people. Let us pray therefore for peace in your land, and we will this day order a mass to be said in St Peter's for the dead. Our thoughts and prayers will be with you, and we will beg the Almighty that the war will immediately cease.'

A pretty speech, regal and appropriate. That would do for Africa. The Archbishop was helped to his feet by his colleagues.

'Holiness, we thank you for your kind thoughts, Africa thanks you for your prayers, but I'm not sure that my request has been understood.'

Ridiculous man, of course it had been understood, and he had received the Church's answer. Our prayers would be with Africa this day. Pius's chins quivered again, and he edged forward in his golden throne. Agnelli seemed contemplative, concentrating on the Archbishop's words, but I knew my friend well enough to know that his contemplations were narcotic, with no view of the African desert. The Archbishop moved closer to Pius, who visibly recoiled from this invasion of his space.

'Holiness, my request, on behalf of my starving brothers and sisters, is for the direct intercession of the Holy Roman Church to help its African family. Holiness, feed the people, save our earthly souls. Look to the children and their mothers, the dying and the half dead. Your holiness can save us. Grant our country temporal aid, feed the congregations of your brothers and sisters in Africa. I beg you, help us.' The Archbishop's empty palms were raised to Pius, demanding to be filled. They would not be.

'Archbishop, these are difficult times for your country. I can understand your needs and wish that it were possible to help you. It is not within the power of Rome to grant your country substantive aid. Our only power is that of prayer and through God's will hope will come to your land. You must trust in our Lord, trust in Jesus, the Holy Spirit, God the Father, Jesus the Son. In God is our trust and with God our hopes for peace in Africa. My son, we will pray for you, and you too must pray, pray that God's wisdom will prevail and peace will enter the gates of your land.'

The African was agitated.

'Your holiness, I thank you for your prayer, but it is not enough.'

Pius did not like to be told that he was wrong, that his prayers were not enough. This was not the way to deal with his holiness. No way at all. Pius swelled, his great Teutonic mass engorged with anger and hostility towards these impudent men. How dare they question papal authority. How dare they? His reply was clipped. 'I'm unsure what you mean, Archbishop.'

The Archbishop, thinking that if he could only make his country's needs understood then his wish would be granted, tried once more to explain the situation to a seemingly uncomprehending Pius.

'Holiness, our needs are direct, our needs immediate. Grant us assistance! Let us go home to Africa with your promise of aid for our dying people. I beg you, feed my people.' His voice cracked and broke with sudden sobbing. He dabbed at his eyes with his sleeve and was clasped in a comforting embrace by a compatriot.

'My lord Archbishop, the Vatican has no funds to assist your country.'

Pius was right, our funds were all tied up in enterprises around the world, and what monies were not were safe in Swiss bank accounts, earning secure interest that kept us here in the Vatican City. There was no money for Africa. The Archbishop spun from his countryman's embrace, and his words were spat from an angry mouth.

'Your holiness, I find that incredible, how can it be true? I look around and I see wealth, in your paintings and statues, in your gold and silver, in your bright jewels and Holy City. Holiness, help us.'

'There is nothing that we can give you.'

'Holiness, one painting, one statue, one holy cross, one tapestry, just one single item could feed a hundred thousand people. Let me remind your holiness of a parable, the parable of the loaves and fishes. Just as one loaf and one fish fed the multitude, let the miracle of one item of the Vatican's collection feed the masses of Africa.'

'We cannot give you the Church's holy property.'

'What use are these piled possessions, these mountains of tawdry trinkets, these encrusted oils, these marble monuments? Where is the breath in an antiquity, the feeling in a reliquary? What is a painting's worth balanced against that of a child's life? Holiness, I beg you, help your people, help your flock.'

'Archbishop, these are not in my possession to give you. I would that I could give them to you. I myself have no need for material wealth. I am a simple man. I live for the Lord and I live on prayer. But these things that you see,' Pius's arm swept the room, 'these are not mine, they are the Church's and it is the responsibility of my office to maintain intact the history of the Church. I am a guardian of the Church's inheritance, a keeper of history. My duty is to conserve, my duty is to maintain. I am the custodian of our civilization, embodied in me, as Pope, is this world, this city. And if I were to disassemble this Vatican, to unload history into the gaping tumbrels of need, our city would fall, cross by cross, carving by carving, and the holy stones assembled over time's ages would crumble and fall. Archbishop, I cannot help you. I have empty hands, but empty hands can clasp together in prayer, and my prayers and those of the Church are with you this day.'

Pius signalled to the captain of the guard. The audience was concluded. The captain marched from the ranks and saluted the African delegation. The deputation followed him from the receiving rooms, and they were a shabby, tarnished group who shuffled away, exhausted despondent, supporting each other, their footsteps out of time with the high march of their tall escort.

Chapter Eighteen

ONASSIS, PASSIONATE prince, king of our dreams, noble warrior, stamper on ingrates, mightier than the mighty, comptroller of the world, how valiant thy sword, how magnificent thy victories, Onassis our first born, keeper of promises, entrusted, righteous! The 1950s and 1960s were a magnificat for Onassis, these two decades had doubled, trebled, multiplied by a hundredfold his wealth. His base metals had become platinum and his gold the furthest brightest stars. His money was our money and the coffers of the Vatican Bank heaved and strained to contain their holiness. How godly was this man, how marvellous his achievement.

From the periphery of legitimacy, Onassis had shuffled his men into power and in America they ruled. From alcohol and drugs, from gambling and the unions his men had moved, sweeping before them scattered bushels of gold into the neat safes of law offices, government, industry and armaments. The roots of this movement from periphery to centre had its vehicle in the Hughes Corporation. Corporate America had been infiltrated through the Texan's business empire. Howard Hughes had been destroyed and in his place a mute substitute planted. This substitute had lived in secrecy and silence, guarded by mafiosi, while rumours of his paranoia, of his obsessive compulsive psychosis, had filled the newspapers, explaining his disappearance from public life and into the shadowlands. Through the Hughes Corporation, Onassis's influence multiplied, generating legitimate business whose profits were ours. Our money was now in aircraft and armaments, in space ventures and pharmaceuticals, and closed were our risky ventures that had grown from prohibition. Onassis's early contacts with Joseph Kennedy burgeoned and together they advanced to control American political life.

Then disaster. Kennedy's stroke removed half of our American political power base, but our confidence for a few moments was emplaced in his son, whom we backed financially in his bid for the highest office. The election was won, but instead of showing loyalty to his father's former partner, Kennedy railed against the Mafia might. Our drug dealers were imprisoned and our union men jailed. This was intolerable and was dealt with justly in Dallas. In true Mafia tradition, our prince took as his bride his enemy's widow. Jackie was his and victory complete.

In order to secure our heroin production in the golden triangle against the Communist advance, Johnson was encouraged to escalate the war effort in South-East Asia. This had a double gain: our armaments industries made enormous profits and our jungle factories were secured.

Johnson was not allowed to stop the war. He had had a mighty lesson, he knew what had happened to his predecessor, realized that Kennedy's destruction had been Mafia-engineered and, knowing this, it took only the breath of a few words for him to be pushed, to be pulled, to move any which way that we and Onassis should desire.

As if to compensate, Johnson tried to secure his place in heaven by doing his best for the poor and the underprivileged, the blacks and the Hispanics, the socially deprived, the homeless and the sick. And in the legislature, civil rights bills and health charters proceeded through the House of Representatives and Senate. Johnson liberalized more than any other President. Johnson liberated, Johnson democratized America. We allowed it. It was a superficial gloss that would wash away in the first rain. We were right: a later analysis showed that in one hundred years of America, there had been no significant movement of wealth. Seven per cent of the nation owned 97 per cent of wealth. The balance of money and the balance of power was secure.

From my command post in the Vatican information centre, I kept an eye on England. Despite my complete immersion in papal work, despite the sublimation of all feelings of my origins into the Church, some traces of nostalgia crept forward when the satellite system beamed in from our abbeys in England. My assistants had the temerity to tell me that I smiled when England announced itself: I did smile.

Matthew spoke of a troubled land, a country of rippling scandal that threatened the government, a Conservative government whose policies we endorsed. The Duchess of Argyll had been caught in a salacious revel, in an orgy of bear-skinned guardsmen that compromised and utterly shocked a prissy establishment. A spying scandal involving a man named Martelli had revealed astonishingly lax security within the Ministry of Defence. Finally, a government minister had been caught with prostitutes procured by a society physiotherapist. He had lied, denying involvement, and his lies had been exposed. These three major scandals brought blustering denials from government lackeys.

Poor England, so soft-bellied the hypocrisy of her perverted aristocrats, so limp her old boy network, so petty her appetites and imaginations. How horrified the people must be pretending to be, bristling in their little houses in the rain. The people could not be allowed to see the great names sullied, the spies victorious, the ministers exposed. It would do no good at all. There was no sense in disestablishing the establishment, in making anxious the people's confident embrace of the state. Let them be quietened, set off an alternate show of fireworks that would make them forget the quick flash of scandal's lightning.

'And what are your plans, my dear Matthew?'

'Cardinal, we have no plan, we are stuck, quite stuck.'

'Well, Matthew, my dear, we must not be stuck, we have to take control, manipulate, organize. We can't have our boat breached by the storm, can we? We must make our own storm that clears our own heaven. So let us conjure a great wind that blows the crests from the roaring waves, quietens the ocean, gives us again a pond to play on.'

'How shall we arrange this, Cardinal?'

'Tell me, Matthew, what else is happening in England? Is there not an easier target for disapprobation? Can we not have a more traditional form of scapegoat? Is there not something else that is irrelevant to politics, to the establishment, that can be exaggerated, something easier for the people to accept? There must be. You must know of some other little event that could be blown up beyond all recognition to divert attention away from these tiresome realities?'

The Abbot did not reply, was quiet for many seconds, reviewing all the peripheral pieces of information filed over the last few months. And then there was almost a cheer, and certainly a very comfortable chuckle, when he found that indeed there was a nice little incident that entirely fulfilled all requirements.

'Why yes, Cardinal, there is.'

'Tell me, Matthew, my dear, do tell me.'

'Well, Cardinal,' and his voice had fire and enthusiasm, where previously there was great fatigue, 'the parish priest in Notting Hill, a district of London.'

'Matthew, I do know where Notting Hill is.'

'I am so sorry, Cardinal.'

'You are forgiven, Matthew, my dear, do carry on.'

'It has been reported that in this area a rather shady character, a Jew of course, ran an unscrupulous business. He bought the freeholds of half-empty properties, buying cheaply because of sitting tenants, and then forced out the tenants by violent means.'

This seemed an entirely reasonable business practice. 'So what, Matthew dear, so what?'

'Cardinal, I'm sorry to be so long-winded. He next moved in West Indians and whores and strong-armed the rent from them. If they failed to pay, they were bullied and terrorized, and they paid or their rooms were broken up, their furniture smashed, their china shattered. They did pay, Cardinal, and our man made more money. The man prospered, but on a small scale. He moved into a moneyed world and became a champagne Charlie. At his parties, the aristocracy stared at the vulgar monster, drank his wine, ate his food, then left and failed to return his invitation. He had a birthday-cake house and married his favourite whore, an auburn-haired wasp with a mouth like an O. Then he had a heart attack and died. He was small time, the house wasn't paid for. He had just £50,000 in the bank and his widow returned to her Shepherd Market parlour, with its Alsatian and duenna. That's it, Cardinal, the story of our Jew. But I must emphasize, Cardinal, that he was only one of many, a small part of a nationwide scandal.'

'I do understand, Matthew, my dear. Is there anything else of interest?'

'Not much, that's it.'

'I think, Matthew, that it does offer an absolutely splendid opportunity. I think that with a little exaggeration it might do. We would need to exaggerate the scale of the racketeering, the violence, the money involved, the numbers of people in a room, add in a few more whores, emphasize the unsavouriness of the individual concerned, that sort of thing, Matthew. And of course he is a Jew, Matthew, and the people definitely would like to hear a little more of bad Jews after that business with them in the war. Frankly there's been too much sympathy as a result of the so-called concentration camps. Camps, Matthew, they were places for good honest work, where just for once the Jews could work for their own adopted countries, the countries that protected them, nourished them, saved them, the countries that they selfishly and dishonestly exploited. It's my sincere view, Matthew, and the view of his holiness too, I might add, that this whole issue of the Jews has been grossly exaggerated by the International Conspiracy of Zionism to attract sympathy for the illegitimate Hebrew state. Yes, Matthew, we have good evidence that the whole camp issue has been used by the Jews to blackmail civilization, first into the establishment of their state itself, with land stolen from the stupid Arabs, and secondly to fund its running by means of these preposterous reparations. And look at the situation that America is in. They have no choice in the United States but to send untold millions to the Hebrews, because, if they don't, they'd be out of government. It's Jew power at its absolute stinking worst. Don't you think, Matthew?'

'Quite so, quite so.'

'Now back to this chap. Are you quite sure he's dead, Matthew?'

'As far as we know, Cardinal.'

'Was there an autopsy?'

'No, Cardinal. His own cousin signed the death certificate. You know these Jews, they're always in a hurry to be buried. Always in a rush to meet their Maker.'

'Yes, they get a discount if they're there before sundown.'

'Very good, Cardinal.'

'His cousin, was it?'

'Yes, you know, Cardinal, second-generation immigrant Jews, they get into portable income, medicine, the law, accountancy, it's salvageable business for when the pogroms come around again. First generation makes the money to educate the second generation.'

'But you're sure it was his cousin?'

'Yes, it's all here, Cardinal. It's in the report. His cousin was a family physician. The wife called him when her husband collapsed. It was the cousin that signed the certificate.'

'Don't you see, Matthew, this is absolutely perfect. The racketeer dies, he leaves an inappropriately small amount of money to his widow, and his own cousin signs the death certificate. It's just right. We can get the papers to suggest that the man's still alive, had his death faked and absconded with an enormous amount of cash, leaving a trivial amount of money in his will to his "widow" for whom he had no love. Matthew, this racketeer is our man. We can use him. All the ingredients are there for us to be able to divert the public's interest from situations that they have no need to be concerned with. Matthew, they don't need to know about government and spies and the frailties and momentary lapses of their betters. Let them forget about these irrelevancies. Let them return to their little lives, their comforts, their homes, their silly back gardens and their summer holidays. Give them this diversion – and how it will divert them – and the world will be secure once more. By the way, Matthew, what was the man's name?'

'Rachman, Cardinal, Rachman.'

'I like it. Matthew, I love it. Rachman, it conjures images of a creeping rat man, the name could not be better, I can see it now as a generic. Mark my words, Matthew, mark my words, in ten years' time that name will be part of your language. Rachmanism. Goodnight, Matthew.'

'Goodnight, Cardinal. Goodnight.'

Chapter Nineteen

THE PAPAL cabinet, council of cardinals, santum sanctorum, was meeting to review policy with regard to contraceptive practice, and to consider the new force of popular music that trampled our world in two-four, three-four, four-four and six-eight time, two fresh verses, chorus, repeat. The wild hymns and dancing psalms were a new religion for the young, its heroes new gods.

We picked at lampreys and the carcasses of turtles, roasted whole and basted in a sweet clear sauce, flavoured with cardamom and cumin. In the smoke of the open fire, in the shivering mist of candlelight, we slumped over our golden bowls and poured our own red wine.

Since Pius XI's death, we had lost only one of our number. Corpulent du Plessis had died in good old age, pleasuring his niece, a divine coquette whom he'd had raised as a sister of mercy. Eighty-nine years old and a glorious death, caught in pleasure, taken in death as he had lived his life. All of our lives seemed to be graced by longevity. There was a strong charm to our Vatican days that kept us here and kept us virile and vigorous. Du Plessis had, of course, been replaced by another Frenchman, Le Fanu, a tiny man of marked paranoia, with a voice of worried whispers, and the reddest hair slicked flat.

The doors opened and the Swiss Guards clanked in to

clear the table of carapaces and bones. A sorbet was served, citron glacé, sweet steel for our palates. Pius was on my right, Van Eyck on my left. Agnelli kept the Pope's right, the lines of the council sweeping out from us. The Pope flicked at the sorbet with his spoon then, plunging his thumbs into the ice for the pleasure of its coolness, pulled out, sucked, then pushed in again. Mannered Agnelli delicately swept sorbet into the tidy corner of his prissy mouth, and Van der Moer seemed to have fallen asleep. Caetano and Costanza were speaking in Portuguese, which was not allowed. Enrico Costa pulled at his neighbour's robe to remind him that Latin was the language of the cabinet, and not, definitely not, Portuguese. Caetano wiped his mouth with his sleeve, and then blew his purple nose into the tablecloth. I really didn't know why we had such a vulgarian in the cabinet. I had never liked him.

The guards cleared the table once more and then the doors opened to a single cook in a white chef's hat who pulled at the reins of a tall stallion. The horse's carcass was stiffened by roasting and his hooves were buried in iron casters that clanked over the marble flagstones. The cook pulled the horse into the room and swung the splendid Pegasus around so that he paralleled the table of cardinals. The horse had been skinned, exposing rivers of seared muscle flowing in anatomic lines, tendons and bones. The animal was rigid in his splendid death, legs splayed, neck arched, nostrils up, and his tail encased in a silver sheath reached to the high ceiling. Very good. And we banged our knife handles into the table top to show our appreciation.

Pius harrumphed, emptied his glass and drummed his fingertips on the arm of his chair. The chef bowed, and unfolded a linen cloth beneath the horse's belly. He gestured to a guard, and the giant stumped forward and slashed at

the beast's belly with the ripping edge of his pikestaff.
Hundreds of tiny birds tumbled out on to the cloth and
formed a crisp pile that buried the horse's hooves. We
banged the table again with our knives, and the chef served
us heaped songbirds and cuts from the horse's plump rump.
As we ate and drank, Agnelli, learned Agnelli, spoke.

'As I view it, there are two major threats to the order of
our good world, threats to the security of our control. The
first is the extraordinary popularity of modern music. This
is a phenomenon that is potentially most damaging.'

Pius XII burped loudly, coughed, and heaved another
goldfinch on to his plate. Agnelli continued.

'I sincerely believe that we have to take an active,
directing influence on modern music. Ignore it, and there
will be dangerous sequelae. During the last forty years
there has been a burgeoning of the media. New forms of
communication systems have been developed, and television
and stereo have become available to the masses. As a result
the people are now able to observe events instantly and in a
way that they have never previously done. Political unrest,
war, intrigue, death and murder are now in the public
domain. We have had to work hard to maintain our control,
and this we have done by the legitimate suppression of
information. The mass of people find politics and economics
dull. Their interest is sparked by their immediate needs,
and a certain prurient curiosity as to the lifestyles and
vulnerabilities of the famous. There has been an unpre-
cedented growth in the popular music business, and this,
for those of you who are not much concerned with television
or radio, generally involves the exploitation of the fusion of
moronic rhythm, a short, oft-repeated tune and a mundane
clichéd verse describing the agonies of love, love rejected,
love found, love in vain, love aground. And the people love

these love songs, for music keys into a primitive part of us all, it's an innate sense like smell, locomotion, taste, vision.'

Pius cracked at the table with his knife. 'Do get to the point, Cardinal. Do get on with it.'

'Certainly, holiness. I'm so sorry to ramble on.'

'Good. Hurry up then. Van Eyck, could you pass me some more of those delicious roast songbirds?'

Van Eyck piled six brittle carcasses on the Pope's plate. Agnelli continued.

'We've always had music. It's been with us from prehistoric time, but never before has it assumed such importance to mankind, and never before have its musicians been popular heroes and attracted so much fame, so much universal importance. These musicians are termed "pop stars" and for these pop stars the entire world has become a stage, and because of the ease with which their music can be communicated by an international media network, the whole world has become the audience for every song. These pop stars have massed armies of fans who crowd forward to buy their records, rush to their concerts and spend their days with music radio. The world has become hypnotized, lost in music, lost to these new demigods, who are mobbed and fêted, lauded and applauded, more important than kings, more powerful than presidents.

'You, of course, appreciate the situation and its potential danger. As long as the musicians sing about love, that's fine, for love is an imagined irrelevance, for poets and magicians, for bitter spinsters and daydreamers. Love is not in our real world. Do tigers love, does gold know love, is there an aesthetic to this mooning stupidity? Of course not, love is for poor fools, easing the passage of the unwashed and the uneducated through life's cold seas. Love is a delusion, love is for the ignorant, the stupid, the dull. Love is ugly, love is

327

a panacea. We, my brothers, have never loved because we have no need for opiate love, for our lives are splendid, rich, incarnate, safe, stately, secure, learned, controlled. However, there is a certain gain to us from this idiot music, it is diversionary, sedative, calming, limiting, and as long as the songs are of love, and love alone, the music will keep the people from investigating more significant issues.

'In a way music might be considered a new religion. The people may be with new gods in different temples, but the essence remains unchanged. In this new faith, the godheads preach love, and by this means deflect discontent, and suppress thought and disorder. There are possible negative aspects to this new faith. The musicians' songs, the musician's catchy tunes, are universally audible and universally sung. But what if these musicians' messages transcend love and become questioning? What if the little tunes, so audible throughout our world, have different catchphrases that speak of the meaninglessness of work, the corruptness of politics, the machinations of industrialists, the poverty of nations, of starvation, of suffering, of the unequal distribution of wealth, of pollution, of deforestation, of our poisoned oceans, of corruption, of the causes of war, of our Church, of food mountains, of covert conspiracy, of power groupings, of pan-nationalism, trilateralism, Bilderbergs, Catholics, Masons, Moslems, the manipulation of the media?'

Agnelli had become animated. Sweating, he had risen from his chair and was gesticulating angrily. He stopped for a moment, drank a full goblet of dark wine, wiped his brow and caught breath. Pius continued eating, and the songbirds' bones cracked and crunched. Agnelli continued.

'I tell you, my brothers, we cannot stand for it.' He smashed at the table with his fist. The plates jumped and Van der Moer jerked awake.

'Because some of the words will stick in the thick ears of the idiot audience. Some of the savages will hear the words, think about the songs' messages, and develop their own views of the world, views prompted by these ridiculous musicians.'

Zu Hohenzollern leaned forward. 'We cannot have this. The music shall be monitored. Convenient plane crashes, mad assassins, drug addiction and overdoses, these can all be arranged to dispose of the unruly. You are right, Agnelli, we must take good care of these bad children.' We nodded in agreement.

Agnelli continued. 'Gentlemen, if I catch the mood of our meeting correctly, it is that we are all agreed as to the danger of music and wish to control its wildness. I don't think that we need to vote on this issue. Does anyone disagree?' We all agreed. 'May I ask you then, Horsmunden, to co-ordinate our forces? I think that you are in the best position to do this as Information Minister.'

I tipped my head, acknowledging this new responsibility. From now on the people would hear only love songs, and the anarchic musicians would be rightly eliminated. We had our agents, and they had their easy ways.

Agnelli sat down and contemplated horse flesh and songbirds. He carved away yellow fat, then delicately chewed, dabbing at the corners of his mouth with a napkin. He had fired us all with the vehement strength of his presentation, and we calmed our indignation with food, pleasantries, and the fine wine. But there was another discussion point for that evening. Le Fanu stood up, hardly taller standing than sitting. He leant forward, elbows on the table, contemplated the reddened flank of the horse's carcass and sighed.

'Contraception, the liberal Catholics' plea for its sanction.' Le Fanu dabbed at the melting hair lotion that dribbled across his brow, his voice high pitched, his phrasing concise, economic, dry. He pushed into the table, straightening his bent back, and pulled himself upright. 'The condom, the diaphragm, the intra-uterine device, the pill, coitus interruptus. Contraception. We cannot allow it.'

He turned stiffly to his left, then to his right, contemplating each of us in turn, taking in the lines of his fellow cardinals, fixing each of us with the blackness of his pig eyes.

'By any of these means, our charges, our Catholics, wish to limit their family size. But there are one billion Buddhists and one billion Moslems. Our Catholic nations are outnumbered, and yet our people wish to limit population growth. It cannot be tolerated. We must maintain balance, and control the good order of the world. Liberal Catholic theoreticians argue that, if population size is limited, then it is possible to limit poverty too. With fewer people, given finite agricultural production, there will be more food for each individual. These idiot theoreticians argue that it is not only food that could be more equably distributed but manufactured products, and not only manufactured products but space and air, earth and water. They claim that if there were fewer people, there would be more for those fewer people. Arrant nonsense. Simplistic rubbish. There are so many other important considerations. Any limitation of population growth has grave consequences for the labour market.'

He dabbed at his brow again, and attention lapsing I looked at my neighbours. Pius was lagging a little in his eating. Toying with his food, he had not torn through the layers of meat in his usual ravenous, ravaging style, but was flipping the songbirds from side to side on his plate with the blade of his knife. Le Fanu continued.

'In order to be competitive, industry requires cheap labour. Limiting population by contraceptive practice leads to labour becoming an expensive commodity. This is against the best interests of the manufacturers and industrialists. These idiot liberals forget that where populations burgeon, where the people outstrip resources, there is poverty, desperation, starvation, and then the scrambling masses turn to religion. Religion is their salvation, hope is their belief, and in the fertile insanitary mud of the shanty towns and slums, nourished by the putrid waters of the open-sewered streets, amid the tin shacks and lean-tos, in the hovels and rotten dwellings, burrow the deep roots of religion that carry the blossoms of redemption, the conviction, the unthinking faith that is our strength. There is our profit. Holiness, cardinals, contraception is an enemy of civilization, a force that limits profitability, destabilizing the precious order of our world. So, let me summarize—'

Pius leant forward, goldfinch carcass waving in his left hand, mouth spatteringly full. 'I don't think that will be necessary, le Fanu, we're hardly idiots, we've all completely understood.'

Le Fanu was open-mouthed. Pius sat back, clutched at his throat, and coughed, and coughed, and coughed. He seemed unable to breathe. Choking, he grabbed at the tablecloth, and silver and china spilled to the floor. He pushed to his feet, knocking his chair over, spluttering and heaving, his face purple blue. What on earth was wrong? We stared transfixed. Amazed. Amazed at Pius's remarkable stamping dance.

'Water.'

He seemed to be wheezing. He collapsed, fell face-down to the floor, and I alone rushed to my Pope to cradle his choking head in my arms and tip water into his rattling

331

throat. He coughed again, gagging, desperate. His thick, caked tongue stabbed out from his mouth. An avalanche of unchewed food spewed on to his white robes, and he shook in the caress of my cradling arms. He was choking, choking to death on the inhaled bones of a songbird. The brittle creature was killing my Pope and there was nothing I could do. Agnelli was now by my side and the Pope's eyes rolled high.

'Bang him on the back, Horsmunden.' We leaned him forward and slapped him hard, but the wheezing and whistling came quicker, more intense. Pius gasped, brief breaths taken in, no air exhaled. My panic was terrible. Pius seemed to expand, ballooning out with each minimal breath. He gurgled, he rattled, and the veins in his thick neck bulged. We were helpless, I could do nothing. Save him, save him. I ripped at the white silk that bound his throat, tore the material, stripped clear his chest, gave him to the cool air that was his, all his. The rattling was horrible, globular, hacking, bubbling, in the empty throat of a diver whose precious gasses were running out. His mouth hung open, and the remains of his meal wobbled among the broken stumps of his worn teeth. Then his limbs were suddenly still. Urine stained his robes and formed a yellow pool on the stone floor.

'Put your fingers into his throat. See if you can clear out the food.' And I did as the looming Agnelli bid, sliding my fingers into the Pope's slimy pharynx, feeling for the morbid asphyxiator, the broken bits of vengeful goldfinch. The Pope heaved. Vomitus filled his mouth, and gurgled on to his robes. He clawed for desperate air and vomit, burgeoned and blew from his dead-end mouth. The cardinals watched as Agnelli and I struggled with the thrashing heaviness of the breathless Pope. They surveyed the scene as they would a film, in their seats, intent, passive, leaning, lolling, wondering, fascinated, and we banged Pius's back, we thumped at his chest, we pulled at his lolling tongue, we did our best, but our God on this empty earth choked to death, twitched and died, twitched again and died again. A body, useless in torn white, heaped dead flesh, dead, all dead, a minute away from life and long gone. I banged at his chest, feeble, pathetic, useless cardiac massage, and all that echoed was death's empty drum. The corpse folded into the ripple of my fist and turned to death's colourless dust.

Chapter Twenty

AND SO it was Agnelli's turn, Pope John Paul, Pius's successor, wise Jesuit, declared heir, elevated from crimson to white, ordained, crowned, glorious. He wore the white well in a world apparently more open, but as closed and unchanged as the dark ages. He wore the white well, held himself above the scandal of the Vatican Bank and our dangling banker. He wore the white well, far from the Star War profiteers and their toy President. He wore the white well, detached from the massacre of priests and children in Tibet and Tiananmen Square, distinct from the issues of the Middle East, uninvolved and failing to comment on torture and oppression in South America, unconcerned with famine and its relief in Africa, unaffected by the great floods that swept through Bangladesh and the AIDS plague that escaped from the confines of a CIA experiment on green monkeys in Equatorial Africa.

Let the people do as they will and let us continue in our own way speaking with our friends, feasting in our palaces, being pleasured by our catamites, cosseted by our slaves, living with our treasures, holding on to our wealth, enjoying our time, safe and secure.

I loved John Paul and the people of the Catholic nations loved him too, seeing in the mirror of his avuncular features their own grandfathers, wise, sensible, all knowing, all

334

forgiving, comfortable, gentle, understanding, loving. And many of these things certainly John Paul was. There was the evidence of grandchildren, the wisdom of his Swiss investments, the sense of his judgements, the comfort of his insights, the gentleness of his forgiving hand on his mistresses' breasts, the understanding and love that he had for the Vatican's money and history. The people were right to put their faith in him, for he was the wisest Pope since the Borgias.

And time's tireless tramp had promoted me, and I, in my turn, was next in line, heir to the sorrow of secrets, first son of two millennia's sterile days.

John Paul watched me, fostered my minutes until it was almost my hour, and, when he saw that I was strong, he claimed me, as the centuries had claimed a hundred others before. It was my time and he took my hand, led me through the darkest corridors of our strength, through the stone hollows of our foundation, under the flickering light of an ancient torch, into the sullen lands of an ancient maze, in the darkest air, empty of winds. In silence, we passed down through fractured forests of stalactites and stalagmites under the stare of frozen trolls, and a hundred blind wolves howled to a nation of hyenas' callous calls. On shivering stones we passed deeper and downwards to where malice screamed from vultures' walls. A rusting portcullis rose and fell, and dank drops of acid dripped from a canopy of fire. Onwards through the wavering shadowlands into the far darkness, where the silent screaming of tortured Medusas seared from eternity's prisons. Onwards, and we dragged through the cold waters of underground rivers where blind fish squelched under our blistered feet. Down and down into the deepness, and the heaviness of our Vatican castles were martyred mountains above us. It was hot and it was cold, and the light of a thousand darknesses was a fluorescent route map for John Paul before me.

Through a carousel of dreams, he pulled me, a boatman on an eternal river. Of love and life he whispered not a thing, but of death and darkness, every grey detail. Taking me by the hand, he talked of bitterness and as he spoke the bats of envy fluttered and misery and sorrow drew their sobbing strangled breath. Onwards and downwards we descended through seams of iron and coal, and the silver bands of bright minerals shone in a shower of reflected sparks in twilight torchlight. Through the layered alluvium we fell. Our ears held no sound, our eyes no vision, and our shadows clutched at our feet for fear of the rank darkness. From blackness to infinite blackness, past the swollen cells of the prisons of wrath, along the contused corridors of the bloody catacombs of Rome's dead history, I was led, how I was led, and the perfume of putrescence and the screams of the world's tortured were bitter company with pain and fear. The pulse of hard time pounded sorrow's cruel heartbeat, and the wild storms of tomorrow's tears broke on sour beaches of dead ice. Living on each moment, swinging on the long pendulum of seconds, I followed the definite footsteps of a whispering old man. Lost in the darkness, I reached for his claw hand to save me, and he pulled me through a quagmire labyrinth that spun and deceived. Between whispers, he murmured, 'Ours is the great secret and closed are our memories, the world is our mystery which to us chosen is unfurled. Unloved, we are loveless and silence is our solution, splendid is our fortune and paradise our mansion. Ours is all inheritance and how comely our property, divine our inspiration and voluptuous our degree.'

He pulled me on a clanking tumbrel, and we lurched

over jarring rocks, floundering on innocence, sanctity and surcease. Down, down through the hanging caves of darkness, to the cesspools of sorrow, the cesspits of vile disease. Onwards we shambled, and, brushing aside cobwebs of malodour, descended deep into the dangling well of larceny and deceit. About us flew no living thing, nor paced a creature pure and we sank down among the riven beasts, the hollow, false and raw.

We passed on and on through stinking swamplands, tiptoeing over mushroom stepping stones, past the sleeping heads of crackle-skinned salamanders and slithering, snapping serpents. We walked in a crying country where the bleeding air burnt and a sharp wind stung. Through the darkness my master led me, hand in hand into the crust of the earth, squeezing through a blind mole's burrows, sucked into the tallest chambers by drooling pools of whirlwind air. In silence, without echoes, down we went, on and on. Across a giant's causeway, a shivering spine of tingling arching rock that spanned a plummeting, falling valley, in whose molten shivering depths was the bubbling lava of the earth's boiling, burning core.

Lost were my footsteps. I could feel no land, and only the strong clasp of my master's hand kept me from spinning away into the hideous wind. On this screaming tightrope causeway, bordered by blackness, under the shivering light of my master's whispering torch, into a hostile swamp. To my left and to my right, no boundary. Ahead and behind, curving narrow stone. Beneath and above me, vision's only limit, the wind. And as we moved onwards, he spoke of a Jew.

'Born of a virgin, born in a promised land, he came for the Pharisees, he came for the Sadducees, he came for the Essenes and the Samaritans, for the Israelites and the

337

world. And the Jew spoke of love and loving and the people gathered amid his words. In peace they came from Israel's corners, and the fields were emptied of useless toil. He showed them how little each man needed and that there was plenty in the land. But there came a clamour unto Tiberius, to rid Israel of this man. So Tiberius sent to Pontius Pilate to crucify the gentle lamb. And Pilate's loyal legions hammered the lord Jesus on to a cross of fractured glass and deceit.'

Yellow-grey, sulphurous cloud wheeled over us, and the stone bridge was no more, the night covered my eyes and in my ears hissed panting death. I reeled, nigh unto fainting, but suddenly the choke of fumes cleared. John Paul pulled me on, on unto the causeway's end, where massive keystones sank into mountain rock. He turned to me, his face impassive, turned to continue his litany, while over us the twisting overhang swayed.

'Resurrected, immortal, Jesus lived on, and under his direction, the people's movement grew. Through the towns and villages of the Roman Empire, Christianity flourished, and for every burnt martyr of the early Church there were a thousand converts. From Sidon through Samaria, from Avignon through Gaul, the word spread on. The rule of the masters trembled, and the people were enthralled, captured by truth and loveliness, caught by the Preacher's holy call.

'Jesus lived on in the Holy Land, organizing his Holy Campaign, and the forces of darkness gathered to destroy his inspired plan. For they could not countenance the major changes in the order of their world, the movement of the people from the dominion of established empires, the collapse of inheritance, the decline of their power, the dominance of the Messiah and His Gospels of love and peace. His doctrines were pervasive, inspired, salvational, made tender the people with his word. His doctrines were revolutionary, disruptive of established hierarchies. Without greed, there was no oppression of work, and with love, grace for every being. The farmers' lands were untilled. The sedition of the Son of God was a light for Europe. And darkness retreated, beaten back by a soft army of marching gentleness, kindliness, godliness.

'In the palaces of their power, the princes plotted with their bankers, the politicians with their generals, the wizards with the warlords. How could they counter the dangerous armies of Christ's love, the encroachment of Jesus's religion on the Roman Empire? And Constantine saw the tide of belief that flooded his kingdoms, saw that the waters of this new religion could not be dammed. He counselled the princes and the bankers, the politicians and the generals, the wizards and warlords that this new religion must be taken and used, used to reassert Roman power, re-establish Roman rule, bring back the people to the Empire, the lost lambs into their fold.

'And Constantine "came" to Christianity while his men searched Jerusalem for Jesus. Captured in the catacombs of the Church of the Holy Sepulchre, the Son of Man was taken to this city, to Rome. He was brought in secret procession here to this Vatican hold. The Roman Empire was succeeded in turn by the Holy Roman Empire, and Christ's religion was deftly altered, his Gospels wrought anew. And justly, with great integrity and foresight, Christianity was a weapon for the Emperor, a means of consolidating control. Order was brought to Europe and quiet was the land. Poverty was proclaimed to be godly and the serfs returned to their fields. The people were pacified by the promise that earthly suffering guaranteed heavenly paradise. By these means, the world was restored to legitimacy, to honour, to safety and to wisdom, to the dominion of those born to rule.

'And as Constantine had established our Church so Christian ideals became our property. Emperors, priests and kings became God's earthly emissaries, and to question their authority was to question God's right, to dispute our laws and testimonies was sacrilege indeed. Europe was still, and the logical victory of the Church brought prosperity, restored civilization, created an atmosphere that allowed the evolutionary progression of mankind to the state of dignity and sensibility that is ours today. And we, my dear Cardinal, are the keepers of civilization, the upholders of morality, the custodians of mankind's destiny. It is to us that the generations before have entrusted this inheritance, this responsible power. Without us there would be chaos and savages would rule our lands. We are keepers of courage, upholding the fate of grace, responsible for the world, responsible for its state. We have, my dearest Cardinal, inherited the earth. And our inheritance is good, our role divine. Without us there would be no structure and disintegration and madness, barbarism and decay would take the land.

'In my time, John, von Rumbold took me, took me through the foundations of the world to this secret place, as I, in my time, now take you. We two men are appointed to uphold the order of the world, and as the Popes before us we are divine. You are my appointed heir, and your inheritance is here.'

John Paul swung around to the rock and from the folds of his papal white pulled out a strange and beautifully wrought golden key. A cold fear took me and I shook. My poor flesh quivered and my pounding heart beat hard. John Paul felt the surface of the rock before him, a blind man feeling for an identifiable Braille. His fingers brushed against the rock face and found their place. Into the stone he plunged the golden key, a sword in its scabbard. He twisted the key, and a heavy stone doorway made itself known, opening on ancient hinges.

Torchlight held high, John Paul beckoned for me to follow, and we passed through the sharp lines of the dungeon doorway into the cave within. I followed my master and his shivering light, down deep into the prison earth, down into a hollow of blackness, down into the darkest of terrains buried within the pillars of stone that held the lands.

We walked on into a flint-chipped chamber where John Paul placed his burning torch in a twisted sconce high on oily stone walls. I looked up, drew my eyes from the plague-pit floor, looked up with terrible fear to a heavy shelf of rock mounted into the far rough wall. John Paul walked forward and my hand in his I stumbled on.

High on the stony ledge there was a shape, a blur, a softness covered with a cotton shroud. John Paul stooped and folded back the shroud. And on the shroud was burnt the prisoner's image. The torchlight quivered in a sudden gasping draught, caught and soared bright. I leaned on John Paul, gathered strength to look at our prisoner. Beautiful man, the loveliest Word made Flesh, gentle, quiet, pure. Christ, pale, eyes blue and open, seeing, watching, noting, draped in rusting, mewling, stringing, catching, cauterizing, burning, barnacled iron chains, blistered manacles pegged into the igneous rock.

And from his stone bier he saw me, caught my eyes as he must have caught the eyes of two hundred fledgling Popes before me and I felt his sadness, felt as never before, felt for the first time in my long unfeeling life. And with his eyes he found my soul, found my soul at last, and I was his, caught by his gentleness, gathered by his honesty, his truth, his great goodness, rescued at last by his love. And I felt for my great crimes, trembled, catching their sense, knowing at last my wickedness, my manipulation of the million souls that were in my charge. And I looked again at Jesus in chains and his eyes gave me meaning, freed up my burning soul, to feel, to know, to have, to care, to share, to give, to suffer, to lay bare. Love is what he gave me in that moment with his eyes, and with his glance I travelled a lifetime, from boyhood to adolescence, to adulthood and middle age and now, on the borders of my dotage, the shutters of feeling had been thrown open, and I knew love, and was not scared.

I knew love, love transcending, love translucent, love substantial, love that made humanity pure. Those eyes so pale, that flesh so pure, lying before me. And in those eyes there was understanding, a sympathy for what had gone before, a knowledge of my stony childhood, the torture of my early dawns, and in his glance, there was my mother and my father and the warmth of man. And in his gaze there was forgiveness, even for me, unholiest of men. For in those eyes there was all knowledge, a humanity unknown to the church. He was not our prisoner, even though he bore our chains, for his sanctity transcended hard iron, and stretched beyond these dungeons of steel. His holiness was lightness, ethereal, evaporating between the links of chains, condensing in the goodness of hearts and brains. And John Paul saw me flounder, thought for a moment he'd lost his man, and it was all that I could do to gather up my bones, and look away from the God of Man. John Paul covered up Christ, drawing the imprinted shroud over his breathing, living body, covering love, sealing again our shame. He straightened up and clasped me to him.

'It's for the best, John, for the best. We must carry on.'

We came from the room, and I looked on and trembled as the door shut on Our Saviour, the golden key turning the clanking gates of the prison's locks.

We traced back over the causeway, through the swamplands, through the burning, leering quagmire, through the graveyards of memories, through the darkness of stinking hell, and with each pace my thoughts became clearer. I knew my life's new task. I grew strong again, healed and whole.

We were within a few footsteps of the doors to the Vatican when I clubbed John Paul on the back of his head, hit hard and deep and strong. He fell, and I tore at the chain of his neck and pulled away the traitor key.